Selected Praise for Megan Hart's
Precious and Fragile Things

"Hart plunges into the mainstream fiction genre
with this haunting, devastating, heart-wrenching tale.
She masterfully weaves every off-hand mention of a seemingly
incidental detail, every potentially eyebrow-raising plot point
together in service to her story and the resulting dramatic climax,
which then becomes believable, thanks to Hart's skill. This story
will stay with you long after you reach the last page."
—*RT Book Reviews*

"This isn't like the previous books I've read from Ms. Hart
and I've definitely learned to expect the unexpected from her....
I know this book will speak to others differently; it's that kind
of read. For me it was dark, disturbing, difficult, uncomfortable,
heartbreaking, and finally, redemptive and life affirming....
It's not easy to try and face those dark nooks and crannies
in our hearts and minds we prefer to pretend don't exist."
—*Manic Readers*

"*Precious and Fragile Things* is an emotional ride
where every page delivers a new facet of the story....
The details of each character are so honest and deep that
they draw the reader in and keep you turning the pages.
I found myself riveted, unable to put the book down and at the
end of the book wondering, if I was Gilly, could I have taken the
same actions. The book was very enjoyable and thought-provoking."
—*Night Owl Romance*

"An expertly titled and disturbing tale
about the complexities of motherly love, loss, and the
relationships that change our lives.... I couldn't tear away
from the interaction between Gilly and Todd. The overall concept
was fascinating...an excellent pick for the right book club."
—*Reading for Sanity Book Review*

MEGAN HART

all fall down

MIRA®

MIRA®

Recycling programs
for this product may
not exist in your area.

ISBN-13: 978-0-7783-1306-9

ALL FALL DOWN

For questions and comments about the quality of this book please contact us
at Customer_eCare@Harlequin.ca.

www.Harlequin.com

Printed in U.S.A.

First Printing: January 2012
10 9 8 7 6 5 4 3 2 1

This book is dedicated once again to my family and friends—
always there to support me. Special thanks to my sister Whitney
for making time to read this book in advance.

To my first pass readers, the ever fabulous Lauren Dane and
the wonderful JNB, as well as my hardcore gang, The Bootsquad—
I rely on you all to make sure I'm doing something right
even when I feel like I'm doing it all wrong.

To the readers who've given my books a chance
and come back for more.

To my agent Laura Bradford for holding my hand when I need it.

To my editor Susan Swinwood
for making me be better at this writing thing.

To the MIRA art department for consistently giving my books the
most beautiful covers, ever. *All Fall Down* is exquisite.

To my children, who've long outgrown naps
but are now blessedly able to make their own breakfasts.

And of course, as always, to Superman,
who listens to me talk endlessly about plot points
and reminds me I CAN do this writing thing.

all
fall
down

ARRIVING

"Get up, Sunshine."

Sunny didn't want to get up. She'd only just started dreaming. She hadn't had more than a few hours of sleep at a time for the past three weeks. Tugging at the blankets, she shifted on the thin pad of her mattress and burrowed deeper into her pillow.

"Sunshine. Now!"

Sunny rubbed at her eyes, listening. No babies were crying. No alarms were ringing. She heard only the soft breathing of her sleeping children and her mom's urgent whisper.

"Sunny. Get up. C'mon. It's time for you to go."

Sunny sat up then, eyes wide and blinking in the darkness. A tiny crack of light shone from under the door, then the unfamiliar glimmer of yellow from the flashlight her mom held tight against her body, fingers cupped over the lens. Her hand made a shadow like a giant spider on the ceiling. Sunny looked immediately to the crib where baby Bliss lay sleeping. Happy's cot was empty.

They'd taken him.

Sunny was up and out of bed, across the room and tearing at the blankets before her mom could grab her.

"Hush! He's here, with me. He's ready to go. You need to help me now, Sunny. You get the baby. I'll take care of Peace. Now!" Her mom's whisper hissed, harsh, not like her normal voice at all.

Sunny's heart pounded. Her palms were sweaty, and she scrubbed them against the soft flannel of her nightgown. The light from the flashlight swung as her mom set it on the cheap dresser missing a leg. The light wouldn't stay steady.

"Mama? Is it time for the rainbow?" The wobbling light hurt Sunny's eyes. Disoriented, sluggish, she could think of only one reason why her mother would've woken them. "Is it time to leave?"

"Sunshine." Mama's face was even harder than her voice. "Hush. You need to get yourself and the babies out of here. Don't ask questions. Hush and do as I say. Listen."

Sunny hushed, going still and quiet. She listened with her heart, as she'd been taught. To obey.

Her mother took both of Sunny's hands and brought them to her lips. She kissed the knuckles. In the pale and trembling light, Sunny's mom looked pale and trembling herself. She looked too thin, her cheeks hollow. There were shadows under her eyes that had been there for a while but now looked extra dark. She pulled Sunny into a tight hug, crushing Happy between them. The boy didn't cry out. He was listening, too.

"Get out? I don't understand." Sunny was awake now. Wide-awake. She moved to the crib to change Bliss's wet diapers and dress the baby in a fresh nightgown. Also the socks her mom tossed at her. A knit cap. A blanket, wrapped tight around Sunny's now-waking daughter.

Sunny's mom grabbed her by the upper arms, turning her. "I have money. Here."

She pressed a soft wallet stuffed with folded bills into Sunny's hands. "I've packed your bags, just one backpack for you and Bliss and Peace. Happy's a big boy, he can carry his own bag, can't you, my sweetheart?"

"I can, Nana."

Sunny looked at her son. At four, he was just starting to lose the baby plump in his cheeks, but it seemed like only yesterday that she'd held him the way she was holding Bliss now. She looked at her mother. Her heart skipped at the weight of the money in her hand and the baby in her arms. With the heaviness of knowledge.

The alarms blared. The lights in Sunny's tiny, concrete-walled bedroom came on overhead, bright enough to startle Bliss fully awake and into a scream. Sunny closed her eyes against the glare.

"No time for that! Come on! Let's go!"

Sunny's mom tugged her forward to sling a backpack over the arm not cradling Bliss. In her cot, Peace sat straight up, small mouth in a frightened O, while Happy struggled into his own backpack. Sunny's mother helped Peace out of bed. She tugged a sweatshirt over the little girl's head and shoved her feet into shoes while Sunny grabbed the blanket up from her bed and slung it around Happy's shoulders. He had no winter coat. None of them did. No boots either, though Happy wore a pair of battered sneakers two sizes too big, the laces shredded and knotted so tight they couldn't be undone. Sunny had a zippered sweatshirt, ragged at the sleeves, the strings of the hood missing. The zip would go only halfway up, and it was impossible to make it go farther with one arm cradling a baby. Maybe not even with two free hands to tug it.

"It'll have to do. We don't have time to get you anything else." Her mother paused to press her fingertips between her eyes, a habit she'd taken up over the couple years that had become so second nature she didn't notice she was doing it... but Sunny did.

It meant her mom's head was hurting her again. Maybe bad enough she'd have to lie down in a dark room. It might even be so bad that John Second would let her miss chapel if this were during the day, but never a summons in the middle of the night. Not when it might be time for the rainbow.

Papa's voice came over the speakers. The commands of a dead man, speaking calmly. "Listen now, my children. Listen with your hearts. The time has come. The time has come. Listen now, family. Listen with your hearts."

Sunny clutched her baby to her chest as her mom shoved Sunny's feet into a pair of men's work boots. Sunny looked down at her mother kneeling, the top of her head, her blond hair shot thickly with silver. When had her mom's hair gone so gray? Her mom looked up at her, and Sunny was alarmed to see tears streaking her cheeks. Her mother never cried. They weren't allowed to cry.

Her mom got up. From the hallway outside came the steady sound of marching feet. Never running. Running was for people who had something to run from, those were Papa's words, even to the children who were found playing tag in the hallways. One foot in front of the other, that's how the family walked, with quiet and careful steps to keep the world from ever thinking they were afraid.

Sunny was afraid.

A knock on the door had Sunny reaching for the handle, but her mother was too quick. She pushed Sunny's hand aside before Sunny could open it. Pressed a finger to Sunny's lips and shook her head.

Sunny didn't move. Bliss wriggled in her swaddling, and Sunny quickly undid a few buttons on her nightgown to slip her breast free, letting the baby suck to fend off her cries—not that anyone could possibly hear an infant's sobs over the blare of the alarms and Papa's steady, unending drone.

"The time has come, family. It is now. Listen with your hearts. Come to the chapel. Come to the chapel."

Sunny's mom cracked open the door and peeked out. In the hall, the white glare of the emergency lights flashed, bright and piercing. They made shadows, black and white. Light and dark. She lifted Peace onto her hip and took Happy's hand. Sunny followed her into the hall, where Peace clapped her hands over her ears at the noise. They'd done this hundreds of times, dozens in the past few weeks alone. Woken from sleep to the ringing of alarms, the glare and flash of lights. More times in the past few weeks, almost, than Sunny could remember in her whole life.

Ever since Papa died, it had been John Second's voice over the speaker system. John Second telling them to listen with their hearts, to go to the chapel where they'd be given the rainbow and tested to see if they were all pure enough to leave. How only when they were truly ready, truly pure of heart, without the weight of their misdeeds, would it be time to leave. Every time, they'd failed and been sent back to their beds, sometimes to be woken again within an hour to the same commands. Maybe two hours. Other times they were allowed to sleep until the bells rang for the morning gathering.

Now, instead of going down the hall toward the chapel, Sunny's mother pulled her and the children in the opposite direction. Through the fire door and down the steep metal stairs, where the lights still flashed in a constant, eye-straining pattern but the voice of Papa was muffled behind the heavy metal doors and concrete walls. At the bottom of the stairs was a set of double metal doors, EMERGENCY EXIT in bright red letters above them. The sign on the door said Alarm Will Sound, but wasn't the alarm going off already?

Mama put Peace down. She pressed a piece of paper into Sunny's hand the way she'd put a wallet of money a few minutes before. "You get out. Go back around the garden and the greenhouses. Stay in the shadows, Sunny. Stay away from the windows. Don't go out the front gate, you find the back fence near the creek. There's a hole. You run as fast as you can. You don't stop for anything or anyone, you hear me?"

"But…Mama, why aren't we going to the chapel?"

Her mom's tears had vanished. She looked hard again, blue eyes glinting and her mouth a thin, grim line. She shook her head. "No more. Not for these sweet babies. You go, Sunshine, and don't you argue with me!"

"But where?" Sunny cried finally, no longer able to listen with her heart. No longer able to simply obey. "Where do we go?"

Her mom crushed Sunny's fingers around the paper in her palm. "You go to your father."

The lights kept flashing. The alarms kept blaring. The steady, muffled voice of Papa continued to murmur on… but Sunny's world broke and crumbled all around her. "John Superior is my father."

"No, Sunny. Your real father. This is his name and address. There's a map and directions to get there. It's not very far from here. It will be hard, but you can do it. You have to do it!"

Sunny looked at the crumpled paper, the words smeared, the lines blurred in the shadows. "How?"

"You go there. You take the babies. And you never come back here! Ever, you hear me? No matter…" Her mom's voice, so much louder now that all the rest of the noise had gone muffled and far away, cracked. She pulled Sunny against her again. She kissed her cheek. "No matter what."

Her mom pushed open the door. Another alarm began ringing, though it was lost in the noise from the others. She pushed Happy out through the door and into the dirty snow. Then Peace. And finally, she shoved Sunny out, too.

"Go," her mother cried. "Run, Sunny. Run!"

Sunny lingered as both her daughters began to sob in the frigid night air. "What about you, Mama? Aren't you coming?"

"No, my sweetheart." Her mom drew in a shaking breath, her eyes again bright with tears.

"Why not?" Sunny cried.

Her mother hesitated, eyes shifting back and forth. Her face creased with pain. "I can't go with you, Sunshine. It's better this way, for me. I'm already… I will…" Her fingers pressed again to her forehead. Her mouth went hard. She shook her head. "It doesn't matter. You go. Now. No arguing, you go!"

Sunny's mother bent to hug Happy to her once more. Then Peace. And finally, Sunny. She kissed baby Bliss, ignoring the squalling and snot. Then she stepped back into the building and closed the door behind her.

Sunny grabbed for the handle, but there wasn't one on the outside, just a smooth metal plate. Her ears still rang with the sound of the alarms, but out here in the freezing night the noise was nothing more than a dull and faraway bleat. A gust of wind came around the corner and took Sunny's breath away, sent her coughing and startled Bliss into a gasp and then silence. Sunny pulled Peace close to her and looked into the night-black backyard. The greenhouses were there, off to the right. The barn just beyond it. There was a path under the snow, which was deep enough to come to her shins.

Peace sobbed, clinging to Sunny's knees, but Happy only looked up at her with solemn eyes. Sunny's arms and back already ached from her thin mattress and the way the springs dug into her, from the hours of scrubbing floors and toilets on her hands and knees and even longer hours of listening on the hard chapel floor. Her muscles pulled and strained now from the weight of the bag her mother had packed and Bliss's solid, squirming weight. With Peace clutching at her, Sunny felt off balance, ready to tumble off this small concrete slab and into the snow-covered grass. For one horrible moment, everything around her spun. She thought she might have to turn her head and vomit, but Happy's small face settled her.

She straightened. Her mother had said to run, but she didn't think they could. Not through the snow and ice. They'd slip and fall, hurt themselves. Get wet and even colder. She looked again across the backyard toward the barely visible humps of the greenhouses. Beyond that was the high chain-link fence topped with barbed wire. It was supposed to keep out anything or anyone that wanted to hurt them. It did a good job of keeping them all inside, too. But there *was* a hole in the fence there, near the creek where the drainage pipe ran. Sunny had found it once while running after some of the chickens that had managed to escape their pen; she had no idea how her mom had known about it.

"Come on, my sweethearts. Happy, take Peace's hand. Hold it tight. Peace, hold Mama's hand."

"Told!" Peace cried. Twin runners of snot crept down her upper lip. "Mama, I told!"

"We're all cold, my sweetheart," Sunny said. "Mama's going to take you someplace warm."

But could she? That was the question. This was stupid, ridiculous...terrifying. She should take her children and go around the front of the building. Bang on the doors if they were locked, demand to be let back in. Everyone would be in the chapel, but surely someone would be missing them. Someone would come to the door to let them back inside.

Except that her mother had told her to run, and Sunny had listened with her heart the way Papa had taught them all to do. And her heart said her mother was right.

Sunny ran.

Gripping her children's hands tight, slipping and sliding in the slush and ice, she ran as fast as she could across the yard. Past the greenhouses, silent and still but alive on the inside with the promise of spring. Down the hill toward the fence and the creek. To the hole by the drainage pipe, where they all stopped to sob for breath and shake, their clothes no help against the cold.

Behind them, the building that housed the entire Family of Superior Bliss blazed with heavy-duty security lights. They'd run far enough that the faint sound of alarms from inside had faded even more, but now Sunny heard shouting voices. Again, she thought of waving and shouting them over. Anything to get back inside where it was warm, where her feet weren't frozen inside boots that were too big and her children weren't wailing and quaking with terror and cold. It was only a few more hours until sunrise. There'd be oatmeal for breakfast. Hot tea. The children would be put down for naps, and she could possibly sneak some sleep while pretending to listen…except that wasn't what would happen. If John Second knew they'd been trying to run away from Sanctuary…

"Mama?"

"Under the fence, love. Go." Sunny pushed at the metal links. Her bare fingers froze at once, ripping the skin when she pulled them away. Happy scrambled through with Peace, no longer weeping aloud but simply shaking, following close after.

Sunny bent with Bliss cradled in one arm while she used the other to shove up the metal fence. She couldn't get through. With the pack on her back, she was too big. Her feet in the oversize boots slipped on the icy ground. She was caught, and she pushed, struggling. The fence tore through her nightgown, then the flesh beneath. She fell, shielding her baby, but hit the ground hard with her arm.

She muffled a scream of pain and bit her tongue. She tasted blood. She pulled herself through the opening and rolled onto her back, the baby on her chest. She closed her eyes, breathing hard, thinking there was no way they'd get free. Whoever had come out after them would have had to see their tracks. They'd be found at any second. Caught. Brought back.

Punished.

She'd never missed a rainbow drill. Sunny knew what happened to people who didn't obey. She thought she'd be able to take a switching, the time spent in the silent room. But her babies couldn't.

She hadn't chosen this; her mother had chosen it for her. But now Sunny had no choice. If she wanted to save her children from being taken from her, beaten, tossed in a tiny holding cell where they'd go without food and water and sit in their own filth for hours at a time…if she wanted to protect her babies, she would get herself off this frozen ground and move. She would move.

There were so many stars tonight, bright cold points against a black sky. Sunny took strength from their beauty. Stars burned, that's how they made their light. They were millions and millions of miles away, and they burned so hard people on earth could see their light. If a star could burn, so could she.

She got up, her leg on fire with pain that echoed in her back and arms. She gathered her children to her, and together they slid down the bank toward the creek. It was never deep, now no more than a trickle, but their feet punched immediately through the thin crust of ice. They were soaked. Peace screamed. Sunny grabbed her up, the baby in one arm and Peace on her hip. Her pack dragged her backward so she thought she might fall, but she caught herself before she could.

"Go, Happy. Past the pipe, up the hill."

They struggled their way up the slippery hill, Sunny at one point on her knees, unable to stand. But they made it. Down the other side, toward the highway. No cars. Nothing but the dark strip of road leading away from the compound, away from the family. Away from everything Sunny had ever known.

"Hold on to my hand, Happy. Hold on tight."

Sunny's feet hit the pavement. She found her balance. And she ran.

Chapter

I

Liesel Albright liked to run.

She ran outside every morning when the weather was nice, up and down the hills of her neighborhood, passing houses with their windows often still dark and inhabitants blissfully asleep. When the weather was bad she ran inside on her treadmill while she streamed old television shows from Interflix on her computer monitor. She didn't like this as much, because running at home meant Christopher could and would stop in to interrupt her with questions about things he could surely have figured out for himself, if only she weren't so deliciously accessible. He also liked to kiss her before he left for work, and it was never the kisses Liesel minded or the sentiment behind them, but the simple fact that it was impossible for her husband to properly kiss her while her feet were steadily chewing up the miles that never took her anywhere. She always had to stop running in order to offer him her mouth, and she hated the way he squeezed her when she was all sweaty.

Running outside was better.

Outside, she ran with her headphones on and listened to anything she wanted without worrying what anyone might think about her penchant for the latest pop hits or retro songs from her youth. Even from her parents' youth. Audiobooks, podcasts. Occasionally her iPod shuffled a movie while she ran, and sometimes instead of skipping it Liesel listened to the dialogue from her favorite films. She covered a lot of distance with Han Solo and Luke Skywalker cheering her on.

She wasn't a spectacularly fast runner, and she'd never gotten herself all worked up about running as a sport. No marathons for her, no fancy equipment like pedometers or sweatbands that wick away the moisture. She invested in the best sneakers she could justify buying and made sure her running clothes fit well so they didn't chafe or have her risk an injury, but beyond that, Liesel simply woke every morning a spare half a minute before her alarm went off. She got up, brushed her teeth, slipped in her contact lenses, tucked her hair under a knit cap if it was cold, went outside…and ran.

The benefits of the exercise were, of course, obvious in the physical. A tight butt and belly that looked okay in a bikini even if her thighs would always jiggle too much for her taste. Liesel had never been a fan of miniskirts and Daisy Duke–style shorts, but she liked knowing that if she wanted to wear outfits like that, she could get away with it even though she was inching out of her thirties.

Beyond the physical, though, were the mental benefits she gained from the exercise. While she was running, it was not only possible for Liesel to put aside everything that was in her head, it was nearly impossible for her to do anything else. No worries about the mess the world was in and how her donations to charities were useless when people were still dying every day from disasters both natural and man-made, and they always would. She didn't have to think about the holidays, how much money to spend on gifts to do her part in stimulating the economy so that she could stop worrying about *that*… putting one foot in front of the other, faster and faster, the slap of her sneakers on the pavement the only sound that mattered, Liesel didn't have to worry if her house was clean enough or if she ought to pull out the fridge and get underneath it with the mop.

When she was running, Liesel was free.

Not that she'd ever have said so to anyone. Most of her girlfriends worked out, sure, sweating away on the stair-steppers and elliptical trainers at the gym or bouncing along to exercise classes. But they all professed to hating it and looked forward to the days they could be "too busy" to get to the gym. They laughed at her, fondly but with a faint lift of the eyebrows, when she said she loved running.

"The only time I'll run on purpose is if something's chasing me," her best friend, Becka, was fond of saying. "Or unless maybe Enrique Iglesias is running in front of me. And probably not even then."

Becka had married her college sweetheart, Kent. They had three sons and a spoiled but adorable daughter, Annabelle, who Liesel liked to borrow for girlie outings like pedicures and Disney cartoons. Becka knew Liesel better than anyone in the whole world ever had, at least once upon a time, but that same time had put a distance between them now. If Liesel told Becka she liked to run so she didn't have to worry about anything, Becka would laugh and say, "Honey, what on earth do you have to worry about anyway?"

Christopher wouldn't understand either and would probably take offense to the idea that Liesel had anything to escape. He'd take it personally, she knew that, the way he was so sensitive to everything. When she filled the fridge with fruits, veggies and low-fat yogurts because she was trying to eat healthier, he bemoaned the fact she thought he needed to lose weight and plunged himself headfirst into a bag of cheese curls. The truth was, Christopher worked out even more religiously than Liesel, not because he liked it, but because in his mind, it was a necessity. He probably assumed the same of her, though he often encouraged her to "mix up" her "workout" the way he did, with strength-training in addition to the cardio. Sometimes she did it, just to keep him happy and because it turned her on to watch her husband shirtless and sweaty, arms corded and bulging as he lifted.

But not today. Today, Liesel was running. Because it was Saturday she'd taken her time, waiting until after lunch when the sun would've warmed the air to a tolerable level. Down the long and winding driveway, careful to avoid the patches of ice, and onto the street. There'd been a couple decent snowfalls interspersed with warmer days, so the roads were covered with layers of salt and grit mixed into puddles that might freeze later but for now just sent splashes of dirty water up against the backs of her calves. She started off at a slow jog, wary of ice that could be hidden, but soon she warmed up and started to move faster.

It took her twenty minutes to jog to the Rails-to-Trails path that ran along an old railroad line. In the summer, spring and fall it was almost worthless to try to run there because she had to fight for room against all the bikes, but in the winter she usually had the trail to herself. Though the trail wasn't salted or even plowed, the gravel underneath the snow had heated enough on the warm days to melt a clear path. She felt safer running there than on the road, where passing cars paid no attention to her, and she could end up in a pile of snow or a ditch on the side of the road. All it would take was one careless driver answering a text message or skipping around the channels on the radio, and she'd be Stephen Kinged.

But then she was worrying again, and Liesel wasn't interested in worry. She drew in a breath of February air several degrees more bitter than she'd expected, slipped in her earbuds and turned on the music. Oh, there was that cutie Enrique, crooning to her about all the dirty things he'd do—that song had been a gift from Becka, who'd had a proclivity for songs with filthy lyrics ever since she'd stolen her older sister's copy of Prince's *Controversy* album.

One foot in front of the other. Fast and faster.

Her breath puffed out of her in thick white plumes. Alone on the path she pretended she was a dragon snorting fire. The music on her iPod shuffled through to some death-metal ballad with lyrics so emo they made her laugh, but with a driving, grinding beat that got her blood pumping.

Fast and faster.

Here in the trees the sun hadn't warmed the path as much. She had to swerve around bigger piles of snow and even occasionally half-frozen puddles. Even as she knew she was just asking for a wipeout, Liesel was reaching that state of gorgeous blankness when all she could focus on was her heartbeat thumping in her ears, the taste of the wind on her tongue and the burn of it in her nostrils. When her knees rose and dropped, her feet slapped the ground and her fists pumped back and forth. Some people called it a runner's high, but Liesel had been high a few times and this was nothing like that muzzy-headed, twirling and sort of delirious feeling she'd gotten from weed. This was something else, something better, and she pushed herself toward it, flying down the path toward the bridge that spanned the rural highway.

As it turned out, the signs warning motorists that Bridge Freezes Before Road also applied to runners. Liesel was three

steps onto the bridge when she hit the first patch of ice. Two
more steps took her, arms flailing and back wrenching, to the
guardrail. She hit it with her shoulder, then her head, hard
enough to clack her jaws together. Her teeth barely clipped the
tip of her tongue, but the pain was instant and excruciating.

She ended up flat on her back with the world spinning
above her, the sound of traffic below her very loud. "Shit!"
Shit. Shit, shit, shit.

Oh, this hurt like a mother, as Becka would've said, except
something like this would never happen to Becka because
she only ran if something was chasing her. Liesel groaned
experimentally. Then again, louder. It didn't make her feel
any better, but it gave her the motivation to heave herself up
off the ground. She used the guardrail and then clung to it,
her mittens scarcely any protection against the sting of the
cold metal. Her butt hurt. Her knees hurt. So did her lower
back and the shoulder she'd hit. Her head seemed fine, but
her tongue ached when she scraped it against the back of her
teeth. The pain didn't stop her from doing it again, though.
Then again.

"Damn it," Liesel said aloud. She tested each of her arms
and legs, but nothing seemed broken. She'd torn the knee of
her track pants and her sneaker had come untied, but that was
the extent of her damage.

It was going to be a long walk back home. As she fumbled in her jacket pocket for her cell phone, two ambulances
and three cop cars flew past on the highway, heading out of
town. They all had their flashing lights on, but no sirens.
She watched them disappear over the hill. It wasn't as if she'd
never seen an ambulance or a cop car before, but so many at
once was strange.

She tried the house first, but got no answer. Christopher
must've already left for his Saturday racquetball match or

whatever he had going on. As she waited for the call to go through, Liesel watched another ambulance speed down the highway in the same direction as the others. This one wasn't local, but from the next town. It was followed by another going just as fast, from a different but also nearby town.

Christopher wasn't answering.

"C'mon," Liesel muttered. Her bones were already creaking. "Pick up."

He didn't. She leaned against the guardrail, assessing the damage, and decided she could probably make it home. Slowly. Painfully. She started walking, the pain easing as she worked her joints, but Liesel knew it would get much worse later.

Twenty minutes running was closer to an hour walking, especially with a limp. By the time she got home, all Liesel could think about was a hot bath, some ibuprofen, assorted ice packs and the comfort of her couch. Stripping out of her clothes on the chilly bathroom tile floor, she got a good glimpse of herself in the full-length mirror. Bruises were already forming on both knees and the shoulder that had hit the guardrail.

The trickle of blood down her inner thigh shouldn't have surprised or shocked her. After all, it had happened every month since she was fourteen. She sank onto the toilet seat and put her face in her hands, her elbows pressing on her sore knees. She breathed in slowly through her nose and out through her mouth, forcing away the sobs the way she'd fight off a gag. It didn't work.

Liesel wept.

It wasn't the pain in her knees, her back, her shoulder. Not even the creeping, growing ache in her guts that would get worse instead of better for the next day or so. Those were physical pains, and just as the benefits of running were twofold, physical and mental both, so was this pain.

It was made more so because she ought to have expected it. She'd been tracking her consistently irregular periods for the past year and a half with the help of an ovulation-tracking website, and though her body stubbornly refused to conform to any set pattern when it came to timing, she'd carefully marked the possible dates of ovulation on her calendar. Problem was, she and Christopher hadn't made love that week—he'd been out of town on business. Still, simply because of the irregularity, she'd held out hope that just this once the timing had been right.

It had been a foolish hope, and this was proof of it. She didn't want to sit here naked on the toilet in the chilly bathroom, every inch of her aching, and cry. She wanted to get into a hot bath with some scented oil and soak away the disappointment and the pains. Most of the time she dealt with this monthly reminder that she wasn't going to be a mother by being practical, matter-of-fact, even forcefully optimistic that though her clock was ticking, ticking, time was far from run out. But for now, in just this moment, all Liesel could do was sit and shiver and sniffle. A runner of clear snot dripped from her nose, and she wiped it with the back of her hand, not caring about the mess.

She couldn't even share her disappointment with Christopher, and that somehow made it all worse. He didn't want children and had made that very clear over the years. They cost too much, got in the way, ruined vacations, took up too much time. Children smelled bad and were too loud. He wasn't, he said, cut out to be a dad.

He knew she'd stopped taking her birth control pills, and they never used condoms. Liesel knew her husband understood the risks of sex without protection, but they never discussed the consequences of it. It was unspoken, the knowledge that she wanted a baby and he did not, but that whatever happened would happen, and they'd deal with it then. Not that it mattered, since every month passed with another week of blood and cramps and silent tears she couldn't share.

The doorbell rang.

Liesel swiped at her face, listening. They lived too far out in the woods to ever get random guests, not even by proselytizing religious groups. She wasn't expecting a package delivery.

The doorbell rang again, then again. Liesel quickly got a tampon and took care of herself, wiping her nose with tissue this time. She washed her hands quickly and threw on a robe, belting it as she hobbled down the stairs. She thought for sure whoever was interrupting her self-indulgent weepfest would've left by the time she got there, so when she opened the door and saw the young woman standing there holding a baby, two small children beside her, Liesel blinked several times. The vision didn't waver or disappear, which meant it was real.

"Hello?" Liesel said. "Can I help you?"

The girl, who couldn't have been any older than sixteen or seventeen, opened her mouth but no words came out. She wore a nightgown and a hooded sweatshirt with a broken zipper. Work boots that were too big for her, Liesel noted with growing concern. The baby in her arms had no coat, just a ragged blanket tucked around it. The kids, a towheaded boy and a matching little sister, weren't dressed any better.

Liesel clutched the throat of her robe closer to her neck. "Are you okay? What's wrong? Can I help you?" she repeated.

"I hope so," the girl said finally in a hoarse voice that sounded as if she'd spent her share of recent time crying, too. "I'm here to see Christopher Albright."

Chapter
2

Sunny is thirteen when the new girl arrives with her mother in Sanctuary. New people do show up sometimes, but it's usually single women or men, not families. The women are almost always already pregnant from one of the Family Superior men. That was how Sunny's mom had joined the family. It wasn't a secret or anything. John Second had brought her to the light, and it was the best thing that had ever happened to her, that's what Sunny's mom says. Always with a smile.

The new girl doesn't smile very much. She's tall, with supershort hair like a boy's that she wears spiked up for the first few weeks, until she runs out of the hair gel she hides under her bed and discovers wet soap doesn't work the same. She has freckles and dark eyes she smudges with lots of black liner until John Second calls her up to the front of the chapel and makes her wash her face in front of everyone. Women in the Family of Superior Bliss don't cover what the Maker gave them with makeup that hides their light. The girl definitely doesn't smile then. She cries, loud and long and hard, and they make her go to the silent room for it. When she comes out, she talks even less than she did before.

There are lots of kids in the family, but all of them, like Sunny, were born into it. This new girl's name is Bethany, and she doesn't change it. Her mother changed her own name from Joyce to Joy. Nobody made her, she just did because she said she wanted to fit in. Her daughter doesn't seem to care about fitting in.

This fascinates Sunny, who's never had a choice about fitting in or not. She does what she's told. She lets her hair grow long and braids it, she dresses modestly, she keeps her face clean and scrubbed. But secretly, down deep inside the place she would never let anyone see, she wants to be more like Bethany and less like Sunshine.

Bethany won't talk to Sunny. Not even to say "leave me alone," though it's obvious that's what she means when she turns her back and walks away without even looking at what Sunny's holding in her hand. It's a cookie Sunny pinched from the kitchen, not a homemade kind but one from the stash way back in the pantry, behind the bulk bags of flour and rice. Sunny doesn't actually like them. The cream in the middle is too sweet, the outer chocolate cookies almost bitter compared to the ones Neveah makes from oats and peanut butter, honey and raisins. Sunny stole the cookie for Bethany, who eats hardly anything and complains all the time about how much she misses McDonald's. Sunny's never eaten there, though she's passed the golden arches and knows what it is. It's junk food. Bad for the vessel, bad for the soul.

Sunny thought Bethany would like the junk-food cookie that's hidden away from everyone. Nobody's supposed to know it's for John Second to nibble at along with his equally secret coffee in the morning. When Bethany walks away, her shoulders hunched, her once-spiked hair flat down on the back of her skull, Sunny follows her.

"Wait," Sunny says.

Bethany pauses.

"Where are you going?"

"I hate it here." It's not the answer to Sunny's question. Bethany still doesn't turn, but her voice gets harder. Rougher. Her shoulders shake and her fists clench. "I hate it. I want to go home. Living with my dad would be better than living here!"

"So…why don't you?" The cookie is half crumbled in Sunny's palm. "Go home, I mean."

Bethany turns then. "Are you kidding me? You're kidding, right? I mean, even you can't be that stupid."

Sunny blinks rapidly. Takes a step back. Her mouth opens and shuts without letting out a single word.

Incredibly, Bethany laughs, though it sounds awful. Like hinges squealing. "First of all, my dad doesn't want me to live with him. He got remarried to a complete bitch, and they have some kids now. Together. There's no room in his house for me. Second, don't you get it? Walk away from this place? How'm I supposed to do that?"

"The front gate," Sunny says.

Bethany shakes her head. Laughs again. It sounds worse this time. "You think I could just walk out the front gate?"

"Well…" Sunny looks down at her hand. Crumbled cookie. Smears of dark, white bits mixed in it. "Why not? It's how you came in, right?"

"You're an idiot."

Sunny blinks again, feeling the sting of tears and forcing them away. "You shouldn't call names."

"Right. You'll…what? *Make a report* on me?"

Sunny shakes her head. "I won't."

"It won't matter if you do. Go ahead."

"I don't want to," Sunny says. "Really, I don't."

"Why are you so sweet?" Bethany shouts, sending Sunny back another step. Then another. And another. "You wacko? You believe in all this stuff? You like it here, you love it! You love this place!"

"Of course I do!" Sunny's not sure she's ever shouted, not in thirteen years, though probably as a baby she screamed, at least a little. Babies do that before they learn to hush and shush. It hurts her throat to shout, but not as bad as the pain inside her from what Bethany is saying. "Of course I love it here. It's my home!"

"You like going to bed with old men? You want to be what...the one true wife or whatever it's called?" Bethany's mouth twists, making her ugly. "You like getting knocked up with their babies, right? You like spending every day in this place scrubbing floors, starving or eating spoiled food? Well, I don't! I hate it! I hate it!"

"So leave!" Sunny cries and claps a hand over her mouth. Words squeak out between her fingers anyway. "If you hate it so much, then leave."

Bethany walks away.

Two days later, she's gone. John Second calls a meeting in the chapel while Papa looks out over all of them with bleary eyes. Papa stares at them a long, long time without saying anything, though his mouth is open. Papa coughs so hard he drools. Finally, he crooks a finger; John Second leans close and listens.

When he straightens up, he says, "If anyone knows where she went, you'd better make a report now."

Saying nothing would be as bad as speaking with a liar's tongue. Worse, even, because John Second's asked right out loud for an answer. Besides, Bethany said Sunny was stupid. Sunny tells them about Bethany's dad's house. This makes Bethany's mother snort with laughter. Bethany's dad lives four hours away. Without money or a ride, there's a good chance her daughter didn't get very far.

Not far enough, anyway. Sunny doesn't know how they find her, but they bring her back and put her in the silent room. Bethany isn't quiet. She screams for a long time while the rest of them pretend they hear nothing. They walk past and ignore the shrieks and sobs. They make their faces like stone.

When the crying stops, John Second says there will be another day before they can let Bethany out, so she understands what it really means to be silent and learn to listen. And the day after that, Sunny is in the wrong place at the right time to see them pull Bethany out of the silent room. She's limp and still and pale except for the parts where there's blood.

Nobody speaks of it. Ever. Not even Bethany's mother. It's like Bethany never existed except in some made-up place inside Sunny's brain, and she knows that can't be true because if she'd made her up, Bethany would never have called Sunny stupid. She'd have been Sunny's friend. And she wouldn't have killed herself, either. She'd have stayed inside Sanctuary the way Sunny does, scrubbing floors and waiting for the rainbow to take them through the gates.

Sunny has thought of Bethany often over the years. Her freckles. Her smudged eyes. Her hair. Most of all, the things she'd screamed when she was in the silent room, about how she hated the family. Hated Sanctuary. She'd screamed out lists of places and things she *didn't* hate. McDonald's, Starbucks, Hersheypark, Walmart, Ocean City. Cheeseburgers, cable television, rap music, video games, Coca-Cola, sugar, cupcakes, French fries. Eyeliner, lipstick, tampons, birth control.

Those were worldly things, and Sunny thought of them now. What had been so wonderful about worldly things that had made having them so much better than being in Sanctuary? What was it about the world that had made Bethany willing to give up any chance she had of going through the gates?

Here in this tiny, pink-painted bathroom in her father's house, her *biological* father's house, the man she hadn't even known existed before yesterday, Sunny wondered how long it would be before John Second discovered where she'd gone and came to take them back to Sanctuary. She washed her hands over and over again. They were almost raw with clean, but she washed them again anyway. Her children were in the kitchen with her father's wife. Her children were outside, and Sunny was inside, and she should go to them, but instead she squirted more soap into her palm and ran the water so hot it turned her skin red.

She ought to go out, but all she could do was look at her face in the mirror and wonder what in this world was so wonderful it was worth dying for.

Chapter

3

"Here," Liesel said to the little boy sitting propped up on one of the kitchen bar stools. "Do you like chocolate milk?"

"He's never had it. But he will probably like it. It's sweet, right?" said the boy's mother doubtfully.

She'd been in the bathroom so long Liesel had started to worry, but now she was out. She'd said her name was Sunny. Sunshine. It was a ridiculous name but suited her, with the blond, blond hair and those blue eyes.

Chris and Liesel both looked at her. It had taken him almost forty minutes to get home, and that had been after twenty minutes of Liesel trying to reach him. Close to two hours had passed since Liesel had opened the door to find Sunshine and her children on the doorstep, and it already seemed like a lifetime.

"Yes," Liesel said. "It's sweet."

The little boy's name was Happy. Liesel had misunderstood

at first, thought the girl said the boy was happy. She'd laughed when she saw Sunny meant it was his name. The baby sleeping in her arms she'd called Bliss, and the toddler sacked out on the leather couch in the family room was named Peace. Liesel wasn't a fan of trendy, strange names—if she ever had a baby, she intended to go with something classic. Maybe Ava for a girl. Edward for a boy.

"Babe," Christopher said. He leaned against the counter with an empty bottle in one hand, looking as if he wished it were a bottle of whiskey. "Can you get me another beer?"

Liesel opened the fridge and handed him one, then focused on her husband's daughter. His *grandchildren*…bitterness rose in her throat, but she swallowed it. Hard.

Happy sipped cautiously at the milk. He touched the tip of his tongue to the milk, then looked up at his mother. She smiled at him.

"Is it good, my sweetheart?" Sunny asked.

He nodded with a grin, then tipped the cup to his mouth and drank. When he took it away, he left a creamy brown mustache behind. His mother leaned forward to wipe it clean with her thumb, which she then licked. Liesel's mother had done the same thing to her as a child. Liesel had always been repulsed, but knew she'd probably have done the same if it were her son.

"Mmm," Sunny murmured. "It *is* sweet."

Liesel found her voice again. Too bright, too shiny. Her mouth tasted metallic from it. "Happy, would you like to watch some cartoons while your mommy talks to me and Christopher?"

The little boy looked to his mother for confirmation. She bit her lower lip and pushed her waist-length braid over her shoulder. "We don't watch television," Sunny said.

Liesel shot Christopher a look. No television? She ran a

hand over Happy's hair, blond and long like his mother's, though his hung in thick curls just past his shoulders. Her husband ran a hand over his own hair, grown a little longer in the front than his usual style. It kept getting in his eyes.

Christopher's daughter drew in a breath. "But I guess it would be okay. Go ahead, my sweetheart. Mama will be right over here."

Liesel took the little boy by the hand, the cup of chocolate milk in the other, and led him over to the television in the family room. She set it to the cartoon station. Sunny twisted on the bar stool to watch them, but seemed satisfied enough that her son was safe to turn back to look at Christopher. Her father, Liesel thought as she heard Sunny talking. Christopher was her father.

"He'll probably fall asleep like Peace did. We're all very tired."

Christopher drank deeply from his bottle of beer. Probably one too many for him. Liesel didn't like it when he drank too much. He started telling jokes, thinking he was funny. Getting frisky and fumble-handed, but his kisses were always sour.

"I made up the guest bedroom for them," Liesel said when he didn't speak. "Sunny, maybe you want to take a shower or something? I have some clothes that will fit you. I don't have anything for the kids—"

"I brought some things for them. Just a few. We didn't have much time." Sunny's voice cracked, and for the first time the cool mask of her expression crumpled. She put a hand over her eyes and drew in a few hitching breaths.

Liesel looked at her husband again, trying to tell him something without saying it out loud. Like that ever worked. When he didn't say anything, she rolled her eyes and turned to Sunny.

"Shh. Don't worry about it. The guest room has a queen bed. You'll be okay until we can make other arrangements." Liesel squeezed Sunny's shoulder again, waiting until the girl took her hand from her eyes to look at her. "Sunny. Everything's going to be okay."

Sunny blinked rapidly, her eyes large and so, so blue. The shape of her eyes was different than Christopher's, but the color was the same. An unusual shade of blue with white spangles around the iris—a family trait he'd told her had been shared by his father and two of his uncles. Liesel had always hoped to see eyes that color in a child of her own.

If there was any doubt this girl belonged to Liesel's husband, those eyes chased it away. Christopher had given some other woman what he was willing to give his wife only by a lack of prevention, not effort. How many times had he told her that he didn't want children? That he didn't like kids. How many times had his lip curled at the sight of a toddler running rampant in a restaurant while he pointed out to her that was exactly why they were better off without any rugrats. A thousand memories washed over her like waves of broken glass, each one stinging and leaving behind a wound.

"Thanks, Liesel. Christopher," Sunny said quietly. "Thank you."

Liesel didn't ask him to help her with Sunny or the kids. Cartoons forgotten, she took them upstairs and showed them the guest bedroom, which had been used only the few times when her mother came to stay. It seemed suddenly too small, stuffed with three children and a young woman who seemed also very much a child.

Liesel went to the windows to open the curtains and let in the light. "The bathroom's through this door, the shower—" Liesel stopped, stunned when she turned around to see Sunny had already begun stripping out of her clothes. The casual nudity was surprising enough, but the scars were really what set her back a step.

White slashes like claw marks on Sunny's pale back.

She turned, giving Liesel an eyeful of her nipples while the baby in her arms sucked greedily from one of them. Her tuft of pubic hair was thick, ungroomed; Liesel couldn't remember the last time she'd been face-to-face with a naked woman who'd had more than a landing strip.

"I'll take Bliss in with me," Sunny said as though nothing at all was out of place. "Happy, Peace. Come with Mama and wait in the bathroom while I take a shower, okay?"

Happy and Peace stared at Liesel without smiles. Big wide eyes, solemn faces. Peace had a finger stuck in her mouth. She hadn't spoken a word the entire time she'd been here.

"The shower has to run for a minute or two before it gets hot," Liesel managed to say. "There's soap, shampoo, towels and stuff under the sink. I'll be downstairs with your...with Christopher. Will you be okay?"

Sunny stared at her so blankly, Liesel knew she'd asked a stupid question. What did okay even mean to a girl like Sunny? Instead, Liesel backed out of the room and went downstairs to her husband.

"I'm sorry," Christopher said before she could even speak.

Liesel's laugh was low and without much humor, but it surprised her anyway. "I just don't get it, Christopher. Why didn't you tell me?"

His mouth worked, and he drew in a breath or two. "I didn't really know."

There'd been a number of times in their marriage when he'd pissed her off. Mostly doing the sort of dumb stuff husbands always do that rub their wives the wrong way. He never answered his cell phone and he made plans without asking her first; he couldn't put a towel in the hamper even if it would've saved a basketful of kittens. But she'd never thought he was in the habit of lying to her, at least not about important things. So as soon as the words slipped out of his mouth, she knew he could tell she thought he was so full of shit his eyes had turned brown.

"Not really," he added quickly, like he could somehow salvage this.

There was no saving it. Liesel gave him a look of such bone-deep disgust her face ached with it. Her lip actually curled.

"I never... I didn't... I'm sorry," Christopher said miserably. "There's not even any proof she *is* my daughter."

Again, it was the absolute wrong thing to say. "All you have to do is look at her. Or her little boy. Christopher, my God, he looks just like that picture of you, the one your mom had framed in her living room."

Christopher shook his head, fingers squeezing Liesel's arm until a glance from her made him let go. "I mean, Trish told me the baby wasn't mine. She swore to me that she'd been sleeping with that guy she ran away with, that the baby was his. She never told me otherwise, how was I supposed to know? She never came to me for money or help or anything."

Trish. Christopher's first wife, the one he never spoke of, not even in the most casual of ways that Liesel sometimes talked about her college boyfriend. Stories about places they'd gone, things they'd done together, in that time before she met Christopher. It wasn't that she hadn't known about Christopher's brief first marriage. Just that she'd never really had to deal with it. With Trish.

"She never came back to me, Liesel. Once she left me, that was the last I heard from her. All I knew was that Trish had gone off with that guy, and they were living in that...place."

"That cult," Liesel whispered. "We all know that's what

it is. I mean, they say it's a church, but you know it isn't, not really."

"A cult is technically a church, I guess."

"What, for tax purposes?" Another humorless laugh wormed its way out of her. "You've driven past there, the big gates and that fence all around it. I've heard that the police have been out there half a dozen times on reports of child abuse and stuff. They don't send their kids to school or to the hospital if they're sick or anything."

She thought of the marks on Sunny's back. The thought turned her stomach. "Oh, God, Christopher, do you think those children have been abused?"

Christopher pulled her close so that her cheek rested against his chest. "I don't know."

She shuddered. "She has marks on her back."

"What kind of marks?"

"Like scars. Like…whip marks."

Christopher grimaced. "God."

"She says you're her dad, that her mother told her to come here. If they were being abused it makes sense that she'd send them here."

"There has to be a way to find out."

"If they were abused? You can't just…blurt it out. I don't think you can just ask them." She shuddered again. "I wouldn't even know where to start."

"No. I meant a way to find out if she's really mine."

Liesel frowned. "Like what, a DNA test or something?"

"Sure. Of course. Something like that."

Liesel pushed away from him, her frown twisted into a scowl. "How can you say that? Even if she's not genetically your kid, Christopher, she *thinks* you're her dad. Her mother obviously thought so. And you can't just… What are you going to do? Turn them away? Put them out? Oh, my God, you can't even think of that!"

Christopher shook himself and reached for her, though she didn't let him touch her. "I didn't say that. What the hell kind of man do you think I am?"

"Apparently," Liesel said coldly, "the sort who had a kid almost twenty years ago and never bothered to have anything to do with her."

"That's not fair." His jaw tightened. He emptied his bottle into the sink and tossed it into the recycling container, where it landed with a clatter. "So not fair."

She softened, but didn't touch him. "I'm sorry. You're right. It's not fair. None of this is. You didn't know. But they're here now. She came to us. We're not turning her out, at least not tonight. Not until we find out more about what's going on."

Her husband frowned. "I didn't say I thought we should turn them out."

He didn't have to say it. She could see it in his face. Still, she let him lie, just this little bit, so that neither of them had to admit he was being a bastard. She nodded once, sharply. Above them, the shower stopped. Silence.

"I'm sorry," Christopher said again, no lie in him this time. "I really am."

"Can you heat up some soup or something for dinner? Make some grilled cheese. I'm sure they're probably starving. I'll go check and make sure they're okay." She paused, then stood on her toes to kiss his cheek. At the sound of small feet on the ceiling, something lifted inside her that had been heavy for a very long time.

"They can stay until we figure out what's going on," he said. "I'll try to get in touch with Trish… Ah, shit. Shit."

He looked so miserable she had to take pity on him, even as something went a little gleeful inside her at how stricken he seemed to be at the idea of even calling Trish on the phone. She squeezed him.

"It's too late now to do anything tonight except let them get some sleep. They're exhausted and honestly, so am I. We can work this out in the morning."

"Yeah," her husband said. "Okay."

On the way upstairs, a slow wave of cramps rippled through her guts, the monthly aches in her womb sudden and pro-found. Every part of her still hurt from her fall, but the pain inside her was worse than any of them. Liesel thought again of those tiny faces, the big eyes. What had she been hoping for so desperately? And what had shown up, literally, on her doorstep?

It was either the answer to a prayer Liesel had been very bad at making, or it was a punishment for asking in the first place.

Chapter
4

Everything was going to be okay. That's what Liesel had told her over and over, but Sunny didn't believe it, not for a second. Nothing would ever be okay again. How could it be?

Happy and Peace were sleeping, both of them curled up tight like kittens on the huge bed that was way too soft. Sitting on it was like sinking into…what, Sunny didn't know, just that compared to hers in Sanctuary this bed squished too much. Bliss was snuggled against Sunny, still sucking every once in a while though she'd fallen asleep a while ago. Sunny didn't have the heart to take her off the breast. She sat in a rocker in the corner with a thick knitted blanket over both of them, but her feet stuck out. Her toes were cold. She didn't want to squirm around to tuck them beneath her in case she woke the baby, but the soft pajama pants Liesel had given her weren't long enough to tuck around her feet the way her nightgown had been. The material clung to her legs, between them, pressing against her bare flesh. It made her too aware of herself, just the way Papa had always said it would, which was why women in the family never wore pants.

The kids slept restlessly but hard. Exhausted. Sunny was tired, too, but couldn't sleep. She couldn't shake the feeling that all of this had been a dream. She'd close her eyes and wake to flashing lights and the constant mumble of John Second's voice over the speakers. Or Papa's. Why hadn't John Second been the one talking? Why had he used Papa's recorded voice to bring them all to the chapel?

Before Papa had died but after he'd gotten sick, he'd often used the recording instead of his own voice. It had been easy to tell the difference because the voice over the speakers calling them to the chapel for the drills was strong and vibrant, full of confidence and authority. The voice of the man who greeted them from his wheelchair when they got there was whisper-thin, raspy and shattered by coughs.

Tears burned behind her lids; she closed her eyes tight to keep them from slipping out. No crying, even without anyone to see and make a report. Crying was weakness and would blemish her vessel from the inside. Bliss protested with a small squeak when Sunny's arms tightened around her, and Sunny relaxed her grip so as not to wake her daughter.

What now? What could the four of them do here in this house with a man she'd never known as her father, and his wife, who stared at Sunny's children with eyes so hungry it was like she wanted to gobble them up. What could Sunny do anywhere? She had just a little money, no clothes except what they'd been wearing and the few items her mom had packed for them. Worse than that, it had been years since she'd been beyond the fences of Sanctuary.

At fourteen she'd been assigned to go outside and sell literature. She'd been awful at picking out potential seekers from the crowds. Even worse at asking people for money in exchange for the pamphlets that encouraged them to adopt Papa's teachings. She'd been punished many times for not meeting her quota. The punishments had been worth being released from having to sell. She didn't really like being on the outside, where women dressed so immodestly and everyone stared at her. There was temptation at every turn. She'd always much preferred staying in Sanctuary, taking care of the children or cleaning. Anything was better than standing on street corners or lingering in shopping malls, trying to entice people not only to take the pamphlets, but also to actually pay a dollar for them. Sunny had come home too many times with nothing but crumpled pamphlets that had been shoved back into her fists by people who laughed or sneered at her when she asked them to pay for what they'd taken out of pity, never real interest.

Once, she'd tossed all the pamphlets in the garbage and lied, saying she'd given them all away but that nobody had paid. She'd been put in the silent room for that. John Second himself had come to stand over her, watching as she ate from a dog bowl. He'd been the one to explain to her how important it was that the world have the chance to learn about Papa's message—but also how important it was that they pay for the privilege.

"People cherish what they pay for, Sunshine," John Second had told her. "It's only a dollar to them and to us, but believe me, when they pay for something, they take better care of it. No matter how little it is. And where do you think we get the money to pay for the food you and your mother eat? You don't want your mother to starve, do you? Tell me now that you understand how important it is for people to pay for the pamphlets, and that you'll work harder next time, so we never have to have this conversation again."

Since John Second had never been required to canvas the streets or solicit, and since he'd never watched people with pity in their eyes give her a dollar or sometimes even more, then immediately toss the pamphlet in the trash without even glancing at it, Sunny thought he didn't know what he was talking about.

But still, she'd been the one hoping for a bucket so she didn't wet herself, and he'd been the one handing it to her.

John Second played at being kind, but even though his mouth smiled his eyes hardly ever did. When Papa had meted out punishments, it was always with a sad smile because he said disciplining his children hurt him as much as it did them, and that he did it out of love. So that they'd be prepared when the time came to leave their vessels and go through the gates. He didn't want anyone left behind.

Except that Papa himself would be left behind. Somehow, his children had failed him. They hadn't meditated enough, hadn't been good enough to the earth, had let temptation lead them astray. Had not listened hard enough with their hearts. Something, anyway, because instead of leaving his vessel voluntarily when the time came for all of them to leave, Papa had simply died, leaving his two true sons to hold the family together.

Except they hadn't. They'd fought. They'd broken it apart.

There'd been loud voices, shouting, she remembered that. Some of the family had left to go with Josiah when John Second threw him out. She remembered that, too. How John Second had shouted, told them all they'd suffer when the time came to leave and they had to stay behind with all the blemished. There'd been days and days of lockdown, being forced to sit in the dark while she tried to keep her children from crying too loudly so they wouldn't attract John Second's attention.

Of course her mother had stayed behind. John Second had been the man to take her from being blemished to a daughter of the family. Sunny's mom had liked to say that before she met John Second, she'd wasted her life trying to get things, and when she found him she'd been given everything.

When Josiah had come around to everyone asking and even then begging them all to reconsider, to come along with him to the outside world, he'd lingered extra long with Sunny's mother. But she hadn't gone along, and so neither had Sunny and her children. Josiah had taken fewer than half the family with him, and John Second had declared that anyone who spoke of Josiah would be punished more severely than a switching or going without food or being sent to the silent room.

Nobody had dared find out what punishment could be worse than the ones they already had, and so nobody spoke of Josiah at all. It was as if he'd never existed, not even in the texts that told the story of how Papa and his one true wife had come to form the family. John Second had taken them all away and burned them, replaced them with new versions of the texts the way he'd replaced Papa.

But Sunny's mother had kept one of the original books. She'd never said why. If John Second had discovered it, certainly he'd have punished her even worse than anyone else. Sunny had found it once while putting away laundry and shown it to her mother, thinking it had been a mistake.

"It's not good to forget things just because we don't like the way they were," her mother had said. "You can make a report on me if you feel you must, I won't blame you. But I kept that book because it's important, for me anyway, to remember that things change and not always for the better."

Her mother had been talking about the man she loved, Sunny thought as she sat and rocked with Bliss. In the bed across from her, her two other children still slept. They wouldn't be woken tonight by flashing lights, alarms, John Second's or even Papa's voice.

At least for tonight, there was that.

Chapter
5

Liesel woke with a start to find a small face peering into hers. Instinctively, she batted at the blankets weighting her and cried out. The little girl who'd been looking at her so intently stumbled back and began to cry.

"Oh…honey…Peace," Liesel said. That was the little girl's name. Everything came flooding back to her, and she managed to sit up in the bed while her head still whirled. "Shh, honey. I'm sorry. I didn't mean to scare you."

She'd slept too deeply, hadn't noticed Christopher getting up. Usually Liesel was up before Christopher, even on the weekends because she liked to get up and run, and he preferred to stay in bed. Caught between the sobbing child and her husband's strangely empty side of the bed, Liesel twisted until she'd made a mess of the sheets.

"Peace," she repeated, unsure what to say or do. "Hush."

Amazingly, the little girl did. Her eyes were still bright with tears welling up and sliding over those perfect, plump cheeks, but her small mouth closed up tight. She blinked rapidly.

Liesel swung her legs over the side of the bed and held out a gentle, careful hand. She glanced at the clock. It wasn't even seven o'clock in the morning. Where was Christopher?

"Where's your mommy?"

"Sleeping." The word came out with an adorable lack of anything resembling an *L,* closer to something you'd do with a broom than in a bed.

Liesel smiled. "She probably really needed it. And your brother? Is he sleeping, too?"

Peace nodded, then whispered, "I hungry."

Liesel's fingers inched closer to the toddler's. She thought Peace must be about two, no older than two and a half. Liesel was pretty impressed such a little girl would leave the safety of her mother's side to trek around through an unfamiliar house to find a stranger. She must really be starving.

Small, warm fingers linked with Liesel's, and she was even more impressed. And touched. To be trusted by a child had always seemed such an honor to her. She grinned.

"C'mon. Let's see if we can find you something to eat, okay?" And find Christopher while they were at it.

Peace nodded. To Liesel's surprise, she held up her arms to be lifted. Liesel did, hefting the child's weight onto her hip. She was so tiny, almost frail. Not much like Becka's daughter, Annabelle, who'd come into the world like a can of solid-pack pumpkin and hadn't changed much since. Sturdy legs, sturdy bum and belly. Lifting Peace, by contrast, was like lifting air.

The faint odor of urine drifted up, but the tiny bottom beneath the long nightgown wasn't squishy with an overflowing diaper. As she headed down the hall toward the stairs, Liesel flipped up the nightgown's edge to check. Bare skin beneath.

"Peace, do you need a diaper?"

The little girl simply stared.

Liesel paused in the guest-room doorway. The door was ajar, but it also creaked like most of the others in this house. She could see just inside to the bed, where a huddled lump and shock of blond hair showed her Happy was still asleep, at least. From this angle she couldn't quite see if Sunny was still in bed, but since the only sounds in the room were the soft, in-and-out sighs of breathing, she figured the girl probably still was. Which meant that unless she wanted to wake them, no diaper.

Ah, well. She'd have to make do. In the kitchen, she settled Peace on one of the bar stools at the counter and poured her a plastic cup of milk. "What kind of cereal do you like?"

Peace stared, then pulled the cup closer to her. She sipped it cautiously, then drank back a gulp that had her sputtering. Liesel grabbed a clean dish towel and wiped Peace's face, then tucked it around the little girl's neck as a bib. Peace ignored the entire process while she concentrated on drinking the milk as fast as she could.

"I have Froot Loops and Cap'n Crunch," Liesel said as she looked in the pantry. "Those are Christopher's cereals. Christopher, your..."

Grandpa? Pappy? Pop-Pop? What on earth were these kids going to call him? At just past forty, Liesel's husband wasn't old enough to be a grandfather. She sagged against the wire shelves in the pantry for a second. Yesterday had been like some sort of TV-movie drama, the sort she watched on the rare days she stayed home sick. Today it hit her even harder.

Liesel drew in a shuddering breath and looked over her shoulder. Peace was still busy with the milk. Some of it had spilled. Liesel pulled the plastic container of Froot Loops from its place on the shelf and poured some into a bowl. She added milk, found a spoon. She pushed the bowl in front of the little girl.

"Here, honey. Try that."

Annabelle would've dived into that bowl like a starving wildebeest, but Peace first pressed her hands together and bent her head. She waited a second or two, then looked at Liesel with a question clear in those bright blue eyes, so much like Christopher's that Liesel was too distracted to realize Peace was waiting for something from her.

"Bwessing?"

It took Liesel a second to interpret. "Oh. Blessing… You want to pray?"

Peace nodded, solemn.

Liesel's parents were nonpracticing Jews who made much of their cultural heritage but hadn't done much beyond the bagels and lox. Christopher's family were Christians of various Protestant varieties, with a few far-flung Mennonites in the mix. She and Christopher didn't put up a tree or light a menorah, but they exchanged gifts on Christmas Day, and if they weren't traveling to New Jersey to spend the holiday with his mother and sister, Liesel usually made a turkey.

She couldn't remember the last time she'd said a blessing over anything, or even if she ever had.

"Um…" Liesel's teeth caught her lower lip, and she forced herself to keep from giving in to the bad habit of biting it. "God is great, God is good, let us thank him for this food?"

Peace's brow furrowed. Her tiny rosebud mouth pursed. "That not what we say."

Liesel didn't mean to laugh at the little girl's disdain, but a chuckle slipped out. "Okay. Why don't you tell me what you usually say?"

Peace sighed, very put out. "Fank you for de winds dat

blow, fank you for de seeds dat grow, fank you for de earth to plow, fank you for de love you show."

Then, using the daintiest of touches to pinch one neon-colored circle between her thumb and forefinger, Peace lifted it from the bowl, smelled it, let her tongue come out to taste it. She looked up at Liesel with wide eyes, then put it in her mouth as cautious as she'd been with the milk. Happy had done something similar the night before, been so careful with the chocolate milk before he drank. Apparently, the food suited, because Peace lifted the spoon and started eating.

"Careful, honey." It was useless to tell a little kid not to spill, Liesel knew that much. As soon as you said it, that's just what they did.

Peace ate with the spoon as daintily as she'd done with her fingers. Liesel leaned with her elbows on the island to watch her. The perusal didn't seem to bother Peace at all. She hummed under her breath as she ate and ignored Liesel.

The girl had the same downy blond hair as her brother and several shades lighter than their mother's, though her tangled mess of curls wasn't quite as long. Soft, though, under Liesel's palm when she stroked it. So soft.

Liesel hadn't ever imagined she'd be the sort of woman to get the baby bug. In fact, when Becka had started "breeding"—her term for it, not Liesel's—Liesel had been a little appalled at how easily her best and oldest friend slipped into the role of mother. They'd become wives around the same time and that change hadn't made much of a difference in their friendship, but that first baby had come between them in a big way.

Dexter had been a cranky kid, now grown to a cranky teen, who took after his dad in looks. Becka had been smitten at once, talking endlessly about the color of poo and sleep training and dozens of other things Liesel hadn't given a damn about, but pretended to because she loved her friend. There'd been times in their friendship when one or the other of them had fallen hard for a guy who'd stolen most of their attention, but this was way worse than that. Liesel had never felt she needed to compete with a boyfriend, because no matter what happened it had always been sisters before misters.

There'd been no competing with Dexter.

So, sort of like the time Liesel had taken up with the teammate of a minor-league baseball player Becka was dating, not because she was into sports or even the guy, but because it meant more time with her friend, Liesel took up…babies.

She grew to appreciate, and in fact, love, the sweet smell of a baby's head. The weight of an infant sleeping bonelessly in her arms. The sheer joy of being the one to elicit a tiny baby giggle.

As Becka kept breeding, Liesel's baby envy grew. By the time Annabelle was born, Liesel had decided she was ready to become a mother herself. Maybe not to four kids, that was a little too much, but at least two. Two sweet and perfect children with Christopher's eyes and her hair. His sense of humor and her creative streak.

Only it hadn't happened. She'd gone off the Pill, taken her prenatal vitamins, kept track of her ovulation. Nothing. They'd been at a baby impasse for a few years, and now…

This.

Peace finished the cereal and now tipped the bowl to her mouth to slurp at the milk. "More?"

"More? Really?" It had been a pretty big bowl for such a little girl, but who knew what she'd been used to eating? Liesel poured another half bowl of cereal and added milk.

Peace didn't go through the ritual of the blessing or smelling and tasting the food before she ate it. This time, she dug right in. She crunched happily, still tunelessly humming and kicking her bare toes against the island.

"Honey, I'm just going to go look for Christopher. Are you okay here?"

Peace crunched away, not looking bothered at all at being left alone. Liesel hesitated, but it wasn't as though Peace was an infant. Besides, she wasn't going to go far. Even if the little girl fell off the stool, Liesel would be close enough to get to her in half a minute.

"Okay," Liesel said. "I'll be right back."

She found her husband where she'd expected to, feet up and reclining in the battered easy chair that had been his dad's. All the other furniture they'd had before they got married had been replaced over the years, but Christopher refused to let go of this chair.

Liesel understood the sentiment. She held on to things, too. Ticket stubs, postcards, matchbooks. It wasn't that she hated the chair, even though it *was* the ugliest thing she'd ever seen. What boggled her mind was how he could fall asleep in that dilapidated, uncomfortable relic while watching television, which was what he did a couple times a week. Usually she woke him before she went upstairs, and sometimes she stumbled down to the den with bleary eyes to shake him awake enough to spend the rest of a too-short night in bed, but last night he must've gotten out of bed after she fell asleep and come down here.

She found him with his eyes closed and mouth open, the TV tuned to some sports station showing something obscure, like curling. In the early-morning light streaming in through the floor-to-ceiling windows they'd paid extra to put in, his face looked slack and disturbingly old. His hair was shaggier than he usually wore it, and Liesel caught a glimpse of silver in the blond. Liesel had never met Christopher's father, who'd died young, just fifty, of a heart attack brought on by too many cigarettes and cheeseburgers. She'd seen pictures though, and her husband looked a lot like his dad.

For an instant, she froze. Fifty used to seem so old, but Christopher was only ten years away from that. Fewer years than they'd been married. He took care of himself better than his dad ever had. Didn't smoke, worked out regularly, and aside from his addiction to cheese curls, didn't indulge in fast food. There was no reason for Liesel to think she'd end up a young widow, but all at once it was all she could do to stop herself from running across the room and shaking him awake just to make sure he was still alive.

"Christopher," she said in a low voice instead of shouting it the way she'd felt the sudden impulse to.

He startled awake in a way that would've been comical if this were a normal day. The recliner rocked as he flailed. Then he scrubbed at his face, letting out a sigh, and leaned forward to put his feet flat on the floor.

"Jesus," he said. "What time is it?"

"It's almost eight."

"In the morning?" He looked disgusted and added a garbled sound of distaste as he stretched and winced.

His question didn't require an answer other than "duh," so she kept quiet. Christopher looked up at her, then past her. He sighed.

"Where are they?"

"Peace is in the kitchen. She woke me up a little while ago. She was hungry, so I'm giving her some breakfast. I guess Sunshine and Happy are still sleeping, the baby, too."

Christopher sighed again and got up, his back snap, crackle, popping as he twisted it. His neck the same way. He had a monthly appointment with their chiropractor, courtesy of that recliner.

He blinked and used the heel of one hand to press against his eyes. "I need a shower."

"Christopher," Liesel said quietly and stopped, not sure of what she meant to say, just knowing there were a lot of words waiting to be spoken and not all of them nice.

"Not now, Liesel."

"Now," she said. "We have to talk about this now."

He sat back heavily in the recliner and waved at the couch across from it. "Fine. Whatever. I could use some coffee and a hot shower first so I'll be a little better at giving you whatever it is you want, but whatever, go ahead."

Liesel's teeth clicked down, biting back a sharp retort. "What *I* want?"

He gave her a weary look. "I'm exhausted, okay? My mouth tastes like shit, I have a headache and my back's killing me. This is the kind of conversation that ends with us talking about what 'we're' gonna do—" he used air quotes for emphasis "—which really means whatever *you* are going to do. So let's just cut to it, okay? I'm a lousy jerk for having a kid and never telling you about her. Okay?"

She knew better than to poke him when he woke up grumpy, but that didn't stop her from replying, "No, you're a lousy jerk for having a kid and never knowing about her."

Christopher stared at her, hard. Then he crumpled. He scrubbed at his eyes again before propping his elbows on his knees and putting his face in his hands.

"We have to talk about what we're going to do with them, that's what I meant, Christopher."

He shifted to look over at her. "You want to keep them."

"Don't you?"

He leaned forward. "They're not puppies, for Chrissake, Liesel."

"No! They're children!"

"She's not," he pointed out. "If she's mine, she has to be at least nineteen years old, probably almost twenty."

"That's still practically a child! I was in college when I was twenty, living at home with my parents and working part-time at the grocery store to earn textbook money. Twenty's barely old enough to be married, much less be a parent."

"I was married at eighteen."

"And look how well that worked out," Liesel retorted. "You were only married for three years."

Christopher flinched. He looked away from her, a hand scraping through his hair. Her sharpness embarrassed her, made her feel like the sort of sniping, shrewish wife she'd never wanted to be. It made her sound…jealous.

"I'm just saying, it's not that young," he said after a moment. "You weren't much older when we met."

"I was twenty-five when we met, but I was twenty-seven when we got married," Liesel said. "We'd both finished school. Had jobs. We didn't have kids—"

"Apparently," Christopher said, "I did."

It was her turn to flinch. "She has *three*. She's not even twenty years old and has three kids. Happy's what, four years old? Which means she started having babies at fifteen? And living in that place… My God, Christopher. Everyone knows they're crazy over there. You've seen them downtown, handing out their pamphlets. Have you ever read one of them?"

Christopher's lip curled. "No. Have you?"

"As a matter of fact, I have. I felt so bad for the kid who was trying to sell them I gave him a five-dollar bill. He gave me the whole pile." Liesel frowned. "I think I still have them somewhere."

"Why would you keep that crap?" Christopher shook his head and tossed the hair from his eyes. Just as seeing him sleeping had reminded her of the photos of his dad, seeing him flip his hair that way took her back to when they'd first met. He'd worn his hair longer then and had flipped it back a lot.

"I don't know. I put them away in my desk when I got home and just forgot about them. That's not the point," she said. "The point is, this is your daughter. And her children. And clearly she's got no clue, Christopher, about how to take care of them, or herself, outside the confines of those walls."

"She got them here, didn't she?"

"Three kids in the middle of winter with almost nothing but the clothes on their backs. And dressed completely inappropriately, for that matter. How'd they get here without a car? Walk? It's got to be at least ten miles away. God. Did they hitch?"

Christopher smiled faintly. "Sounds like she knows how to take care of herself to me."

"Don't you want to help her?" Liesel cried, accusing. "Or would you rather pretend you didn't know she exists, just like you did for the first nineteen years of her life?"

Silence swirled after she said that. At least her husband looked a little bit ashamed, but she felt just as guilty for saying something so mean. It had been true, she saw that on his face. But still mean, and sometimes what saved a marriage wasn't love or patience or mutual respect, but the ability to simply not be mean.

"What do you think we should do?" Christopher said after a moment.

"Well, you said you would get in touch with her mother, find out why she sent them here."

Christopher said nothing, which wasn't strange. What was odd, though, was how easily and quickly his expression became blank. He'd put on a mask of Christopher's face, but the man beneath it seemed like someone else.

"It's not like I can just call her up," he said after a moment.

"There has to be a way to get in touch with her. With them. Maybe you have to go out there, I don't know." Liesel paused, trying for honesty. "Look, it's not like I'm all rah-rah-rah about you hooking up again with your ex-wife."

First he looked startled. Then guilty. That told her more than anything else, and a stone settled in her gut.

"Until then—" she continued to push past what had risen up between them "—they can stay here."

"We don't know anything about them."

Liesel frowned. "She's your *daughter*."

"She's Trish's daughter," Christopher said.

More silence.

"I don't blame you for thinking I'm a jerk," he said after another few long seconds. "But this isn't something we should just rush into. Anyway, who knows. Maybe she only wants to stay for a few days."

"We'll see." Liesel stood. "And I don't think you're being a jerk."

Before she could say anything else, a piercing scream ripped through the house. Christopher was on his feet before Liesel could even turn, through the door and into the hall. She heard another garbled scream and took off after him, catching up to him just as he hit the kitchen.

Peace had gotten down from the stool and stood in the middle of the kitchen, eyes wide. She wasn't the one scream-ing. That had come from upstairs. Sunny, then. There was a pounding of feet on the stairs, and Sunny flew into the kitchen, too, her bare toes squeaking on the tiles.

"Oh…" She sagged in the doorway. "Oh, thank goodness. I got up, she was gone, I was confused. I thought they took her."

"Who took her? Where?" Liesel tried to catch Christopher's eye, but he was looking away.

Sunny shook her head, her long blond hair falling over her shoulders. She looked apologetically at Christopher and Liesel. Her face had been the color of chalk, but now her cheeks bloomed with pink.

"I'm sorry. I was dreaming. I had a nightmare. And then I woke up, and Peace was gone. I'm sorry I scared you."

Peace burst into tears just as the patter of liquid on the tiles came from beneath the hem of her nightgown. Urine spread in a swiftly growing puddle around the little girl's feet, then the soft plop of something worse.

"Oops," Liesel said.

"What the—!" Christopher leaped across the room like he was going after a racquetball on the court to grab up a handful of paper towels. He tossed them onto the puddle, then took the entire roll and dropped to his knees. "Hey, kid, cut it out!"

That's when Peace threw up on his head.

Chapter
6

"This is all you brought?" Liesel looked over what Sunny had laid out on the guest bed.

Heat settled in Sunny's face again. It was bad enough that she'd embarrassed herself by screaming this morning when Peace had only been in the kitchen. Not stolen away by John Second to make sure Sunny understood how important it was to obey. It was worse that Peace had puked on Christopher and all over herself. The floor, too. Christopher was still in the shower, and Sunny had insisted on mopping the floor, but there wasn't much to be done about Peace's clothes.

Bliss was sleeping in a makeshift crib of pillows, and Happy had been sent downstairs to watch more television. Peace sat on the bed, hair still wet, tucked into a towel after the scrubbing Sunny had given her in a tub so big and shiny bright it had been intimidating. The nightgown she'd been wearing was in the laundry, and the clothes she'd been wearing the night before were filthy as well from the run through the woods. Liesel had put everything in the washer.

"I… We left in a hurry." Sunny didn't know what else to say. Liesel was blemished. Sunny shouldn't talk about family things with her. Within the walls of Sanctuary it had seemed entirely normal that nobody had more than a change or two of clothes accessible to them at any time, but Sunny knew that out here in the blemished world things were different. Here, people indulged in excess and greed, the accumulation of material goods. Out here, people relied on *things* for comfort instead of listening with their hearts.

"Sunny, look at me."

The zipper of Sunny's sweatshirt was still stuck halfway. She tugged it over Peace's head. The girl would swim in it, but it was better than nothing. She looked at Liesel…at her step-mother, she thought. Liesel was her father's wife and therefore had an authority in this house that Sunny needed to respect.

"We can go to the store and buy you some new things for the kids. For you, too."

At Liesel's kind look, sharp and shameful tears pricked at Sunny's eyelids. She took a deep breath to push them away. "Oh, no. I couldn't have you do that."

"Sunny, all of this—" Liesel gestured at the bed, where everything that had been stuffed into both their knapsacks had made only a tiny pile on the soft comforter "—I don't mean to hurt your feelings, but it's worn-out. And dirty."

Sunny nodded, biting her lip, and concentrated on tugging a borrowed comb through Peace's curls. In Sanctuary, clothes were shared and then recycled when they became too worn to wear. But at least there they had other clothes to wear while dirty outfits were being washed.

"I have money," Sunny said.

Liesel hesitated. "Of course, that's fine. But if you don't have enough, I'm sure your…dad…and I can cover it."

Sunny smiled faintly at that. "I can't think of him as my dad. I'm sorry. It just sounds funny."

"It does, doesn't it?"

Liesel smiled. This time the warmth welling up inside Sunny wasn't from embarrassment. She smiled back.

"You don't have to call him Dad if you don't feel comfortable," Liesel said. "I think he feels strange about it, too."

Sunny smoothed Peace's hair through her fingers to get at a particularly bad tangle. Peace wriggled, complaining at the tugging. "Hush, my sweetheart. Just a bit more."

Sunny looked up to see Liesel watching her closely, her head tilted a little. Liesel, caught, didn't look away. She leaned against the dresser with a small smile.

"This is all a surprise to us. A good one," Liesel added quickly. Sunny didn't think she was telling the whole truth about that. "It's just that we didn't know."

"I didn't know, either." Not that it would've mattered. The man who'd fathered her was blemished, not part of the family. Even if her mother had told her about him long ago, Sunny wouldn't have considered him her father.

"She didn't tell you about him? I mean, not ever?"

"Not until she told us it was time to go." Sunny finished with Peace's hair. "Do you have to use the toilet?"

"She doesn't need a diaper?" Liesel sounded surprised.

Sunny looked up. "I know she had an accident in the kitchen, but she was just scared."

"No, I mean… Never mind. It was an accident, I know that. I'm not upset." Liesel laughed softly.

Liesel spent a lot of time saying things she didn't mean, Sunny thought. Or thinking of things she meant to say but didn't. Either way, it was clear she didn't spend much time

listening with her heart, because while Sunny might sometimes let her thoughts fly out of her mouth before she could
restrain them, she always meant whatever it was she actually
said. Liesel didn't seem so certain of herself.

"Christopher might take some time to recover, though."

Sunny winced, thinking of how he'd shouted and the disgust on his face when Peace had thrown up. Only a little had
gotten on him, most had been on the floor or down her own
front, but even so it had been bad, especially with the rest of
the mess. "I'm sorry."

Liesel shook her head. "I'm not upset about it. I'm just
surprised that she's not in diapers, that's all. She's so young."

Sunny considered this. Peace was just over two years old.
"She's been using the toilet for a few months now."

Clearly, this wasn't something Liesel had expected. She
shook her head slowly. "Wow. That's some accomplishment."

What did that mean?

Liesel must've seen her confusion. "None of my friend's
kids got out of diapers until they were over three years old."

Sunny had been reprimanded many times for her inability
to hold her tongue, and she was no better at it now. "That's
ridiculous!"

Liesel laughed and shrugged, though she did give both
Peace and Sunny another curious look. "That's what my friend
Becka said about it when she was trying to get them out of
diapers. But I think that's normal, isn't it? Never mind. That
was a dumb thing to say."

It was normal for the children in the family to be using
the toilet by Peace's age. Sunny'd already said too much. She
found a rubber band in the pocket of one of the backpacks and
slipped it onto her wrist while she quickly braided Peace's hair
into a smooth twist, then used the band to secure it tightly at
the nape of her neck. She should do the same to her own hair.

Leaving it unbound and uncovered this way made her feel more naked than if she'd taken off her dress, but the rubber band she'd been using had snapped this morning.

"Do you have another rubber band?"

Liesel put a hand to her own hair. She wore it short, cropped like a man's. Like Bethany's. "Oh, sorry. I don't have any hair bands or anything like that. We can get some from the store. We can leave the kids here with Christopher while we go shopping. It'll do him some good."

Bliss was still sleeping, and Sunny paused, remembering his reaction to Peace's accident. At home she'd have thought nothing of leaving her children in another's care, just like nobody there would've blinked at leaving their children with Sunny. Everyone shared the responsibilities. But, as with everything else, Sunny was immediately reminded that *here* was not *there*.

"It'll be fine," Liesel reassured her. She'd turned to look into Sunny's face. "Christopher's a good guy. He can't handle puke, but he's a good guy."

Sunny nodded uncertainly. Bliss would probably sleep for another hour, then wake hungry. "I should take the baby, though. She'll need to eat."

Liesel chewed at her lip for a second. "Right. Right, I didn't think about that. And you don't have a car seat for her or anything, right?"

Sunny shook her head. "I can hold her on my lap."

"Oh, wow. No. That's against the law, Sunny." Liesel shook her head harder than Sunny had.

"I didn't know."

"How'd you get here?"

Sunny was silent for too long, she could see that in Liesel's face. "We walked. And...a man in a truck gave us a ride. He didn't say anything about a car seat."

He hadn't said much of anything. It had been sort of scary, as a matter of fact, the way he'd looked them over before opening the door to let them in. He'd asked only where they were going, driven in silence and dropped them off at the bottom of the driveway without waiting to see where they went.

Liesel visibly flinched. "Oh. How'd you get her home from the hospital? Didn't they give you a car seat then?"

Sunny blinked. "She's never been in the hospital."

"But surely when she was born—" Liesel stopped. "You didn't have her in a hospital."

"Hospitals are places the blemished go to die," Sunny blurted, then bit down on her tongue. Hard. She cast her face in stone to keep from betraying anything else.

"The blemished? Is that what you call us?"

Sunny nodded.

Liesel murmured something Sunny couldn't quite hear. "I guess it's better than some of the other things we could be called, huh?"

Sunny lifted a hand before she thought, but kept herself from touching Liesel's shoulder. "It's just that you're not one of us. That's all. It's not meant to be disrespectful. You can't help it."

"Let me call my friend," Liesel said after a moment. "I think she has a car seat and some baby clothes she could lend you."

She'd said *lend,* but Sunny knew Liesel meant *give.* This generosity pricked tears into Sunny's eyes that she refused to let fall. It wasn't that she was unused to being given things. Papa had said there was never any shame in taking what other people didn't want or couldn't use, whether it be from local charity organizations or Dumpsters behind the shopping malls.

People threw away so many things with life still in them, it was more shameful to let them go unused than to take them.

This felt different. It felt like pity, and no wonder, because it was pitiful to show up on someone's doorstep with three kids wearing dirty, worn clothes. Like refugees.

Papa had said the blemished were greedy, selfish, full of the need to take and acquire, but all Liesel had shown Sunny so far was the desire to give. She didn't know what to think about this, just that it embarrassed her to have Liesel think she didn't know how to take care of herself or her children.

But…wasn't that the truth?

"That would be great," she said. "If your friend has those things. I can pay her for them, I have money."

She'd said that already, and in fact hadn't actually counted the money her mother had given her. She had no idea how much was in the wallet. She didn't really know how much things cost when it came right down to it, because she'd never been allowed to handle money for spending.

"Oh, honey, don't you worry about that. Becka's my oldest friend, she's like a sister to me. Which means she'll be happy to help you. That's what happens when you're like…well. You're family. Right?"

To this, Sunny had nothing to say. She had a family, and her mother had forced her to run from it. Still, she managed a small smile. "Sure. Thanks. Right."

It was a lie, and Liesel seemed to know it. She didn't say anything though, just nodded and gave Sunny's shoulder a squeeze. She touched Peace's curls lightly, twining one around her finger. "Let me call Becka."

Sunny nodded. Forced a smile. She had no other choice.

Chapter
7

Kmart wasn't Liesel's top choice of stores to buy fashionable clothes, but it was the closest place, which meant they could get there and back as fast as possible. And, judging by the clothes Sunny and her kids were wearing and what they'd brought with them, fashion wasn't really a priority.

Living in Pennsylvania Dutch Country with its large Mennonite and Amish populations, Liesel was used to seeing women dressed "plain." For the Amish it was black dresses, while their more liberal Mennonite sisters wore dresses in different colors but all the same style. They all wore "coverings," mesh caps worn over hair scraped back and rolled on the sides to be secured at the back in a tight bun. Sometimes they wore braids, the way Sunny had plaited Peace's hair and her own. All of them looked like high-fashion models on a Paris runway compared to Sunny, who wore a long-sleeved, high-necked shirt and an oversize jean skirt that hung shapelessly to her ankles. She'd let Liesel give her one of Christopher's old college sweatshirts to replace the one with the broken zipper, and it further obscured her body.

Now, standing in front of a rack of sweatpants and turtle-necks, Sunny shook her head and stared at Liesel with bleak eyes. "I can't wear any of this."

"What's wrong with— Ah. You don't wear pants. We can get you some skirts. Don't worry."

They'd already been up and down the children's section, loading the cart with things for Happy. Becka had stopped by earlier with an old car seat and a couple bags of clothes for both Peace and the baby, along with a few toys her kids had outgrown. Ever the true friend, she'd given Liesel a look that said "call me later," but hadn't asked any questions.

Sunny stopped in front of another rack. This one had long, elastic-waisted skirts in dark colors. She held one up. It hung from her hips to her toes. She scrutinized it, mouth pursed, and held it up to the light. She fingered the material, then shook her head.

"It's very thin," Sunny said.

"We can get you some winter-weight tights. That'll keep you warm." Liesel tried to give her an encouraging smile, but Sunny wasn't looking at her.

She spread her fingers under the material, showing Liesel how the hint of her flesh showed through. "It's immodest."

A funny complaint coming from a girl who'd stripped down seemingly without a second thought in front of a stranger, Liesel thought. "We'll buy you a slip."

Beyond them and across the aisle in the electronics department, all of the flat-screen televisions had been tuned to the same local channel, now showing the news. A petite brunette bundled into a trench coat and scarf stood in front of a tall, chain-link fence. The sound was off, but Liesel could see the banner running across the bottom of the screen.

ONE HUNDRED DEAD IN CULT SUICIDE

Sunny dropped the skirt and ran toward the televisions, leaving a stunned Liesel alone. She followed quickly, pushing the cart. By the time she got to Sunny, the girl had begun frantically pushing the buttons on the biggest television.

"Make it louder," she said. "I need to hear what they're saying!"

Liesel pushed past her gently to turn the volume up, her stomach already sick with anticipation of what they'd hear. The reporter gestured at the fence, emblazoned with Keep Out and No Trespassing signs. She pointed at the gates, wide open, and the cluster of buildings barely visible at the end of the long driveway.

"That's Sanctuary," Sunny said in a strangled voice. "Oh. They did it. They did it. Oh, no. They left. They all left."

"Did what?" Liesel asked stupidly, since the explanation was right there in the reporter's clipped nasal tones and the banner still running along the bottom of the picture.

CULT LEADER ORDERED MASS SUICIDE, AUTHORITIES BELIEVE

"They left," Sunny whispered. She pressed her palms flat against the TV set for a second, and when she pulled them away, left a wet mark behind that for an instant made the picture beneath it extraclear before it faded.

Liesel didn't know what that meant, but suddenly the reason that Sunny's mother had sent her and the children to Christopher was no longer some strange secret or whim. "Oh, my God. They're all dead?"

"They did it," Sunny repeated and turned a stricken, vacant-eyed face to Liesel. "They left without us."

Chapter
8

They drank the rainbow and went through the gates, just the way Papa had said they all would. Her mother had spoken with a liar's tongue and sent Sunny and her children away. Why would Mama have wanted them to be left behind?

Had her mother known of all the dark things inside her, the ones Sunny hadn't made reports on? All those thoughts and desires Sunny knew were wrong—her craving for a meal from McDonald's, for one thing. How once she'd taken the money from selling her pamphlets, only two dollars, and spent it on a cheeseburger. It had been the best thing she'd ever tasted, but she'd been so nervous about eating it she'd thrown it up almost at once. Maybe her mother knew about Sunny's hatred of John Second. Her mother loved John Second. Maybe she'd somehow known how Sunny had dreamed so many times of what might have happened if she'd gone with Josiah when he left the family.

Maybe it was something else so dark and rotted that Sunny couldn't even imagine it.

All dead in cult suicide.

That's what the television said. All dead. Suicide. They made it sound so nasty, something terrible and shameful. They didn't know anything about the family, she thought as the buildings outside the car window became empty fields, then trees. This was the road she'd stumbled down so early in the morning. Or maybe it was another one, so many places in this world, so many things to see, and she was still alive to see them all.

Josiah had been on the TV screen. A woman had been shoving a microphone toward him. His familiar face had been more than serious, grim even, but he'd looked out from the TV as though he could see Sunny right through it.

"Sunny, are you... We'll be home soon. We'll get you home."

Liesel wasn't taking Sunny *home*. Home was Sanctuary. Liesel was taking Sunny and Bliss back to the big yellow house at the top of the steep driveway, where she would feed Sunny's children junk and sedate them with television. Where Sunny would sleep in a bed so soft it had to be made of sin.

Sunny curled her fingers against her palms, feeling the sting of her nails in her skin. Pressed harder. Small pain, getting deeper. She pressed so hard her fists shook, and she tucked them between her knees to keep them still.

Sunny thought again of Bethany, the things she'd shouted about the world. Sunny had made her own lists over the years of wordly things she wanted to taste or touch or smell or try. She'd drifted to sleep at night imagining the tug of denim between her legs instead of her own flesh pressing together beneath a long skirt. She'd lifted her hair from her neck, thinking how it would feel to cut it all off. Pinched her cheeks and bit her lips to take the place of cosmetics.

That was why she'd been left behind.

"We're here," Liesel said as she pulled into the garage. She twisted in her seat to look at Sunny with wide eyes. Her mouth had thinned with a grief Sunny didn't understand. Liesel hadn't known any of the family. "We're home."

Liesel was waiting for something, though Sunny didn't know what it was. More tears, probably. Shame, prickling, heated her face at the memory of how she'd lost control in that store. Mama would've been ashamed.

From the backseat, Bliss let out a cry, so Sunny had the excuse of focusing on that. She got out of the car to unbuckle her daughter from the complicated straps of the seat they'd forced her to use. She pressed her face to Bliss's sweet baby head, nuzzling the fine hairs before cradling her. Liesel was still staring as Sunny lifted Bliss out of the car.

"I'll be okay." Faced with Liesel's obvious anxiety it seemed the thing to say, and the words tripped easily enough from Sunny's lips. "We'll all be okay."

Liesel nodded. "Yes. You will."

They were both lying. Her mother had sent her out into the world, and that had been bad enough. Sunny'd been found unfit, left behind, abandoned. That was worse. But the worst part of all was not that she'd failed to make her vessel pure enough to leave with the others. The worst part was knowing she'd been given what she'd always secretly hoped for, she was out here in the world, and nobody was coming to take her home.

Nobody ever would.

Chapter
9

At the sight of his mother, Happy jumped down from the stool and ran to her with a cry. She got on one knee to greet him, holding him at arm's length and studying his face. She looked up at Christopher with a faint smile that didn't reach her eyes.

"Peanut butter?"

"Yeah…is that okay? They're not allergic or anything, are they?" Christopher looked back and forth from her to Liesel, who'd gone to the fridge with a glass to get herself some crushed ice and chilled water.

Sunny shook her head and stood, holding on to Happy's hand. "No. They like peanut butter."

"He wouldn't eat it. Said it wasn't dinnertime," Christopher said with a self-conscious laugh that didn't sound like his. "I guess you have pretty strict rules where you…live."

The ice crashed into the glass. Sunny looked at Liesel. "I

need to feed Bliss, and Peace probably needs a nap. Maybe Happy, too."

Liesel nodded. Her smile felt like a grimace. "Sure, you go on. I need to talk to Christopher."

When Sunny had taken the kids from the room, Christopher looked at Liesel. "What the hell is going on? Did you guys have a fight or something? She's definitely a little weird, I know that—"

"They're all dead."

Christopher blinked. "What?"

Liesel swallowed frigid water, thinking it might somehow make the words easier if they fell from a numb tongue. "All of them, in that compound. They're all dead. They killed themselves yesterday in some sort of mass suicide. Some cult thing."

A broken, strangled cry tore from her throat. She clapped her hand over her mouth and went to the sink to dump the water down it. The clink of the glass against the stainless steel was very loud when she put it down. She turned to him.

"It was all over the news. We saw it on TV *at Kmart,* for God's sake. And yesterday, when I was running, when I slipped on the ice? I saw the ambulances and the police cars heading in that direction. I saw all those cars, but I didn't think… I didn't know—"

"Hey. Shh, hey." Careful not to press her bruises, Christopher took her in his arms again. "Slow down. How do you know they're all dead?"

"The reporter on the news said so. The paper, too. A hundred people, all dead. They didn't release how it happened, just that they found them all together. Dead. Don't you get it? That's why Trish sent them to us. She must've known." Liesel swallowed convulsively, nausea rising. "Oh, God. We have to call the police, don't we?"

All those people. Dead at their own hands, dead like those poor jerks in Jonestown who drank the Kool-Aid. Was that how they'd done it? Or had they put themselves to sleep with plastic bags over their faces and matching sneakers like those Heaven's Gate fools?

"Did the news say what happened?"

"Just that the police found only bodies. No survivors."

Above them, the ceiling creaked with footsteps. Both of them looked up, then at each other, connected by something more than twelve years of marriage and familiarity. Christopher pulled her close.

"There were at least four," he said.

"I think we have to call the police, Christopher."

"Yeah. I guess we have to."

Liesel swiped at her eyes. "Sunny didn't seem surprised. Do you think she knew? I mean, ahead of time. Do you think she left that place knowing?"

"If she did, then she's smart, don't you think?"

Liesel pressed herself against him with a soggy sigh. "All those people. There were children in there, Christopher. The news didn't say how many, but there had to be kids."

His hands rubbed her back in slow circles. She waited for him to say something comforting, but he stayed silent. She looked up at him, thinking how he would kiss her and tell her everything was going to be all right, and then he'd do something to make that true.

"Christopher?"

"I'll call the police." He kissed her forehead. Then he let her go.

Chapter
10

Mama shakes her awake and says, "Come on, Sunshine, wake up, it's time."

Mama means it's time to leave. Papa's voice is talking over the speakers. Mama pulls a sweatshirt on over Sunny's nightgown and takes her by the hand, out into the hall.

The lights are too bright, the sounds too loud. Sunny hangs back and Mama tugs her by the hand. No time for dawdling. You never, never run, but you don't dawdle, either.

In the chapel, they take their places on the hard wooden floor. It hurts Sunny's knees, hurts her bum. There's a splinter in her finger, but she doesn't dare cry. She puts it in her mouth to suck it, feels the sharp piece of wood sticking out and tries to catch it with her teeth but can't.

John Second has a tray with paper cups full of juice. White pills, red pills, some blue, a few are yellow or green. Papa always calls them the rainbow, but it's not really. Not enough colors for a rainbow. John Second holds up the tray to show them all. Mama and Sunny are near the front, so they can see. What about the people in the back? They are far away. Can they see what John Second is showing them?

Mama pinches her. "Turn around. Pay attention."

Papa is very tall. He stands with a hand on Josiah's shoulder. Papa's two true sons take the cart with the trays. Up and down, up and down the aisles while Papa talks.

Take a cup, hold it up. Fill it from the pitcher. Maybe, Papa says, the rainbow is dissolved into the juice tonight. If it is, are they ready to leave? Who's ready to leave tonight and go through the gates? You have to be ready, your vessel prepared, you have to be ready to go without anything on your conscience.

"If you have something to report," Papa says, "now's the time. Because you can't get through the gates with a dirty, broken vessel, and what breaks your vessel faster than the weight of your bad behavior?"

The splinter pricks and stings. Thief's hands. That's what Sunny has. And a liar's tongue, because even though Papa says it's time to report, she says nothing. Not about the food she steals from the kitchen, not about anything. Nothing.

Other people report. Papa listens and nods. Sometimes he points to the stick on the wall, and John Second takes it down to use. Tonight nobody's sent to the silent room. That's good.

Sunny drinks the juice. She watches as the rest of them do, too. Watches as they all fall down. She waits and waits to fall down herself, but nothing happens.

"Get down here!" Mama has a rasping, angry whisper, but her eyes look scared. They look toward John Second, who is staring their way. "On the floor, Sunshine!"

And then she knows it's just another practice. The rainbow wasn't dissolved in the juice, they're just supposed to pretend it was. Her face is pressed to the dirty wooden floor so close she can see the splintery bit that poked her finger. She hopes it won't poke her eye. That will hurt way, way worse.

"So," Papa says, "it's not time to leave. We can't get through the gates. They're not opened. They're still closed, because at least one of you has a vessel that is still not ready. Who here has not made a full report?"

And though Papa waits and waits, nobody else says anything. They look at each other until finally someone steps up and makes a report about someone else. Then another. And then it seems everyone has something to say about someone else, and Papa looks pleased even though the juice is all gone and the sun has come up and it's still not time to leave.

Lots of people talk about other people and themselves, admitting to every small thing, but nobody says anything about Sunny, and she says nothing about herself.

And she knows it's her fault they didn't get to leave.

Chapter

11

Christopher stood like the floor felt too slick, like he might slide and fall if he moved too fast. Sunny knew that feeling. She stood beside him, still. Quiet. The coroner spoke in a quiet voice. Respectful. He seemed to think there should be tears from at least one of them, and Sunny couldn't tell if it offended the man that there were none.

"This is your mother, Patricia Bomberger?" The coroner twitched the sheet to reveal a fall of blond hair streaked with silver.

Christopher took a step back.

"You okay?" the coroner asked, as if he was ready to catch Christopher if he fell.

Christopher nodded. "Fine. Sure."

Sunny looked at the woman on the table. Same hair. Same face. The same mouth that had smiled at her so many times, now gone slack. It was only her mother's vessel; the important part of her mama went through the gates. But that wasn't what the man was asking. She looked at the coroner. "I didn't know that was her last name."

"It was Albright," Christopher said hoarsely. "We were married. Her last name was Albright."

The coroner raised his bushy white eyebrows in Christopher's direction, but Christopher had nothing for the guy. No sympathetic shrug. No understanding smile. Christopher looked almost as blank and loose as the empty vessel on the table.

"All I know is what was in the letter she left behind," the coroner said. "Look, Mr. Albright. I know the circumstances were a little...unusual. I just need to make sure she's identified correctly."

Christopher had already signed all the paperwork guaranteeing he'd take care of the burial arrangements. Sunny had been adamant the body be buried in a plain pine box with no restoration and minimal preservation. That there be no ceremony. Christopher hadn't argued about any of that.

"Yes. That's my mother's vessel." Sunny looked at it again. She felt the weight of both men staring at her. She looked at Christopher. "Is that it? Can we go now?"

The coroner shook his head as he tugged the sheet back up over her mother's face. He cleared his throat. "Just to let you know, in cases like this, we always do an autopsy to determine the cause of death."

"What difference does it make?" Christopher asked in a low voice. "She's dead. They're all dead. Right?"

"We do it anyway," the coroner said. "There has to be an investigation."

"I can tell you how she did it," Sunny told him. "They dissolved the rainbow in the juice, and she drank it. They all did. That's how she left her vessel."

It was more important to understand why, not how. That

it wasn't death, which was involuntary, something that happened to people who weren't ready to go through the gates. Her mother and all the others had left. There was a difference between leaving and simple death, but the coroner was blemished. He wouldn't understand. Sunny stared at him until he looked away.

"There's an investigation," the coroner said again. "To make sure that it was…voluntary."

Christopher let out another low sound, like a groan. He turned and took two shambling steps away from the gurney before stopping to put both hands on the countertop by the sink. His shoulders hunched.

"The others," Christopher asked without turning around. "What about them?"

"We were able to get positive IDs from their family members." The coroner cleared his throat again. Sunny wished he'd just cough already, instead of trying to talk around whatever was caught there. "It seems they were all extremely… organized. Left notifications for their next of kin. Specific instructions for the burials."

"They'll all want the same thing," Sunny said in a flat voice. "They've left their vessels, it's important they be used to nourish the earth as best they can."

Christopher and the coroner exchanged a look she didn't miss.

In the hall outside, Christopher tried to touch her, but his fingers skated along her sleeve without grabbing hold. Before he could say whatever it was his brain had convinced him was necessary, a tall man stepped in their way.

"Chris."

She hadn't thought he might like to be called Chris instead of his full name. Liesel called him Christopher. He still wasn't "Dad."

Chris sighed. "Hi, Mr. Bomberger."

The men stared at each other, Sunny between them. Not like a prize to be fought over, but something else. She paused and looked at Chris. Then the older man.

"This is your mom's father," Chris told her. "He'd be your—"

"So. It's true?" Mr. Bomberger didn't even look at her. Not a glance. Not a shift of his eyes. Nothing. "She's dead."

"I'm sorry," Chris said.

The other man's gaze went dark. "She died for us a long time ago. I just wanted… I had to know for sure. My wife wanted to know."

"This is Trish's daughter, Sunshine," Chris said quietly. "Mine, too."

But Mr. Bomberger kept his gaze fixed firmly on Chris's face. "She died for us a long time ago," he repeated.

He turned on his heel and stalked away down the long, echoing corridor while Sunny and Chris stood watching without saying a word.

"I need to use the restroom." Chris didn't wait for her to reply, just left her standing there as he ducked into a bathroom smelling strongly of some caustic chemical.

Sunny waited for a few minutes, but the grinding, desperate sound of sobs echoing off the tiles was too much to stand. She hurried down the hall, seeking daylight. Needing fresh air.

She found her mother's father just outside the doors to the parking lot. The smell of smoke clung to him in a cloud she could actually see as he exhaled a wreath of it. The cigarette in his fingers made more. She stepped back until her rear hit a metal handrail, one foot going down a step but the other staying put.

"Smoking's bad for you," she said after a long minute had passed without him saying a word.

Mr. Bomberger looked at her with narrowed eyes and lifted the cigarette to his lips again. He drew the smoke in. Let it out. "Your mother used to say the same thing to me."

"She was right." Sunny looked up at the gray sky. Maybe rain. Maybe just clouds.

"You look like her."

She looked at him. "I do?"

She'd never thought so. Her mother was pretty. Petite, blonde, graceful. Her mother was a good woman. Quiet and respectful. Good with her hands; she could make things. She could sing.

He nodded. Smoked some more, then tossed the cigarette onto the concrete step and ground it out with his toe. "Yes."

"I'm sorry," Sunny told him.

His shoulders bent. He was an old man, she realized. Not as old as Papa had been when he died, but he had the same kind of wrinkles in his face. He looked faded.

"For what? Did you kill her?"

Sunny looked again at the sky. "Nobody killed her. She didn't die. She left, to go through the gates. It's a good thing. You should be happy about it."

"Well," he said, "I'm not. Are you? Really?"

"No," Sunny whispered without looking at him.

He started down the stairs. Sunny went after him. He turned to look at her, one hand held up as though she'd tried to grab him, when she hadn't even made a move to touch him at all.

"Don't."

"You should tell your wife not to be sad," Sunny said.

"I won't tell her anything. All of this is bad enough, I won't tell her any sort of crazy talk." The old man's lip curled. His eyes opened wide. He stabbed a finger at her. "And don't go getting any ideas, either. About coming around. We don't know you. You're nothing, you hear me? You're not anything to us! So don't you think you can come around and stir up a lot of old memories."

This time when he walked away, Sunny didn't go after him. The door opened behind her. Chris, eyes and nose red, jerked his chin toward the old man getting in his car across the parking lot.

"What did he want?"

"Nothing," she said. "I was trying to tell him not to be sad, but he didn't want to listen."

"He never liked me very much," Chris said. "I'm not surprised he wasn't nice to you. He should've been, though. I'm sorry, Sunny."

She looked at him, surprised that he could take blame for something that had nothing to do with him. "Why?"

Chris looked surprised, too. "Because…he's your grandfather. He's your family. He should be happy you're here."

"Are you happy that I'm here?"

"Of course I am." He put a hand on her shoulder, strong fingers squeezing. Sunny thought he would pull her close for a hug, but he didn't. He released her with a sharp nod, as though they'd shared something significant.

Maybe they had.

Chapter
12

The doll's name is Baby-Wets-a-Lot. Grammy sent it for Liesel's birthday. Mom laughs at the bright pink package, and when Liesel pulls out the pack of special diapers, she makes a face.

"Just what we need, right? More pee-pee and poo-poo? Hey, Liesel, Mommy has a real Baby-Wets-a-Lot right here." She hikes baby Robbie higher on her hip. "Any time you want to change a diaper—"

"These are special diapers," Liesel says.

"Believe me," Mom says, "your brother's are pretty darned special, too."

Robbie needs feeding and a nap, so Mom leaves Liesel and Gretchen to coo over Baby-Wets-a-Lot's cute little outfits and her special bottle that you fill with water to feed her so she pees. Gretchen has lots of doll babies, but Liesel grew out of them a couple years ago. At least, she thought she did, but faced with the excitement of a doll with real bodily functions, she discovers a newly maternal desire.

"Let's put her in my carriage," Gretchen suggests. "We can take Baby for a walk in the yard!"

Liesel shakes her head. "Her name's not Baby."

"It is! Mommy said so!"

"Nope." Liesel really likes to tease Gretchen, who's only two years younger but still acts like worse of a baby than Robbie sometimes. "Her name's...Prunella."

Gretchen wrinkles her nose. "That's a bad name."

Liesel makes a shocked face and cradles Prunella against her. "Shh! Don't hurt her feelings!"

It's just a silly doll, but Gretchen will believe it has feelings. She still talks to her stuffed animals and arranges them every morning on her bed. She pets them, or in the case of the plastic ponies, brushes their hair while she sings to them. Grammy really should've sent Gretchen the doll.

But she didn't. Prunella belongs to Liesel. Gretchen frowns and crosses her arms, but there's nothing she can do about it. Liesel takes Prunella out into the yard anyway, under the big shady tree. There she takes off the doll's dress. She and Gretchen marvel at the doll's plastic nipples. Then at the small hole between the doll's legs.

"That's where the pee comes out." Gretchen sounds amazed.

Liesel already filled the bottle with water. They take turns feeding Prunella, until a minute or two later, the diaper gets wet and soggy. Then they change it. That's fun for about another minute, but then Liesel's bored. They go inside the house to get some lemonade, because that will make the pee yellow.

"I think we should make her poop." Liesel whispers this with glee, but Gretchen looks horrified.

It doesn't really matter, because Liesel can get Gretchen to do anything she wants her to. That's how Liesel makes her sister climb up into the cupboard to get the box of chocolate pudding. They mix it up together in Liesel's bedroom while Mommy is taking a nap with Robbie.

The "poop" goes in, but it doesn't come out.

"Maybe she needs more to drink." Gretchen fills the bottle with more lemonade. They force it into Prunella's mouth.

They wait.

And then…

"Poooooop!"

It dribbles out of the tiny hole in Prunella's butt and into the diaper. Gretchen and Liesel dare each other to taste it, and Liesel sticks a finger in it. She chases Gretchen down the hall, both of them screaming, until Mommy comes out of her bedroom with that face on. The one that means they're in trouble.

Liesel doesn't find the doll again until a few weeks later, under her bed, and only then because of the smell. She sneaks it into the garbage when her mother is busy with Robbie. Prunella's ruined, and even though Liesel doesn't like dolls very much anymore, she cries when she stuffs stinky, moldy Prunella under the banana peels and eggshells and coffee grounds. It was the last time she'd played with a doll or changed a diaper until Becka's kids came along.

Now, Liesel held a squirming, sobbing infant who refused to be soothed no matter what she did. She'd changed Bliss's diaper, rocked her, tried to give her water, since that was all she had. Sunny had agreed to leave the baby behind when she went with Christopher to the morgue, but had seemed appalled at the suggestion Liesel give Bliss some formula while she was gone. Liesel understood breast-feeding was natural and everything, but it didn't do her much good with Bliss red-faced and furious from hunger. The other two kids had settled happily enough in front of the television in the den with bowls of dry cereal, but the baby was inconsolable.

"Shh," Liesel said. "Shh, shh."

She tried to remember a lullaby her mom had sung to her, but all she came up with was a slowed-down and way less falsetto version of Prince's "Kiss."

The wailing didn't even turn Happy's or Peace's little heads, but it was starting to set Liesel's jaw on edge. She sang under her breath as she paced in front of the living room window, bouncing the baby in her arms until, finally, Bliss collapsed in exhaustion against her. Then she pressed her lips to the baby's soft head and breathed in. She expected the sweet baby smell of powder and wipes, but coughed instead on the sour stink of a dirty diaper and unappeased fury.

It reminded her of that long-ago doll she'd tossed aside under the bed in favor of other games. Liesel gathered the boneless, sleeping baby closer instinctively, though she'd never told anyone what she'd done with that doll and there wasn't anyone here to judge her anyway.

Christopher pulled into the driveway. Minutes later, Sunny came into the kitchen, then through to the living room. Liesel wouldn't have thought the girl would have many smiles after identifying her dead mother, but Sunny's face beamed when she held out her hands for her daughter.

"How was everything?" she asked.

Liesel's bruises still ached, and the unaccustomed weight of a twelve-pound infant in her arms for hours had exacerbated the pinching warmth in her neck, shoulders and back. Her belly still griped with cramps. Still, she smiled. "Great. Everything was great."

Christopher's face showed it hadn't been as great for him, and when Sunny took Bliss upstairs, Liesel followed him into the den with a cold bottle of beer. He'd already poured himself a glass of whiskey from the decanter they hardly ever used. When she slid onto his lap, he shifted to hold the glass out of the way.

"Hey," Liesel said. "How was it?"

For a moment she thought he wasn't going to answer her. He drank first. The smell of the whiskey, thick and peaty, reminded her of their wedding night. Christopher's kiss had tasted of liquor and they'd laughed and laughed about sneaking away early from the reception to get into their suite.

"How do you think it was?"

His answer made her feel stupid and like the weight of her on his lap was too much, so she got off to prop herself on the arm of the chair instead. She sipped at the beer she'd brought for him, though she didn't care for the taste.

"She's dead," he added, though she hadn't said anything else. "That's it, it's done. That's all there is to it."

"What about the funeral?"

"No funeral," he said. "She left a letter. They all left letters. Christ, Liesel, it was like something out of a horror movie. I recognized her handwriting. She always made this little half circle instead of a dot over the *i* in her name. She knew what she was doing."

Liesel rubbed his shoulder and after a hesitation, Christopher leaned against her. She kissed the top of his head. "I'm sorry."

But she wasn't, not really. She was sad for him and for Sunny, and those three children, but only because they'd all lost someone who'd meant something to them. She was sad in a vague way and sick to her stomach at the thought that a group of people could be so easily led into taking their own lives for some reason she couldn't begin to process. But sorry about Trish specifically? Not really.

Still, she tried. "Do you want to…talk about her?"

"Nothing to say." Christopher got up, shaking the chair and making it feel so unsteady beneath her that Liesel got up, too. He poured himself another measure of whiskey, though this time he swirled it in the glass, holding it to the light, and didn't actually drink.

"Do you want to talk at all about any of this?"

He scrubbed at his eyes with the heel of his hand. He drew in a breath, then another. And another, his shoulders lifting. She'd never seen him off balance about anything—she was the one who freaked out about fender benders and giant spiders, while Christopher dealt with whatever life pitched at him by hitting it out of the park.

Christopher sighed and held out an arm. She went to him for a hug and warmed herself in his embrace. In silence, he rested his chin on top of her head.

"This could turn out to be a good thing, Christopher." When he didn't answer, she took his hand. Squeezed it reassuringly. "A really good thing."

Chapter
13

The uniformed man sitting across from her seemed nice enough. His name was Officer Smith. He had a friendly smile. Kind eyes. Sunny didn't trust him at all. Papa had often warned them to avoid the cops when they were passing out literature, because they could be arrested for soliciting without a permit. Sometimes the police had come to Sanctuary to investigate complaints about different things, and when that happened, it had always been bad for all of them. There'd been punishments. To keep them safe, Papa said. To make them extra-aware of how their behavior outside could bring trouble inside.

"Let's go over everything again, just to make sure I have it all straight. We're just trying to figure some things out. Okay? Just a few more questions."

Sunny nodded. Liesel and Christopher had taken the children into the other room, and her lap felt empty without a baby on it. She had a mug of hot tea on the table in front of her, but she didn't want to drink it.

"Your mother woke you, is that right? Your mother is…" He looked at a small notebook. "Patricia Bomberger?"

Sunny nodded. "Yes."

"She'd already packed for you?"

Another nod. "Yes. She gave me a backpack with some clothes in it. And some money."

"Where'd she get the money?"

"I don't know." It wasn't a lie. It hadn't occurred to Sunny before, but her mother must've stolen it. Probably from John Second. Sunny swallowed, hard.

"She told you to take your children and get out."

"She told me to go to my father's house."

"And you'd never been here before? You had no previous relationship with your father? That would be Christopher Albright."

"My mother left him before I was born. I never knew him," Sunny said quietly. "The only father I ever knew was John Superior."

"John Alvarez," said the cop's partner, Officer Dugan, reading from his own small notebook. "Also known as John Superior, John the Prophet and John Mashiach."

"I don't know if he had other names. He was John Superior to us."

"Your children called him Papa," said the cop.

Sunny hesitated. "Yes, we called him Papa. He was our spiritual father."

The cops exchanged a look. "And John Alvarez had two biological sons, is that right? John Alvarez Junior and another son? Josiah? He's the one who notified the police about what had happened."

Sunny hesitated. She'd said nothing about Josiah to them,

but they already knew. They'd already known a lot of things about the family. "How did he know? He left a long time ago."

"He and—" Officer Dugan paused to check his notes "—John Alvarez Junior had a falling-out? They fought?"

"After Papa died, they didn't agree on Papa's teachings. So…" She looked back and forth to the police. "How did he know what had happened?"

Silence. The cops looked at each other again, then her. Officer Dugan cleared his throat. "We're really not at liberty—"

"Apparently, John Alvarez contacted his brother to tell him the…plans." Officer Smith leaned forward just the slightest bit. "Unfortunately, Josiah Alvarez didn't get the message in time and wasn't able to notify the authorities before…well…"

Sunny tried to make sense of this. "Why would John Second have called him?"

"Miss Albright—"

Startled, she looked up at Officer Smith. "What?"

There was no need for last names in the family. It had never occurred to her they would think of her as Christopher's daughter, with his name. It had never occurred to her that legally, it probably was.

"Had John Alvarez Junior, alias John Second, been behaving erratically or…um…was there a change in his behavior?" This came from Dugan, who wasn't quite as nice as Smith.

Sunny thought about the lockdowns. The forced fasting. The punishments had become more frequent, more severe over the past year. "John Second was angry that some people thought Papa had lied to us about what we needed to do to get through the gates. He said we all needed to work harder, that it was our fault Papa hadn't left the right way. He blamed us."

Officer Smith gave her another kind smile, but this one

didn't reach his eyes. "Did you know he was going to order everyone in the compound to kill themselves?"

"We had drills." Sunny drew in a breath and fought to keep her voice steady. "Rainbow drills. It was important that we be ready."

Dugan sighed. "Ready for what, exactly?"

Sunny lifted her chin. They were blemished; of course they'd never understand. "To leave. Ready to go through the gates."

"By killing yourselves?"

"Physical bodies can't reach the spiritual plane." Papa's words sounded strange in her voice. Tasted weird. "Our physical bodies are the vessels we use to contain our spiritual bodies until the time comes to go through the gates. That's why it's so important to take care of them, because a flaw in the physical can scar the spirit."

She'd said too much, she saw it in both their faces. Skepticism. Disdain. Pity. She'd seen it before, on the faces of the people she'd offered literature to.

"I need to ask you again, Sunny. And you need to answer me honestly, okay?" Officer Smith leaned forward just a little, those kind eyes sincere but digging far too deep inside her. "The night you left, did you know that John Second was going to order everyone to take the pills that would kill them?"

Sunny shook her head. Her throat ached and her eyes burned, but she lifted her chin and took some more deep breaths to give them nothing but a face of stone. "No. I didn't. I thought it was just another drill, like all the others."

Officer Smith stood, and after a second, so did his partner. "That's all we have to ask for now."

Sunny didn't stand. She warmed her hands on the mug. "What's going to happen to me? And my children?"

The officers exchanged glances. Once again it was Officer

Smith who answered her. "Your father and his wife have already assured us that you all have a place here with them. The social worker who was here earlier—"

"Mrs. Umberger." That had been the woman's name. She'd had kind eyes, too, but her gaze had been sharp enough to pick out anything dirty, unsafe. Sunny'd seen social workers in Sanctuary, checking to make sure they weren't living in squalor or beating their children. This woman had looked around Liesel and Christopher's house as though it were a dungeon made from a garbage heap.

"Yeah. She'll have to write up a report—"

"A report?" Sunny frowned. Report was what they did in Sanctuary when someone chose not to share their discretions and needed someone to do it for them.

"That's right. A report about whether or not she thinks your children will be protected here with you."

Sunny's fingers tightened on the mug. "Of course they will! I love my children!"

"Nobody doubts that," said Officer Smith. "And I'm sure Mrs. Umberger will put that in her report. And since your dad and his wife have assured us and Mrs. Umberger that you'll be taken care of, I'm sure it will all be fine. You and your kids are very lucky, Sunny."

With that, they left her sitting at the table. Not even the hot mug could warm her. She hadn't known it wasn't just a drill, Sunny thought. But she should have. John Second using Papa's voice instead of his own should've told her that. Or else she should have known when she listened with her heart. There should've been the small, still voice Papa had told them would let them know when it was time to leave, except that Sunny had heard nothing.

Had her mother heard it?

"Sunny? Hon, are you okay?" In the doorway, Liesel held Bliss. "Did they leave?"

Sunny nodded. "Is she hungry? I can take her."

Liesel looked into the baby's face with soft eyes and a small smile. "Yeah, I think she is. What a little cutie. I changed her diaper, too."

"Thanks." Sunny held up her hands to take the baby as Liesel handed her over. "Happy? Peace?"

"They're fine. They're playing Candy Land with Christopher." At what must've been a confused look, Liesel chuckled. "It's a board game. They're having fun. They're okay. They're just in the den. I know it must be weird for you, all of this. If you want to talk about it, hon…I'm here."

"I don't have anything to talk about." Sunny put Bliss to her breast, noticing how Liesel's gaze slid away, as if it embarrassed her to watch. The blemished were okay with parading women's breasts across billboards to sell cars, but feeding children with them seemed to be completely out of line. "Thank you, though."

"More tea? I can warm it up for you."

"No, thanks."

Liesel looked as though she was about to say something else, but then didn't. "I'll just go check on Christopher and the kids. Give you some privacy."

Sunny fed her daughter. This house was cleaner than any place she'd ever lived, even despite the hours she and many of her sisters had spent on their knees scrubbing floors. It was warm, too. Smelled nice, like flowers, even though it was winter. The water was hot, the food was plentiful and varied.

They'd bought her clothes. Given her toys for her children. Disposable diapers, which went against everything Papa had ever taught them about being kind to the earth, and yet were so much more wonderfully easy to use than the cloth diapers she'd used for all her kids.

This could be a good place for them, she thought. Except she couldn't stop thinking about Sanctuary. After years of preparation, training that had gone on as long as Sunny could remember, John Second had actually done what his father had always promised was coming.

Her mom. John Second. All the men and women Sunny had thought of as her brothers and sisters, no matter if they didn't share actual parents. Everyone was related in the family.

And the children.

Oh, the children. A strangled sob tore at her throat, and she pressed her lips together to hold it inside. Why had her mother sent her away if she knew John Second was going to have them all leave, make it more than just a drill? Sunny slipped cold fingers over the top of her infant daughter's head, and thought she understood.

Chapter
14

"She's not a baby. She has three kids of her own, Christopher." Liesel rubbed lotion into her elbows and arms, then squirted another palmful and started to work on her thighs and calves and butt. Her skin got so dry in the winter, itching, and it drove her crazy. "I'm sure she'll be fine here by herself."

Christopher looked at her from over the top of his glasses. He had a finger shoved into the middle of a thick book, a biography of some rock star whose music he didn't even listen to. "Yeah, and she escaped with her life from a crazy cult that just all offed themselves only what, two days ago? I'm just saying, I don't think it's a good idea for her to be left alone."

Liesel flipped back the comforter and slid beneath the flannel sheets. "Lower your voice! Do you want her to hear you?"

Her husband would certainly never win any awards for subtlety, but at least he managed to drop his voice to something just above a whisper. "You're the one who thought it would be such a great idea for her to stay here. And I'm not saying you're wrong," he added before she could interrupt. "I think we're the only place she has to go. But there's no question that she needs some attention. I mean, for God's sake, the police will probably want to talk to her again, and didn't they say something about the possibility of another social worker coming out for another inspection or something? Didn't you see her face splashed all over the TV? They're calling her the Angel of Superior Bliss or some such shit. Soul Survivor. Christ. What a bunch of crap."

Reporters had been calling, too, though so far none of them had shown up at the house. Liesel and Christopher had let the phone ring without answering. Their voice mail had filled up with messages.

Her neck and shoulders still ached. The bruises from her fall had bloomed spectacularly. Yesterday and today had been spent dealing with all the official stuff that went along with the tragedy. Another day at home wouldn't be such a bad thing. It just wasn't as easy for her to get time off as it was for Christopher, who got vacation and sick time.

"You should do it," she said, leaving the reason unspoken because she'd said it so many times already. Sunny was *his* daughter. *His* responsibility.

Again he peered at her over his glasses. "I have meetings. I can't just cancel a national conference call to stay home and play patty-cake."

It was so much more than that, but she could see by the set of his jaw that he wasn't going to budge. Liesel sighed. "You know what a hassle it is if I call in. They count on me there."

Christopher rolled his eyes. "It's not like we're going to go hungry if you miss a few days' pay."

His comment probably hadn't meant to sound as derisive

as it did, and Liesel tried hard not to take it that way. "Wow, thanks."

Christopher shrugged. "Maybe if you miss a few days, they'll see how much they need you there and appreciate you more. Did you ever think of that?"

She found a laugh for that. "Oh, that's hardly likely."

Liesel had been working at a local print shop for what felt like forever. Owned by a husband-and-wife team who'd been in the printing business for thirty years, the shop did a little of everything, from mugs to T-shirts to calendars, and Liesel did a little bit of everything for them—some accounting, some sales, almost all the design.

"I told you. I've got meetings. I can't miss them," Christopher said flatly. "Besides, you're better with all that...stuff."

"You're going to have to find a way to be better with it, Christopher."

He shrugged, focused on the book she knew he wasn't really reading.

"You were okay with them when I took her shopping. You had a good time playing Candy Land with them, didn't you? They're sweet kids."

He shrugged again. "They're fine."

"They're your grandchildren," Liesel said.

He looked at her. "And she's my daughter. Yeah. We've been over this. Get off my back, okay?"

"I didn't mean to be on your back about it." Liesel scooted closer to him to put her head on his shoulder. He warmed her better than the blankets did. She let her icy toes slide along his warm calves and laughed a little at his muttered curse.

Christopher sighed and stuck his bookmark in to mark his place. "This is all a real mess, you know that, right? I mean, this isn't normal. It's bad enough she shows up here after almost twenty years, but with three kids in tow? How the hell are we supposed to cope with that?"

"We'll manage. Have you called your mother yet?" She let her hand rest on the tiny slip of belly exposed between his T-shirt and his pj bottoms. She was still itchy, despite the lotion, so she scooted back across the bed to get another couple of squirts. She pulled up her pajama shirt and rubbed, then looked over her shoulder to find her husband grinning at her bare chest. "Focus, Christopher."

"I'm focusing."

"On what I asked you, not my boobs."

When the phone rang, they both looked at it. Liesel glanced at the clock. It was just past 9:00 p.m. Nobody ever called them after nine.

"It's your mother," she said, checking the number on the caller ID. "Let me guess, you didn't call her."

Christopher's mother had moved in with his sister a few years ago after their dad died, but stories like this traveled. It had made the national news. And of course, Liesel realized with a small curl of her lip, her mother-in-law would've known all about Trish.

Funny how she'd never been jealous of her husband's first marriage before, and now the thought of it made her want to kick something. Christopher had been married right out of high school, a concept so foreign to Liesel she'd been able to pretend it hadn't been real, a feat made so much easier by the fact he never talked about Trish. Ever. She might as well never have existed, except for the four people in Liesel's guest bedroom.

He sighed. "No. I haven't. Did you call yours?"

"I did, actually. Left her a message to call me. But you know, Sunny's not her granddaughter. She'd be a lot less… invested."

Christopher hooked the phone off the cradle. "Mom."

Liesel pressed her grin flat. She liked her husband's family just fine, but they exasperated her husband constantly. Probably the same way her own parents worked her very last nerve yet barely bothered Christopher at all. They were lucky, she thought, watching him. She knew a lot of people who hated their spouse's family.

"Yes." Christopher swung his legs out of bed. Then, incredibly, he got out of bed altogether, and stalked into the dressing room. He closed the door behind him.

Liesel stood at her side of the bed, her hands still full of lotion she rubbed quickly into her skin so she could pull down her shirt. She could hear her husband's voice, muffled through the door, but not exactly what he was saying. Just the fact he'd felt the need for privacy told her more than anything else.

Her stomach cramped with a slow, rolling wave of something close to, but not quite, nausea. With all the excitement she'd forgotten to be mournful about her period. Liesel got into bed, under the blankets, and pressed her palms to her belly to ease the pain. If it got worse she'd have to get out the heating pad, maybe even take some medicine. But that would mean passing through the dressing room to get to the bathroom, and she didn't want Christopher to think she was spying on him, desperate to hear what he was saying, even if that was pretty much the truth.

During the first few years of their marriage, Christopher's dog had liked to try to get into bed with them at night, so they'd gotten into the habit of sleeping with the door closed. Buster had died three years ago and neither of them had felt the need for another pet, but the habit had remained. Tonight though, Liesel had made sure to leave the door cracked open a little bit so she could hear if Sunny or the kids got up or needed anything in the night.

It hit her hard, this sudden punch of a realization that an open door now meant something so much more than a matter of preference. Beneath her palms, her belly ached and cramped, then a sharp pain pricked at her deeper inside.

Half giddy, half terrified, Liesel had a realization. Something that hit home harder than anything had yet. Leaving a door open in the night to hear if someone needed her. This was what it was like to be a mother.

Chapter
15

Sunny woke, but didn't get out of bed. Blinking, she tugged the blankets up to her chin and listened to the silence in the room. Soft breathing, the familiar snuffle of her baby dreaming. What did babies dream about, anyway? Eating, sleeping, pooping?

She'd been dreaming of her mother laid out on that gurney like some broken doll nobody had bothered to fix. Her mother's vessel, she corrected herself, and if she'd ever doubted Papa's words they'd hit her right in the face when that doctor had pulled back the sheet. There'd been nothing left of her mother in that empty container.

The room was still dark, and she had no clock to check the time, but she figured it was probably around five-thirty or so. At home she'd have been up half an hour ago for the morning meditations. Lying in bed now felt indecent. She'd gone to bed with the children last night about eight, far earlier than she was used to, and had been woken only once by Bliss, who hadn't really needed to nurse but wanted to anyway.

It was the longest Sunny had slept without interruption since childhood. Maybe her entire life. So why was she still so tired? The bed was so soft, the blankets so heavy, the pajamas Liesel had bought for her so thick and soft and warm and comfortable.

She really needed to get out of bed.

Without waking Happy and Peace who shared the bed with her, Sunny put her feet over the edge. The floor was cold on her toes, but she was so toasty warm everywhere else that it hardly mattered. She yawned and stretched.

There was nobody here to notice or care if she did her morning meditations. There'd be no punishment for missing them. But *she* would know. The Maker would know. And if there was nobody here to make a report on her, force her into the silent room or heap her with extra chores, that didn't mean there wouldn't be any consequences.

Quietly, Sunny dressed in the new clothes Liesel had bought. They felt wrong on her skin. The fabrics scratchy. The skirt too heavy, the blouse too light. Her fingers fumbled on the buttons and smoothed the material over her belly, tucked it into her waistband. She had trouble with the zipper, felt guilty even for wearing a skirt so fancy, but there'd been so little choice of what was acceptable that she'd had to make do with what she could find.

She found a place for herself in the living room. Unlike the family room off the kitchen, everything in this room matched and was perfectly in place. The white carpet, thick and plush, had no footprints on it. Sunny stepped carefully to the middle of the room. She sat cross-legged on the soft carpet and let her hands fall, palms up and fingers open, onto her knees.

"Thank you for the winds that blow, thank you for the

seeds that grow, thank you for the earth to plow, thank you for the love you show."

That was the simple part. Now came the more difficult bit. Listening.

Sunny closed her eyes. Drew in a breath. She listened with her ears first, of course, because she couldn't help it. In the chapel there was always some sort of noise like the shuffle of feet or snuffle of breath. The children were impossible to keep completely silent, so there was often a baby's cry or a small child's whimper. They were supposed to be able to push all that aside, but it took longer for some than others. It had always taken longer for her.

Here, though, the house was quiet. The sound of her own breath whispered very loud in her ears, along with the steady *shush-shush* of her heart that was very much like the noise she'd heard long, long ago when she held a shell to her ear. They were hundreds of miles from any ocean, but the rush and roar of it had filled Sunny with delight and longing. She'd never seen the sea.

She imagined it, though. How the waves would curl, then break and toss themselves up on the sand. She'd seen pictures of it, and once, a very long time ago, she'd heard the sounds the ocean made on an old record album John Second had played while he had sex with her mother when Sunny was supposed to be sleeping.

Someday, she thought, she'd go to the ocean.

But for now she sat as still as she could and focused on listening with her heart. Without the words of Papa or even John Second to guide her, it was hard, but Sunny did her best. She breathed, she listened. The floor beneath her fell away.

She floated.

Her eyes snapped open, the floor rushed up to meet her, and she tipped forward with both hands out to catch herself though she wasn't really even falling. She coughed, her breath sharp in her throat. She swam against the carpet.

"Sunny?"

Blinking and swallowing a rush of spit, Sunny looked up to see Liesel in the doorway. She wore a knit cap, mittens, a heavy coat. Her cheeks were pink. She smelled like fresh air.

"Are you okay, hon?"

Sunny blinked again and looked down to where her fingers had curled into the carpet. It was so thick they disappeared up to the first knuckle. A few stray hairs had fallen out of her braid and tickled her cheeks. She sat up, brushed them away, uncrossed her legs to stand on numb feet. She stumbled.

Liesel reached to catch her, but Sunny righted herself before she could. "Sunny?"

"I was meditating. I'm sorry, I guess I got a little dizzy." Sunny looked at the spot on the carpet marked by the weight of her body. She'd been floating. Papa had said he'd been able to do it in his private meditations. He'd said they all could do it, if they listened hard enough to the secrets of their souls. John Second had claimed he could fly.

"Maybe you need a drink of water. Maybe you're coming down with something," Liesel added, and touched Sunny's arm. "You've been through a lot the past few days. Come to the kitchen with me, I'll get you something."

"Thanks." Sunny followed obediently with a glance behind her at the empty spot.

When you got rid of the weight of your misdeeds, Papa had told them, you could learn to float. Fly. And then you'd be ready to leave and go through the gates. Was that what had happened to her? Sunny shook off the remaining dizzy feeling. Or was she just too tired, too worn-out, like Liesel had suggested?

In the kitchen, Liesel pulled off her coat and hat, tossed

them on a chair, poured Sunny some orange juice and then herself coffee. She sipped it from a mug and watched Sunny over the rim of it. Her hair stuck up in wild spikes.

"Do you meditate every day?"

Sunny sipped the juice. Sweet. It was like drinking…well, sunshine. She wanted to gulp it, greedy, but forced herself to take only the tiniest of tastes, one at a time. "Yes."

"Did you all meditate?"

Sunny looked up, the juice like some sort of key that un-locked her tongue. "Yes. Every morning, afternoon and at night before we go to bed. In-between times we do it on our own, if we need a little extra."

"Extra…what?"

Sunny turned the glass in her hands, feeling the cool glass on her palms. "Extra silence."

Liesel shook her head a little. "I don't get it. I'm sorry."

Sunny looked around the kitchen, then at her father's wife. "In order to leave this life and our physical vessels behind, we have to be able to put aside everything outside ourselves and go all the way inside, to the silence. We have to listen to that silence with our hearts, because that's what tells us how far we have to go."

It was Liesel's turn to blink. She sipped her coffee, then held the mug in both her hands close to her face, as though bathing in the warmth. "So…during the day if you feel you need extra silence, you meditate?"

"People talk too much," Sunny said. "And don't listen enough."

Liesel laughed. "I believe that's certainly true. Yes."

Sunny studied her. She'd gone out on the literature mis-sions but had never been actively sent to recruit anyone. She'd never been called on to explain the family's beliefs to anyone before, though she'd been given the same lectures as everyone else on how to recognize a potential seeker. Papa had said the best way to show someone the path was to walk it. He also said that everyone in the family had the obligation to lead as many people to the light as possible, through words and deeds.

"Do you want to try it?"

Liesel looked startled. "Oh, I…I don't really think…"

"C'mon," Sunny said. "It's not easy, but it's worth it. I bet you'll be good at it."

Liesel looked at Sunny through one squinted eye, her mouth twisted, too. "What do I have to do?"

"Just listen. I'll show you." Sunny took Liesel into the living room and sat, demonstrating.

Liesel followed, but slowly, with a groan. "I might not be able to get back up."

"Meditation helps anything, even aches and pains, whatever's wrong with you. Daily meditation keeps away illness and lifts the spirit." Sunny paused, having spouted what she'd always been told but now hearing her words as one of the blemished might. "It doesn't hurt, anyway."

Liesel laughed and ducked her head for a second. She looked self-conscious. "Okay. I'm up for it. Let's go. What do I do?"

"Mostly, you just listen."

Silence for a minute or two.

"What am I listening for?"

Sunny opened her eyes and smiled. "Not with your ears. Listen with your heart. Inside. Whatever's inside."

"Okay." Liesel looked skeptical and shifted on the carpet. "How long does it usually take?"

Sunny laughed, surprised at how funny she found Liesel's question. "Sometimes, a long time. Give it another few minutes."

They were both quiet, until the sound of footsteps on the wooden floor of the entryway turned both their heads.

It was Chris, dressed for work, brow furrowed. He lifted a coffee mug.

"What the… What are you doing?"

"Hi, babe." Liesel winced and slowly uncurled herself to stand. "Sunny was showing me how to meditate."

Chris recoiled, just a little, but enough that there was no doubt of his reaction. "I'm going."

That moved Liesel forward to tell him goodbye. She followed him out of the hall, toward the kitchen. Sunny heard the low-pitched tone of a conversation that sounded as if it was trying hard not to turn into an argument, the rise and fall of voices in conflict and the mutter of her own name.

And try as hard as she could, she couldn't hear anything else.

Chapter
16

"Liesel, what's going on? They're all dead, my God, we saw it on the news even down here, I had no idea that was close to you at all." Liesel's mother sounded briefly distant, as if she'd taken the phone from her mouth and put it back. "Down! Get down, Rascal! This damn dog, Liesel, I swear to you I'm gonna have him stuffed."

Her mother's constant complaining about her admittedly ill-mannered dog was one of the main reasons Liesel had never lobbied for a replacement after Buster died. She could picture her mom now, scolding the runty mutt with a cigarette in one hand and a glass of iced tea in the other. Liesel missed her mother suddenly so hard and so fiercely she had to put a hand over her eyes to keep herself from bursting into tears.

"How's Christopher dealing with it?" her mom asked.

Liesel paused, not certain what she could say and wanting to be sure she could speak without sounding as though she was holding back sobs. "Okay, I guess."

Her mom snorted. "No, not how well is he dealing with it. I mean, *how* is Christopher dealing with all this? What's he doing about it?"

"What can either of us do about it? They're here, they have no place else to go."

Another snort. "I can't believe he never told you before. That's all. All those years, right in your backyard."

"He didn't know." Before her mom could comment on that, Liesel added, "And they weren't that close. Almost in the next town."

"But they'd been there how long, doing God knows what? Sacrificing stuff, no doubt." Liesel's mother coughed loudly. "Damn it, I thought moving to Florida meant no more winter colds."

It was the smoking, not a cold, but Liesel didn't say so. "They weren't a satanic cult, Ma."

"They all killed themselves, didn't they? What kind of religion makes you martyr yourself to get to heaven?" Her mother paused. "Well, Christianity favors that, I guess."

"They're not Christians either, so far as I can tell."

"You never hear of any Jewish cults," her mother said firmly. "Rascal, for God's sake, get down!"

Liesel peeked through the half-cracked laundry room door to the kitchen, where Sunny and the kids sat at the table, folding towels. Sunny had asked what she could do to help around the house, and all three of them were making a good job of it. Singing, even.

"I'm sure there are some," Liesel said absently. Voyeur, that's what she was, watching them when they didn't know she was. But how else was she supposed to see what they did when she wasn't there?

Her mother made a derogatory noise. "Whatever. Listen, you have them in your house now, what's going on with that?

She's what, almost twenty, you said? With three kids? Oy. I don't think I need to tell you those kids are gonna have some problems."

The children actually looked fine to Liesel. Better than fine, they were the best-behaved children Liesel had ever seen. Compared to Annabelle and her brothers, children Liesel actually loved, Sunny's children were saints, even the baby.

"They're kind of…Amish," Liesel whispered.

At the table, Sunny showed Peace how to fold a tea towel into a neat square, then shook it apart and held it out for the little girl to take. The result was messy, and Sunny laughed, shaking her head, to kiss her daughter's curls before having her do it over.

"See," she said so quietly Liesel had to strain to hear her. They all talked like that, soft and low, not quite whispering but something like it. "Like this."

"I thought you said they weren't Christian," Liesel's mom said.

"They're not. I'm not sure what they are. It's kind of like… I don't know how to describe it." Liesel had found the pamphlets she'd bought so long ago shoved in a desk drawer, but the crumpled papers hadn't done much to enlighten her. "Hippies, maybe? Simple. Plain, like the Amish, but sort of otherworldly, too."

"Oh, good Lord, not like those Heaven's Gate people!"

The pamphlets featured illustrations and had been written by someone named John Superior, the man Sunny had called Papa. Printed on cheap paper with tiny, cramped text, there'd been a lot of information about keeping your "vessel" in the best condition you could. Something about if you put a plant in a pretty pot with good soil, it was more likely to grow and bloom, but if you put it in a pot that's too big or too small, or with poor soil, it would only wither.

"Pot? Maybe they were dopeheads," Liesel's mother said when she described this.

"Shh. She's singing."

Liesel strained again to hear what Sunny was singing. There was an Amish-owned market not too far from here that sold close-to-expiration products, along with banged and bumped things. Liesel had never trusted the dented cans for human consumption, but when Buster was alive had often shopped there for dry dog food. The Amish workers often sang while they worked, harmonizing over their cartons of off-brand canned beans and expired cleaning products. That's what reminded her of Sunny now, along with the clothes and the quiet, almost meek attitude.

"I used to sing to you, Liesel. That didn't make me Amish."

"Shh," she said. "I'm listening."

"…ring-a-ring-a-rosy, pocket full of posies, ashes, ashes," Sunny sang softly, her voice sweetly lilting, out of tune. "We all fall down!"

"All fall down," Happy cried with a giggle and knocked over the pile of washcloths he'd so carefully folded. "Again!"

"Sure, do it again," Sunny said.

How many times would they fold and refold that same basket? Liesel thought just as the dryer buzzed, making her jump. She said a word that made her mother tsk-tsk at her.

"What are you doing, spying on them?"

"I'm just watching." Liesel tugged open the dryer door to let out a waft of heated air that smelled of fabric softener. She began pulling out the laundry and dumping it into the basket. "How do such small people make so much laundry, Ma?"

Her mother laughed. "One of the unanswerable questions of every mother, honey."

Liesel wasn't really anyone's mother. But she thought of leaving the bedroom door open and how that had made her feel. This laundry, these tiny socks and shirts, this soft blanket she held up to her nose to catch a whiff of baby scent even though all she smelled was detergent...those were all part of being a mother, too. Or so she thought.

"Liesel Eloise, are you crying? What's going on?" her mother demanded.

But Liesel couldn't tell her mom exactly why she found herself weeping into a pile of baby clothes because her mother had always been carefully kind enough never to ask her oldest daughter when she might give her a grandchild. "Ma, I have to go."

"Go, go. You call me later, let me know how it all went. Or if you need anything. You hear me?"

"I hear you, Ma."

"I love you, babydoll."

"Love you, too." Liesel disconnected the call, then slipped her cell phone into her pocket. She lifted the basket of laundry, surprisingly heavy considering the size of the garments loading it down, and nudged open the door with her hip. "Whoooooo wants to help me fold more laundry?"

It was a question of the silliest sort—who liked laundry? Annabelle would've rolled her eyes and run away. Peace and Happy, on the other hand, both looked up with bright grins and clapped their hands in what Liesel had to assume was unfeigned excitement.

She looked at Sunny, who had shadows under her eyes and looked only a little less thrilled. "This is the last load."

Sunny nodded. "I don't mind. It's easier than scrubbing the floors."

Liesel looked automatically to the floor, which looked fine to her. "Are they dirty?"

Sunny smiled. "Aren't floors always dirty? We walk on them."

"Sure, but…I mean, they're not too dirty. Are they?" Liesel put the basket on the table with a thump that tumbled one of the piles of washcloths over.

"All fall down," Happy crowed, his little sister repeating it.

"You know, that's a fun game, too. Not just a song. We could play if you want." Liesel tipped the overflowing basket onto the floor next to the window seat.

Sunny gasped, but quieted when she saw Liesel had done it on purpose. "A game? What kind of game?"

"Peace, Happy. C'mere." Liesel gestured so the kids each got down from their chairs. She looked at Sunny with a stupid grin on her face, feeling all at once light and strange. "You want to play?"

"I'll just watch."

"Suit yourself. Here." Liesel took one of Peace's tiny hands, then one of Happy's. "You hold each other's hands, too. And then we do this, ready?"

She began to sing the childhood song as she walked in a slow circle around the pile of warm laundry she'd dumped on her not-too-dirty floor. When had she last played this game? With Annabelle, maybe never. Becka's daughter had been born too sophisticated for games like this. Before that, long, long ago, when Liesel herself had been a toddler, maybe she'd played this with her own mother.

"…all fall down," she cried, and pretended to fall into the pile of clothes.

Peace and Happy stared.

"You do it," Liesel said.

Happy looked doubtful. "Fall into the clothes?"

"Yep. Right in 'em." Liesel shot Sunny another grin, but Christopher's daughter looked as confused as her son had. "Ready? All fall down!"

Peace didn't hesitate this time, just launched herself into the pile with a scream of glee. "Whee!"

Happy looked at Liesel.

"Go on," she encouraged. "It's fun."

Happy let his knees bend, slowly crumpling onto the somewhat squashed pile of laundry. Peace rolled onto her back, little legs kicking, her laughter loud and infectious. Liesel joined her.

Sunny looked disturbed. "That's…a real game?"

"Sure," Liesel said, holding out her hands for both children to grab. "Let's do it again. In the fall we can do it in the big piles of leaves Grandpa will rake up in the yard."

"Who's Grandpa?" Happy's small fingers linked in Liesel's.

Liesel glanced at Sunny.

"She means Christopher," Sunny said. "He's my father, so that makes him your grandfather."

Happy's brow furrowed. "So then…what's you?"

"She Weedul," Peace said, full of scorn. "Dat her name. Weedul."

Sunny burst into a flurry of giggles she tried to hide behind her hand, and gave Liesel an apologetic look with eyes bright above the dark circles. "Oh…I'm sorry, I shouldn't…"

"It's okay." Liesel laughed, too. "I've been called worse, I guess."

"I know her name," Happy said, still solemn. "I mean, what's she called? If he's Grandpa?"

Liesel's laughter faded a little bit, and she wiped at her eyes. She looked at Sunny with a shrug. "What would you like to call me, honey?"

"Weedul-ma!"

Happy shook his head. "No, Peace, that's dumb!"

"Happy," Sunny said sharply. "That's not how we talk. Do you want me to have to make…a report…?"

Sunny stopped, voice trailing off, then drew in a shivery breath. "Never mind that. Just don't talk like that to your sister. Apologize."

"I'm sorry, Peace." Happy hugged his sister far more willingly than Becka's sons would've...and again Liesel was struck with just how good these kids really were.

"You've done such a good job with them," she said impulsively. "They're such good kids."

Sunny looked up, brow furrowed very much like Happy's. Looking again a lot like Christopher. "Happy was quite naughty just now."

"Not terribly." Liesel ruffled his hair.

"Pway again?" This was Peace, tugging at Liesel's shirt hem and looking up with those striking blue eyes. "Pwease? Weedul-ma?"

"Can we call you Nana?" Happy asked.

Sunny drew in a small, sharp breath, and gave Liesel a sad look. "That's what they called my mom."

"Oh...well...Happy, why don't you call me Liesel. Grandma would feel a little funny to me." Liesel took Peace's hand, then Happy's.

"Where it feel funny?" Peace poked Liesel with her free hand.

"In her heart, probably." Sunny cleared her throat as though around emotion, though her eyes were dry. "Liesel's very young to be a grandmother. Aren't you?"

"I guess," Liesel said, looking down at the two children holding her hands, "I'm old enough. C'mon, then. One more time, let's play. Then how about we bake some cookies, okay? That's what grandmothers do, right?"

"Let's pway!" Peace cried, and this time when they came to the end of the song, she and Happy both fell down into the pile of clothes, their faces bright with laughter.

Chapter
17

"Let's play a game." This is John Second, he is Papa's true son, and he's looking at Sunny with a smile that makes her want to run away. "Come over here, Sunshine."

Sunny was going from the chapel, where most people are still listening, to the bathroom, because she has to use the toilet. Mama says Sunny is old enough not to wear diapies anymore, she is a big girl. Too big for games now, not a baby or a little girl, now she can make reports and everything.

"Sunshine," says John Second. He has a big hand and a long arm that reaches to grab her, but doesn't grab. Just curls the fingers like a poke, poke, poke. Like they want to poke her. "I said, come here."

Take a little step, another little step. That's the sort of steps Sunny does, not into the bathroom to use the toilet, even though her belly's hurting from having to go. She would run away from John Second, but he would make a report on her, tell Papa how Sunny is disobedient and how she does not listen when told. He would tell Mama, too, and she would look at Sunny with the sad eyes and be sad that Sunny isn't a good girl.

Not the bathroom, which is far, far away at the end of the hall, but down the other hall and into the bedroom. This is a big, big room, not small like the one Sunny sleeps in with Mama. Sunny's room has two beds, Mama's bed and the one underneath that pulls out when it's time for Sunny to sleep. But this room has a big bed, soft and comfy with the pillows all piled up so high it's like clouds. Papa's true son gets to have the big room with the big bed because his vessel needs a nice place so he can sleep good. He sits on the edge of the bed and says to Sunny, "Now, be a good girl and come here. We're going to play a game."

Sunny knows games. Like Pick Up Sticks and crosses-and-naughts and now this one, whatever it's called. John Second puts a finger on top of Sunny's head. He says, "Spin."

She does in a circle, his finger pointing down hard in her hair and keeping her in one place.

John Second laughs and sings a song about flowers, that's what Mama calls posies. And a fire, too, because he says about the ashes, and that's what fire leaves behind after it's all burned up. They make a fire sometimes in the yard in the summer to burn the garbage, and sometimes they let the kids poke long sticks into the hot dogs and they eat them all cooked up like that from the fire, but only sometimes, because hot dogs aren't good for their vessels. Hot dogs are for when they don't have other food and it's what the food bank sends.

"Get ready." John Second hums and hums the song, and when he gets to the end, oh, what a surprise! Instead of falling down, he picks Sunny up, up high, so that she's afraid her head might hit the ceiling. He's laughing, and he tosses her down onto that big soft bed like it's made of clouds, and he falls down, too.

It's not a very nice game, but John Second has lots of other games to play. Sunny doesn't like any of them. And one day, when she's older, he says to her, "Sunny, you come with me now," and she stands in front of him with her belly all smooth and round and fat even though she's been put on rationed dinner because she can't sell all her pamphlets.

And that was Happy.

Happy, her sweetheart. He was working very hard with a ball of soft clay. No, not clay, dough for playing. It was bright red and smelled strange, almost like it would be good to eat, but when Sunny took a surreptitious lick it was all salty. Happy had already rolled out several long strands. Now he braided them together to make a rope of dough. This he circled on the plastic mat, building it up to make a basket.

"Wow, look at that. So clever." Liesel came in from outside, her cheeks pink, her hair standing on end when she took off her hat. She'd been running, which she said was exercise.

Exercise was good for your vessel. Sunny looked at the clock. An hour had passed, a whole hour, and what had she done that entire time? Nothing but sit on this kitchen chair and watch her son make braids of dough. Peace had fallen asleep in front of the television, her thumb in her mouth, snoring lightly. Sunny shouldn't let her watch so much TV or suck her thumb, both were bad for her vessel. One would rot her brain, the other her teeth. But somehow she hadn't managed to even notice the time passing or what her child had been up to while she…what?

While she remembered.

Blinking, Sunny shook her head and bent to pick up the

plastic container that Happy had dropped, so she didn't have to look at Liesel. Liesel might see something on her face and ask her what was wrong. Sunny breathed in, pushing away memories and listening hard with her heart for any sign of a still and silent voice, but finding none. She heard the rush and roar of her blood pounding its ocean-beat in her ears, and when she sat up the world spun a little crazily, but that was all.

"What should we make for dinner?" Liesel asked as though only a couple seconds had passed instead of the eternity it had taken for Sunny to lift the plastic cup to the table.

Maybe that was all the time it had been.

Disoriented, Sunny reached to roll a piece of dough in her palm. More listening, that's what she needed. They'd been here in her father's house for only a couple weeks. Already everything they'd lived with their entire lives was managing to fall away. They went to bed and woke up at strange times. Meals were just whenever Liesel served them instead of strictly at seven, noon and five. There was always too much food and things they weren't used to eating.

"I was thinking pizza," Liesel said. "Sort of a celebration, what do you think?"

"A celebration?"

"What's a celebration?" Happy asked.

"It means when you're excited or happy about something," Liesel said.

"I'm always Happy."

Liesel laughed. "Yes, buddy, you are."

"What are we celebrating?" Sunny squeezed the dough into a circle, poking it with a fingertip.

The poke left a hole. She smoothed it over and pinched off another bit of dough, adding it to the ball in her palm. This piece was white, and where it smooshed together with the red, it made pink. How hard would she have to mix it to make it all red? Or would the white always be there, making the red a lighter shade? How much white would it take to turn this ball white?

Liesel shrugged. "There's always a reason to celebrate, if you think hard enough. We could celebrate you being here with us. That's something, isn't it?"

Sunny looked up. She curled her fingers over the ball of dough, then mashed it back into the container. A couple weeks ago she'd been living with her mother, her family, and she'd known exactly where and how every piece of her life fit against the other.

"It's nice you like having us here enough to want to celebrate."

Liesel studied her. She did that sometimes when she thought Sunny couldn't see her doing it. Sunny was used to people on the outside staring like that, all sideways and squint-eyed. But now Liesel did it right up front and without pretending she wasn't. That was harder to take, so Sunny looked right back without flinching, cast her face in stone, listened with her heart about how she should react.

"Pizza it is. I'll order it, have your dad pick it up on the way home. We don't get delivery out here, but I guess you're used to that." Liesel paused. "Do you eat pizza?"

Sunny had eaten pizza lots of times. Fresh dough, tomatoes from the garden, garlic. Lots of cheese. "Yes. It's good. Thank you, it will be great."

"You know, Sunny…" Liesel sighed a little bit and gave Happy a look, like maybe she didn't want to say something in front of him, but did anyway. "It's okay to say something if you don't like it. We don't have to have pizza. We could order subs, or even get burgers or something. Sushi."

"I don't know sushi."

"It's raw fish with rice. It's so, so good."

Sunny recoiled. "That's silent-room food!"

Liesel chewed her lower lip for a second, then crossed the kitchen to sit at the table next to Sunny. "What's the silent room? You want to talk about it?"

Sunny most definitely did not want to talk about it, but something in the way Liesel had asked made it clear she wanted to hear about it. Papa had said, "Don't turn away the seeker."

"The silent room is where we go when we've been too busy being loud to listen with our hearts. It's a place to be silent, to listen for the still voice inside that counsels us about how to behave."

"The…silent room. Is it a nice place, then? Like a place where you meditate?"

Sunny shook her head. "No. It's not a nice place. But it's a necessary place."

"And they fed you bad food there." Liesel's face looked hard, like maybe she was casting her face in stone, too. Maybe she was trying to listen with her heart.

Sunny nodded. "It helps us to think if we're hungry. Fasting clears the brain. So you get food, but it's…well, like you said, sushi."

"I'm pretty sure it's not sushi," Liesel muttered. She took some dough from the container and rolled it in her palm the way Sunny had before.

Sunny smiled at that, how even Liesel liked to play with the dough, which was really for children. Happy had made a nice basket, though it was soft and wouldn't hold anything. Now he'd moved on to other colors, shaping them with the plastic tools that had come in the big bin with all the containers of dough.

"Is that why you're so careful about tasting everything first?"

Sunny had to think a moment about what Liesel meant, but then understood. "Not because of the silent room. But sometimes the food…it could taste bad."

She thought about the bowls of oatmeal sprinkled with salt instead of sugar. Milk gone just barely sour, not enough to make you sick but definitely tasting bad. Cold pasta, the noodles orange with congealed powered cheese.

"John Second said the best way to appreciate what you have is to understand what you could have, instead." Sunny rubbed her palms together to clean them of the tiny scraps of leftover dough.

Liesel made a soft noise from the back of her throat. "And he's the one who made you go to the silent room?"

Sunny nodded after a hesitation, but looked into Liesel's eyes. Seekers asked questions because they needed answers. Sunny could not presume to know all the answers, but she could try to find some. "It was his job when Papa died to make sure all of us would be ready when it came time to leave. He fought his own brother for that responsibility and threw him out. He was Papa's true son."

Liesel looked blank, an expression Sunny knew well. Then faintly disgusted. "So he made you eat spoiled food or sometimes starved you? To teach you a lesson?"

Sunny shifted in her chair, trying to find the right words that would make Liesel understand. "When Papa died, John Second was all we had. He did what he thought he had to do to make us ready. It was his duty, as the father of the family, to make sure we all did the best we could. My mother said..."

She paused, but Liesel gestured.

"What did your mother say?"

"Mama said when a man loves his family so much he would do anything for them, we should do the same for him. We should obey him, because he knew what he was doing." Sunny paused again, thinking of the rise and fall of voices behind John Second's closed door. Her mother had been the only one who ever dared argue with him. "She should've been his one true wife."

"But she wasn't?"

Sunny shook her head. John Second had wanted a one true wife who could give him sons. Or maybe he hadn't wanted a one true wife at all.

"Sunny, there's no silent room here."

"I know that."

"I would never put you in a place like that. Never. And anyone who would..."

Liesel's fierce tone took Sunny aback, until she realized Liesel was not angry with her. Angry...for her? Maybe?

"Nobody got put in the silent room who didn't deserve it," Sunny said.

Liesel's hand closed over hers. "Sunny. Listen to me, and believe me when I tell you, there's nothing that any of you could have done that would've made you deserve something like that."

Sunny looked at her fingernails, the tips dark with red dough beneath them, and at Liesel's fingers over top of them. Liesel kept her nails short, too, square, and without the fancy polish Sunny'd seen on so many of the blemished women outside. She looked at Liesel's face, her nose and cheeks red from running, her hair a mess. Liesel had kind eyes, and the way she was looking at Sunny made her see two things.

One, that Liesel really was angry that someone could've put Sunny or anyone else in the silent room. And two, that maybe...well, maybe Liesel was at least a little bit right about it being wrong.

"Well, it's gone now, anyway," Sunny said. "Everything is."

Liesel squeezed her hand. "No. Not everything."

Chapter
18

The folder of paperwork slapped onto Liesel's desk with the sound of a hand on a cheek, so loud Liesel jumped in her chair and twirled to face the person who'd tossed it down. "Rod! Jeez, you scared me."

Rod, her boss, looked at her from squinted eyes above plump cheeks gone red with the effort of climbing the stairs. Beads of sweat had pearled in the edge of his butch cut, and as Liesel watched, one slid down his temple toward his jaw.

Amazing. It was freaking freezing in here, and he was sweating. Liesel's brows rose. "What's up?"

"Rush job. Some guy needs T-shirts for his kid's party next week. I told him we could get something made up for him superfast. These are the specs, there's some graphics stuff in there he'd like to use. Do what you can with it."

She looked at the folder, notes scribbled in Rod's atrocious handwriting that he'd expect her not only to decipher, but transcribe. She glanced at the clock. An hour before she was due to leave. Of course.

"I'm working on the price quotes for the Ebling job," she said evenly without putting a finger on Rod's folder. To touch it was to commit. "I'm still waiting on a few numbers back from that new vendor. And I have the Wentzel job in the pike, too."

Rod took a folded white hankie from his back pocket and mopped at his face. "Good. That's good. But you can take this, too, can't you? C'mon. You're my best girl."

"Funny how you say that all the time except when it's time to give me a raise." Liesel didn't love being called Rod's best girl. It always meant more work for her. At the same time, she knew it was a compliment, and he was right. She really was the best one on the minuscule design team. "I'm not sure I'll be able to get to it today, Rod. I really have to leave on time. I have my husband's daughter and her kids at home with us, and I don't want to leave them alone for too long."

"Yeah, yeah, I know. You took two weeks off, remember?" He blotted more sweat from his face, but it just kept rolling down.

Liesel looked at the clock again. Five minutes had ticked by while they had this little conversation. She didn't touch the folder. "Rod, you know I leave at three."

"What?" His expression clearly showed he did not know, apparently, because he always made sure to bring her work that needed to be rushed just before she left.

"Three o'clock," Liesel said patiently. "In about forty minutes, I need to get out of here."

She'd stayed late to help out with last-minute projects so many times that she supposed she couldn't blame him for looking as if she'd just started spouting off in a different language. It was the curse of being reliable. And talented, she thought, peeking at what she could see in the folder. She could whip up this design in an hour or so, while the same task would take Rod or one of the other guys half a day.

"But…who else will I ask, if you don't do it?" Rod insisted. "If we don't get this design finished by the end of today, we won't have time to run the shirts."

He gave her a long look. "It's for a kid's birthday party, Liesel."

Liesel sighed and took the folder. "I'll see what I can do."

Rod nodded and left her office. When she heard the heavy thud of his feet on the metal stairs outside, Liesel picked up the phone. First she dialed Christopher, but he didn't answer his cell and she hated going through his secretary. Beth always made her feel like a dunce, like Liesel didn't know where her own husband was or what he was doing. Like she had to line up to get a piece of his attention. She sent him a quick text instead, asking him to call her. Then she dialed the house phone.

She hadn't told Sunny not to answer the phone or anything like that, but when it rang four times and went to voice mail, Liesel wondered if the girl would pick up. She might feel uncomfortable answering the phone in a stranger's house. Or worse…did she even know how to answer the phone?

Liesel shook her head, scoffing. Of course Sunny could answer a phone, for goodness' sake. Even the Amish, who didn't allow phones in their houses, surely knew how to use one—no matter how Sunny had been raised, in what strange circumstances, surely she can't have been so out of touch as that. Liesel disconnected, dialed again, let the phone ring four more times before it switched to voice mail. She wished for the old answering machine they used to have. That at least would've let Sunny hear Liesel's voice leaving a message, so she could either pick up or understand what Liesel was calling about.

No answer.

A small edge of unease pinched at her, but she forced it away. She'd been the one to reassure Christopher that Sunny and the kids would be fine at home, especially after two weeks of settling in. It had been a bit hellish, even though it had gone better than she'd expected. Sure, there were some weird things here and there—his mother had taken the news of her previously unknown granddaughter particularly hard. She'd been on the phone with Christopher almost every day but had claimed to be "too nervous" to speak to Sunny. Not that Sunny would've been that great on the phone anyway. But all things considered, the week had passed without anything too out of control.

Her cell phone rang and she snatched it up, thinking it would be Sunny and realizing that was silly. Maybe Christopher. But no, it was Becka.

"Hey, girl, what up?"

Liesel had to laugh at Becka's heavy-toned slang. "Working. You?"

"Like a mother-effing-dog. Like a DOG."

They both laughed at that. Becka had quit her full-time job as a psychiatric nurse when Annabelle was born, because she'd said juggling work, child care and the house along with four small kids at home was driving her almost as crazy as the patients. Liesel knew Becka was full of it—she'd taken to staying home with her kids like she'd spent her whole life yearning to be Suzy Homemaker, complete with her own full-size version of the Easy-Bake Oven and Baby-Wets-a-Lot.

"We're getting a new fridge," Becka said. "I had to pull this bitch out and clean underneath it. My God, you know what sort of crap ends up under the fridge? You don't even wanna know. Believe me."

"What happened to your old fridge?" Liesel glanced at the clock and started typing in orders, glad she could multitask.

"Nothing. But Kent had a boner about getting ice and water through the door, so who am I to deny the man something he wants? And the new fridge, not gonna lie, is sweeeeeet." Becka drew out the word. "I might make sweet love to it, that's what I might do."

Liesel snorted laughter, eyes on the screen, fingers tapping away as fast as she could go. "Um, ew."

"So...that's not why I called. I just wanted to check up, make sure everything in Casa de Albright was on track." Becka paused. "Today's the first day you left them home by themselves, right?"

"Yes."

"No frantic phone calls?"

"No. Actually..." Liesel finished off one file and saved it, then opened the next. "I called home to ask Sunny if she could put some chicken in the oven because wouldn't you know it, Rod needs me to finish up some things here."

"Why don't you just order dinner? Save yourself the trouble?"

"I thought about it, believe me. But Sunny's kind of funny about eating."

"What do you mean?"

Liesel paused, trying to think about how she could describe it without sounding as if she was a little nutso herself. "They taste everything before they eat it."

Becka laughed. "Doesn't everyone?"

"No. I mean...they taste everything before they eat it. Like it's going to bite them back or something. They don't like to eat when it's not the right time. No snacking in between meals—"

"Wish I could get my kids to do that."

"I know they're hungry. That's the thing. They're hungry but won't eat unless it's the right time or the right things. They don't eat candy. And yes," Liesel said before her friend could interrupt, "I know that it's better if they don't eat candy. But isn't it what kids do?"

"I know lots of parents don't let their kids eat candy."

"It's not that she doesn't let them. It's that she looks at me like I'm insane when I offer them a cookie or, God, even a Fruit Roll-Up. She doesn't come off as trying to be judgmental, but she is."

"Most people think they're right about things, that's been my experience. And they want to make sure you think they're right, too."

Liesel rocked in her chair. "It's not really that. It's like she has all these secrets and we're just not privileged enough to understand them."

"Ah."

Liesel sighed. "Yeah."

"Listen...I was thinking about something. If you think Sunny needs to see someone, I can recommend some great docs who specialize in younger patients."

It had occurred to Liesel that they all might need some sort of counseling, but honestly, she'd found the prospect so daunting she'd been unable to face it. "You think they need to see a shrink?"

Becka paused. "Yes. I think that it would certainly help them. At least a psychologist, if not someone who has experience in deprogramming."

Liesel sagged in her chair. Deprogramming, God. "Yeah. Yeah, I think that would probably make sense."

"How does she seem? Sunny."

"Quiet. They're all very quiet. The kids are amazingly well behaved."

"Compared to my monsters, most kids are." Becka laughed. "But honey, you know they had to go through a whole lot of stuff you can't ignore."

"I know."

"So if you want me to recommend someone who can just talk to her a little...anytime...I can do that."

"Thanks, Becka. Shit, I have to get this stuff done. I'll call you later, okay?"

"Fine, fine, I have to finish scrubbing my kitchen floor. So glam, I can't even stand it." Becka paused again. "And Liesel, hon, be careful."

"With what?"

"Just...you don't know what sorts of things Sunny might do, that's all. Oh, shit, there's the doorbell, I bet that's the delivery guy. Gotta run. Call me."

Becka hung up before Liesel could say anything else. She ended the call and turned back to her computer, but the screen blurred and she had to blink rapidly to get her eyes to focus. She rubbed them, the clock her enemy.

What sorts of things might Sunny do?

For a second, Liesel imagined coming home to find her house emptied of every valuable, Sunny and the kids gone off on some wild adventure financed by Liesel's grandmother's silverware and her wedding ring, the one that had gotten too big and that she kept in her jewelry box on top of her dresser. Guilt instead of unease pinched her this time. She shouldn't even think of such a thing.

She dialed again. This time, the phone only rang three times. There was a click, then silence.

Then, "Hello, Liesel."

"Hi, Sunny, it's—" She broke off with a laugh. "How did you know it was me?"

"The phone told me. I mean, it said it here in this little window. Your name."

"Oh, caller ID. Of course." Liesel felt dumb. "How are you doing?"

"We're fine."

Liesel waited a beat, but Sunny wasn't forthcoming with anything else. She cleared her throat. "Listen, hon, I'm really sorry. I know I said I'd be home by four, but it looks like I might not be home until five. I left a couple packages of chicken breasts out to thaw, do you think you could put them in the oven for me? There's a small box in the pantry labeled Onion Soup, you just put that on top with about a cup of water."

Sunny hesitated but said, "I'm sure I could."

"Great. I'm sorry to do this to you on your first day there alone, but I know you don't like to eat too late. How are the kids?"

"Happy and Peace are playing that game you gave them. Candy Land?" Sunny's voice had brightened. "Thank you, they like it very much. They want to know if they can have some candy now."

Liesel chuckled, but ruefully, the conversation with Becka still fresh. "Don't kids always want candy?"

"We don't eat it," Sunny said. "Candy's very bad for our vessels."

"Oh." Liesel bit off her laughter. There it was again, that nonjudgmental judgment. She couldn't tell if Sunny was assuming she was some wild, rampant sugar fiend, or merely stating a fact. "Well, I'm glad they like the game. And you're okay?"

It seemed impossible to Liesel that Sunny could be anything

like okay. Other than her outburst in Kmart, she'd barely shown any signs of grief. Christopher had said she didn't even cry when she identified her mother, who'd been buried without anyone attending. Liesel was no expert on mourning, but it seemed a couple weeks was far too short a time to recover from losing everything you'd ever known.

"Liesel, I can put the chicken in the oven. Bliss needs her diaper changed. Is there anything else?"

Her mind had been wandering, but she was called back now by Sunny's calm voice through the phone line. "Oh... yes. I have some salad fixings in the fridge, and you can pick a vegetable from the freezer to go with dinner. I have potatoes in the pantry, maybe you want to bake some of those?"

"Sure, okay."

"Sunny, you have my cell phone number, right? In case you need anything." Liesel didn't want to hang up without some further reassurance that her stepdaughter was handling things.

Sunny read off the number Liesel had printed on the pad next to the phone. "Right?"

"Yes. That's it. Thanks." Liesel hesitated again. "Okay, well, I should be home by about five. Okay?"

"Okay," Sunny echoed. Then she hung up.

No "goodbye," no "see you later." Liesel stared at the phone in her hand before setting it back in the cradle. She laughed, shaking her head. It was efficient, if not exactly socially savvy.

Then she turned to the folder Rod had left her with a sigh of determination.

Chapter
19

Each to his task and not to someone else's, that was what Papa had taught them. Some do the shopping, some do the cooking. Some the cleaning. Some teach the children. Some, like John Second, handle the money. Some, like Josiah, deal with the blemished, making sure that everything is taken care of in the right ways so that they leave Sanctuary alone. Separation of duties means everyone works together to make Sanctuary a warm, welcoming and functional home, so long as everyone does what they're meant to do and don't try to do anything beyond what they've been assigned.

Sunny's mother works in the gardens. She chooses the seeds that will go into the ground from a large catalog, and she writes their names on a list. She is supposed to give the list to Papa, but Josiah is really the one who takes it. He looks it over and uses a calculator to add up all the numbers in the catalog.

"Lots of tomatoes," he says.

Mama smiles. "We use them for lots of things."

"I like tomatoes." Josiah shrugs and reaches to tap Sunny's shoulder. "What about you, Sunshine? Do you like tomatoes, too?"

The truth is, she doesn't like them raw in a salad or thick in a sandwich, dripping with mayonnaise. She likes ketchup, though. Spaghetti sauce, too. She nods.

Suddenly, the taste of tomatoes floods her mouth. Saliva squirts, bitter in her mouth. Her throat closes and she thinks she might choke on the flavor of it. That's been happening a lot lately. Phantom tastes and smells that leave her stomach churning.

Mama doesn't notice. She's too busy talking with Josiah about the varieties of brussels sprouts and broccoli. Sweet corn. Sunny loves sweet corn, but even swallowing again and again, she can't wash the taste of tomatoes from her tongue.

"You think you might like to help your mom in the garden?"

Sunny turns. She likes Josiah much better than his older brother. Josiah is kinder, for one thing. He laughs a lot. He plays the guitar sometimes. And…he has never touched her the way John Second touches all the girls. Josiah and Papa don't get along very well, though. There's not supposed to be shouting in Sanctuary, but there often is. Now Josiah's staring at her with a smile on his face, his hair long to his shoulders, and Sunny wonders what it would be like to touch his hair. It looks like it would feel soft.

"Papa wants Sunny to share the light," Mama says as she tucks the list neatly into the catalog and hands it to Josiah.

For a moment, Josiah's brow furrows and the creases at the sides of his mouth get deep. "Of course he does. He has all the prettiest girls and boys doing that."

Mama looks surprised, then pleased. She nods, looking Sunny up and down. "Then she's perfect for it."

The taste of tomatoes is back, harsh and thick and stinging. Sunny shakes her head against the flavor, but also in response to what her mother said. Sunny does not like going out into the world to peddle the pamphlets. She doesn't like going in the van that smells of feet and sour breath. She doesn't like being dropped off outside the malls or grocery stores or bank parking lots to stand with her sheaf of pamphlets, begging for a dollar or as much as they'll give her to read Papa's word. The blemished can be mean, sometimes even angry. They can be scary. But most of all, Sunny can't stand being so close to so many things she's not allowed to have and definitely is not supposed to want.

She's not meant to avoid temptation, she thinks. It must be so easy for other people in the family to not look even once at the cases of pastry in the coffee shop and wonder at how they'd taste, or the short skirts and high heels blemished women wear and think how pretty they are. But it's not easy for her.

"It's why Papa chose you," Josiah says to her later, when he catches her after dinner and walks down the hall with her, and something in the way he looks at her makes her tell him the truth even though it's not time to make a report.

"Because he knows I...want? Things?"

Josiah has a nice smile, full of white teeth that have never rotted. "I'll tell you a secret, Sunshine, if you lean in close."

She does, heart skipping a little faster as she closes her eyes. She waits for him to press her to the wall or pull her into a room. To touch her. But Josiah's only caress comes from his breath on her ear.

"We all want things," he says quietly. "It's not the wanting that weighs you down and keeps you from going through the gates. It's when you know something's not good for you, and you do it anyway. Not just once or even twice, but over and over again. It's not doing the best you can for your vessel. That's what ties you down, so you can't fly."

He steps back with another smile she can't stop herself from returning. He's not like his brother. Not one bit.

"You go out and you spread the light, Sunshine. It's what you were meant for. Papa saw that, and I see it, too." Josiah touches his fingers to her cheek for just a second.

She remembered that touch for a long, long time.

Of course, as it turned out, Papa had been wrong about Sunny being meant for leading anyone to the light. She'd failed miserably at selling pamphlets. She'd found her place in Sanctuary, though. Each to his task as Papa said, and not to someone else's.

Hers had most definitely not been in the kitchen. Beyond her sneaking of food now and again, Sunny barely even set foot in the Sanctuary kitchen. She'd never had a need. Others had the responsibility of cooking the meals. All she'd ever had to do was be on time to eat them.

She should've told Liesel the truth, but had been too ashamed to admit it. There'd already been too many things she didn't know how to do. Now the smoke alarm beat out its cry in a steady pattern, with the others in the house blatting out their own shrieks in counterpoint. When they first went off, Sunny had gone to her knees, hands clapped over her ears, certain the next sound would be Papa's voice directing them all to go to the chapel.

That would've been better than what was happening now. Smoke, acrid and choking, poured from the open oven door. Inside, the chicken had become a blackened lump. The potatoes had exploded all over the inside of the oven. Sunny stood in front of it, one hand covered in a red rubber oven mitt, the other in front of her face, waving a tea towel ineffectually at the smoke.

Bliss, strapped tight into her infant seat on the kitchen table, added her screams to the sounds of the alarm. Peace had broken down into wrenching sobs. Only Happy had maintained any sort of calm, though his eyes were wide and frightened, and he tugged on the hem of her blouse.

"Mama? Why won't it stop?"

"Hush, my sweetheart. Stand back. Take your sister away."

Happy took Peace by the hand and backed up a step. Bliss screamed louder, struggling against the straps of her seat on top of the kitchen table, but Sunny didn't have time to comfort her. The grease that had collected beneath the pan of chicken flamed suddenly, and Sunny reached without thinking to grab at the pan. The pain was instant and intense, and she jerked her fingers back with a cry.

"Sunny! What the hell?" She hadn't heard the garage door opening over the sound of the fire alarm, but now Chris ran into the kitchen.

He slammed the oven door closed, went to the stove and turned on the fan over the cooktop. He opened the double glass doors leading to the back deck and grabbed another tea towel. He stood under the smoke alarm and swung the towel back and forth until finally the alarm cut off.

He looked at her. "What the hell are you doing?"

She could still see flames inside the oven. Chris turned off the heat, but left the door closed. Tendrils of smoke seeped out from the vents, but not as much as had been pouring out before.

"I was cooking the chicken. Liesel asked me to cook the chicken." Sunny's hair had fallen into her eyes. She pushed it back and winced at the pain in her hand. Her fingers were blistered.

"Did you burn yourself?" Chris took her hand in his, not

gently enough. "You need ice on that. Go run the water in the sink, cold as it goes. I'll get some ice."

He pushed a bowl under the spout on the fridge to get some cubes from the ice maker. The bowl shook, and the ice tumbled out onto the floor. He bent to pick it up and held on to the fridge-door handle for a second when he came back up. He blew out a breath.

"Here." He gestured at Sunny with the bowl. "Sit down."

She turned off the water and held her hand out in front of her to sit at the table, though she bent first to look beneath it. "You can come out now."

Two blond heads poked out from under the table. Sunny gathered them into her arms, hugged them close and kissed the tops of their heads, then looked up at him with a small, nervous smile as she stood.

"I'm sorry," Sunny said. There was no point in denying anything. "Liesel said to cook the chicken, and I wasn't sure how to use the oven."

"Where is Liesel?" Chris flapped the tea towel again, but most of the smoke was now disappearing.

"She called and said she'd be home late, and could I start dinner." Sunny frowned with a look at the oven. "I'm sorry, Chris," she repeated.

He gave her a long, strange look. "If you didn't know how to use it, why didn't you call her? How the he—heck do you not know how to work a freaking oven?"

Sunny took a deep breath and coughed on the still-thick scent of smoke in the air. She'd made a mess of things, unintentionally, but she had to take responsibility for it. She hugged Happy and Peace to her again, grateful Bliss's sobs had softened into silent, hitching tears.

She bent to murmur into Happy's ear, "Take Peace upstairs into the bedroom. Silent feet. Go, now."

When they'd gone, she faced Chris with a sense of inevitability. "I should have called her, you're right. I was stupid and silly."

"You could've burned the house down," Chris said unnecessarily. He tossed the tea towel into the sink and ran his hands through his hair. Everything reeked of smoke, and he went to the glass doors to take a long, deep breath. He turned back. "Look, Sunshine…"

Chris stopped dead. Sunny had pulled a large wooden spoon from the kitchen tool caddy. She held it out to him, and Chris took it automatically. Sunny turned to the kitchen table and leaned over it. She flipped her skirt up, exposing her plain white panties. Her hands on the table squeaked as she put her palms flat on the stainless-steel surface.

She looked at him in resignation over her shoulder, hoping he'd at least be fast.

Chris stepped back, jaw dropping, mouth dry. "Sunny. What the hell?"

And that was how Liesel found them.

Chapter
20

The first time Liesel Gottlieb looks across the room and sees Christopher Albright, she's not looking for him. Her gaze just sort of snags on his face as she scans the crowd the way everyone does at parties. Seeing who's who.

The second time, though, she's looking specifically for the blond man with the loud laugh who's entirely focused on the short redhead in a dress a size too small. She's all hair and heels and cleavage, and if Liesel were to get much closer, she's sure the woman would be all perfume, too. That's okay. Liesel's a lot more than tits and lipstick, and predatory women like that are lots of fun to usurp.

Liesel waits, though. This party is full of single hotties, and she's not really that into blonds as a rule. There is something about him, though. The laugh, for one thing. It turns heads, not just hers. The redhead can't quite keep up with him, though bless her tiny heart, she's trying.

Liesel circulates. She thinks of leaving. She changes her

mind when she passes by the makeshift bar someone's set up at the kitchen table and finds the blond man struggling with a couple slices of lime and a bottle of rum.

"Mojito?" he asks hopefully.

Liesel eyes the goods and pulls out the ingredients she needs to make up a standard mojito. She mixes the drink and hands it to him. "It would be better with crushed mint and simple syrup, but this will have to do. I hope she likes it."

His gaze shifts toward the living room for a second. "How do you know it's not for me?"

"You don't look like a mojito drinker." Liesel leans back against the counter. "I figure you for a whiskey sour sort of guy."

"Oh, yeah?" He gives her his hand to shake. "Chris."

"Liesel." He has a nice handshake, firm and warm. Not clammy. "Am I right?"

"Whiskey and soda, actually. But you were close."

She laughs. "I tended bar to pay for my last couple years of school."

The conversation moves on from there, one topic flowing into another without any break and sometimes, any sense, though neither of them seems to have trouble understanding the other. They laugh. A lot. He leans in to put a hand on the cabinets next to her head, the drink and the redhead both long forgotten. Liesel tips her head, offers her mouth without a word.

That first kiss goes on and on.

Liesel leaves the party with Christopher, and they kiss again under a streetlight. Again at the corner by the stop sign. Once more on her doorstep, where he leaves her without asking if he can come inside.

She's not surprised when he calls her the next day, or when he asks her out. She's not even surprised how much she likes him, because meeting Christopher is like hooking up with an old friend she's known forever. They just…mesh. They merge.

They were married not quite two years later. Nothing fairy tale about it, no chick-flick drama, just two people who met, fell in love and kept on loving. Facing her husband from across the den, watching him drink his whiskey and soda, Liesel realized how lucky they'd been to have had so few bumps in their road. The problem was, she thought as her husband paced and drank and shut her out, they had no practice at dealing with trouble. It was easy enough to stand together when things were going well. What were they going to do now that things were a little rocky?

Her hands were cold, and she rubbed them together. She leaned on the arm of the couch, not wanting to sit and yet unsure of how long she could keep standing. "You have to talk about this, Christopher."

He sipped at his drink. "I don't know what you want me to say."

"It's not about what I want you to say. It's about what you think or feel or need to say."

He gave her a look. "Really? You want me to talk about how I feel? Or do you want me talk about how *you* want me to feel?"

She wanted to say he was being unfair, but something in his tone stopped her. How *did* she want him to feel? For that matter, how did she feel, herself?

"This is a mistake. We were stupid to think this was the right thing to do. We don't know anything about where she came from, except that those people were a mess. They all killed themselves, for God's sake," Christopher muttered, at least making the attempt to keep his voice down. "And she doesn't seem to see a damn thing wrong with it, Liesel! Who knows how they messed with her head."

"So we'll get her help!"

Christopher tossed back the last of his drink and set the glass on the bookcase with a thud. He paced, hands on his hips, not looking at her. "She almost burned the house down. Did you think about that? How she doesn't even know how to work an oven? We're not talking about getting her a little help, Liesel, we're talking about training her from the ground up."

"She's not a dog!"

"No, and you can't adopt her just like one."

Liesel sighed. "So what do you want to do?"

"We could get them set up somewhere. There are places they can go—"

"Like what? Foster care? Women's shelter?"

"She's a grown woman. We could help her with money. She could apply for help from the state."

Liesel frowned. "You want to send your daughter and grandchildren away to live on welfare?"

"She wanted me to...spank her." Christopher's voice was thick with disgust.

She crossed the room to him, meaning to make this all go away. Make it better somehow. This was her husband in front of her, not some stranger, after all. Yet when she got there to take his hand, it felt different. She kissed the knuckles anyway. "I know."

"It was sick."

"I'm not arguing with you about that. But...she didn't think it was sick. I mean, it must've been something they did there. Where she grew up. I told you I saw scars. And I'm not saying it was right, not at all," Liesel added hastily. "I'm just saying that before we make judgments, before we just write her off, don't you think we should at least try to find out more about how she was raised? What they believed? Don't you feel some sort of obligation to her, Christopher?"

The speech rattled out of her in a long string of words she wasn't even sure made sense, but it felt as if the faster she talked and the more she said, the likelier it would be that something clicked with him. She couldn't even have said why it was so important to her, exactly.

"This isn't about me," Christopher said in a low voice. He backed away from her and rubbed his sweating glass against his forehead. Typical. She was freezing; he was overheated. "And you know it."

Liesel sat up straight, jaw clenching. "I don't know what you mean."

Her husband gave her a long, long look. "They won't be yours. Those kids."

As if she was trying to…what? Steal them? Like some freaky, crazy person who snuck into a hospital and tried to walk off with someone else's newborn? Just hearing him say the words were as bad as if he'd slapped her, and her head rocked back just like he had.

The look on his face was worse.

"How could you…" was all she managed to say out loud before her throat closed up and her teeth bit off the reply. She tried again. "Her mother sent her here."

"Is that what you want to talk about? My first wife?" Christopher paused, then kept on without waiting for her to answer. "What do you want me to tell you, Liesel? She was a crazy bitch who cheated on me, lied to me and raised my daughter as someone else's. She never once bothered to make me a part of Sunny's life. And then when shit went down, Trish sent her to me, and I'm supposed to just…what? Forget all that? Forget about her?"

"No. Not forget. You're supposed to deal with this,

Christopher. She's your child, and she's here now, with us. And we have to find some way to make this work, for the sake of those little ones, if nothing else."

He faced her. "If you had one of your own, would you feel the same way?"

Liesel gaped. "What does that have to do with anything?"

"If you had your own." She'd never seen him look so hard. It turned her stomach, and she had to look away, but he kept talking. "If I'd let you have a baby—"

"Let me?" Liesel's throat closed, the words forced and hoarse. "When have I ever needed you to *let me* do anything?"

But he kept on, not listening to her, or at the very least not hearing. Not wanting to hear. "If you had a kid of your own, would you be so jazzed about having them here in this house? If it was a question of your child's safety over that of some other woman's children…"

She turned, considering clapping her hands over her ears so she wouldn't have to listen. His words followed, poked and prodded. Christopher had a caustic sense of humor that could bite when he was angry. Occasionally he could be insensitive, the way Liesel figured all men could be. He could be inattentive. She'd never, ever, thought of him as cruel. Liesel had never looked across the room at Christopher's face and thought that she might gladly punch him in the junk. Or that she'd simply turn on her heel and walk away without a look back. She'd never imagined she could be angry enough to leave him. Her stomach ached from how easy imagining it became. She wondered if she'd ever be able to forget it. She thought probably she never would.

His words cut at her, not because he was being cruel, though he was. But because inside her, not even in a place that was very deep and not at all a secret, Liesel knew he was right.

"Well," she said finally, when it became clear he wasn't going to say any more, "I don't. Do I? Have my own. And I probably never will. Maybe this is the closest I'll ever get."

A long beat of silence cut her to the bone, until at last he said, "I'm sorry."

Sorry because if they'd had their own it would have been so self-righteously easy to put Sunny and her children aside? Sorry because he understood for the first time how badly she'd wanted a baby of her own? Or simply sorry because they'd tried to do the right thing and now had to deal with the punishment for their good deed?

It didn't matter.

This was a man she loved, who loved her, and even if they'd never had to get through anything difficult in the past, they were going to get through this now. When Christopher put his arms around her, his chin on top of her head, Liesel pressed herself close to him, the beat of his heart familiar and steady under her cheek. Somehow, they would get through this.

Chapter
21

Sunny had messed up again. Burning the dinner had been bad enough, but then when she'd tried to make amends she'd made everything so much worse. It had seemed simple enough to give Christopher the spoon. He was, after all, her father.

Sunny couldn't forget the look on his face. He'd been revolted. Liesel, coming through the door, had actually shouted at him and grabbed the spoon from his hand before Sunny could tell her it hadn't been his idea, but hers. Liesel had backed away from Christopher with a look of disgust identical to his, but within a few seconds of his hurried explanation that look had turned on Sunny herself.

It had been awful.

In the corridor of the morgue, her mother's father had looked right past her as though she didn't exist. That had been better than seeing the faces of the people who were supposed to be her family—her blood family, staring at her as though she were some kind of monster.

She'd tried to explain that because of the mistakes she'd made, and the mess, it was Christopher's job to discipline her. His duty, in fact. The wooden spoon was as close to a switch as she could find on short notice.

Liesel had actually tossed the spoon in the trash and turned to Sunny with her arms crossed across her stomach and hands cupping her elbows. Holding herself, against exactly what Sunny didn't know, but it had shown on her stepmother's expression as sickness. Then Liesel had suggested in a voice that was more like a command that Sunny go upstairs with the children and wait until they called her back down.

She'd expected them to make her leave. She hadn't had any idea about where she might go, but she'd been prepared. Terrified, but ready. Instead, they'd offered her another chance.

Now she couldn't sleep. Bliss had been sleeping without waking in the night more regularly over the past week than she had since she'd been born. Peace and Happy were clean, warm, well-fed and dressed. They had toys to play with, and even as Sunny's conscience poked at her for letting them have such worldly things, such wasteful things, there was no denying that it had made all this so easy. There were no late-night drills, no punishments. Nothing to fear. Everything that had been her life, gone and replaced with what anyone could see was better.

Still, this bed, this room, this house were all too big. Too confusing. She tossed in the warm blankets until her new nightgown tangled around her ankles and she had to kick off the covers and get out of bed.

In Sanctuary, roaming the halls at night could get you into trouble. There were few enough nights, anyway, that they weren't woken for some reason or another. A rainbow drill. A room inspection. When she'd moved from her mother's room into the dorm, it had been common for John Second or one of his friends to come during the night and pick out a girl or two for special "inspections."

It had never stopped Sunny from slipping out into the shadows and creeping to the kitchen for snacks she didn't even want to eat. It was never hunger that drove her. Just the idea that she could get away with it.

She wasn't hungry now, and she knew that even if she was, neither Liesel nor Christopher would deny her something to eat, no matter the hour. Still, she crept from her room on soft feet, easing down the thickly carpeted hallway with her breath captured tight in her lungs. She took each stair slowly, testing with her toes first to make sure none creaked to give her away.

She searched the pantry first, fingertips brushing over the boxes and packages of food. So much of it, and all contaminated with additives and chemicals and things so bad for your vessel they made cancer. In the cupboards, too. Bottles, cans, jars. She pressed a cool glass jar to her cheek to feel the smoothness, but settled it back on the shelf.

A noise froze her in place, hands full of proof she was not the good girl she was supposed to be. Another noise, something like a snore. Sunny carefully replaced everything she'd taken out and shut the cabinet and pantry doors quietly before going down the hall toward the den.

She'd turned the kitchen light on and in the glimmer of it tiptoed just to the doorway, filling the hall but doing no more than peeking inside the den. She shrank back at the sight of Christopher in the chair in front of the television, but it was too late. He'd seen her.

"Come here." His voice was thick, low.

Her feet moved, one step and another, even though she

wanted to go the other way. When she was close enough to him, his hand took her by the wrist, fingers curling tight. He pulled her onto his lap.

Sunny went quiet. Not just silent with her voice, no sound, no protest, nothing to say, but quiet in her head. He would touch her now. Run his hands up and down her body and find the soft and hidden places. Sunny sat loosely, nowhere near calm but letting her muscles be tricked into the pretense of relaxation. It was always better that way, to let herself be limp and placid like a rag doll. Like her body belonged to someone else.

He buried his face in her hair, which she'd taken out of the braid she normally wore. His fingers tangled in it. She could hear the low rasp of his breath and feel the shift of his shoulders as he leaned into her. She thought he might be… crying?

Now she put her arm around him, one hand rubbing his back, the other on top of his head. Her fingers sank into the thickness of his hair. She didn't know this man who was supposed to be her father…but she knew how to comfort someone.

"Trish," he muttered so softly she wasn't sure she'd heard him.

At the sound of her mother's name, Sunny's soothing fingers stopped. "Chris?"

Every part of him touching her tensed and tightened.

"Get up," he barked, pushing at the same time as he tried to stand. "Jesus Christ. Sunny, what the hell?"

She nearly tumbled off his lap, but caught herself. Her feet tangled in the hem of her nightgown, but she managed to keep herself upright as she tugged it free. Her heart pounded. Her head, too. She moved away from him, uncertain and ashamed. Again.

"I'm sorry," Chris said before Sunny could say anything. "I was…dreaming. But I shouldn't have… What were you doing?"

"I was thirsty. I came to get a drink of water. You sounded like you were talking. I came in to see what you were doing." Every sentence slipped from her mouth in a soft, unassuming tone. She waited to see if he'd call out against her lie, but he didn't. "Are you okay, Chris?"

"You should…" She heard the click of something in his throat when he swallowed. "You should call me Dad. I'm your father."

Would that make what had just happened better or worse? "Are you okay…Dad?"

"I'm fine. I was having a nightmare, that's all. I'm… I was dreaming."

Silence.

"You should go back to bed," Chris said.

She wanted to tell him it was okay, that nothing had happened that couldn't be forgotten, but even in the dimly lit room she could see he wasn't looking at her. She wasn't sure he would've taken it as comfort, anyway. When she got to the doorway, his voice made her pause.

"You look so much like her." The words sounded as if they hurt him to say.

She hoped they did, because they really hurt to hear.

Chapter
22

Rod hadn't been happy about Liesel leaving work early, but after the incident with the stove she didn't want to leave Sunny home with the kids all day long by themselves. It had been a little tricky—Liesel didn't want to insult her husband's daughter, but on the other hand it was very clear that even though Sunny'd lived a life that should've made her as much of an adult as someone years older, she was still very much a child. So Liesel had told Rod she'd be working from home in the afternoons until further notice, had dealt with the fallout, and now pulled into the driveway with her trunk full of groceries. At least this time there wasn't any smoke in the garage when she opened the door. That had to be something, anyway.

Laden with plastic grocery bags, Liesel called Sunny's name as she headed down the hall from the laundry room toward the kitchen. She stopped, caught short. Not like yesterday when she'd come home to find her oven on fire. That had been panic inducing. What greeted her now made her instantly, ridiculously angry.

Every cupboard, every drawer hung open. Pots and pans taken down from their usual place on the pot rack hanging over the kitchen island were piled high on one side of the double sink. The dishwasher emitted a steady, low thudding noise that meant something had been placed incorrectly so that the water spray moved whatever it was with every spurt.

Liesel dropped the bags from her hands. They hit the tile floor with a crash, spilling several cans of chicken noodle soup, which rolled across the floor. One bag split, tossing a tube of Pringles chips, and Liesel muttered a curse. Now the chips would be crumbled.

"Sunny!"

"Liesel," Sunny said from her place at the counter. "Let me help you with your bags."

"What's going on in here?" Liesel watched as Sunny knelt in front of her to gather up the plastic bags and take them to the island to unpack. "What are you doing?"

Sunny looked at Liesel over her shoulder. "I thought that since I made such a mess yesterday it would be my job to clean it up. There was a lot of smoke. And dust," she added.

Liesel frowned. She cleaned as often as seemed necessary so as not to live like pigs, and had a cleaning woman come in twice a year to handle the major stuff. She couldn't remember the last time she'd dusted. Then again, she couldn't remember the last time she'd burnt a chicken into charcoal, either.

Liesel looked around her formerly, if not immaculate, at least approximately neat, kitchen. "You've torn everything apart."

Sunny set a can of baked beans on the counter next to the soup she'd picked up. "The only way to do the best job is to start from the beginning."

Liesel shook her head, drawing in a small breath, then another. One at a time, trying not to be too angry. "It's just that...surely you could've cleaned things one at a time. Without making so much of a mess."

Sunny frowned. "I thought I was helping. I know I can't cook, Liesel. I mean, I never had to before. But I can clean. I'm good at cleaning."

"It's not that." Liesel looked around, noticing the cupboards Sunny had already been through. The mismatched plastic containers left over from Chinese takeout and packaged deli meat had been stacked neatly, lids replaced so that each container had one. Liesel was used to having to catch a tumble of plastic storage ware every time she opened the cupboard, but now there was actually extra space.

"I put all the ones that didn't match on the table so you could recycle them," Sunny said when she saw Liesel looking.

"Sunny..." Liesel sighed. "Thank you. I'm just surprised, that's all."

Now that she could really take a look around, she could see that all the places Sunny'd cleaned were clear of smoke, dust and clutter. In better shape than they'd been before the fire. Even the fridge had been wiped down and the magnets rearranged in neat rows.

"Do you have more groceries to bring in?"

Liesel looked at Sunny. "Oh. Yeah. Can you help me?"

"Sure." Sunny smiled, no sign she'd taken any of Liesel's bad mood to heart.

"Where are the kids?"

"Bliss is sleeping. Happy and Peace are supposed to be napping, too, though Happy is probably reading," Sunny answered as she followed Liesel out through the garage and toward the car.

"Reading?" Liesel stopped at the trunk, then forced herself

to grab another few bags to cover her surprise. "He's so young."

"It's important to be able to read so we can understand the letters." Sunny grabbed a few bags in each hand and hung back, waiting for Liesel to go first.

"What letters?"

Sunny followed Liesel back toward the kitchen. "The Superior letters. They're what Papa wrote so that all his children could know his words even when he was unable to say them. Or so if we're away from the family, we can have them."

Liesel concentrated carefully on putting out everything she'd bought at the store. Haphazard, she realized now, setting a can of black beans next to a jar of artichoke hearts. She'd pushed her cart quickly up and down the aisles, unable to remember what she had at home or what she needed, just anxious to get back before something went wrong. She thought about the pamphlet she'd taken once from that wide-eyed, scrawny boy one long-ago summer.

"I thought you didn't leave the family." Liesel pulled a loaf of French bread in a paper sleeve from one bag and put it on the counter.

Sunny shrugged. "Oh…I didn't. Papa wanted his true sons to have their own homes someday, because of course it's important for children to eventually leave their parents, when it's time."

"But so many of you all lived together, didn't you?"

Sunny must've thoroughly acquainted herself with the location of everything in the kitchen, because she moved effortlessly from the counter to put away what she unpacked from the bags. Well, most things. Liesel noticed that the girl studied the labels of every package before putting it in the fridge or pantry, and some things she set aside on the counter as though uncertain about where they went.

"Yes." Sunny was silent for half a breath. "About a hundred."

And all of them except Sunny and her kids had died. Liesel's throat tightened with sympathy. It hadn't even been a month.

"But that's because nobody was ready to leave him. A good father will make sure his children can live the lives he created for them on their own before he'll let them move off by themselves. Papa didn't want any of us to go out on our own among the—" Sunny stopped herself, then said, quietly, "the blemished."

Liesel needed some coffee for this conversation. She pulled down the container and filled the coffeemaker with grinds and water, then took a mug from the dishwasher that had finally ceased its cycle. It was still hot, almost too hot, but the steam bathed her momentarily when she opened the door and the porcelain warmed her hands. She leaned against the counter to watch Sunny gather the plastic bags in one hand.

"Why do you call us that?" Liesel asked quietly, trying to find a way to sound curious but respectful and feeling as though she'd failed miserably at both.

Sunny looked at her, then shrugged hesitantly. When Liesel didn't show any reaction, Sunny looked relieved. She gestured at Liesel, the plastic bags in her hand crinkling. Then at herself.

"Anyone not in the family, anyone who hasn't accepted Papa's teachings or who doesn't live by them, is blemished."

"Does that mean you're...flawless?"

Behind Liesel, the coffeepot sputtered and belched the rich, delicious aroma of the caffeinated beverage. She'd put a vanilla-caramel flavored coffee in because Christopher wasn't here to complain that flavored coffee wasn't "the real thing." She breathed in the smell, and her stomach rumbled. She hadn't eaten lunch and it was now almost three.

At Liesel's question, Sunny looked surprised. "No! Oh, no. Not flawless, not at all. We're all flawed. Our vessels make us flawed. That means our bodies. We're only perfect when we've passed through the gates and left our physical bodies behind."

For a few seconds both women stared at each other across the kitchen. Liesel clutched her empty mug. Sunny held the empty bags.

"I know you think they were crazy," Sunny said. "You can't understand why they did it."

Liesel sighed. "Oh, hon."

Sunny's chin lifted. "The police thought I was crazy when I told them why they did it. The people on the television—"

"I told you not to waste your time with that garbage, didn't I?" Liesel shook her head. "The news just wants to make a big story out of what should've been a private pain. That's what they do."

Sunny's frown deepened. "Papa always said it's not the fault of the blemished if they can't comprehend. It's our job to teach them. Not to hate them, even though they might hate us."

"We don't hate you, Sunny. Not at all." Liesel couldn't quite bring herself to say that she loved Sunshine—she barely knew the girl. "I might be a little confused about what you believe, and I have to confess I don't understand why your family would…do what they did. But that doesn't mean I hate you. Or them."

Sunny nodded without looking at her. She smoothed the bags in her hands. "They've all left their vessels, that's it. They went through the gates and…well, they left us. That's all."

Liesel didn't know what to say to that, so she busied herself with the coffeepot. "Would you like some coffee?"

Sunny crossed the kitchen to stand beside her. "Caffeine's a drug."

Liesel hesitated, the glass carafe chit-chattering on the edge of the coffee mug before the steaming liquid poured out. She filled the mug three-quarters of the way, leaving plenty of room for sweetener and fat-free milk. "Yes, I guess it is."

She looked at Sunny. "You don't have to drink it if you don't want to."

Sunny's brow furrowed. "Patience told me once that Papa drank coffee. So did John Second and Josiah."

"Who's Patience?"

"She was my sister. She's dead now," Sunny said flatly. "She worked in the kitchen. She'd have known how to cook. She wouldn't have set your oven on fire and burned your chicken."

"Oh, hon." Liesel put her mug down and took Sunny's shoulders in both her hands. "Listen, I'm not angry about that. You made a mistake, that's all. Everything's going to take some time to get used to. And...I'm sorry about your sister."

"She wasn't my blood sister. I mean, we didn't have the same mother." Sunny paused. "Or the same father, I guess."

"I'm still sorry," Liesel said.

Sunny's chin tipped up again, and she smiled. It didn't look entirely real, that smile, but at least she was trying. "Sure. I'll have some coffee. That's what people on the outside do, right? They share coffee."

On the outside. The term settled just a little wrong in Liesel's ears. She supposed she could understand it, but it didn't make her feel at ease. "Some people do. Not everyone. My sister, for example, never drinks coffee. She likes herbal tea. Heck, she doesn't even drink caffeinated soda. I can't live without it. Here."

Liesel pulled another clean mug from the dishwasher and handed it to Sunny. She filled it the same as she'd done for her own, leaving room, then went to the fridge to pull out the jug of skim milk.

The fridge was almost empty.

All the jars of pickles, olives, the marinated peppers Christopher loved to put on his sandwiches were all still there, though in different places. The jellies and grilling sauces, ketchups and steak marinades, even the mayonnaise and salad dressings…all gone. Liesel turned with the jug of milk in her hand.

"Sunny?"

"I cleaned it," Sunny said. "You had a lot of toxins in there."

Liesel reminded herself to breathe when it felt a little bit like her ears were starting to buzz. "What toxins? What does that mean?"

For one strange moment she imagined cans bulging with E. coli, salmonella, botulism. Once, as a teenager, Liesel had eaten some bad canned fruit from her grandmother's pantry and had needed to go to the hospital for a few days when she couldn't stop vomiting. Fortunately, she couldn't remember much of the experience beyond knowing it had scared her. But though Liesel shopped often at the bargain store, she never bought dented or bulging cans, and she religiously checked expiration dates.

"Corn syrup," Sunny said.

Liesel paused. "Corn syrup?"

Sunny nodded.

Liesel took another breath, reminding herself that no matter what she thought she might understand about her husband's daughter, no matter how much she wanted to be kind and generous and to do the right thing…she really had no idea and no clue about the young woman in front of her. "Corn syrup isn't a toxin."

Sunny didn't smile. If she'd given Liesel any other look instead of the steady, solemn gaze she was now giving her, Liesel would have jumped to the assumption the girl was playing some sort of joke on her. Not a funny one, more like a trick. Instead, Sunny picked up one of the cans she'd unpacked from the grocery bags and set aside on the counter. She turned it to squint at the label, bringing it very close to her eyes, then holding it farther. She turned it toward Liesel.

"Corn syrup. It's in a lot of things, most everything, and it's a toxin." Sunny said this with the absolute authority of someone who knows without a doubt that she's right. "It makes people sick. It can cause all sorts of problems. It makes you fat, rots your teeth, it can give you cancer."

Liesel had in fact heard something about corn syrup being bad for you, probably in one of those chain emails her mother insisted on sending her. But a toxin? She sighed. "Oh, Sunny."

"It's all right," Sunny said. "I took care of it for you."

Sunny walked to the drawer that pulled out to reveal the garbage can, full of a disgusting, gloppy mess of what looked like everything from tomato paste to canned soup. She turned with a proud smile. "And I recycled all the cans, too. I noticed you didn't have a recycling bin, but I found one in the garage. It had some things in it, but I put them aside. I'd have put them away but I didn't know where you wanted them."

She moved toward the French doors to lift a familiar red-and-green bin Liesel had used to store the Christmas decorations Christopher's grandmother had given them.

"Where did you put the stuff that was in the bin?" Liesel hadn't seen anything that looked out of place in the garage, but then she hadn't been looking.

"On the bench with all the tools."

Liesel went first to the garage to find the dozens of hand-spun glass ornaments, many of them antiques, settled among Christopher's hammers, wrenches and screwdrivers. They all seemed to be still wrapped securely in their nests of cotton batting and Bubble Wrap, but still—the workbench was not the place for expensive heirlooms. Jaw set, she went back to the kitchen to find Sunny holding a can of Liesel's soda over the sink. Cola poured out, fizzing and bubbling. Brown gold being flushed down the drain.

"No!"

Sunny looked surprised and stopped. Then, like a garage door sliding down, her expression shuttered. "What?"

"No, Sunny. Don't you dump that stuff." Liesel yanked the can from Sunny's fingers, but it was already empty. So was the cardboard fridge pack on the counter, the sink full of cans. "You dumped my...oh, God. Oh, my God. Why did you do this?"

"It's poison," Sunny said. "Full of chemicals—"

"I know that!" Liesel cried. "I don't care!"

Sunny blinked and bit her bottom lip for a second. Her brow creased. "It's so bad for you."

Liesel tried another approach, not sure she could even form the words but managing. "That's like tossing money away. You might as well just flush my paycheck down the toilet."

"Why would I do that?"

"Food costs money." Surely the girl understood that. She couldn't be that sheltered...or simple. Could she?

"I know. But it's bad food, Liesel. Corn syrup causes all kinds of disease. It harms your vessel. If you can't grow your own food, fresh, it's best to keep it as simple as possible. Avoid chemicals and toxins."

"It wasn't yours to dump," Liesel said, sounding too harsh, but the sight of her soda swirling down the drain made her want to weep. Even Christopher, who could be incredibly unobservant, knew better than to drink her soda, and Sunny had dumped it all away.

Sunny's expression didn't change except, if it were possible, to get blanker. She backed up a step. Paced a few more, swiveled on her heel. Then back again. Her fists clenched together, fingers linked. She paused, head hanging, the intricate design of her braid somehow making her ears and chin and neck seem all the more exposed.

Liesel fought her own expression, which wanted to twist and turn into ugliness. "Look. Sunny. I know all this is crazy and new to you…"

"It is," Sunny said in a low voice, without looking at her. "We've already talked about this. You're going to tell me you understand, that you know it will take time. That me and my kids are welcome here, in my father's house."

It was exactly what Liesel had been about to say, the same words she'd already said several times over the past few days. "All of that is true."

Sunny faced her. "But you don't understand, Liesel. You can't ever understand, I don't think."

"Because I'm blemished?" Liesel asked wearily.

"Because you've lived your whole life in a house like this!" Sunny cried, her blank mask slipping for a moment to reveal the agonized girl beneath.

From upstairs came a thin wail. Bliss. Sunny let her eyes roll upward, but she didn't move. She looked back at Liesel.

"Why don't you have any children?"

"I… We…" Liesel frowned. "That's not really any of your business."

From upstairs came a series of thumps. Another short cry. Liesel would've been up the stairs by now, but Sunny just cocked her head as though assessing not just the volume of the cry, but its nature. She shook her head a little and pushed away a tendril of hair that had fallen over her face.

"I know you don't have to let us stay here."

Liesel sighed. "Of course I do, Sunny. Where else would

you go? A homeless shelter? Or maybe you'd like to give up your kids—"

"No!"

"Well," Liesel said again with that same harsh tone she was disturbed to realize tasted too familiar, "that's what would happen if you don't stay here. You'll be out on the street. And the state will take your kids from you."

It sounded too much like a threat, and she hadn't meant it to be. It was the simple truth. Hard, unpleasant. But true.

"I'm not a child."

"I know you're not," Liesel said, again too harshly, but unable to stay emotionless. "But let's face it, you're as much to take care of as one."

"I am as a child in my father's house." Sunny coughed against the back of her hand, not looking at Liesel. It sounded like a quote Liesel should know the source of, but didn't. "But that's not what you mean, is it?"

"No. And I'm sorry, I shouldn't have said it."

"You meant it, didn't you?" Sunny shrugged, still without looking at her.

Liesel sighed and put both her hands on the countertop, leaning forward for support, her shoulders tense and back aching. "But I shouldn't have said it. It wasn't nice."

"If it's true, does it have to be nice? If you have something true to say, but you don't say it because you just want to be nice, isn't that sort of like a lie?" Sunny looked at her again, her words a question but her face showing no sign of curiosity.

"Is that what your…is that what Papa taught you?"

"Not to speak with a liar's tongue. Yes. We're taught not to."

"So…you always tell the truth?"

Sunny hesitated. "We're supposed to. If we don't, someone

will tell it for us. You can't go through the gates with the weight of lies and misdeeds holding you back."

Liesel looked around her ruined kitchen, the hundreds, if not thousands, of dollars of wasted food. She thought of three small faces and the clasp of tiny fingers in hers. "Nobody expects all this to just magically be all right for any of us."

"I know that."

"But it will get better," Liesel said.

Sunny looked at her. "Are you saying that because you think it's true? Or because you think it's nice?"

"Sunny," Liesel said with a smile the girl slowly returned, "sometimes it can be the same thing."

Chapter
23

Papa used to be tall and strong, with long white hair and a scratchy beard that tickled on your cheeks when he kissed you. Now he sits in a wheelchair and his hair has gone a dirty yellow color. His fingernails, too.

He hasn't kissed Sunny in a long time, not for ages, but she thinks about the feeling of his beard on her face now. It's time to see if maybe Sunny's going to become Papa's one true wife, to replace the one who'd left her vessel too soon. It's been a long time and he hasn't found her yet, but there's always the chance it could be any one of the women in the family. Maybe Sunny. And once he finds her, then everyone else can take their one true wife or husband, and they'll all be able to go through the gates. But by the time Sunny's mother brings her to Papa's room, he's already started to get tired.

"Sit with me, Sunshine," Papa says from his bed, patting the blankets next to him. "Tell me about yourself."

There's not much to tell. Sunny is fourteen years old and

has moved into the dorm where she'll stay until something else happens to her, like becoming the one true wife or having a baby. She shares the dorm with Patience, Willow and Praise, four beds all in a row, and she misses the trundle in her mother's room. But her mother says she's glad Sunny's moved out to the dorm so she can have a little more privacy—which Sunny knows means time with John Second alone, and that's okay with her because maybe if he has more time with her mother, he won't bother with Sunny anymore.

"You've done well with your lessons, I hear."

She doesn't ask from whom. Anyone can make a report on anyone else, and it could be a good report or a bad report. Mostly bad. People always seem to pay attention to the bad things you do, not so much the good. She nods, shy in front of Papa, though she shouldn't be.

"In another month or so you'll be sent out among the blemished." Papa coughs fiercely, the bed shaking. He coughs so loud and long and hard that Sunny becomes alarmed, though he waves away the glass of water she pours him from the pitcher on the table by the bed. "You'll be an emissary for us here in Sanctuary, Sunshine."

"What's an emissary?"

Papa laughs. "A bringer of good news, I suppose you could say. It'll be part of your job to put my words into the hands of the blemished and hope that some of them become seekers."

Sunny nods, relaxing a little bit. If all Papa wants to do is talk to her…well, that can't be bad. "Like Edwina and Patch."

"Yes. They came to us as seekers and now they've become part of our family. It's a beautiful thing, Sunshine, being able to bring the word to those who don't know about it." Papa coughs again, longer this time, then sags back against the pillows. He reaches for her hand and holds it tight. His fingers are hot and rough, scratching hers. "You're a good girl, Sunshine. Aren't you?"

"I try to be."

"You take care of your vessel?"

"I try, Papa."

"Let me see."

She shouldn't feel shy or ashamed, but she does as she stands to unbutton her blouse and skirt and drop them to the floor. Her mother made her take a long bath before she came here, to wash everything on her body. She trimmed her fingernails and toenails and smoothed every inch of herself with lotion. Now she feels chilly as she stands bare in front of Papa, and she wants to put her arms around herself, but doesn't.

"Turn around."

She does, in a circle, then stops. Her teeth try to chatter, but she keeps them held tight. Her throat works. Her nipples are hard from the cold, gooseflesh pimples her all over. She has the sudden, embarrassing urge to pee.

"You keep your vessel clean, fit." Papa coughs, closing his eyes. "Come here."

She does. She knows what to expect, but instead of doing all the things John Second has done, Papa only kisses her. His hands rub her all over, that scratchy flesh like briars, plucking. Her shiver is from distaste this time, and shame washes over her. It would be a great thing to be the one true wife, perhaps give Papa another true son or even a true daughter. It would assure her a place beyond the gates and would wipe out everything bad she's done that might keep her out.

And…unlike his son, Papa is kind.

"That's it, then," he says as if he's talking to himself. He's done nothing but touch her with his hands and that one kiss. "Get dressed, Sunshine."

She does. Her mother is waiting for her in the hall, sitting in a metal folding chair. She's been biting her nails, the tips are red and raw. Sunny takes her mother's hand from her mouth and holds the fingers closed.

"Mama, don't do that."

Her mother looks sad. "You weren't in there very long."

"He wasn't... He didn't..." Sunny doesn't want to admit that there's no way she will become the one true wife. Her mother will be so disappointed.

Instead, her mother hugs Sunny close. "It's okay. He's an old man."

Papa is more than old. He's sick, too. Now at night when they're woken by the sound of Papa's command, it's always the same words and tone over and over, not his real voice but a recording. When they drag themselves on sleep-stumbly feet to the chapel, Papa sits in a wheelchair, his long hair so thin you can see his scalp. John Second speaks for him most of the time, but not every time.

"Listen with your hearts," Papa says between thick-sounding coughs. He turns his head and spits into a bucket. "The time's coming soon. We have to be ready. You all have to be ready, so listen for the still, small voice that will tell you what to do."

Sunny listens hard, then harder, with everything, not just her heart. She closes her eyes to concentrate on the sound of her breathing, the beating throb of her heart. But all she can hear is Papa's rasping coughs. The shifting of people's butts on the floor. The whimper, quickly shushed, of a baby.

She can't hear a voice at all.

But then...once, long after that day in Papa's room, after Sunny's already had Happy and Peace, and Bliss isn't so far from being conceived...it comes to her, one night after they've been woken twice already and it will be dawn soon. When she's spent the day with nothing to eat or drink but crackers and water because Papa has said they all need to clear their brains. When she's so cold she can't feel her fingers or her toes, or the tip of her nose…

That night, Sunny hears the voice.

She always thought it would sound like Papa, but it doesn't. It's a soft, female voice, and it whispers. It could be her mother's voice, but it's not quite. Sunny strains to listen, and everything else falls away from her. The floor under her behind, the insufficient weight of her sweater, the tickle of her hair against her cheeks.

There is nothing but silence and the sound of that sweetly whispering voice, telling her it's time…

"Time to leave." She's muttered it out loud without knowing it, and her eyes snap open not at the sound of her own voice but because someone has shoved her.

When did everyone stand? Why are they not running, but walking fast? Up toward Papa, who's fallen from his wheelchair. John Second bends over him, shouting. Josiah is bringing a blanket. Nobody's paying attention to Sunny, which is why she's being shoved and jostled as people try to get around her and she stands solid in the way. Unmoving, still caught up in the sound of the voice.

It was wrong, of course. It wasn't time to leave. Not for her, anyway. Or the others. Only Papa had gone that night, and he hadn't left, either. He'd just died.

It was the only time Sunny had ever heard the voice Papa had told them would come to them if they were good enough, took enough care of their vessels, meditated long and hard enough. If they were worthy to go through the gates, the voice would tell them when it was time. Now she thought she'd just wanted to hear it so bad that she'd made it up, because it had never come back.

With her ear to the door, Sunny listened to the rise and fall of voices from downstairs. They were arguing about her again. She heard her name once, then a silence that meant they'd pushed their voices quieter to keep her from overhearing.

In her hands, the long white envelope had gone limp from being folded and unfolded so many times. Her name had smeared, the ink staining her sweating palms, from how often she'd squeezed it in her hands. She'd read it at least a dozen times. She could probably have recited it from memory by now. It had arrived that morning while Liesel and Christopher were out, and though Sunny had been careful to put the magazines and bills and postcards addressed to them in the pile by the telephone, this letter had borne her name and had seemed something like a secret.

She wished, in fact, it was something she'd never known.

According to the letter from the coroner, her mother'd had cancer. Sickness had spread within her and would've killed her if she hadn't gone through the gates when the others did. Sunny turned this information over and over in her head, trying to make it work out. How long had her mother been filled with it?

Mama had complained of headaches, blurred vision and nausea for years. She'd called them migraines or her "special" headaches, which were different from the normal sort everyone else got. Sometimes she'd laughed a little when she told Sunny there were so many thoughts inside bursting to get out they made her head hurt.

But…cancer? Family members who lived by Papa's word and followed the rules weren't supposed to get cancer. They weren't supposed to get sick at all. Mama had always followed Papa's word, but more than that, she'd believed in it. Even after Papa died and she had doubts about the things John Second had done, she believed in the foundations of what

Papa had taught them. If there was anyone in Sanctuary who represented everything Papa had envisioned for his children, it was Sunny's mother.

From behind her came the small giggles of her children, and she turned, tucking the letter deep into her pocket. "Hush."

Happy fell silent at once, small fingers still manipulating the game piece on the board but obeying. Peace was more like her mother and let out another flurry of giggles as she spun the plastic arrow attached to the cardboard square. It landed on red, and she let out a joyful cry.

"Peace," Sunny repeated. Her daughter didn't look up at her, too involved with the game, so Sunny knelt in front of her to squeeze Peace's chin in her fingers. Peace's cry wasn't as joyous this time. "I said hush."

Tears welled up in the big blue eyes and overflowed onto fat cheeks. Sunny shook her head and wiped them. "No crying. Hush when Mama says."

Sunny could remember all too well those same words directed at her from her own mother's mouth. How hard it had been for her as a little girl to keep quiet when she wanted to laugh, to keep dry eyes when she wanted to cry. It had been her mother's responsibility to teach Sunny how to hush so she could listen with her heart, and it was Sunny's duty now to do the same to her own children.

She gripped Peace by the upper arms and pulled the little girl to her feet. Peace wore a pair of pink, glittery sneakers that had been the only choice in her size. Liesel had put them in the cart, and Sunny hadn't protested, but seeing them now, a whisper of disdain hissed in her ears. Worldly shoes. No wonder Peace didn't listen.

Sunny shook her daughter once, twice, until Peace stopped crying and looked at her with wide-open eyes. Tears still streaked her cheeks, and Sunny wiped them away. She pushed the blonde curls from Peace's forehead.

"You must mind me, Peace. When I say hush, you must hush. Do you understand?"

"You must mind Mama," Happy put in. "Or you get the stick."

Sunny had used the stick on Happy only once. Her belly, swollen with Peace sleeping inside, had been in the way when she took it down from the hook in the chapel. That was how long ago it had been. Happy had thrown a tantrum during the evening meditations. John Second had been sitting next to Papa, watching as Sunny tried to hush her son without success. Papa had continued talking even over the child's cries, but his one true son had come down from the pulpit and pulled Sunny to her feet. He'd marched her to the place where the stick, a birch branch about two feet long, hung from a length of braided leather tied through a hole in the thick end of the stick's base.

He'd said nothing, but she'd understood. It had been her responsibility then to make sure her child knew how to mind. How to hush when told. And she'd done it, holding back her own tears at the sight of her son's. Clearly, he remembered the experience as well as she did.

She gathered Peace close to press her lips to the girl's soft hair. It smelled like flowers from the fancy shampoo Liesel had given them. And though it was worldly and not plain and would hold them back from getting through the gates when it was time, Sunny liked the way this shampoo smelled. How it made their hair soft and tangle-free so she didn't have to fight a comb through it. She held her daughter close and kissed her head and closed her eyes against her own tears.

What were they going to do?

Later, when the children had been put to sleep, Sunny again

snuck from her room to travel the dark corridors on silent feet. Not to hunt for snacks this time, not to linger in front of her dreaming father whose touch was too familiar even though she thought he didn't mean for it to be, and she knew he minded what happened far more than she did.

No, this time she ran from the house, knowing she had to get out or bring down the walls with her screams. She looked over her shoulder at her father's house, where she wasn't supposed to be a child. Lights bloomed in the bedroom windows. They looked so warm, and she was cold. Shivering. She'd come out without a coat, hat or gloves, and the boots her mother had given her were still too big and not very warm. That was okay. She deserved to be cold. Sunny tripped down the deck's wooden stairs and into the snowy backyard. Cold wetness went up over the top of her boots and inside, burning first before it numbed. She ran down the sloping hill and slipped in the snow, going to one knee before catching herself.

Where was she going? Where could she go? There was a street and beyond that another. The highway. A town. At some point, she could find her way back home to Sanctuary. The thought made her shudder. Her family was gone and without them, it was just a place.

Liesel had said there was no silent room, not here. Sunny could understand why Liesel had been appalled by the thought of it; it had been a cruel place. Sunny herself still shuddered with memories of the few times she'd been forced into it.

For the first time, Sunny understood exactly what Papa had meant when he said sometimes everyone needed a little silence.

She tried to find some now, but though she tried hard to push aside the world around her and focus on the one within, she couldn't manage to block out anything. She thought about how she'd floated. Too many misdeeds weighed her now. Too many sweet treats, no matter how she'd told Liesel they didn't need to eat them. Too many hours of television programs. Too many hot showers when she ought to have bathed quickly but had luxuriated instead.

Up in the night sky, stars didn't twinkle. They just shone. The night her mother had pushed her out the door, Sunny had looked up at those very same stars, but they looked different now. Farther away. They didn't seem the same as the ones that had watched over her in Sanctuary; although she knew they had to be the same because though there were millions of them in the sky, they didn't change.

She'd only been out here a few minutes, and already she couldn't feel her feet and fingers. Her children were in that house, so she needed to go back inside if for no other reason than that, but it wasn't as if they weren't safe there. Liesel and Christopher wouldn't let anything bad happen to the children. Bliss would probably be crying for her by now, and Sunny's breasts ached, full with milk that let down when she remembered it was long past feeding time. It wet the front of her blouse all the way through her sweatshirt.

At the bottom of the hill, the house looked somehow even bigger than when she'd been right next to it. Here were trees, small ones with cages around them. Maybe the kind that grew flowers. Someone had planted them on purpose, not like the big trees in the woods that grew there all on their own. These were for show, and though they were of the earth, were still material. Still fancy, just for decoration. Not quite as much a waste of resources as some of the other things Liesel and Christopher had in their house, but not as useful as a fruit tree.

A figure loomed up out of the darkness. One hand raised. For a horrifying, wonderful moment, Sunny thought it was her mother and had taken two or three steps toward it before she knew it couldn't be. By that time she'd reached the woman offering her hand to the darkness, and she discovered it was…a statue.

The barest caress of light from the house illuminated her, but Sunny's eyes had adjusted to the dark, so she could see it was a woman's shape. Kneeling, not holding out her hands as she'd thought, but with wings. The woman knelt, her face buried in one arm against a pedestal. She was weeping.

Weary of casting herself in stone the way this woman had been carved, Sunny wept, too.

Her tears were scalding hot, but only for seconds before they froze and plucked at her skin when she swiped them away. She touched the stone woman, who should've been covered with snow but wasn't. The stone was smooth, not rough like Sunny expected. What was she doing here? Why a stone woman in a little grove of trees, set in someone's backyard?

Then it struck her. More decoration. No purpose, no point, no use. Just for show.

Sunny laughed out loud, the sound sort of raw and painful, which was also how it felt. Did it matter what Liesel and Christopher did? If they were wasteful or fancy, even if they raped the earth and used fossil fuels and didn't recycle? If they stuffed their vessels solid full with corn syrup and chemicals? What difference did any of that make, really? It had made none to her mother.

"I miss you," Sunny said. "Mama, I miss you so much, and I don't understand any of this."

"Everything will be all right, Sunshine. Listen with your heart, and you'll be okay." The voice, soft and sweet and purely feminine, whispered like a tickle in Sunny's ear.

She stopped laughing, stopped crying. She gulped down snot and tears, thick and nasty, then spat another mouthful to the side. She touched the stone woman again. She closed her eyes. She listened.

It wasn't Papa's voice, the way Sunny had always thought it would be, and it wasn't her mother's voice, the way it hadn't quite been before. This time she thought she recognized it.

"Everything will be okay, Sunshine."

It was her own voice.

"What will we do?" she said aloud. "What will *I* do?"

What would she do, to stay here with her children? To protect and provide for them. What choices could Sunny make?

The answer came, not in words but in a smooth burst of understanding that dug into her core, husked her out and left her empty...but lighter. So, so much lighter. Light enough to float, maybe even someday to fly. What would she do?

Whatever she had to.

Chapter

24

Working from home wasn't working.

Liesel had spent the day with her laptop, roaming from room to room to find a quiet spot to work and finding none. For children who were so wonderfully well-behaved, those kids made an awful lot of noise. Add to that the fact Sunny seemed too scared to lift a finger to do a damn thing without asking permission, and Liesel had been interrupted ceaselessly.

Christopher, on the other hand, had arrived an hour later than expected, bright-eyed and smelling of sweat because he'd taken the chance to stop off at the gym on the way home. It might've been a fight, but Liesel was just too freaking tired to raise one. That was, until her husband, who'd been listening to her list of complaints, decided he had the solution.

"I don't see any other way to do it." Christopher's voice was muffled from inside the fridge. He came out with beer in one hand and a container of chip dip in the other.

Liesel always bought Heluva Good French Onion Dip for

him, but after the debacle with Sunny throwing out all the food, she'd made the concession of trying to make her own with sour cream and French onion soup mix. It had been nearly impossible to find a prepackaged mix that didn't contain corn syrup or any of the other half-dozen ingredients Sunny had said would kill them. She'd ended up mixing together a random assortment of spices and dried-onion flakes instead.

"Of course you don't." Liesel leaned against the kitchen counter, watching as he went to the cupboard for a bag of potato chips. "Why would you? You're not the one who has to quit."

Christopher settled himself at the bar and tore open the chips. He opened the container without even looking at it, dug a chip in, ate it. Grimaced and muttered a curse. "What's this? This isn't Heluva."

"Does it *say* Heluva?"

He gave her a narrow-eyed look and dug another chip into the sour cream. Tasted it more slowly. "Why didn't you get Heluva Good?"

"I did," Liesel told him. "Your daughter dumped it in the garbage, remember? She told me to make my own, it would be healthier for you."

Her husband took another bite. "Tastes like ass."

"Don't eat it, then." Liesel made to grab the container and toss it in the trash, but Christopher pulled it out of reach before she could. "You could take a leave of absence. Family leave. Something like that, part-time, and—" Even as she said it, she knew he'd never go for it.

He did, indeed, look at her like she was nuts. "Liesel, I make over a hundred grand a year and have terrific benefits, including four weeks' vacation."

That was all he had to say. She made far less than half

of what he did, worked part-time, no benefits, no vacation. The only thing they'd lose if Liesel quit her job was the free T-shirts and mugs she sometimes brought home from over-runs. Oh, and her dignity.

"You don't even like your job," he told her.

"It's not about liking it!" she cried, surprising herself. "It's about *having* it!"

Christopher gave her an implacable look. "You wanted this. Now you have to deal with it, Liesel."

"This is nothing like what I wanted."

"Well," her husband said, "it's what you got."

That he could be so casual left a sour taste on her tongue that made her want to turn her head to the side and spit. He didn't get it, she saw that clearly enough. And she didn't even want to try to explain. "I'm going for a run."

He looked at once toward the ceiling. Everything was quiet upstairs, Sunny and the kids not making a peep. "What about…?"

"You'll be here in case of an emergency." Liesel ignored his grunt of protest and didn't even go upstairs to change, just grabbed her running shoes from beside the door, tugged on a cap and mittens and went.

She ran.

Liesel had always been a working girl, just like Melanie Griffith in that cheesy eighties movie. She got her first job at fifteen, scooping cones in an ice-cream parlor that was only open during the summer. She worked for minimum wage plus tips and never gained a pound because she had to be on her feet for her entire shift. She'd worked in retail, food service and had tended bar. She'd landed her first office job just out of school, a paid internship at a great design firm in Philadelphia that had made much out of its "hiring from within" program.

She'd had to start from the absolute bottom, but there'd been the promise of moving up.

She'd done that, too. She didn't just have a job, she had a career. She had an apartment, a car, nice clothes. Then she'd met Christopher. She'd fallen in love and married him, and they'd moved out here to follow his job, which just happened to be closer to his family and where he'd grown up. It had seemed like a good idea at the time. The cost of living was much lower in Lebanon County than it had been in Philadelphia, and his commute would be shorter. They could afford a nicer house, better cars and vacations. The fact she'd had a tough time finding work hadn't seemed so important right away.

Not until six months had passed with Liesel sending out résumés and going on interviews, only to be at home the rest of the time, twiddling her thumbs. She didn't like to cook and discovered she wasn't very good at cleaning, either. Finally, she took the job at Roy's Printing and Design because even though the money was crap and she wasn't doing anywhere near as much design work as she'd done in Philly, it was better than not working at all.

Working gave her a sense of purpose and worth she would never admit to needing. It defined her as a woman who didn't stay home to rely on her husband for everything, even if the truth was she'd never have been able to afford their lifestyle on her own. Without a job, what would Liesel do?

Who would she be?

Liesel pushed herself a little faster. Harder. Her breath burned in her lungs as she pushed herself up one of the steeper hills in the neighborhood. She usually ran the other direction, but today she was heading for the outer limits and the woods beyond. There was no through road back here, though an east-west rural highway was close enough to glimpse through the trees at the edge of several backyards. There were, however, a number of footpaths worn by runners like her, as well as bikers and hikers and the occasional hunters and horse riders who frequented the game lands that pushed up against the neighborhood.

She took the path through the woods, looking at her feet as she leaped a gnarled tree root that could've sent her onto her butt. She didn't need that again, not with her bruises just barely healed. She'd bought those sneakers with her own paycheck. Swiped the credit card in her name and paid the bill when it arrived with a check from her personal account, the one she'd had since before she got married. She'd added Christopher to it, just as he'd added her name to his, but he never added or took money from it.

"Her" money had always been for special things. Gifts at holiday time, weekend trips, that new pair of running shoes she didn't need but really wanted. Losing her money wouldn't mean they had to give any of that up, but it meant a whole lot more than simply switching which account she paid the bills from.

Below her, cars and trucks whizzed by on the highway as she kept up her run along the footpath through the trees. At one point, the path dipped to road level and she crossed to take a series of paths on the other side of the highway. There'd been a quarry here once, now filled in with water, and lots of talk about building an indoor water-park resort around it with, so far, no progress. A bunch of new houses here, too. Bigger than hers, with longer driveways and gates at the end. Fancy houses she'd toured during the annual Parade of Homes. She and Christopher had marveled at the things people spent money on that seemed so frivolous. Small, odd-shaped rooms with limited functions, extravagant closets and bidets and pot fillers and potting counters.

Liesel ran past them all, not even looking to see if anyone stared out at her from the windows. Her sides hurt and so did the knee she'd twisted. She pushed on anyway. She ran and ran, sweat streaking down her back.

And then, she stopped.

Panting, bending to put her hands on her knees, Liesel blinked away the black-and-red spots in her vision. She'd forgotten to bring water. Stupid. She stood too fast and had to bend over again to keep herself from fainting.

When at last she caught her breath, she stared across the highway at the high metal gates that had once closed in the place where Sunny had been raised. She called it Sanctuary, but there were no signs to label it that way. Lots of no trespassing and private property notices, though.

She'd been so close, always so close, and Christopher had never known.

Liesel crossed the highway. She ignored the signs—the gates weren't locked and there wasn't any police line tape to worry about. She jogged more slowly this time, down a long gravel driveway that became bare dirt. She stopped far away from the buildings, though. The entire compound was deserted and creepy.

People had died in that building. Four stories and built of gray concrete, it looked more like a barracks than a house. She supposed that was probably what it was more than anything. There were a couple barns and some greenhouses, too, but she kept her eyes on the gray building. That's where Sunny and her kids had grown up.

There weren't any clues in it.

Not in looking at it, anyway. If she'd gathered the courage to snoop around, who knew what she'd find. But Liesel had never been a fan of horror movies, and she wasn't stupid enough to go inside looking for ghosts. She shifted from foot to foot, cold now that she'd stopped running and the sweat had begun to dry. She didn't even really know why she'd come here, unless it was somehow to prove to herself that it was as awful as she'd imagined. She didn't have to go inside to see that.

She ran home, but at a much slower pace. It took her twice as long, and by the time she'd stumbled out of the woods and onto the street, every part of her felt sprung and sore. Night was falling. She couldn't push herself to run, so walked the rest of the way home.

Christopher had left the lights on for her. There was that, at least. She let herself in through the front door and followed the sounds of childish laughter into the kitchen. Peace and Happy sat at the table, playing Candy Land with Christopher, who got up when he saw her.

"I was getting worried," he said.

She let him hug her though she was covered with sweat and desperately wanted a shower. She felt, as she always did after a good long run, wrung out and sort of jittery. She kissed him, then went to get a cold drink.

"How were things here?"

"Good. We played games. Sunny is upstairs with the baby."

Liesel nodded. "I'm going to shower. Did you make anything for dinner?"

"Grilled cheese. I can make you one, if you want."

She shook her head. "I'll grab something when I'm done."

She didn't think about kissing him again before she went upstairs, but some impulse moved her feet toward him instead of away. He'd just flicked the spinner with his finger to make it land on a new color, and he looked surprised when she bent to press her lips to his forehead.

Upstairs, she heard the murmur of Sunny singing in her

bedroom, and Liesel paused in the doorway to peek inside. "Hi."

Sunny, sitting in a rocking chair that had been Christopher's grandmother's, looked up from nursing Bliss. She smiled, though it looked wary. "Hi."

"Can I come in?"

"It's your house." The way she said it came out less like a sullen teenager and more like she was surprised Liesel would even ask such a thing. In her arms, Bliss gurgled and snuffled before latching on again.

Liesel sat on the edge of the bed, too aware that she must look terrible and smell worse. "The kids seem to be having fun with Christopher."

"He's been playing with them for a while," Sunny said after a tiny hesitation. "We had dinner. I gave them baths. You were gone a long time."

"I went for a run, just a couple of hours. I like to run. Sunny…" It seemed they'd had the same conversation over and over; all at once Liesel didn't have anything else to say.

"My mother had cancer."

Liesel wasn't sure she'd heard Sunny right. "What?"

"I got a letter," Sunny said in that placid, unaffected manner she was so very good at. "It came in the mail. From the coroner's office. The results of her autopsy."

"Oh. God. Sunny, I'm sorry, your dad didn't say anything to me—"

"He didn't see the letter," Sunny interrupted. "I got the mail, and I found it, and it was addressed to me. It was mine. Was it wrong to read it? It had my name on it."

"No. It wasn't wrong. I'm just sorry you had to find out that way…it must've been difficult." Liesel struggled for something to say that didn't sound lame and could only come up with, "I'm so sorry."

"The cancer didn't kill her," Sunny said. "The rainbow did. The drugs, I mean. She took them the way everyone else did, and that's how she left. But they discovered a tumor in her brain that probably would have killed her in another few months."

Sunny paused to draw a hitching breath. "She had headaches."

Liesel thought she should put an arm around her, offer some comfort, but Sunny didn't seem open to that, and Liesel wouldn't have known how to, anyway.

"She knew she had cancer, I think. She knew something was wrong. Looking back, I can see she must've known. But she didn't say anything to me about it. I didn't know." Sunny cleared her throat. The baby had gone limp, slack mouth still suckling though she'd fallen away from the nipple. Sunny tucked her shirt closed.

"I'm so sorry," Liesel said again, thinking that if she knew she had a brain tumor that would kill her in a month or so, she might well have been persuaded to down a toxic cocktail of chemicals, too. For the first time, she felt a surge of sympathetic warmth toward her husband's first wife. "At least she isn't in any pain."

"I don't know what she is," Sunny said flatly. "Her vessel wasn't pure. She didn't die, she left. So, did she go through the gates? John Second said you could only go through the gates if your vessel was pure and you drank the rainbow, but Josiah said Papa was sick and died, just died. Not that he'd been taken in advance by special forces the way John Second told us. It's why John Second made Josiah leave the family."

Again, Liesel wasn't sure what to say. Her clothes were starting to stick to her, and her hair was stiff with sweat. She itched. "Are you worried your mother didn't…go through the gates?"

"How did she get cancer," Sunny replied evenly like a statement, not a question, "if she lived a pure life, in superior bliss, the way Papa taught?"

"I don't know." Simple answer, complicated question. "I think a lot of people wonder how they or someone they loved could get cancer."

Sunny shook her head slowly and looked down into her sleeping daughter's face. "I don't expect you to understand. It's okay."

"I'm sorry, I don't." Liesel stood, bone-weary, to look at the baby. She touched the soft hair.

From downstairs came another trill of laughter that dug at her heart. She had the chance right here in front of her to have everything she'd wanted so much for such a long time. Not in the way she'd wanted it, but that wasn't important.

"Everything's going to be okay, Sunshine," Liesel said, the words familiar, repeated so often they'd become nonsensical.

Sunny looked up at her with that implacable stare, so much like her father's, unbroken even by the faintest hint of a smile. "I know."

STAYING

Liesel looked out Sunny's window to the backyard to check on the kids playing in the grass. April showers and higher-than-normal temperatures had made it grow in thick and green. Christopher would need to mow it soon. She smiled at their high-pitched squeals as they ran and jumped through the sprinkler. They'd be filthy and exhausted later, but for now they were having a blast.

Farther down in the yard, close to the garden, she spotted Sunny walking with Bliss in her arms. She couldn't hear what Sunny was singing, but if she squinted, Liesel could see Sunny's lips moving a little bit and could imagine it was one of the tunes Sunny frequently hummed. "Simple Gifts," maybe, or her new favorite, "The Sound of Silence." Liesel had never been a huge fan of Simon & Garfunkel, but Christopher loved them. Like father, like daughter. As Liesel watched, Sunny settled on the curved stone bench next to the weeping angel statue that had been an anniversary gift from Christopher two years ago.

Someday, instead of letting whatever wildflowers came up on their own overtake it every year, Liesel would really get out there and work in the garden she'd laid out when they moved into this house. Maybe put in a pond with some koi. She'd had fantasies of sitting down there on that bench or even in a pretty garden swing with a book, listening to the sound of running water with that angel there to keep her company. As it was, she hadn't even been down there since last summer.

Well, once she got this last load of laundry in the washer she could walk down there and sit with Sunny. Tickle Bliss's fat chinny and make her giggle. They'd talk about what to make for dinner, maybe. Or maybe just sit and watch the kiddies play until Christopher got home and they could convince him to take them all to the Jigger Shop for burgers and ice cream.

Sunny was careful about putting the dirty clothes in the hamper, but the kids hadn't been so tidy in their excitement about putting on their bathing suits. Liesel bent to pick up a pair of Peace's shorts and Happy's T-shirt. The edge of a cardboard container caught her hand from just under the bed. She snagged it as she stood.

Ritz Crackers, the box half-full. Two of the wax paper tubes were missing, with one full one left and another half-eaten with the wax paper carefully twisted shut. Frowning, she bent to look under the bed. A bag of chips, held shut with a plastic clip. Also an unopened container of soy milk.

Huh.

Straightening, she tossed the packages into the laundry basket and took it downstairs with her to put away. She loaded the washer and filled the soap dispenser, added some color-safe bleach and turned the machine on. The pounding of little feet on the deck outside caught her attention and she went to the French doors.

"No running," she warned. "You'll slip and fall. And what happened to your bathing suit?"

Peace, completely naked, giggled and danced, shaking her little tushy. Happy still wore his bathing trunks, thank goodness. He'd been a little easier to keep in clothes since it got warm outside, but not much. His sister, on the other hand, had been nearly impossible to keep clothed. Apparently, the Family of Superior Bliss had some weird ideas about modesty— clothes, particularly for women, had to be severely plain, but casual nudity was all right for both genders and all ages. It had taken a few embarrassed moments for Sunny to understand Liesel, and especially Christopher, required a knock on any closed door before entering, but as far as Peace was concerned, the second she could get naked, she did.

"Took it off," Peace crowed.

"I see that." Liesel shielded her eyes to look across the lawn. "Where's your mama?"

"Talking to the angel." Happy pushed his wet hair out of his eyes. "Can we go back in the sprinkles?"

"Peace, put your… Oh, never mind." Liesel sighed. The suit would be off in another few minutes anyway, and what did it really matter? They were in the privacy of their own backyard, and Peace wasn't even three years old. "Yes, go play in the sprinkler. Maybe in a few minutes you can have a Popsicle."

The kids danced at that, which made her smile and hug and kiss them, though she knew their mother would frown about both the bribery and the treat. Sunny wouldn't say anything. She hardly ever did anymore. Knowing she didn't approve made Liesel feel just a little guilty at promising them the treat, but…darn it, wasn't that what grandmas were for? To spoil their grandkids?

She left the kids dancing in the water droplets and went across the green lawn, down the small slope of the hill toward the garden. Last year in the spring, she'd had Christopher lay out gravel on the path and it crunched now under her flip-flops. A lot of weeds had grown up through the stones, and Liesel sighed. One more thing to feel guilty about.

"Hey," she said when Sunny looked up. "The kids are having a great time."

"Yes, I can hear them. Bliss, no-no." Sunny took a handful of gravel from the baby, who'd been doing her best to get it toward her mouth. "She's going to be ready for solid food soon."

"She's only eight months…" Liesel stopped herself. Bliss was Sunny's child, her third. Liesel, as she was so constantly reminded, had none.

Sunny gave her a curious look. "Yes? Almost nine."

"It's just that…well, aren't you supposed to wean babies at about a year old?"

Sunny appeared to think on that. "I don't know. Are you? We always nursed the babies until they could eat solid food. Some took to it sooner than others. But when they are able to eat solid food, why would they need to nurse anymore?"

That made sense.

Mostly everything Sunny said made sense because she said it so matter-of-factly. Even the wackiest details sounded so legitimate that Liesel had to wonder if she was the one out of line.

"I guess not." Liesel laughed briefly. "But what do I know?"

"Oh, Liesel. You know so much! About all kinds of things." Sunny again took a handful of gravel from Bliss's questing fingers.

"That's nice of you to say, but some days I sure don't feel like it." The sounds of childish laughter drifted down to them over the hill. Liesel closed her eyes and tipped her face up to the late-afternoon sunshine, red behind her lids. She'd get freckles. Couldn't, just then, bring herself to care.

"Well. You do."

Liesel cracked open an eye. "How are you, Sunny?"

Sunny looked up from where she'd been bending to let Bliss stand holding on to the bench. "Fine."

Liesel didn't miss the way the girl's gaze shifted, but she didn't press. Dr. Braddock, the psychiatrist Becka had recommended, had told her and Christopher there might be some things Sunny would never be good at sharing, including her emotions. "Good. I'm glad to hear it."

Sunny looked down at the baby again. "How are you?"

The question took Liesel by surprise. "I'm fine, too."

"You haven't found another job yet."

"No." Liesel grinned. "Maybe that's why I'm fine. This is the first summer in a long, long time I don't have to get up early and go to work."

"You get up early to run."

"Totally my own choice. There's a huge difference."

Sunny smiled. "I guess there is."

"Sunny...I just wanted to tell you..." Liesel hesitated. It had only been a few months, and so much change had happened. In most ways, she felt as if she was still looking at a stranger. The children, she knew and understood. Loved.

But Sunny was still different.

Sunny lifted Bliss high in the air to blow raspberries on the baby's belly, and with infant laughter between them, Liesel didn't have to say anything more. Sunny was so good at that. Deflecting conversation.

"It's been good having you here," Liesel said.

Sunny pressed her face to her baby's belly, then looked at Liesel while Bliss sunk tiny hands into her mother's hair and tugged. A silver strand of drool dripped from Bliss's mouth, and Sunny ducked from it with a laugh. She wiped it with her thumb as she settled the baby on her lap.

"Thanks, Liesel."

"I just wanted you to know. That's all."

When Sunny smiled, she looked so much like Christopher that it sort of hurt Liesel's heart. Not just because she was jealous about Trish. Mostly because Liesel loved her husband and seeing his face in his daughter's reminded her of just how much. Lately it seemed she needed more and more of those reminders.

A scream, not exactly of pain but certainly of anger, drifted to them. Sunny stood, eyes searching. Liesel stood, too.

"It's Peace," Sunny said. "It looks like… Happy! Don't push her!"

But of course it was too late, the kids were tussling for some reason and Sunny was striding across the grass with Bliss on her hip, leaving Liesel behind to sit on the stone bench. Liesel got up, too, to help separate them, the promised Popsicles forgone as punishment for the fighting, though later when Christopher came home he brought ice-cream sandwiches to spoil them with.

Sitting on the back deck eating burgers they'd cooked on the grill that were better than any from a restaurant, watching the children play and Christopher chase them in the grass, Liesel didn't realize until much, much later that she'd forgotten to ask Sunny about the food she'd found stashed beneath the bed. And by then it was time for bedtime baths and stories, for tucking in sleepy heads and lullabies.

And by then it hadn't seemed quite so important or necessary to ask.

Chapter
25

Sunny had woken early so she could shower and wash her hair. Now it hung down her back, heavy and wet. Her shirt clung to her skin, uncomfortable and damp in the house's sterile and too-chilly air. Outside, the summer sun was just rising. The grass would be wet, and the air might still be cool before the heat hit. It would be better than how it felt here inside with the air-conditioning on.

Bliss woke with a yawn instead of a cry. She kicked her feet in the air and rolled over to pull herself up in the crib, then held up her arms for Sunny to lift her out. The diaper change took only a minute or so, and as Sunny put the wet diaper into the bucket to soak, she made a mental note to be sure to run a load of laundry later so Liesel wouldn't have to. Later, when Sunny got home from work.

Oh. Work.

Her first day. The thought sent a shiver all through her, sort of a good kind and yet scary, too. She'd had a week to get used to the idea, but now that it was here she wasn't sure how she felt about it. It would be good to get some experience in the world and have some money of her own. That's what Chris said, and Sunny knew he was right.

It didn't make it any less terrifying.

Chris had found her a job at a coffee shop downtown, just a few days a week. She'd work from eight in the morning until four in the afternoon. He'd drop her off and pick her up, since she didn't have a driver's license. He would teach her to drive, Chris had said. Maybe get what he called a "junker" for her to ride around in, like he'd had when he was young.

Chris often seemed to think she was a lot younger than she was. He didn't remember that when he was Sunny's age, he'd already been married to her mother. And, while it was obvious he knew, intellectually, that Sunny'd already borne three children who were his grandchildren, Chris seemed happy to let Liesel take over anything to do with them as though they were simply some small strangers who'd invaded his house. He didn't ignore them. In fact, he played with them quite a bit if he got home from work before they went to bed, which wasn't often. He said it was because he had to work longer hours now to take care of the days coming up when he would have to leave early to come get her, but he often smelled of alcohol when he came home on those later nights. Liesel never said anything about it, not where Sunny could hear, but she knew her stepmother smelled it, too.

Sunny knew the coffee shop from before. The owners, Wendy and Amy, had never allowed the family to post their pamphlets inside or stand outside to sell them, but if they remembered the few times Sunny had wandered past in search of a spot to rest or to use the bathroom, they didn't say anything about it. Just like the smell of booze on Chris's breath that his wife knew about and ignored, though, Sunny knew Wendy and Amy knew where she'd come from.

It seemed like everyone in town did, because of how Sunny's face had been splashed all over the local paper and TV stations. Chris and Liesel had tried to keep her from knowing about it, but they hadn't been able to stop the police from questioning her a few more times about what had happened. She hadn't been held to any sort of blame, and she'd cooperated as best she could, but some of the news stories had still made it sound almost like she'd gone into the chapel with a bucket and a funnel and forced everyone there to drink the rainbow herself.

Chris and Liesel had asked her if she wanted to get a job, and Sunny'd said yes only because she knew they wanted her to get one. She knew it was important, just the way so many other things were. Studying to get her high school degree, learning to use money, how to use the oven and the stove, how to drive. She did her best to pretend that none of those things terrified her, even though everything did.

In an hour or so she'd leave her children behind with Liesel to watch them while Sunny went out into the world. They'd be well cared for, and certainly they were used to being left with people other than their mother. In Sanctuary, she'd left them with other mothers all the time without even the "practice runs" Liesel had insisted they have. Sunny wasn't worried at all about the children. No, she was worried about the other people.

The blemished.

Months and months had passed, and she still thought of them that way. She didn't say it out loud, not to Chris or Liesel and not even to Dr. Braddock, who'd made it so clear Sunny could tell her anything, no matter what. Sunny told Dr. Braddock a lot of things, but she never said aloud that she still thought of herself as something separate from the rest of them.

With the baby on her hip she leaned close to her window, open though she knew Liesel didn't like it that way even when Sunny carefully closed all the vents in her room and kept her door closed so she wasted as little electricity as possible. It was the air-conditioning that was really wasteful, not Sunny's open window, but still, she closed it before she went out, just in case Liesel came in.

Liesel liked to say she respected Sunny's privacy and would never go into the room they'd given her without Sunny's permission, but that was silly and not completely true. Sunny knew Liesel went inside to gather laundry or for other reasons she didn't know or care about. Sunny knew something Liesel didn't—privacy was something Sunny appreciated but didn't necessarily expect. She was glad for it certainly, especially when it came to things like the bathroom. Not having to share a shower with anyone was wonderful, even though she knew it was just as wasteful to spend half an hour in the hot water as it was to use the AC. Maybe even more, because it was not just a waste of energy but of water well beyond what was necessary to keep her vessel…her body…clean.

But expect? No. In fact, since Peace and Happy had moved into their own rooms, the space left for Sunny and Bliss seemed way too big. The bed, too huge. She stretched out in it every night like a starfish, arms and legs reaching to all four corners yet unable to touch. There were many nights she took Bliss into bed with her even though the baby no longer even woke at night to nurse.

But what could she say?

Please put us all back in the same room because it's too hard for me to sleep by myself. Please inspect my room to see if I've disobeyed you by opening the window though you've asked me not to, because if I made a report to you on myself, you'd just look at me like I was crazy.

Dr. Braddock had said, over and over again, that Sunny was not crazy. She had not said that Papa was crazy, but Sunny knew that's what Dr. Braddock thought. It's what everyone thought on the TV and in those articles in the magazines Liesel had thrown in the trash but Sunny had seen anyway.

John Second. *He* was crazy. And cruel. Dr. Braddock had convinced Sunny of that. All the things he'd done to her, those bad things when she was a child and even later…and finally the bad thing he'd made the rest of them all do…he was crazy. He'd taken his father's words and ruined them, Sunny had no doubts about that. But some of Papa's words, the things he'd taught them about respecting and loving the earth and taking care of their vessels, most of that still felt right to her. Even if her mother had gotten cancer. Even if instead of vessel she was supposed to think "body."

"By calling it a vessel, Sunshine, it makes it too easy to believe that taking your own life is a valid choice." That's what Dr. Braddock said. "When you call your body a vessel, you separate yourself from it like it's an object you can easily replace. When the truth is, your body is as much a part of your existence as your soul. You need your body."

Her body. Sunny looked down at her wrists and hands exposed below the buttoned sleeve of her lightweight blouse as she quietly pulled her door closed. Liesel had picked out this blouse, which was so pretty and yet still in keeping with the family's ideas of modesty that Sunny wanted to wear it every single day. She would've, too, but Liesel frowned on that. More waste, washing clothes after wearing them only once, though Sunny couldn't deny she loved being able to slip into fresh clothes smelling of laundry detergent.

Sunny could no longer deny a lot of things.

Every day that passed took her further away from her life in Sanctuary. Some days it was almost as if she'd dreamed all those years living there. The things that had happened. Certainly her dreams were full of memories that Dr. Braddock had encouraged her to explore, remember. Write down. Talk about.

Purge.

So it wasn't any wonder that with all that talk and the dreams that lingered occasionally after she'd woken, Sunny had trouble being certain of what was real and what was memory. When she felt as if she'd always lived here, it was so much easier to pretend everything else that had happened to her was like something from a movie or a book.

Except…that was a lot like saying vessel instead of body, wasn't it? Calling people blemished. Making it easy to keep it separate from herself. From the truth.

She still needed the silence she found in meditation. Without Papa's words to rely on for comfort, she had to find some other way to keep anxiety from overwhelming her. She'd never floated again the way she had in those first few days. It was the weight of the hot showers, the sweets, the mindless television, the dozens of wasteful, wordly things she allowed herself that kept her stuck so firmly to the ground. But she didn't give up. She listened with her heart as often as she could, even when for days and days the voice never spoke a word.

Sunny paused first at Peace's door to peek inside. Her small daughter slept sprawled the way her mother did, but not because she was trying to take up as much space as possible. Peace loved her white bed frame with the princess canopy of mesh Chris had hung for her. She slept there without any sort of self-consciousness or even fear—Peace would forget her life in Sanctuary sooner rather than later. Sunny saw it in her already.

Happy's room wasn't quite as decorated as his sister's. Liesel had offered to paint it for him, to buy him the same sort of wall stickers Peace had picked out at the local Lowe's, but in a boy-friendly pattern. He hadn't wanted it. He'd hung his walls with his drawings, instead, and slept in plain blue sheets with a matching blue comforter that was all he wanted from the store. It would take him longer to forget.

Bliss batted at the front of Sunny's shirt, and for a moment she considered unbuttoning it and allowing the baby to nurse, but the fact was, Bliss really didn't need breast milk anymore. She was entirely on solid foods now, fruits and veggies and pasta. No meat yet, but she'd been making grabby hands at the meatballs Liesel had made for dinner a few nights before, and it wouldn't be long before Bliss was eating everything along with all of them. Sunny slipped a finger in Bliss's mouth, felt the tiny nubs of teeth both top and bottom that were trying to break through.

"You," she said to the baby, "are growing up so fast."

Sunny grabbed a few slices of bread and spread them with organic strawberry jelly while Bliss made grabby hands at those, too. Then a glass of her favorite orange juice—she still couldn't get used to knowing that she could eat or drink whatever she wanted from the fridge whenever she wanted to. It was wrong to steal food from the cupboards and hide it away, she knew that, but her stomach still too well remembered being empty. And it wasn't for her, she thought. It was for the children. If something went wrong, she couldn't let them go hungry. Bliss's feet drummed on Sunny's thighs as she reached for the jelly toast, and Sunny broke off a small piece for the baby to gum.

"Hush," she said to the baby, who didn't hush the way both

Happy and Peace would've. Well, Happy would. Peace was her own girl, and while part of Sunny was proud to see her young daughter so independent and sure of herself, another part reminded her that it was good for children to obey their parents.

Outside, the sun had risen higher, but the grass indeed was wet on her bare feet as she made her way across the yard. She left footprints behind her as she went, though Sunny didn't bother looking over her shoulder to where she'd been. Only where she was going.

Liesel had always wanted a garden, she'd said. She just didn't have the time for one. The soil in this neighborhood was rocky, thick with clay, lacking nutrients for fruits or veggies. Squirrels and deer ate most decorative plants. Wildflowers grew like the weeds they were, but though Liesel had tried to plant roses once shortly after they'd built the house, only one raggedy bush survived. It didn't bloom very well.

Sunny liked the garden anyway. She'd never spent time in the greenhouses, and though she'd done her share of weeding in the vegetable patch in Sanctuary, she hadn't been the one to decide what to plant or how to take care of the plants. She thought Liesel had been disappointed to learn that, the way she'd been so surprised Sunny didn't know how to cook. Sunny was better now, because Liesel had taught her, but since neither of them understood how to fix the garden it had stayed overgrown, sort of forlorn, full of rocks.

And of course, the angel.

The stone angel, weeping about what? Liesel hadn't known, had looked to Chris for answers since he'd been the one to buy it for her. He'd only shrugged and said he bought it because he liked some program on television about a doctor with no real name. Liesel had laughed, shaking her head, told him he'd better not blink. She'd kissed him, making a private moment right there in front of Sunny like she was invisible, and it should've been fine since it certainly wasn't the first time she'd watched a man and woman kissing, but somehow had been awkward.

Sunny could think of lots of reasons about why the angel was crying, but the one that felt the best to her was that the angel wept so Sunny didn't have to. The angel's voice, when she spoke, still sounded exactly like Sunny's own, only from a Sunny who was a lot older and more mature, one who had a good handle on things in a way she really didn't at all. She liked listening to the angel more than she'd ever enjoyed listening to Papa.

"Hush," she told Bliss as the baby bounced on her lap, now reaching with those same grabby hands for the stone angel. "Listen, Bliss. With your heart."

Sunny listened, too.

Chapter
26

Sunny's first day. In a way, it would be Liesel's first day, too. She'd heard the shower running way earlier than normal, and she knew Sunny had spent some time down in the garden again. That was becoming a habit, but Liesel supposed it was good that at least someone was getting something out of the garden other than guilt at how overgrown it was. She hoped whatever Sunny did down there brought her some comfort, anyway.

Now Chris had taken Sunny off to work at the coffee shop, and Liesel had the entire day at home alone with the kids. She'd been making mental lists since learning Sunny would definitely be working at least three and sometimes four days a week. Everything Liesel wanted to do with the kids, all the places she wanted to take them. Everything she'd planned for years to do when she had children of her own.

This was going to be fun.

Liesel's days had been so taken up with everything that

she'd never realized would need taking care of, she hardly had time to miss her job, though the idea that what she did wasn't "work" still niggled at her sometimes, usually when she was pulling out her credit card to pay for one of the many, many things the kids needed. Her husband made appreciative noises about the lunches she'd begun packing for him, the dinners she spent hours preparing…when he made it home in time for them. But it wasn't the same, always starting tasks and never finishing them. Not being the best at what she was doing, that was hard, too.

The past few months had been an adjustment for all of them, and sure, there were days when she opened her closet and looked inside at all the lovely clothes she used to wear, but the truth was, the dress code at Roy's had been permanently casual. The days of Liesel in designer heels and a briefcase were long over before Sunny and the kids arrived.

Liesel had a new life now.

She hadn't managed to get in a run this morning, not with everything being a little rushed and confused, but that was to be expected. She needed a shower, though. Couldn't start the day without one, and she'd been so caught up in making sure Sunny had everything she needed for her first day there hadn't been time for Liesel to jump in the shower before she left.

Bliss had already gone down for an unexpectedly early-morning nap, so Liesel popped her head into the den to tell Peace and Happy what she was going to do. "What are you guys watching?"

"Cartoons." Happy pointed. "Tom and Jerry."

"I used to watch Tom and Jerry." Liesel smiled. Both of them were sitting so close to the TV there was no way they could possibly be comfortable. Liesel scooted Peace back. "Happy, sit back here. That's too close. Listen—"

Peace's gaze twitched her way, but Happy twisted completely to stare at her intently.

She'd forgotten exactly what "listen" meant to them. Not that she was entirely sure she understood. She gave him a smile she hoped would set him at ease. "I'm going to go up and take a shower. Then we're going to do some fun things today, okay?"

Happy nodded. "What things?"

"I thought we could go to the park." The next town had a huge wooden play park complete with castles and a pirate ship. Liesel had never taken Annabelle there because she'd been too old by the time it was built, but Liesel had often driven past it. "And later, there's a great program at the library I think you'll like a lot."

Happy nodded again, but his eyes went wide and his lower lip trembled. "Do we have to?"

"No, of course we don't have to, honey. But I think you and Peace would really like it." Liesel paused, watching his reaction.

A lot had changed in the past few months, but even so, conversations with these kids and Sunny could be like navigating a minefield. There was still so much hidden. One wrong word could blow everything up.

"Happy, do you even know what the library is?"

"It's Papa's room with books in it. It's where the door is to the silent room. You have to be quiet, quiet, quiet in the library." Happy hesitated. He didn't weep, but it was clear he was upset. "Quiet, or they put the tape on your lips."

Liesel attempted an uneasy laugh, but it got stuck in her throat and came out sounding like gears grating. Just as well. Somehow she didn't think Happy would really understand her attempt at humor to diffuse the pain.

"Honey, that's not the same kind of library. This one has

books, yes, but they're for kids and grown-ups to borrow to read. Today they're having a really neat show just for little kids like you and Peace. It's with puppets." Liesel wanted to hug him, but Happy wasn't huggable. He'd let her, of course, but he'd stay stiff-armed, suffering rather than taking comfort from the embrace. "And no silent room. You have to be quiet so other people can enjoy the books, but not because you're in any kind of trouble. I promise. No tape. Nothing to hurt you."

He looked so relieved, Liesel wanted to cry. "Not in trouble?"

"No, honey. Of course not." She did hug him then, just briefly. She kissed the top of his head and caught a whiff of sour little-boy smell. "Oof. You need a bath, kiddo."

Peace tore her attention from the TV long enough to bounce. "Me, too? Me, too! In the big tub? Pwease?"

Liesel laughed. "Sure. Okay. Both of you, in the big tub. Let's go."

Bliss needed a bath, too, after the huge diaper blowout she had when she woke up. By the time Liesel bathed all three kids and grabbed a shower herself, everyone was hungry. That meant what the hobbits called "second breakfast," because one thing she did know was that it was stupid to head out the door with children who were already whiny with hunger.

She'd planned to get to the playground by 10:00 a.m. They pulled into the parking lot just before noon. Who planned a playground without a single bit of shade? she wondered sourly as she hauled Peace out of her car seat, then helped a squirming Happy get unbuckled before finally pulling a grumpy Bliss from her infant seat. Not a tree in sight, and with the sun directly overhead, the only shadows were inside the castle and the pirate ship…both places she couldn't fit inside with the baby.

As it turned out, also places neither Happy nor Peace would go into. Though the playground teemed with roaming packs of children who didn't seem to care about the heat, Sunny's kids wouldn't leave Liesel's side. She'd found a spot on one of the red metal benches close to the sandbox where Bliss could sit and dig. And eat the sand.

"Go play," she said irritably to the older kids as she stopped Bliss from putting a second fistful of sand in her mouth. "We came here so you can play."

When she looked up, Peace was sucking her finger and looking with wide eyes at the swings. Happy was staring at a group of boys playing tag in and on the huge castle structure. But neither of them were moving.

Oh, shit. They didn't…they didn't know how to play with other kids?

"Guys," Liesel said so they'd look at her. "You don't have to stick by my side. You can go play with the other kids."

"We don't know those kids," Happy said.

Peace took a hesitant step and gave the swings another longing look, but Happy put his hand on her arm. She pouted, but stayed put.

"You can go meet them, Happy. Go ahead. I have to stay here with Bliss."

Happy shook his head, small fingers gripping down so tight on his sister's arm she whimpered and tried to pull it away.

"Happy, let go of her." Liesel pried his fingers off Peace's arm, then rubbed the red marks and tried to soothe the little girl, who was sniffling. "Why would you do that? Peace, honey, if you want to go play on the swings, you can. I'm right here."

"No!" Happy's cry was so agonizing it turned the heads of several of the mothers sitting on the next bench over. "No!"

"Happy. Hush." Sunny's command slipped from Liesel's

lips and a pang of guilt stung her at how easily manipulated he was, but he did go quiet. "Happy, I promise you, nothing bad will happen to you here. It's a playground, it's a special place for kids to play. It's… You'll have fun. Okay?"

Peace pointed at the swings. "Wanna do that."

"You can. Go ahead."

With a significantly triumphant look at her brother, Peace skipped off toward the swings. Liesel scooped Bliss out of the sand to keep her from shoving more grit into her mouth, then turned to Happy. He'd gone white-faced and sweating, and Liesel pulled out a bottle of water from the diaper bag. She pressed it into his hand.

"Happy. Drink this."

He did, so automatically it was disturbing to watch. Liesel's heart hurt for him in that moment, more than any other since the first time she'd opened the door and found them on her doorstep.

She stroked his sweat-soaked hair back from his forehead. "I know this is scary, sweetie."

Happy's eyes were glued on Peace, who'd managed to get her little butt into one of the rubber swings but hadn't managed to figure out how to get herself to move. "She should come back here."

"It's really going to be all right. Look at me."

Reluctantly, he did. Liesel pulled him closer, not quite onto her lap. Bliss let out a squeak of protest that caught Happy's attention, and he kissed the baby's head. Liesel put her arm around him, felt the trembling in his small shoulders.

"Why are you afraid?" She didn't expect an answer. The kid was four, it was ridiculous to think he'd be able to articulate his fears when he might not even understand them.

Happy looked at her with wide eyes. Christopher's eyes. "They'll take us away."

"Who? The other kids?"

He shook his head and jerked his chin toward the other mothers, who'd turned back to their conversation. Liesel sighed, uncertain of what to say. She gently squeezed Happy's hip.

"They won't. Those are other mommies. They're here with their kids, just like I'm here with you and Peace and Bliss. They're not here to take away anyone but the kids they brought with them."

"Peace!" Happy shrieked and broke away.

A well-meaning mother had settled her son into the swing beside Peace, and now was taking alternative turns pushing each of them. She caught Peace's swing and pulled it back, up high, then let go. Peace screamed as she swung forward. Liesel couldn't tell if it was in terror or joy, but either way, Happy was running as fast as he could toward her.

"Happy! Wait!"

Too late. He'd thrown himself toward his sister, right in the path of the oncoming swing. It missed him, but barely, and the other mother was quick enough to grab Peace on the backswing and keep her from moving forward again. By the time Liesel got there, her arms aching from clutching Bliss, Happy had put his arms around his sister to stand off with the woman he thought was trying to hurt her.

"I'm sorry. I'm so sorry," Liesel said. "He thought you were trying to…"

Ah, shit. What could she say? The expression on the other mother's face was clearly judgmental, verging on disdain.

"I was just pushing her."

The unspoken criticism, that Liesel's "son" needed to take a chill pill both rankled and embarrassed her. "I know. I'm sorry. He was just worried about his sister."

The other mother nodded with a small, tight smile and

helped her son get off the swing. She spoke over her shoulder as she led him away. "No problem. Kids get crazy ideas sometimes."

"Yeah. Thanks, sorry again." Liesel knelt to force Happy to look at her. "Hush."

He did, though his eyes were still wide, lips still trembling. He blinked rapidly. Still no tears. Totally unnatural. Liesel sighed.

"Happy, you're fine. Peace is fine. Bliss is fine. I'm fine."

He nodded slowly. "That lady was going to push Peace off."

"No, honey, she was just pushing her on the swing. That's what you're supposed to do. Want me to show you?"

"Yes!" Peace cried.

But Happy shook his head. Liesel sighed again. Bliss was making cranky noises and squirming, rubbing at her eyes like she was tired again.

Liesel pulled Happy close enough for a hug and kissed his temple. He surprised her by putting his arms around her, holding almost too tight. She heard the sharp whistle of his breath in her ear.

"Maybe another time," Liesel said. "We can come back another time."

Chapter
27

"Sunny, Sunny, Sunshine." Josiah's broad, white smile is impossible not to return. He's wearing a white shirt open at the throat, sleeves rolled up to his elbows. His jeans are worn, the hems ragged. His wheat-colored hair is too long, falling just past his shoulders, and he wears a beard even though most of the other men don't. "How are you doing?"

Sunny gestures at the stack of pamphlets she's been bundling and rubber-banding together. The ink has smeared on her fingers, turning them black. She has five hundred to sell, an impossible number, but since yesterday she didn't sell her hundred and the day before that she didn't sell her hundred either, John Second says she has to do extra or face the consequences. She's already facing them. Rationed dinner. Being made to stand for hours, hands linked behind her head, until the world spins and knocks her over. Not the silent room.

Not yet.

"Getting ready," she says.

"Not *what* are you doing. How." Josiah looks over the stacks on the table, touches one to flip the edges of the pamphlets with his fingertip. "My brother expects a lot from you."

He and Sunny are alone in Papa's library. John Second had brought in the box of pamphlets and told everyone to portion theirs out. The van will be leaving in an hour. Then they'll drive another hour to find places to canvass. Sunny's the only one who didn't finish in a few minutes, but she'd had to leave the room several times to go to the toilet. She thought she was going to be sick, but since today breakfast had been only a couple pieces of dry toast, she'd had nothing to bring up. She's eaten next to nothing over the past few months. Her stomach constantly feels raw and rumbly, but her clothes are a little too tight around the middle no matter what she does.

"That's too many for you though, no matter how pretty your smile is." Josiah's smile tempts her into another. "And you look…tired."

Under his scrutiny, Sunny wants to shrink. John Second looks at her with flat snake eyes, but Josiah's gaze is always much warmer. It makes her cheeks hot. He's looking at her that way now, something curious in his eyes.

"My brother…does he…" Josiah shakes his head with a frown, but stops himself.

Does he what? she wonders. Does he know she hates selling literature? Does he know she snuck a jar of peanut butter from the kitchen last week, that it's hidden under her bed in case she's ever hungry again? Does John Second know of the other things Sunny's done but hasn't made a report on?

John Second comes through the doorway and gives his brother a sideways, sneering look. "Sunshine. Let's go."

"I'm almost ready."

"We're waiting for you."

Sunny stands and gathers her bundles of pamphlets. Papa's

words. *The Story of the First Father and His One True Wife. The Story of the Two True Sons. Living in the Light.* She's read them all so many times but could never repeat them aloud, because every time the new boxes come out of the print shop in the big barn, the words have changed. Sometimes a little, sometimes a whole lot. Nobody's supposed to notice, but Sunny always does.

"It's too cold out there for her, brother." Josiah moves in front of John Second when he tries to grab Sunny by the arm. "Look at the kid, she's about ready to keel over from exhaustion."

"Sunny's job is to bring the light to seekers. That's her job." John Second spits his words like they taste bitter, even as he grins. "Papa put me in charge of the task distribution. *Brother.*"

"You have enough kids out there working the streets, don't you? How many do you need, anyway? If you're not careful you'll have the police down on us again—" Josiah deals with the blemished all the time, making sure the paperwork is filled out that tells them the family children don't need their schools, their vaccinations, their hospitals. If he says the police might come, he knows what he's talking about.

John Second doesn't care. Sunny is a prize between them, something to be fought over. All she wants to do is curl up and take a nap in warm blankets, but she doesn't move. Doesn't make a sound. Draws no attention to herself; this is their battle, not hers.

"She goes." John Second yanks her arm.

Papa has always called Josiah *The Miracle* because of how many years had passed between the births of his sons. He's nearly fifteen years younger than his brother, which makes him only ten years older than Sunny, but just now he doesn't seem younger at all. John Second's the one acting like a child pouting over a toy he's been denied.

Josiah puts his hand on Sunny's shoulder, but doesn't pull her. "Take another look at her, brother. Take a good, long look."

"Sunny, you come with me now."

"*Look* at her," Josiah says again. "Take responsibility for what you've done, John."

Sunny puts her hands on the smooth, round bump of her belly and understands, suddenly, what she ought to have figured out a long time ago. Someone should have, anyway. Mama should have known, should have told her.

"You can't send her out there on the streets like that, John. You want to bring the authorities down on us? She's what, fifteen years old?" Josiah squeezes Sunny's shoulder gently to tug her back a step, then another, from his brother. "She needs to stay here, not be out where people can see her like this."

Sunny's fingers twitch and she lets her hands fall to her sides. Josiah talks like she should be ashamed of carrying John Second's baby. John Second's eyes narrow. He looks her up and down.

"We don't want the police here."

"No," says Josiah. "Of course not."

"Sunny. You're off street duty. You can start in the nursery." John Second barks this before turning on his heel to leave them in the library.

Sunny can't believe her luck. She turns to Josiah, unable to stop herself from grinning. "Thank you! I hated it! I hated it so much!"

"You should never do what you hate. You should love everything you do." Josiah looks troubled.

Sunny meant selling literature. She thinks Josiah means the games John Second has been playing with her since she was much younger. She thinks Josiah means the baby in her belly—but she could never hate a baby. Not her baby.

"Whatever task you're set, you should find some way to love it," Josiah continues. "I'm sorry, Sunshine, you should never have been forced to…do anything."

Josiah's lived in the family longer than Sunny has. How can he not understand it's impossible to love everything they're forced to do? Yet those are the words that stick with her in the long weeks after Papa dies and the family breaks apart.

Whatever task you're set, find some way to love it.

Sunny wondered if Josiah's words applied to standing with a face of stone so the person in front of her wouldn't know how much she wanted to scream.

"It *is* her." The fat woman said this to her equally obese friend, the pair of them in denim shorts that showed off too much of their thighs and rear ends. She lowered her voice, but just enough to make it seem as if she didn't want Sunny to know she was talking about her, when it was clear to anyone with a brain cell to spare that there was no way Sunny wouldn't be able to hear. "That survivor."

"I read on the internet they made blood sacrifices there," said her friend without trying to be quiet at all.

Sunny had been clearing away the table next to theirs. Paper napkins, plates, mugs still half-full of coffee. The blemished made so much waste. Papa might've been very wrong about a lot of things, but he was right about that. She turned so she wouldn't have to look at them.

It didn't stop them. They kept up their overloud whispers, louder and louder, in fact, until it would've been impossible for them to believe she couldn't hear them. Maybe they thought she was deaf. Or stupid.

"I can hear you," Sunny said finally, flatly, stopping next to their table with her hands full of other people's garbage. She tipped it into the can next to the counter and turned back to face both gape-mouthed women. "You should stop talking about me. Gossip is worse than speaking with a liar's tongue. You should be ashamed of yourselves."

The first woman had blond hair with black roots, and along with her immodest clothes, she wore too much lipstick. Her eyebrows were skinny caterpillars that rose high as her eyes got wide. "We didn't mean anything by it."

"You didn't mean it when you said you heard my family killed goats to appease Satan?"

"I…" The woman's cheeks colored. "No, I guess not."

"Then you spoke with a liar's tongue?" Sunny persisted. Her face felt hot, her jaws tight, teeth clenched. She moved closer, sad to discover how much she enjoyed the way they shrank from her. "For shame!"

Her friend piped up, "Well, did you?"

Sunny looked at her. "We had goats and chickens and two cows." She paused at that, wondering what had happened to the animals. "But we didn't believe in Satan. So no, we didn't sacrifice animals to appease him." Another pause. "Why, do you?"

Both women gasped audibly.

"You need Jesus!" cried the blonde.

Sunny'd heard that before, from many people who'd passed up buying her pamphlets. "I don't believe in Jesus, either. Maybe you need something other than Jesus, have you thought of that? I mean, if you're so unhappy with your own selves you have to speak poorly of other people."

The words tumbled out of her, tasting like freedom. She'd gotten in trouble so many times for speaking her mind. Right now, she didn't care.

When Wendy called her back into the office, though, Sunny hung her head and spoke before Wendy could even begin. "I'm sorry. I shouldn't have been rude to your customers."

"Those old biddies?" Wendy had a loud, hoarse laugh. "Nah, believe me, I've heard it all from them myself. You'd think anyone so uptight about what other people do in bed wouldn't want to buy muffins from us, but hey, their money spends just like anyone else's."

She meant because she and Amy were partners. Romantic partners, not just business partners. Sunny chewed the inside of her cheek, not sure what to say. She'd never known women could be with women that way, or men with men, until leaving Sanctuary.

"I did want to talk to you about your work, though."

Sunny's stomach fell. She'd been doing her best, trying to keep up with everything they wanted her to do, but she wasn't surprised it wasn't good enough.

"Amy and I think you've been doing a great job here, and we'd like to give you some more responsibility. How would you feel about opening the shop a couple mornings a week?"

Sunny blinked rapidly, trying to focus on what Wendy had just said. "You want me to...open?"

"Yep. Of course, we'd give you a raise. Train you. All that good stuff. What do you say? You want to talk to your dad and stepmom first?"

"I... Yes, sure. I mean yes, I'd love to!" Sunny's grin felt a little twisty-turny on her lips, but in a good way. "Yes, I'll have to talk to them, make sure Liesel can help with the kids, but yes, Wendy. That would be great."

"Good. Let me know tomorrow, okay? And...Sunny, I know it's been tough adjusting." Wendy looked at her carefully. "I knew your dad and your mom in high school, did you know that?"

"You did?" Sunny let her tongue stroke the bitten spot, tasting a tinge of blood. "Oh."

"Yep. Your mom, she was a nice girl. Fun. She had a great sense of humor. You—"

"Look like her," Sunny said. "I know."

Wendy nodded. "But I see a lot of your dad in you, too. But what I was going to say was, you have her sense of right and wrong."

Sunny thought about that. "I do?"

"Yep. Your mom was one of those do-gooders, even back then. Belonged to the debate team, always picked the topics about equality and stuff. She was big on equal rights for women, minorities, everyone." Wendy hesitated and looked at Sunny, taking in her clothes, her hair. "She was a real feminist back in the day. Not so much later, I guess."

Sunny wasn't sure what a feminist was, but she knew about equal rights. "We're all equal in the Maker's eyes, that's what...um, that was what I was taught. It's what you choose to do with your life that sets you above or below anyone else."

Wendy looked thoughtful. "We were all really sorry to hear about your mom."

"She had cancer," Sunny said without thinking. "She'd have died anyway."

Wendy's mouth twisted. "I'm still sorry. It must be pretty hard for you."

Sunny'd used up all her words and could only shrug. Everything was hard, and she knew she should try to love it anyway. "Should I get back to work?"

Wendy gave her a curious look, but then nodded. "Sure. You go on ahead. Don't let them bother you."

"I won't."

The women were gone by the time Sunny left Wendy's office, and she was glad. Still, hearing what they'd thought about what Sanctuary had been like stuck with her. She'd always known the blemished didn't understand the Family of

Superior Bliss, but she hadn't understood just what sorts of misconceptions had run so rampant.

Sunny finished every day at four, but always went to the library a few blocks away to wait until Chris picked her up at a little after six. Liesel could've come for her, but it interrupted nap times, and it was a huge hassle to get all three kids in the car for a fifteen-minute drive. Besides, Sunny liked the library. In those two hours, she could study for her GED. She could sit and read, uninterrupted, which was a luxury she'd never known in Sanctuary. Novels, magazines, newspapers, nonfiction texts on subjects she'd never heard of. She struggled sometimes with the bigger words, because though she'd been taught to read well enough to get through the family literature, reading for pleasure had been discouraged. She struggled more often with references to events and situations she didn't know. History she'd never been taught. Slang she'd never heard.

She could also use the library's computers to get on the internet. She'd have been allowed to use the computer at Liesel and Chris's house, but there never seemed to be any time and Sunny felt funny asking permission to use what seemed like such a personal possession. At the library, she watched videos of funny kittens or penguins getting tickled or babies laughing. She watched television commercials for products she'd never heard of and caught pieces of movies and TV programs that made little sense. The comments left on these videos made her feel just as confused. The blemished seemed to make a habit out of being anonymously cruel.

Liesel said *The Wizard of Oz* had been her favorite movie as a little girl and had played it for the kids and Sunny. Navigating this new world made Sunny feel like Dorothy stepping out from her black-and-white house into a world of color so bright it didn't seem real. Everything in this world seemed like a dream.

Sometimes she left the library with her head aching, too full of information she didn't know how to process. Other times she turned new concepts over and over in her mind and meditated on them until the voice of the stone angel whispered and helped her piece together what had become a very, very big quilt of ideas. There was so much to learn, so much she'd been denied, and she wanted to fill herself up.

Today at the library, on the internet, she searched for information on the Family of Superior Bliss. One site had long lists of accusations about the family, none of which were true, including the idea that they sacrificed animals to Satan. Sunny could only laugh at such blatant misconception. Another site showed photos of family members, including the only picture of Sunny herself, the one the newspeople had used. It had been taken during one of the visits from the social people who came to make sure the children were safe. Sunny clicked away from that site fast. Too many memories. And then, finally, scrolling through pages of links that had nothing to do with her family but another with a father figure that people had labeled a "cult," she stopped on a simple website detailing local Lebanon County religious history.

This site had pictures of Papa as a young man with his wife next to him, baby John in her arms. Pages of text detailing Papa's background and how he'd founded the family. She found copies of his early words, so different even from the stories she remembered that had changed during her lifetime. The internet called Papa's teaching his "doctrine," and described how it had changed over time, beginning as a simple dictate to live a life closer to the earth and as natural as possible and becoming something "twisted," was what the website called it.

Sunny felt twisted, reading that. Her fingers moved the mouse, clicking and scrolling, until she had to close the pages and leave the computer to stop herself from feeling sick. If she was still seeing Dr. Braddock, she might've asked for advice on how to filter all this, how to file it away into sections that made sense, but Sunny had stopped her appointments when they decided she should get a job. She wasn't sad about it; Chris and Liesel and Dr. Braddock had met with Sunny and asked her how she felt about her life, and that she should know she could talk to any of them at any time. None of them understood she didn't need to talk to them when she had the stone angel to listen.

The stone angel wasn't real. Her voice was Sunny's voice. She knew that. Just like she knew from deep inside her heart that not everything Papa taught was wrong. Here in the library was a big can with Reduce, Reuse, Recycle printed on the lid. Liesel talked about being "green," which didn't mean a color but things like turning off lights or buying vegetables from the stands on the side of the road.

And yet…so much of what she'd been raised to believe was wrong. It had to be. Why else would her mother have gotten cancer? Why else would Sunny have three children by the time she was nineteen, something that had seemed natural and normal in Sanctuary and was definitely frowned upon out here. The blemished might be obsessed with sex, but not when babies resulted from it. Why else, she thought as she logged off the computer to go to the parking lot to wait for Christopher, would Papa have died?

The temperature outside the library was hot. Sunny'd grown too used to air-conditioning. She pulled a bottle of cola from her bag, too used to the sweet taste and bubbles to give it up in place of water. She looked up at the summer sky, blue and cloudless, and breathed in the scent of hot asphalt. Car exhaust. Her own sweat, which she knew enough now to find repulsive and cover with deodorant, though she hadn't managed to find the courage to utilize antiperspirant. Too many chemicals, the lingering fear of cancers that started when you blocked your body's natural functions.

All these things were part of her new life, the one her mother had insisted she have. Sunny'd thought maybe it was so she could bring the light to Liesel and Chris, maybe even lots of other people, but it had been too difficult to convince anyone else, when her own faith had been so shaken. Now she wasn't sure what her task was supposed to be.

And how was she supposed to love what she wasn't sure she was supposed to do?

Chapter
28

Date night. It had been too long since they'd gone out to dinner together like this, and Liesel was determined to make the most of it. That dress she knew Christopher liked, pulled from the back of her closet. High heels from way back in her Philly design-firm days. They pinched her toes now, but she'd deal with it. The price of beauty.

She did feel beautiful, too, holding on to her handsome husband's arm as he helped her walk across the gravel parking lot to the deck. She could hear live music playing and caught a scent of something mouthwatering. She was going to order the biggest steak they had. Onion rings. Screw the calories and the extra lumps on her hips that had appeared since she'd been unable to find the time to run as long and often as she'd used to. Tonight was a night out away from Candy Land and macaroni and cheese (made by hand because the boxed kind was, of course, full of chemicals). Tonight she was going to be a grown-up.

"What?" she said twenty minutes after they'd been seated under the huge tree around which the deck had been built. Christopher had been drinking a beer, and Liesel had finished off her first margarita while they waited for their meal to arrive. She'd been talking a lot, she guessed by his expression. "What's so funny?"

"Not funny. Just…even when we're out, you can't stop talking about them."

Liesel paused, running over everything she'd said. In the car she'd given him the rundown on clothes and shoes, since the kids had all needed new things. Sunny had convinced her to shop at the local thrift stores instead of buying new, pointing out how fast the kids grew out of clothes and how much better it was to recycle. It had been an adventure. Led by Sunny, they'd all trooped up and down the aisles, pulling out the most ridiculous outfits they could find and laughing hysterically. They'd come home with two huge bags of clothes for less than forty bucks.

Since sitting down at the table, Liesel'd covered the plans to get Happy into preschool in the fall and how it was going to be complicated because he didn't have a birth certificate or social security card. She'd talked about Bliss getting teeth and learning to crawl, how they had to be so much more careful now about leaving small toys on the ground where she could put them in her mouth. She had, she realized, talked nonstop about her days, her life, and hadn't asked a word about his.

"Sorry," she said, chagrined. "How's work?"

Christopher shrugged. "It's fine."

So much for that. Liesel tried to think about the last time they'd had a conversation that didn't revolve around the house or Sunny or the children and was ashamed to realized that she was unable. She reached across the table to link her fingers through his.

"I love you," Liesel said.

"Love you, too." Christopher smiled and brought her knuckles to his lips to brush them with a kiss.

"How *is* work?" she repeated. "I know you were talking about that sales conference a couple weeks ago. How did it go?"

"Fine." Christopher withdrew his hand and shrugged again. "Work's fine. Same old stuff."

Liesel sat back and sipped from her margarita. The slush had softened, turned to liquid. She licked the salt from the rim of her glass and sighed, tipping her head back to stare up through the tree branches. She couldn't see the sky.

The waitress brought their food and a couple more drinks. They ate huge steaks with all the sides, and Liesel tried hard not to overwhelm her husband with the minutiae of children and housework, even if that was all she really had to talk about. Then, with her stomach so full it bumped out the front of her dress, Liesel reached again for her husband's hand.

"Let's dance."

They hadn't danced together since... Well, she couldn't remember. Maybe the the last company holiday party they'd gone to, which wasn't this past Christmas but the one before. Christopher was a good dancer, light on his feet, and Liesel happened to be a little bit tipsier than she'd expected. She stumbled, but he caught her. She lifted her mouth for a kiss, which he gave her.

It was sweet.

Everything about the night was sweet, including the ride home with the top down, the wind blowing her hair, the stars in the dark sky above. The dark and silent house, almost like they were alone again, and the way he pushed her up against the counter in the kitchen to kiss her. Tongue and hands roaming, when was the last time her husband had kissed her with this much passion? When was the last time she'd wanted him to?

In the past they might've made love right there on the kitchen table, but while the quiet house might have tricked them, the sink full of plastic cups and bowls didn't. Instead, Christopher took her hand and they tiptoed up the stairs, past the rooms of sleeping children of all ages. Giggling, Liesel stopped to tug off her heels and toss them to the side as he closed their bedroom door.

Something about having to be quiet made this seem so urgent, almost furtive, like the days back in high school, making out for hours. Liesel'd never had that with Christopher. Neither of them had been virgins when they met, and though they hadn't fallen into bed with each other without a thought, they hadn't held off very long, either. Now they kissed and kissed and kissed in the same bed they'd shared for almost thirteen years, but when he ran his hands up and down her body, it felt like it could've been the first time he'd ever touched her.

When they had finished, Liesel lay sated in the tangle of their sheets while her husband padded naked to the bathroom. She heard the rush of water as he used the toilet and flushed, then a clatter. A curse.

"Liesel!"

She got out of bed to weave her way around a couple baskets of laundry she hadn't had time to sort, through the dark. She stubbed her toe. The bathroom light hurt her eyes. "What's the matter?"

He'd kicked over the bucket of water in which she'd been soaking her "fluff," which was what the Etsy vendor had called the reusable cloth pads. Pink water and soaked flannel pads had spread across the tile, and Christopher stood in the mess with his bare feet.

"Don't move," she said and grabbed a towel to toss down. "What the hell is that?"

Liesel uprighted the bucket and began tossing the fluff into it. She'd added some detergent to the water, and it had made the floor slick. Her fingers, too. She mopped at the mess with the towel, waiting for Christopher to bend down and help her. Of course, he didn't. She looked up at him, her earlier good mood slowly starting to get nibbled away. "They're my pads. I forgot to throw them in the washer."

It had only been a couple days since her last period, and she'd meant to do it, but had become distracted by other tasks. Always distracted, that's how she felt these days. And now, annoyed.

"You're…"

Watching him hop away like he'd stepped in a pile of manure should've been funnier.

"What the hell?" Christopher turned on the shower. "Why do you have a bucket full of…those?"

Liesel put the rest of the fluff into the bucket, got up and used her feet to push the towel around to collect the water. "Your daughter didn't want to use store-bought pads because they take up room in landfills and are bleached with chemicals. She was using rags, real rags because she didn't have anything else and was too embarrassed to ask me for something different. When I found out, I looked up reusable pads online because she'd said they used to make them for themselves where she lived, but that she didn't know how to sew. I found them online, and I ordered some. And I thought I'd try them out."

The shower had begun to steam, but Christopher didn't get in. "But…why?"

His plain disgust shouldn't have bothered her. After all, Liesel had felt the same way upon learning that Sunny didn't want to use regular pads and throw them in the trash. But, just as with the many other changes that the household had made, once Liesel really thought about how much better for the environment it would probably be to wash and reuse pads, it hadn't seemed gross at all. Just…sensible.

"Why what?"

"Why are you using them?"

"Because that's what happens to a woman when she's not pregnant," she said snidely. "She gets her period."

She tossed the towel into the hamper, making a mental note to make sure that load went into the washer first thing in the morning.

Christopher let out a long, low hiss of dismay. "Whaaat are you doing? You wash that stuff with all my clothes?"

Liesel had gone to the sink to wash her hands, thinking that if he didn't get in that shower soon she'd get in ahead of him. Now she paused. Turned. "Of course I do, how else would I wash it?"

"But it's…" He wisely shut up after that and got in the shower.

Ten minutes ago Liesel would've joined him, but now she waited until he'd finished before hopping in herself. She stayed in there until the water got cold, knowing she'd regret it in the morning when the kids woke her earlier than she'd like. In bed she stretched out to touch him, thinking of how once they'd have snuggled up naked for the rest of the night, maybe even woken to make love again in the morning. Everything had changed.

"Maybe you shouldn't let her convince you to do all this stuff," Christopher said.

"Who, Sunny? What stuff?"

"All this freaky stuff. Cloth diapers, reusable…things."

She'd never known him to be squeamish about feminine

things before. Maybe he had been and she hadn't noticed. "I don't get what the big deal is, Christopher. You know I like to be as green as I can."

"Shopping totes, sure. Recycling. Whatever." He paused. "Don't you think maybe you're taking it too far? We're supposed to be helping her adjust to a normal life, not letting ourselves get sucked into something else."

"Is that really what you think is happening?" Liesel rolled onto her side to look at him, wishing she could see his face, but it was blocked by shadows. "I mean, if you just talked to her about this stuff…"

His low snort gave her pause.

"You do talk to her, don't you? I mean in the morning when you drop her off and then when you pick her up again. You talk to your daughter, Christopher, don't you?"

"You want me to talk to her about her period?"

"You can talk to her about whatever you want," Liesel told him. "I can't believe you don't talk."

He made another low snort and shuffled onto his side. He'd be asleep in a minute or two. Snoring. Liesel touched his shoulder, but he didn't turn.

"Maybe you should spend some time alone with her. Just you and her. Take her out to dinner or something—"

"Like what, a date or something? Christ, Liesel." He shrank from her touch.

Confused at his vehemence, she scooted closer, but he didn't bend to her the way he usually did. She pressed her lips to his shoulder. "Dads do take their daughters out to spend time with them, you know. You spend time with the kids on your own."

"She's not a kid."

"Why should that matter?"

He said nothing for so long she was sure he'd fallen asleep, but then he said, "I don't have anything to say to her. That's all."

"Maybe you should find something," Liesel said.

Christopher made a low noise, deep from his throat. Like a grinding. His voice came out sounding gritty. "She looks like her mother."

"She looks a lot like you, too—" Liesel began, but Christopher cut her off.

"She looks like Trish. Just like her. She has the same laugh as Trish. She…she has the same gestures. When I look at her, I see Trish. Christ, she even smells like Trish."

Liesel swallowed hard, fighting to find words. Her husband shrugged and turned from her, shoulders hunched, head hung. If he thought she would comfort him, he was wrong, she thought. Liesel couldn't even move.

"She's not Trish, Christopher. She's your kid, for God's sake. Not your first wife."

Christopher said nothing. After a minute of silence, he rolled onto his side and faced away from her. Liesel listened to the sound of his slow breathing, but wondered if he was faking sleep the way she was, or if he also lay awake, staring into the dark.

In the first few months of their marriage, they'd shared a double bed before finally getting the king-size they'd slept in ever since. It hadn't mattered at first, sleeping snuggled up tight and close with barely any room to turn over without pressing up against each other. They'd been newlyweds, making love more nights than not. The bigger bed had seemed vast and expansive, an excess of space between them, but after years of having so much room in which to spread out, sharing a smaller bed had become almost intolerable. They'd ended vacations early when the only accommodations were a double or even a queen-size bed instead of a king.

Their giant bed was the perfect size for two, Liesel thought as sleep refused to take her, no matter how many sheep she counted. But it was way too small for three, and that's exactly how many people were in that bed. It didn't even matter that one of them was a ghost.

Chapter
29

She might always be better at mopping the floors and cleaning the toilets than brewing the coffee or kneading the dough, but at least she could do those things when she had to. And she liked to, Sunny thought as she looked over the list of things Amy had left for her to do. It was a big responsibility, opening the store, but Sunny liked that, too.

Amy and Wendy obviously trusted Sunny enough to give her a key to the store. Sunny'd never had a key before. Heck, she didn't even have a key to Chris and Liesel's house, now that she thought about it. Oh, they'd give her one if she asked, that wasn't a worry, she just hadn't ever needed one. And there was one tucked into that clay pot by the front door.

But it wasn't at all the same as a key to the store.

It meant they trusted her. It meant they thought Sunny not only *could* do the tasks set out for her, but that she *would* do them. And of all the things Sunny had come to accept and even sometimes embrace and enjoy about her new life outside, trust was what she treasured the most.

This morning, Amy had left a list detailing the expected deliveries. She'd also written the names of the new sandwiches and left Sunny an unopened package of those fun markers that drew so prettily on the blackboard. The other stuff on the list was nothing special—stock the bathroom and napkin holders with paper products, fill the sweetener and creamer containers on the self-serve coffee station. That sort of thing. Tally the drawer and mark down any change needed, that could be a tough one. Fortunately, Amy wasn't any better with doing math in her head than Sunny was, and never made fun if Sunny used a calculator.

During the day, Amy and Wendy controlled the music, usually playing their favorite internet radio station. They both favored current pop hits like Liesel did, music that left Sunny cold. Before Amy and Wendy came in, though, Sunny liked to switch the station to something called Oldies Hits or Indie Rock. Simon & Garfunkel was her favorite.

The first song played today was "The Sound of Silence," and Sunny hummed along with it as she swept the tile floor before taking the chairs down from the tables. Whoever had closed the night before was supposed to sweep, but she liked to do it again just to start the day off right. With only a couple hours between her arrival and the official shop opening, she didn't really have time to create extra chores for herself, but she liked knowing that when she turned the sign on the front door from Closed to Open, she'd made the Green Bean the cleanest and most welcoming shop anyone could ever ask for.

She made the first pots of coffee, measuring the beans and grinding them. The water. Filling the big jugs. She loved the smell of coffee but not the taste. Probably never would, and not just because of the caffeine she knew was no devil's tool but still wasn't good for her vessel.

Her body, she reminded herself as she washed her hands to start some prep work on the few salad items that would go into the deli case. Not her vessel, but her body. And no, caffeine wasn't good for it, but drinking coffee wouldn't keep her from…well, from whatever there was for people after they died.

It was hard, this constant reminder that the things she'd always thought of as her entire world weren't real or true. That it wasn't even a matter of faith, as Papa had always told them, because Sunny had learned there were all sorts of faiths in the world, and none of them seemed any more right than the other.

Orange juice, though. That she could never get enough of. Orange soda wasn't the same, though she liked that, too, and drank a lot of it during the day because Amy and Wendy had said it was included in her employee benefits even though juice wasn't. She had to be careful, though, to brush her teeth to get rid of the sugar. It made her feel less guilty that way.

She allowed herself a glass of orange juice in the morning though, when she came in to open the shop before anyone else arrived. Just one, a tall glass of it, swimming with pulp. She liked to squeak the little bits between her teeth. The cool air from the fridge bathed her face when she opened the big metal door, and Sunny closed her eyes to lean into it. Just for a second or two. The hum from the fridge was loud enough to sound like the sea. And the cold air felt good after she'd been sweating with all the sweeping and lifting of boxes and stuff.

When she closed the door, she wasn't alone. A man stood in the back door, which hung open, spilling in the light from alley. The jug of orange juice slipped from her suddenly numb fingers. It bounced on the floor, the cap flying off, and landed on its side with a glug-glug-glug of juice spilling out, but the jug itself didn't crack open. Sunny snatched a dish towel from the prep counter and tossed it on the puddle, then pulled the jug off the floor. The cap had rolled too far for her to reach. She stood, her back against the prep counter.

She was startled, but not surprised.

It was Josiah.

"Hello, Sunshine." Josiah had a smooth, low voice. Sort of creamy. He had the same soft, wheat-colored hair, the same blue eyes that looked right into hers and saw everything she'd been doing since she left Sanctuary.

"What are you doing here?"

Josiah looked around the kitchen and held out his hands, palms up, as if he meant to hold something in them but had found only air. "I heard you worked here."

"From who?" It was a silly question. He could've heard it from anyone. Lebanon wasn't very big, and she already knew she'd been the subject of a lot of gossip. Sunny bent again to pick up the sodden towel, dripping orange juice. She took it to the sink and rinsed it, wrung it out. She picked up the bottle of spray cleanser, but moving back to the spill would put her right in front of him, and she didn't want to get that close.

"You act like it's a secret. Is it?" He tilted his head to look at her, up and down. "A secret even from me?"

"It's not a secret. It's just…you shouldn't be here."

"Why not?"

Because she didn't want him there, she thought. Sunny shook her head. "You just shouldn't. What do you want?"

"To see you. Make sure you're okay."

"I'm fine."

"Outside," Josiah said quietly. "Living with the blemished. How can you be fine?"

She felt her jaw go tight, her teeth like a cage to keep inside the words, like beasts. "Why are you here?"

"I told you—"

"No. I mean why are you *here?* Why aren't you…"

Josiah waited for her to finish, but it seemed she couldn't quite make herself say it. "Dead? Is that what you mean, Sunshine? Why didn't I leave my vessel the way my father told us to?"

"Yes," Sunny said.

Josiah laughed. He spread his hands again, holding on to nothing. "My brother…he wanted to live the way our father had told us. He's the one who thought it was time for everyone to leave their vessels…but he was wrong."

"Of course he was wrong!" Sunny shouted. "He was crazy! Just like you all were!"

Josiah looked sad. "Oh, Sunshine. C'mon. That's not you talking. Those aren't the words of a daughter of the family. Those are the words of the blemished. But it's all right, I understand. You just have to remember something."

She eyed him, suspicious. The thunder of her heartbeat had stilled as every second passed without him moving toward her. "What's that?"

"We still love you. We haven't forgotten you."

"Who?"

"I haven't, for one." He gave her a smile that reminded her of Papa's, only nicer. "Everyone who came with me when my brother forced me from my father's house."

"The police will want to talk to you." Sunny had no idea if that was true, but it sounded like it made sense. They'd wanted to talk to her plenty.

Josiah laughed gently. He'd always been the nicer of Papa's true sons. He'd played games with the kids and was never afraid to speak out to Papa and John Second against punishments. He'd always been the only one. Josiah had once given her an extra portion of oatmeal and toast when she was pregnant and had felt faint between lunch and dinner. Funny how she thought of that now, when she hadn't thought about anything nice that had happened during her time with the family in a long while. Lots of the bad things, but not the not-so-bad.

"I've spoken to the police. But I didn't do anything wrong. I was long gone before my brother decided to preemptively encourage everyone to leave their vessels." Josiah looked sad again. "I explained to the police that the reason I left Sanctuary was because I didn't think it was time for us to go, that a lot more had to happen in the world before we'd have to leave it. And that it had to be a choice for every single person, not something anyone should force on anyone."

"They said you knew."

Josiah hesitated. "My brother called me. Yes. But he called me a lot of times before, Sunshine, to tell me he was going to make sure everyone left, and he never went through with it. I didn't know that this time he meant it."

The orange juice would be sticky by now, and Amy was due in about half an hour. She wouldn't be happy Sunny hadn't bothered to clean the mess. Sunny took the damp dish towel and the spray cleanser and knelt to wipe up the rest of the spill. She was very aware of how close Josiah was, and how it felt to be on her knees in front of him the way she'd been so often in front of his brother. She kept her eyes on the spill, swiping and wiping, spritzing it with cleanser and folding the towel so she could use the clean parts to get every last drop of juice. It had splattered quite a bit.

"The police can't do anything to me, Sunshine, because I haven't done anything wrong."

"What John Second did was wrong. What Papa did…that was wrong, too."

"My father and brother did a lot of things that were wrong. I agree. Absolutely."

It was too hard to be terrified of a man who spoke so kindly. Josiah hadn't taken so much as one step toward her. He tilted his head again to look down at her as she looked up, then he squatted onto his heels.

Papa would never have lowered himself that way. Not John Second, either. Sunny, cloth in one hand and spray bottle in the other, stood. Now it was Josiah below her, looking up. Again, he spread his fingers, the backs of them pressed against his knees with the palms up, like an invitation for her to take one of them.

"What do you want from me, really?" Sunny went back to the sink to rinse the towel. And again. Over and over, the water running so hot it turned her hands red and there was nothing left to wring from the towel but clear water, and still she kept going because with the rush of the spigot she could always pretend she didn't hear what he had to say if she didn't like it.

"Like I said, I just wanted to make sure you were all right. And to let you know you were missed, and that you don't have to be alone."

"I'm not alone."

He sounded like he was smiling again, but because she refused to look, Sunny couldn't be sure. "Of course not. But… you're lonely. Aren't you, Sunny?"

Sometimes, yes she was.

She didn't answer him. Not even with a shrug. In Sanctuary she'd have been punished for the disrespect of giving him her back; ignoring a direct question was a sure way to get some time in the silent room. But she wasn't there, she was here.

And when she turned around to tell him that, to make sure Josiah understood that no matter how many times she still woke from dreams in which she'd returned to Sanctuary, Sunny knew the difference between there and here, the family and the blemished…

Josiah was gone.

"Hey, Sunny. What's up?" The boy at the counter gave her a smile so bright she could only look at it from the side instead of straight on.

His name was Tyler, and he went to summer classes at the college across the street. He hung out in the Green Bean with a bunch of other kids who also went to that school. Tyler liked to buy a bottomless cup of coffee and sometimes a bagel with salmon cream cheese. He sat in the front window with his books and computer when he was alone, toward the middle at the biggest table when he was with his friends.

Today he was alone.

"Hi, Tyler." His name tickled her tongue so much Sunny was always afraid she'd get tangled with it. Stutter. Almost two months' working here, and still she found herself stumbling over simple, stupid things. "I'm fine. What's…up with you?"

"Just working on a couple papers. Can I get—"

She was already pushing his mug toward him. He took it with another of those smiles that made her feel dazed, like she'd just stared a little too long at the sun. He had beautiful white teeth. Straight. And dimples.

"Thanks." He handed her a couple of dollar bills and put the change she gave him into the tip jar. "That's for you, make sure they let you keep it."

Sunny glanced over her shoulder toward the kitchen. Amy and Wendy always shared out the tips, even when Sunny didn't work at the register. When she looked back at him, he was still smiling. She hated the blush that crept up her throat and into her face, but Tyler didn't seem to notice. He took his mug and headed for the front window, where he sat facing the street, silhouetted in the light from outside.

Sunny liked knowing he was there, even if she didn't talk to him. The days Tyler came into the shop with his friends were a little stressful. They were all so loud, laughing, the girls always dressed with so little modesty. Sometimes sitting on the laps of the boys, doing silly things like playing with the buttons on the front of the boys' shirts, or their hair, or leaning close to whisper in their ears.

It was hard to believe she was their age. Even a little older than one or two of them. Sunny had nothing in common with any of those kids, though they seemed to think of her as... well, not one of their own, exactly. Not with her long skirts and sleeves, the way she wore her hair and didn't use makeup. They were nice to her, but they thought she was Mennonite or something.

She didn't fit in with them either, those young Mennonite women in their matching dresses and hair coverings. A lot of them had children, just like Sunny, but that meant they also had husbands. Homes of their own. A church and faith to support them.

She didn't have much in common with anyone.

No, she much preferred the days Tyler came in by himself. Some days the shop was empty for hours with just him sitting in the window, tapping away at his computer. He'd told her he was an English major. He wanted to be a teacher. Tyler knew what he was doing and what he wanted, and Sunny admired that.

"You okay out here?" Amy poked her head through the swinging door to the kitchen.

"Yes. It's slow today."

Amy looked out at the empty room, caught a glimpse of Tyler and grinned at Sunny. "I see your favorite customer's here."

More heat flooded Sunny's face, and she quickly wiped at an invisible spot on the counter. Amy liked to tease. "I like all the customers."

Sunny watched her return to the kitchen. When she turned back to the counter, there was Tyler with his empty mug. Sunny was still smiling, couldn't stop, and he seemed a little surprised. Just at first. Then he smiled, too.

They looked at each other across the counter for a few seconds that felt much longer, until finally Tyler handed her his mug. Sunny took it, imagining the heat of his fingers on the porcelain. She thought he'd walk away then.

Instead, Tyler shuffled a foot on the wooden floor. His sneakers squeaked. He rubbed a hand on the back of his neck, head tilted with one eye shut as he looked at her. "Sunny."

"Yes?"

"Do you wanna see about doing something sometime?"

It took her several more long seconds to understand what he meant. She put the mug down so hard she was afraid she'd cracked it. "With you?"

He laughed. "Sure. With me."

"Something…like what?"

"We could see a movie," he said. "Maybe go to dinner?"

"A date," Sunny said flatly.

"Sure." Tyler hit her with another smile, but hers had faded. He looked a little confused. "No?"

"I just… I'd have to ask my dad."

His laughter slid away the moment it left his mouth when he saw she wasn't laughing along. "Really? You're kidding."

She shook her head.

"I figured you were my age."

Sunny didn't want to talk about this anymore, but he was still looking at her. "I'm going to be twenty."

"I just turned twenty," Tyler said. "I don't ask my parents if I can go out. Is it like…some religious thing?"

He meant the clothes, she thought. Or maybe her past clung to her like a stink. Sunny shook her head. Then nodded.

Tyler's smile was half of normal, but it still warmed her. "Okay. So. Ask your dad."

She opened her mouth to say no. What came out instead was, "I will."

Chapter
30

Liesel's mother is about to scream. Liesel can see this by the furious way her mom's trying to light her cigarette, but her shaking hands are making it impossible. Robbie cringes behind Liesel, and Gretchen is stone-faced, though her eyes are glittery with tears and her cheeks are bright red. Liesel hasn't started to cry yet, but she does want to run away.

Fast.

"How. Hard. Is. It?" Mom's words crack on Liesel's ears the way stones shatter glass. "How many times do I have to say it?"

Robbie lets out a little whimper. Liesel wants to poke him, tell him to shut up, because when Mom gets like this, she's like one of those lionesses in the grass on one of those nature programs the family watches on Sunday nights. Don't draw her attention to you, and you might escape alive.

"You kids," Mom says, "are driving me crazy. You know that? How many times do I have to ask you to pick. Up. Your.

Crap! Pick it up! Don't throw your shoes and coats on the floor! Hang them up, put them in the closet! If something belongs to you, put it away, for the love of God!"

Liesel can't be sure what prompted the tirade, but she's pretty sure it was Gretchen. She always comes in the front door from school and dumps her stuff on the dining room table so she can run downstairs to watch that stupid cartoon all of her friends are so into. It could've been Robbie, he never puts away his shoes. Or his toys. His stuff is always all over the place.

"Liesel!" her mother cries loud enough to snap Liesel's attention back toward her. "This isn't brain surgery!"

Her mother points at the kitchen sink with one perfectly manicured fingernail. She's finally managed to light her cigarette, and she draws in the smoke now, eyes narrowed against it. She holds it for a second, so when she talks she sounds harsh and breathy.

"Dirty cups go in the goddamn dishwasher!"

"Oh." Liesel's stomach sinks. Yes, she'd had a drink of water from the faucet and had put her cup in the sink, not the dishwasher. "But it was full!"

Her mother hits the latch and the door to the dishwasher falls open. Her mother points again. "Yeah, with clean dishes. If you see that? Here's a small clue. Put the dishes away. Then put the dirty dish in the dishwasher! This is not difficult."

She points at Gretchen. "You. Go get all your crap off the table, or I swear by all that is holy I will throw it all in the trash."

At Robbie. "You. If I find one more dirty sock anyplace other than the laundry—if I find any single article of your dirty clothes, for that matter, in any location other than the appropriate laundry basket—I will take one dollar out of your allowance for every single thing. Do you hear me?"

Robbie and Gretchen nod. Liesel has already moved toward the dishwasher. Her mother takes in another long drag and lets it out, the smoke rancid and making Liesel want to choke.

"Are we all clear on everything?"

The kids nod. It's better not to speak. Nothing they say will make any of this better. Besides that, they know they're wrong. Mom *does* ask them all the time to do exactly what she's asking now. But it doesn't seem fair that she gets so darned mad about it.

"Good." Mom stabs out her cigarette and takes a deep breath. "We all live here. Right? And I know you have this crazy idea that I just love cleaning up after you, but the fact is, I do not. There is more to my life than doing your laundry."

Liesel can't imagine what else her mom might do all day other than laundry and clean, but wisely, she keeps her mouth shut. She considers herself lucky that she got away with only having to unload the dishwasher—she could've been grounded. That would've sucked.

Mom sighs. "And really…I hate yelling like this."

"I'm sorry, Mommy." Robbie is kind of a suck-up, but when he squeezes Mom around the waist she does smile.

Phew. The worst has passed. At least until tomorrow when the same conversation probably will happen all over again.

That was what Liesel thought of when the words popped out of her mouth. "There is more to my life than cleaning up after you."

Peace, hands and mouth smeared with chocolate pudding, blinks and says nothing. Happy frowns. Bliss, firmly ensconced on Liesel's hip, babbles something so cute and precious it would be nice to take a second to appreciate it, but Liesel is caught between her genuine and somewhat frightening fury and her shame at realizing that she's turned into everything she swore she'd never be.

"Happy, didn't I ask you to watch your sister?" Ten minutes, that was all it had taken for Liesel to take the baby upstairs to change her diaper. Ten minutes and thirty seconds that had apparently been long enough for two kids to destroy the kitchen.

Half-gallon of milk on the floor, mostly spilled. Two glasses half-full, contents slopped on the table. Chocolate pudding cups completely emptied, though it seemed more of the pudding ended up all over Peace's face and clean shirt than in her mouth.

"Peace was thirsty," Happy said. "I had to get it for her."

Liesel knew the kids were a little wild with the idea that they were allowed to help themselves to stuff from the fridge, and the last thing she wanted to do was have Peace revert to asking her every twenty minutes if she could have a drink or something to eat. Happy wouldn't—he was still very much attached to the idea of a schedule. But he'd help his sister do whatever he thought was necessary to keep her content. It was sweet, actually.

Just messy.

Liesel sighed, bouncing Bliss on her hip. "I have to put Bliss down for her nap. Why don't you go in the den and play."

Upstairs, Bliss fussed when Liesel put her into the crib, though it was at least half an hour past the time she normally went down for a nap. It was the second day in a row Bliss had fought going to sleep in the morning, and Liesel really hoped this meant she wasn't trying to give it up. That hour in the morning had become precious to her, one of two times a day when she could set the other kids in front of the TV and grab a shower. Or God, just go pee by herself.

She hadn't shaved her legs in two weeks. No time, and

when she thought of it, she was usually too tired to bother. Her hair was in desperate need of both a trim and a color touch-up. No time for that either, unless she wanted to drag three kids along with her to the stylist, who never seemed to have any appointments available on the days Sunny didn't work or after she got home. Liesel hadn't yet broken down enough to go to one of those mall salons, but it was getting close. There was only so much a couple of bobby pins or a baseball cap could handle.

None of this had been anything like she expected, which was stupid on her part since she'd certainly been privy to Becka's grousing about how hard it was to be at home with kids. But somehow Liesel'd thought things would be… different. Because they weren't her children? Because she wanted this so much? Or because it was the only way she could stop herself from dwelling on the fact she'd quit her job and it was the first time in her entire adult life she hadn't had a paycheck to call her own.

There was a lot of good in not working, sure. The longer she was away from the print shop, the more she realized the good parts hadn't even come close to making up for the bad. And the rewards of hearing Happy teaching his sister her ABCs from a book Liesel had ordered online, of watching them slowly blossom from the frightened children they'd been at the playground that first day to kids confident enough to run and play and swing…there'd been nothing like that in her life before now.

It was all the rest of it she couldn't quite manage. The constant noise. The mess. The lack of bathroom privacy. Hell, the lack of any privacy. Leaving the door open a crack in case of cries in the night had become second nature, just like any small sound had become an interruption to whatever few-and-far-between intimacies she and Christopher managed.

Even when Sunny was home, it wasn't much easier. The kids had started turning to Liesel first before anyone else, so even with their mom in the house they went to Liesel for snacks, drinks, to put a new movie in the DVD player, to get out the games from the cupboard.

Sunny's days off from the shop were Liesel's days off from child care and housework, at least ostensibly. But with Sunny on her hands and knees scrubbing the floor in the kitchen, Liesel couldn't exactly plop herself down on the couch with a bucket of bonbons to glut herself on daytime television. First, she'd have had to wrestle the remote away from Peace and Happy who'd become addicted to sickly sweet kiddie programming that made Liesel want to poke out her eyes. Second, Sunny never complained about cleaning no matter how messy the house got, and that made Liesel feel like she shouldn't, either. Sunny was in the bathroom right now, scrubbing the toilet and the shower. Singing while she did it. The lilting melody of "The Sound of Silence" filtered into the hall. Liesel hadn't run in a week.

Stupid. Bliss, Peace and Happy were Sunny's children and her responsibility, and there was no reason why Liesel should feel one second of guilt about leaving her here alone with them. Especially because it had been months since there'd been any need to worry about something going wrong. Yet there Liesel was, rushing through showers, forgetting to shave her legs, foregoing her daily run, all in order to get back out there and help Sunny with the cleaning and the kids and everything else.

It was amazing, though, what just an extra pair of hands could do. In a couple of hours Sunny and Liesel had managed to clean the whole house, feed the kids and even fold and put away three baskets of laundry. Both the washer and dryer were still going, but as Liesel looked around her newly cleaned kitchen, she felt as if she could take a full, long breath. The first in days.

Sunny had taken Peace and Happy outside to play, and Liesel drank in the quiet. She mixed up some lemonade using real lemons, scrubbed to make sure they were clean from pesticide, and real sugar because chemical sweeteners were full of...well, chemicals. Sunny was a walking encyclopedia of what food was good and what was bad, but Liesel had to admit, homemade lemonade tasted better than any powdered substitute. She took it out to the deck along with a plate of crackers and cheese. The kids were playing tag and Sunny was sitting next to the angel, so Liesel poured two tall glasses of lemonade and took them down to her.

She handed one to Sunny. "It's hot out here. Have some lemonade."

Sunny took it. "Thanks."

Liesel looked at the angel and her poor, sad garden. "Maybe she cries because there aren't any flowers."

Sunny looked startled. "What?"

"The angel." Liesel gestured. "Maybe she cries because I haven't planted any real flowers."

Sunny looked around at the garden. "I like the wildflowers. They grow however they want to. And they come back all on their own."

Liesel sat on the warm stone bench and sipped cold lemonade. "They're weeds, mostly."

"I don't care. They're still pretty."

Sunny looked...edgy, was the only way Liesel could think to describe it. Cagey. A little shifty, even.

Dr. Braddock had told them it was okay to ask Sunny if she was all right as many times as it seemed necessary, but to be prepared for her to resent it. She'd also told them to be ready for Sunny to push at boundaries and rules the same way the children did. So far, nothing like that had happened, but Liesel kept waiting.

She should ask Sunny what was bothering her, but then Liesel would know, and she'd have to figure out a way to help Sunny solve all her problems...and right now, sitting in the hot sun with cold lemonade, the only problem Liesel wanted to solve was how to find a way to take a nap. They sat together in the hot sunshine and drank lemonade while the children played. Liesel basked in the sun, letting it paint the inside of her eyes with crimson.

She'd thought wanting this so much would make it all easier, but none of it was.

Chapter
31

Liesel went for a run after dinner, leaving Sunny to clean up the dishes. She didn't mind. Bliss was happy enough on Chris's lap, while Peace did her best to talk his ear off from his other knee. Happy had been a good helper, clearing off the table and loading the dishwasher. He sat at the table now, coloring in one of the many books Liesel had picked up for him. He sat close enough that Chris could comment on what he was doing. It warmed her to see that closeness, because although Chris never seemed thrilled about having her there, it was clear that he loved her kids.

She'd brought home some leftover chocolate cake and pastries, bought with her own money and her employee discount. Silly things, not at all healthy, but knowing she'd paid for them with money she'd earned herself made them taste so much sweeter. Maybe knowing they were bad for her did, too.

"I can make some coffee," she said.

Chris looked up as though startled she'd spoken to him. He probably was. They hardly ever talked. Well, he barely spoke to her, and she'd taken the cue from him. Their morning and afternoon car rides were spent listening to the radio with only an occasional comment in between. He always said "have a good day" when she got out, but he never asked how her day had been when she got in again.

"I learned how at work," Sunny told him. "I'm pretty good at it."

"Sure. I'd like some coffee. That would be great."

He hardly looked at her, either. It was because of that night when she'd come across him in the den, when he'd pulled her onto his lap. She'd assumed he was the sort of man who would do that to a girl, even his daughter, but she'd learned since then he wasn't. She wondered if he'd ever be her dad.

She made the coffee while she finished up the last of the dishes, then brought him a cup fixed the way he liked it. "Sugar and cream, right?"

"Yeah...thanks." Chris nudged Peace off his lap and put Bliss on the floor to follow her. Now that she'd learned to crawl, you couldn't keep her still. "Go play. This is hot stuff."

"C'mon, Bliss. Let's play with the blocks." Peace could be inconsistently kind to her baby sister, but now she patiently waited for the baby to crawl after her across the tile floor and down the hall.

"Be careful," Chris called after them. He looked at Sunny. "Will they be okay?"

"We've put everything Bliss can get into up high, and there's a baby gate to keep her from the stairs. They'll be okay." Sunny took a mug of coffee for herself. She always thought she'd learn to like it. Maybe she would, eventually.

After dinner, if he was even home for it, Chris usually disappeared upstairs to work out or into the den to watch TV, since he could close the door against the kids. Tonight he sat with his mug in his hands, spinning it slowly on the tabletop.

"So," he said, "how's...work?"

Surprised, Sunny wasn't sure how to answer. "I like it."

"Good."

So many of the blemished didn't know what to do with silence. Sunny'd learned that well enough at the coffee shop, where people insisted on talking, talking. To be "social," they said, but she thought it was because they didn't really know what to do with themselves if they had to listen to what was in their heads instead of what came out from their mouths.

"I'm sorry," Chris said suddenly. "I'm bad at this."

She had no idea what he meant. Chris was good at lots of things—he'd fixed the sink when it broke and he had a real knack for getting Peace to calm down when she was wound up about something. He was bad at lots of things, too, like picking up after himself and turning off lights and closing cupboards. She looked around the kitchen now, trying to see what he was talking about.

"At being your dad," Chris said.

"Oh." Her voice sounded smaller than usual, and Sunny focused on her mug. "Well...I've never really had a...dad, Chris. If that helps any."

"Liesel said I should talk to you more."

Sunny laughed. "About what?"

He shrugged. "About anything, I guess."

She considered this. She and Liesel talked all the time, about the children, the house, grocery lists. What would a daughter talk to her father about? Something important? She thought about telling him Josiah had come into the shop, but what could she have said about it? He came in, talked to her, left.

She didn't want to tell Chris about Josiah.

Still, he was looking at her expectantly and also a little fearfully. "Well, there is something."

Chris cleared his throat. "Hit me."

"There's a...boy."

"What kind of boy?" His brow furrowed, eyes narrowing.

"He comes into the shop," Sunny explained. "His name is Tyler. He goes to the community college."

"Is he bothering you? I'll talk to Amy and Wendy." Chris frowned.

Sunny shook her head. "No. Not bothering me. He's...nice. He asked me to go to the movies and dinner with him."

"Sunshine, that's—"

"I don't have to go anywhere with him," she put in quickly. "I know it's not really appropriate."

Dating wasn't something she'd ever even heard about until she came out into the world. In Sanctuary such a thing didn't exist. When she was a little girl, she'd thought about what it would be like to be the one true wife. Nobody else could marry until Papa found her. When she got older...well, by the time Sunny was old enough to even care about boys, she'd already had Happy, who'd been a blessing to her in so many ways.

After Happy came, John Second had left her alone.

"Why wouldn't it be appropriate?" Chris asked.

She turned her head toward the blare of cartoons coming from the den. Then she looked at her son, still so diligently coloring. She touched his hair.

"Because."

The silence between them was perfect, no need to speak for the sake of speech itself.

Happy looked up. "Mama?"

"Yes, my sweetheart."

"Are you going away?"

Sunny shook her head. "Of course not."

"I think going to dinner and a movie would be fine," Chris said.

Sunny's smile twisted, and so did her fingers, linking with each other. "I really like him, Chris."

"Then you should go."

Happy frowned. "Mama, you said no."

"Just out with a friend, that's all," she told him. "But you'll stay here with Liesel and Chris, and that will be fun, won't it?"

Happy nodded, looking solemn. He showed Chris the picture he'd been working on. "The lady was pushing Peace, and I thought she was pushing her down, but Liesel says it was just for fun."

That sounded like a story, but not one Happy wanted to continue, because he hopped down from the chair and left his crayons and book behind to go in search of the cartoons. Chris and Sunny sat in more quiet, something that had been awkward eased between them.

"We'll want to meet him first, of course," Chris said after a pause.

Sunny laughed. "You will?"

"Sure. Of course."

"But…you don't mind? Really, you think it would be okay?"

Chris reached across the table to take her hand, stilling her twisting fingers. He cupped both her hands with his. "I think it would be okay, Sunny."

A key turned inside a lock, something inside her she hadn't known could even open. Sunny drew in a hitching breath that hurt her throat. Her eyes stung. Her lips moved, forming words she didn't even know she wanted to say aloud until they forced their way up from her throat in a guttering rasp.

Chris pulled her chair closer to him. He hugged her hard. One hand stroked down her back, over and over, slowly. Her mom had done that for her, a long, long time ago, when Sunny was very small. She missed her mom more than ever.

This was so different from that first time, in the dark. Sunny closed her eyes and pressed her face to the front of his shirt while she fought to keep herself from shaking in her grief. When his hand moved along her hair, it was too much. She wept.

It felt good; she knew then why crying had been so discouraged in Sanctuary. Not because it made you weak, but just the opposite. Holding in your sorrow was what weakened you. Hiding your feelings never kept you from having them.

She cried for just a few minutes, but hard enough to wet the front of his shirt. Chris gave her a napkin from the table, and she blew her nose. Wiped her eyes. She didn't move away, though, and he didn't push her. They sat like that for what felt like a long, long time.

"Wendy said she knew you in school."

"Yeah, I knew Wendy back in the day." Chris rubbed slow circles on her back.

"She said...she knew my mom, too."

The motion of his hand slowed, then stopped. "Yeah. She knew your mom, too."

"Do you miss her?"

It seemed like a normal enough question for her to ask. He'd been married to her mom, after all. Even if it had been a really long time ago, even if they'd gotten divorced and he'd married Liesel, that didn't mean he couldn't miss her.

"Papa always said the people we love leave a spot on our hearts," Sunny said when Chris didn't answer right away. "When I was small, I thought he meant like a bruise on an apple. I was sort of silly."

"It was just like a bruise on an apple." Chris's hand moved again, this time up and down, before he let it rest between her shoulder blades for a second. Then he pulled away to look her in the face. "I loved your mom very, very much."

He paused. Lowered his voice. "Don't tell Liesel I said that."

Sunny pondered that. "She won't ask me if you said it, I guess. So…I wouldn't have to lie or anything."

"I don't want you to lie. Just… She wouldn't be happy to hear I said that."

"But even if she's not happy about it," Sunny said, "it's still true."

Chris laughed with a grimace. "Yeah. I guess so. But I love Liesel, too. Don't want her to be upset, right?"

Sunny thought again. "No. Of course not."

Both of them looked up at the scrape of shoes on the tile floor of the hall. Liesel came through the arched doorway to the kitchen, her face red and gleaming, her hair stiff with sweat in the front and great rings of it under her arms. She went straight to the fridge to grab the pitcher of lemonade and poured herself a tall glass, drinking it down without a word.

Chris moved away from Sunny without saying a word, making a space between them. She took the hint and moved, too, got up to take the mugs to the dishwasher, where she almost bumped into Liesel putting away her glass.

"Did you have a good run?" Sunny asked.

Liesel looked at her without expression. "It was good. Not long enough. But good."

She looked at Chris. "I'm going up to take a shower and get to bed early. Sunny, you work tomorrow, right?"

Sunny nodded, but Liesel wasn't looking at her. Instead, she pushed past Sunny and barely gave Chris a nod before leaving the kitchen and them behind. At the table, Chris let out a long, slow sigh.

It seemed there should be something for Sunny to say, the silence not as perfect now as it had been just a little while ago. Without a word, Chris got up and left the kitchen, heading toward the den. Then she was left alone.

Chapter
32

While helping Christopher's mother clear out some boxes in preparation for her move to New Jersey, Liesel had found a whole box of Christopher's high school memorabilia. Stuck in the very bottom was a white faux-leather album filled with wedding photos. None of them professional, not like Liesel and Christopher's posed portraits with every stray blemish and those few extra pounds erased. These were snapshots of a much younger Christopher and his beaming bride in a dress covered in frills and lace.

Trish had been so…pretty. In those snapshots, Liesel saw her husband in love with the sort of woman she'd never been and never would be. They'd cemented to Liesel that she was not the first woman her husband had loved enough to marry. She'd never, until now, even wondered if he'd never loved her as much.

Her mother had always said you never heard anything good when you listened at doors. Liesel had discovered that, all right. And what could she have said to her husband about it? Trish was not only long gone from his life, but she was also dead. That there was a living, breathing reminder living in their house with them was whose fault? Who'd wanted it? She had. And now she had to, as Christopher had so sweetly pointed out to her, deal with it.

"Christopher said a boy from work asked you to go out with him. When are you going?" Liesel tried to keep her voice light, unaccusing. She'd been the one to tell Christopher he needed to talk to his daughter. What kind of bitch would she be to be angry with him now that he had?

"I don't know. I told him I would, but he hasn't been in since then." Sunny looked at Liesel. "Maybe he won't ask me again."

"He asked you already, right? Why would he change his mind?"

Sunny shrugged. "Maybe he didn't mean it."

Liesel could remember that feeling. Liking a guy, not sure if he liked her in return. Hoping, but not convinced. "I'm sure he did."

Sunny shrugged again. "He doesn't know anything about me. Or...what if he does?"

Liesel kept her attention on the pile of laundry they were folding. Something in Sunny's voice sounded precarious, incapable of facing a direct look. "So, he'll get to know you."

Sunny hesitated, then shrugged one more time.

"You know, Sunny," Liesel said carefully, "it's really okay to leave the past behind. You don't have to forget it. But you don't have to carry it along with you forever, either."

Another pause.

"Maybe you want to start seeing Dr. Braddock again? She helped you a lot before, didn't she?" Liesel matched socks. Folded small T-shirts into tidy bundles.

Sunny was working on the towels. The basket was fuller, but the work was easier, and Liesel couldn't stop a stab of annoyance that once again she'd ended up with the more difficult chore.

Sunny smoothed a tea towel across her knees. "If you think I should."

"No. I mean, I only want you to if you think you want to. If she'd help. Or you can talk to me, to your dad—"

Sunny's sharp laugh cut off Liesel's words. "It's not talking that's the problem, Liesel. It's the listening."

"We'd listen."

Sunny smiled. Shrugged again. She folded more towels while Liesel dug around to find the counterpart to too many tiny socks and came up missing.

They worked in silence after that, until Peace tripped and bumped her head on the edge of the counter and needed an icepack and some cuddles that Sunny gave without even a grimace. So easy. So calm. Was it because she'd given birth to them? Was that what made it easier for Sunny to handle three kids? Or was it that she'd grown up without having to worry about anything other than the straight and simple tasks set in front of her, and she still didn't. No worries beyond what was right in front of her.

Envy tasted sour, the bitterness lingering even when Liesel drank to wash out her mouth. More guilt. Sunny'd been through a lot more in her life than Liesel ever had or would ever want to.

Sunny'd never gone on a date. She'd had babies, but no boyfriends. Now a boy liked her, and it would've been, should've been the most normal thing in the world for her to giggle over him with Liesel, but instead she'd acted as though she didn't even freaking deserve to be liked.

She didn't even know how beautiful she was, Liesel

thought, watching Sunny wash Peace's face at the sink and send her back off to play. She didn't know how to be pretty, and whose job should it be to teach her? Her mother's, of course, but she didn't have a mother.

She had Liesel.

"I have an idea. Something that might make you feel a little better about your date."

Sunny straightened, her smile wry. "The one I might not have?"

"The one you will have," Liesel told her. "C'mon upstairs with me."

In her bedroom, she opened the closet, then looked at Sunny over her shoulder. "Let's give you a makeover."

Sunny's brows rose. "Oh…Liesel. I'm not sure…"

"Nothing crazy," Liesel promised. "But I know I have some things in here that I haven't worn in a while. They'll fit you."

Most other girls Sunny's age would've turned up their noses at hand-me-downs, but Liesel had learned that the concept of new clothes, new anything when there was an alternative, made Sunny anxious. Now she tugged out a lightweight summer dress with a matching shrug to cover up the bare arms. It had an empire waistline, which had never been flattering on Liesel.

"Try this."

Ten minutes later, Sunny stepped shyly in front of the mirror. With her long blond hair piled on top of her head, just a few ringlets escaping around her face, and the long dress, she looked like a character out of a Jane Austen novel. She turned slowly back and forth, looking at her reflection.

More envy, the pang of it sharper this time. Sunny was lovely in a way Liesel had never been. Feminine, delicate. Not that Liesel was some great galumphing beast or anything like that. But she'd never look like that. Never like Trish had.

"You look so pretty," Liesel said.

She did. Tall, slim, blond, skin like peaches and cream. Sunny's beauty was effortless and therefore shouldn't have been enviable. But it was.

Sunny smoothed the front of the dress. From down the hall came a set of suspicious thumps from Sunny's room. Before either of them could react, there was a much louder thump and a scream. Liesel was halfway out the door behind Sunny when she recognized the screaming as laughter, at least not pain or terror. Thank God. But when she rounded the corner and stared through the doorway into the guest bedroom, she let out a scream of her own.

Bliss had pulled herself up against the side of the portable crib with Happy and Peace standing in front of her. All three kids looked as if they'd been dipped face-first in a bath of chocolate, a real Willy Wonka explosion. All three of them were grinning.

"Bliss made a poop," Happy said. "We tried to change her diaper."

Sunny had made it through the door before Liesel, but now she sagged back a few steps so her shoulder hit the door frame. She let out a low noise Liesel couldn't identify. Her shoulders shook.

Oh, God. It was shit? Everywhere was shit. All over the sheets and blankets, the children. Even on the white curtains hanging just over the crib. The smell of it rose thick and rich from across the room, and for the first time in her life Liesel truly understood the term *miasma*.

She let out a strangled sound of her own and fought a gag. Sunny turned to her, face red, eyes bright. For an instant Liesel assumed Sunny was weeping, ashamed at how horrible her children had behaved, but before Liesel could bite out a lie and tell her it was okay, she saw it was just the opposite.

Sunny was laughing.

"This is it!" Liesel shouted.

Instant silence. No more giggles. No hitching breaths as Sunny tried to hold in her laughter. Even baby Bliss looked up with surprise, tiny eyes wide, before bursting into a wail.

"This is…abominable. Outrageous. It's disgusting!" Liesel screamed, far from proud at how Peace and Happy both flinched, clapping their hands over their ears. "What is wrong with you?"

The question was more like what wasn't wrong with her. What wasn't wrong with any of them? Liesel backed into the doorway, her stomach clenching, and wondered if she was ever going to feel like her life was back to normal.

Sunny had retreated, scuttling across the carpet to get to her kids. She stood in front of them, protective, not seeming to care that she was getting feces all over the back of Liesel's dress. They stood like that for a half a minute before Peace was the next to burst into tears.

"Hush," Sunny said. The little girl didn't hush, but despite the stench, the confusion, Sunny didn't lose her temper. "I said hush."

The four of them stared at Liesel, who realized she was making a strange, low growling. She forced herself to stop. She covered her mouth and nose, trying not to breathe.

"It's only poop," Sunny said as though she was trying to comfort Liesel. "I know it's gross, but poop washes off."

The children and all the clothes and bedding needed to be washed; the question was, which could she stand to deal with better? "Run a bath in the big tub in my room. You bathe the kids, I'll do the wash," Liesel said.

Sunny nodded, no longer laughing. She lifted the baby, holding her away from her body, though it didn't really matter. The dress was covered in crap all along the back, and it was of a dry-clean-only material. They'd probably just have to throw it in the trash. Sunny murmured, calm as she ever was, and took the children from the room, leaving Liesel surrounded by filth.

She couldn't do anything but stand there for a long time. Hands shaking. Not really angry. More ashamed at her reaction than anything else. Sunny had handled it so easily. So simply. *Poop washes off.*

Of course it did.

Yet as Liesel looked around the room and the mess the children had made, all she could think of was how everything had turned to shit.

Chapter
33

Liesel, car keys in hand, met Sunny at the door with Bliss in her arms and passed the baby off with little more than a mumbled greeting. She barely kissed Chris, who'd come in the door behind Sunny. "Going shopping," she said and then was out the door and in her car, backing out of the garage.

"What the hell is her problem?" Chris muttered.

"Hi, baby," Sunny said to Bliss, who'd started babbling and was now waving chubby fists around. "You telling me a story?"

In the kitchen, Chris muttered again, "No dinner?"

Sunny looked around as she settled Bliss into her high chair. She could hear the sound of cartoons from the family room. "Happy! Peace!"

Happy came at once on skipping feet to give her a hug. Peace didn't. Sunny thought of shouting for her a second time, but then if Peace still didn't obey she'd be forced to punish her. Sunny didn't feel like punishing or even disciplining her daughter, a fault of her own and one that would've meant her own punishment back in Sanctuary.

But...she wasn't in Sanctuary.

"Happy, you need to clean off this table so we can have some dinner. Put all your cars in the box. The puzzles, too." Bliss banged her hands on the tray, and Sunny rubbed the baby's head. "Yes, my sweetheart, I'll get you something to eat."

To Chris, who'd taken out a bottle of beer and stood in front of the sink, looking out the window while he loosened his tie, Sunny said, "I can make some dinner."

He turned, bottle at his lips. "Maybe we should just order a pizza."

She didn't blame him for being wary. "Chris, really, I can make us some sandwiches, and I know there's pasta salad in the fridge because I made some yesterday. I learned how at work. I'm not so bad at cooking anymore."

She wasn't up to the challenge of anything complicated, but she wasn't totally helpless, either. Chris drained his beer and tossed the bottle into the recycling bin, then nodded. He pulled his tie free of his shirt collar with a sigh and looked down at it in his hand like it might turn into a snake and bite him.

"Why don't you go take a shower," Sunny suggested. "Change your clothes and stuff. I can handle this. Really."

He gave her a faint smile. "Sure, okay."

He paused to kiss both Bliss and Happy on their heads as he passed and then stopped in the family room to call Peace over for a hug and a kiss. Watching them, Sunny's heart twisted. Peace jumped into his arms with a cry of glee, her little arms and legs wrapped around him while he spun her.

This...was home. This was what a normal life was like, she thought as Chris put Peace down with a pat on her bottom to send her into the kitchen to help Happy clean off the table. Family who loved each other.

"Mama?" Happy tugged her sleeve. "What's-a-matter?"

Sunny shook her head and took the time to hug him close and stroke his blond hair from his face. Liesel had taken Happy for a haircut that he'd asked for. It had broken Sunny's heart to see him without his long curls, but apparently the other kids on the playground had called him a girl once too often. She kissed both his cheeks.

"Nothing's the matter, my sweetheart. Let Mama make the tuna salad, okay? If you're finished putting the toys away, you and Peace can go play. Turn the TV off," she added when Peace headed straight for it. "Play a game or something."

Happy sighed but nodded. Peace, on the other hand, stomped her feet and crossed her arms over her belly. She grimaced.

"Nooooooooooo!"

Sunny's brows lifted. "Peace, hush."

But Peace didn't hush. "NOOOOOOOOOOOOOO!"

Sunny straightened. In the drawer, the wooden spoon. Her child's shoulder, bones small and fragile in her fingers. Soft hair falling down the girl's back, covering Sunny's hand as she shook the girl into sobs. Happy's wide eyes, solemn face, and the pound-pound-pound of Bliss's fists on the high-chair tray.

No.

No.

The angel's voice that was really Sunny's own whispered, soft in Sunny's ear. A phantom touch on her cheek. She closed her eyes for a moment, listening, but there was nothing more to hear.

Sunny put the spoon away. She knelt to take Peace more

gently by the shoulders and wiped her face with a napkin. "Peace. Hush."

Peace let out another series of strangled sobs. Sunny gathered her close, rocking the girl back and forth while she shushed her. When Peace's sobs had faded, Sunny pushed her away to look at her again.

"Go play," she told her. "No television. Play a game with Happy, or with your babies. Do you hear me?"

Peace nodded, cheeks stained with tears, small mouth still pouting. "I wanna watch 'toons."

"Later. But when you cry this way and don't listen to me, you don't get what you want, do you understand?"

Peace didn't understand, clearly, but she nodded after half a second. She stomped away, not at all pleased with the situation, but in front of the TV she hesitated before pushing the button to turn it on. Instead, she went to the bin containing her dolls and pulled one out.

Sunny drew in a breath. Then another. There wasn't time to think this over, because Bliss had started to whine as well as thump her hands. Upstairs, the hissing of water in the pipes stopped. Chris would be downstairs in a few minutes, and she hadn't even started the sandwiches. There wasn't time for Sunny to ponder how she felt about almost beating her child with a spoon for the sin of back talk.

That she had not done it was more important than the fact she'd wanted to, she told herself as she went from cupboard to counter to fridge. A can of tuna, some mayo, some mustard, a few stalks of celery and half an onion went into the mixing bowl and she stirred it up. She hadn't done it.

The food was ready just as Chris, hair wet and wearing sweatpants, came into the kitchen. Sunny'd set the table and added a basket of sliced bread, a platter of tomatoes, some carrot sticks and fresh fruit. It wasn't a bad meal at all, she thought as Chris called the kids to come to the table. In fact, it was as good as anything Liesel could've done.

"Looks good," Chris said, and Sunny beamed.

Chris usually didn't talk much, but without Liesel here to keep the conversation going, it fell on Sunny to ask him questions about his day and to share pieces of her own so they could find something to talk about. She'd seen her mother do it with John Second enough, this drawing out of a man who wasn't in the mood for chatter. Sunny wasn't nearly as good at it. Conversations were still so often like a field full of stones that stubbed her toes or tripped her up when she tried to be clever. Still, she made him laugh with a story about something that had happened at the coffee shop, and she considered that an accomplishment.

When he winced, though, rolling his head on his neck with a grimace, Sunny frowned. "What's wrong?"

"Neck hurts. Back hurts. Getting old, I guess." Chris shrugged.

The meal finished, Bliss put to bed and the other kids sent to play in the family room, Chris grimaced again as he was helping her load the dishwasher. Sunny gestured. "Sit down. I can help you with that."

He tried to put her off, but she insisted until he sat in the kitchen chair, still protesting. "Hush," she told him, and surprisingly, he did.

She felt the knot as soon as she put her hands on his shoulders. A thick bulge of too-tight muscle just at the base of his left shoulder and a spot just a little higher on his neck that made him hiss when she pushed on it. She eased the pressure and used the tips of her fingers to find the edges of the tension.

Chris groaned, leaning forward with his hands loose and open on the table in front of him. "God. Ouch."

She paused, but he shook his head. "No, it's a good ouch. Right there, it really hurts."

"John Second," she said, and stopped herself short before she could tell him John Second had been the one to teach her just how to squeeze and roll her fingers to soothe sore muscles.

Chris suffered her attentions in silence for a minute or two before he said, "John Second was the man who convinced your mom to leave me. Right?"

She was glad she didn't have to look at his face when she answered. "Yes."

Beneath her working fingers, Chris's shoulders tensed again. "Was he good to you?"

The angel whispered again, another single word. The same as before. Sunny spoke it aloud. "No."

Chris twisted in his seat to look at her, one of his hands pressing on hers to keep it from moving. "You want to talk about it?"

Sunny pulled her hand away, gently, not a yank. "No. I don't have anything to say about it. He wasn't a good man. That's all. And he's gone now."

She didn't want to think about John Second, or Sanctuary, or her mother, but Chris who hardly ever spoke had found his voice and came after her with it.

"Was she happy? Your mom. Was she happy?"

Sunny leaned against the counter with her arms crossed over her belly. She thought of her mother, laughing at something the children had done. Her mother's eyes closed, mouth moving but curved in a smile as she said the blessings in silence.

That was the worst of it, she thought, remembering how Mama had lit up from inside when she listened to Papa's words, or when John Second had pulled her aside to whisper in her ear. She'd had a glow around her, her eyes full of love for him and the life he'd brought her to. She'd turned those eyes away from him though, when he did bad things, so she could pretend she didn't see.

Her answer caught in her throat, hooking it like a thorn. "Yes. She was happy."

"I should've been there for you, Sunshine." Chris closed his eyes, swallowed hard.

"It's all right. You didn't know."

Chris shook his head, and she could see even after the few minutes of work she'd done on his neck that he was moving more easily. "I should've known. I knew she was pregnant when she left me. I knew you could've been mine. I just didn't want to know, I let her tell me lies…"

Sunny backed away with a shake of her own head. She didn't want to talk about it. She didn't want to hear how her mother had lied and stolen Sunny away from her real father and her real family, or how different Sunny's life could've been had her mother not been shown the light.

She didn't want to talk about the things John Second had done to her.

Chris was on his feet though, coming after her to snag her wrist and keep her from getting away. "Sunny. Listen. I'm sorry."

"You don't have to be sorry, Chris. It's not your fault."

He shook his head again, his fingers loose enough she could pull away if she tugged just a little. "I know you miss her, too."

Sunny didn't want to know this, either. She backed up a step. Then another. His hand fell from her wrist, and he didn't try to reach for her again.

"I don't miss her," Sunny said. Then, louder, "I don't miss my mother."

Liar's tongue.

The angel's voice was hard and cold. Unkind, the way the truth could be.

The cell phone Chris had given her buzzed from Sunny's pocket, and she put a hand over it, startled. Chris looked at it. He shook his head, passed a hand over his eyes. He rubbed the spots on his neck and shoulders she'd massaged, then he looked away.

Sunny pulled the phone from her pocket. "Hello?"

She listened for a minute, the words coming through the phone stringing all together into sentences that made sense and yet she still had trouble understanding. She murmured an answer and closed the phone to slide it back into her pocket.

"Tyler," she said. "The boy from the coffee shop. He wants me to go out with him and a group of kids to a carnival tomorrow. He said he'll pick me up after work and bring me home."

Chris cleared his throat, his gaze bright until he blinked and blinked again. "Sure. Okay, that'll be fine."

"It's time for me to put the kids to bed."

He nodded, silent. Sunny took her children and bathed them, dressed them in their pajamas and tucked them into their beds. She whispered the blessings her mother had said to her every night in their ears and kissed their foreheads the way her mother had always kissed hers. Peace fell asleep before Sunny'd even finished, sprawled across her mattress without a care. Happy, though, curled tight onto his side and clutched his pillow as she stroked his hair over and over until at last his eyes reluctantly closed.

"Finally asleep?" Liesel had come up the stairs just as Sunny left Happy's room.

Liesel had complained often about her hair over the past few months as it grew longer. It hung to her chin now, and she'd done something different to the shape of it. Soft bangs, some layers cut so that it framed her face. She'd colored it, too. Lighter.

"Yes. Your hair looks pretty," Sunny told her, wondering why Liesel had felt the need to change it.

Liesel touched the fringes around her jaw and gave a self-conscious laugh. "Oh. Thanks. I thought I needed something a little different, easier to take care of. It's not quite long enough to pull back, but at least I don't have to worry about getting to the salon every month to keep it short."

"It looks nice." She didn't look like Liesel anymore.

"Where's Christopher?"

Sunny paused, listening for the sound of him downstairs. "I don't know. I guess he went out."

Liesel sighed and put a hand on the wall, her head ducked for a moment before she pushed past Sunny to head for her bedroom. In the doorway, she paused to murmur, "Good night," before closing the door behind her.

Chapter
34

"Welcome to the world of motherhood." Becka winked as she said this, then pulled out a bottle of tequila from behind her back. "Look. The good stuff. Patrón, honey, not some cheap-ass bottle of Cuervo or whatever that swill is you think counts as booze."

Liesel had been hanging over the sink, gripping the stainless steel and fighting back a scream or sobs—she still wasn't sure which—when Becka let herself in through the back door. She turned now. "Oh. God. I can't drink that."

Becka frowned and looked at the bottle. "Huh? Why not? It goes down like silk, I promise."

"Yeah, that's what I'm afraid of." Liesel pressed the heel of her hand to her eye socket, just briefly, then cocked an ear to listen for any sounds coming from the den. The kids had been quiet for the past ten minutes. Too quiet, too long.

She couldn't face going in there just now.

Becka set the bottle down and helped herself to a couple

of glasses from the cupboard. She looked at Liesel over her shoulder. "Does not compute."

"If I get started—" Liesel's laugh came out more like a growl "—I might not stop."

"That sort of day, huh?" Becka sounded sympathetic, but she gave Liesel another wink as she poured a finger of tequila into each glass. She handed Liesel one, kept the other. Lifted it. "Cheers. Down the hatch."

That sort of day? Talk about that sort of year. Liesel looked at the glass. "I don't think—"

"Listen. Some days a shot of tequila is the only damn thing that kept me going. Drink it. One isn't going to kill you. It won't even make you drunk, unless you're a pansy light-weight, and girl, I know you can handle your booze a little better than that. By the way, love the new hair."

Liesel clinked her glass against Becka's, and before she could stop herself, she tipped it back. Oh, that was good tequila, smooth like gold. It left a line of fire down her throat and into her gut, but it was a good kind. She licked her lips.

"Thanks. At least you noticed it. Christopher didn't say a damn word about it."

"Typical male. Are you surprised?"

Liesel held out her shot glass for another, but for sipping this time. "Pissed off, more like it. I should know better. Any time a woman does something to her appearance for a man instead of herself, it's always a wasted effort."

"Deep. Very deep. A little bitter, but deep." Becka put the cork top back in the bottle and pulled open the drawer of Liesel's freezer to tuck it in behind the bags of frozen green beans. "There. My gift to you. Keep it in there, nobody will find it."

Liesel's laugh was only a little better this time. "I can't be drinking tequila every day."

"I'm not kidding, hon, that stuff saved my sanity."

Liesel paused before pouring. "You're not kidding?"

"Nope. Children are seven kinds of pain in the ass."

"Only seven?" The words came out before she could stop them, and Liesel shut her mouth tight before anything else could slip out.

"Maybe it should be sevenfold. It's a lot, that's for sure." Becka laughed and shook her head. "Your hair's super cute, by the way, though I have to say I never pictured you as a blonde."

Here it was, the moment of truth, but if you couldn't admit your stupid motivations to your best friend of forever, who could you admit them to? "*She* was blonde."

Becka's brows lifted. "The first wife?"

Liesel nodded, ashamed. "Yeah. Blonde and tiny and pretty, just like her daughter, who I've been so encouraging my husband to spend more time with. He took her out driving last night. I mean, she needs to practice so she can get her driver's license, of course she does. But he takes her out, they're gone for hours…"

Liesel stopped, even more ashamed. "I sound like I'm jealous of her."

"Are you?"

There were some things that couldn't be admitted to.

Becka didn't push. From the grocery bags she'd brought along, she pulled out a loaf of frozen garlic bread, a jar of spaghetti sauce, a box of pasta. Some bagged salad.

Earlier, Peace and Happy had been jumping on the couch in the living room, even after being told not to. The collision of their heads had resulted in a bloody nose, two screaming kids and a woken-from-nap baby. Liesel had spent forty minutes getting them all cleaned up and calmed down. She'd be able to shampoo the rug, but the white couch was probably ruined. She wasn't thinking too hard about it now because she might just cry. That couch had been the first piece of "real" furniture she'd ever bought.

Becka had called somewhere in the middle of everything and had listened for half a minute to Liesel's description of the scene before simply saying, "I'll be over in half an hour." True to her word, here she was, with booze and food.

Liesel still wanted to cry.

"How's she doing with the GED?"

"Good. She needs some tutoring. There's only so much Chris and I can do. I mean…new math, forget it. They have math so new I don't even know where to start." Liesel found another laugh. This one hurt her throat. She thought about another shot of tequila…but no. That was trouble. "She's a bright girl—"

"Oh, that's obvious," Becka said.

Liesel sighed, watching as her friend made herself comfortable with pots and pans and the oven. She should step in and at least offer to help, but she'd known Becka so long she also knew it would be a wasted effort. Becka was in full-on caretaker mode, and frankly, Liesel was in the mood to be taken care of.

"And she's motivated. I guess it had never occurred to her that she might actually deserve an education. We haven't talked about college yet. That's too much at this point. But she could go, Becka. She should go."

Becka slipped the garlic bread onto a baking stone and put it in the oven. "Of course she should."

"Anyway. Her job's been good for her, too. Gives her some experience. Some spending money."

"Some time out of the house. That's good for her, too, I'm sure." Becka turned to face Liesel. "But what about you, hon?"

Liesel pretended she didn't know what Becka meant. "What about me?"

Becka gently moved Liesel to the side so she could fill a pot with water. She didn't look at Liesel, though they were practically shoulder to shoulder. "Is it good for you?"

Liesel waited until Becka had put the pot on the stove and turned on the burner before she found the words to answer. "She needs this, Becka. The girl's been through… I can't even begin to imagine everything, and that's with knowing some of what she's had to deal with."

"Sure, she's had it rough. That's for sure." It wasn't like Becka to be so deliberately neutral. She leaned against the table to look at Liesel. "How's the counseling going?"

"It was great. Dr. Braddock was fabulous. Sunny really liked her."

"Yeah, Jean is great." Becka's smile didn't quite reach her eyes. "But she's not going now?"

Liesel hesitated, but it wasn't as if she'd never bitched to Becka about Christopher before or listened to her friend complain about Kent. "I think she should go back. She's just not quite…right."

"Are you afraid she never will be?"

That was it, right there. Liesel let out a long, hissing sigh like air from a balloon. "Christopher says, why should we force her into some Judeo-Christian box that neither of us believes in ourselves?"

Becka's brows rose. "Wow. Heavy."

"Who knew, right?" Liesel was tired of trying to force laughter, so didn't bother. "I didn't know he had such an opinion about religion. I mean, at first he was all over me for making accommodations for her with the food stuff, the meditation, whatever. Now he says we shouldn't expect her to just drop everything she ever believed just because it's different."

"But you think she should?"

"Not entirely. Some of the stuff she says makes sense, I can see where she's coming from. But other things…"

"Like offing yourself in order to get to heaven."

Liesel looked at her. "That. Of course that. And this thing she does with the listening. It's more than meditation, which I always found interesting, how people can lose themselves in their heads like that. But she does something else. I mean, she really…listens. And I think she hears things."

Becka's mouth pursed. "Like what kinds of things?"

"I don't know. She told me the problem with so many people is they don't take the time to listen to silence, or something like that, and I get what she's saying. God, there are days when I'd kill for some quiet. I get it, I totally do. But it's more than that. Maybe…" Liesel laughed, embarrassed. "Maybe I *am* jealous. That she can just find someplace inside and go away, even for a little while."

"Hell, sign me up for that, too." Becka smiled.

"I should check on the kids," Liesel said suddenly. It had been quiet for too long.

"Sure, you do that. I'm not going anywhere." Becka cracked open the sauce jar and found a pot for it.

Liesel shouldn't have worried. Peace had passed out, thumb in her mouth, legs sprawled. She still had the bloody twist of tissue stuck up her nose. Happy was quietly coloring in the jumbo drawing pad Liesel had picked up at the dollar store. He bent over the picture, tongue caught between his teeth in concentration, pudgy fingers gripping the cheap crayon so tightly it was no wonder that it snapped as Liesel watched.

"Oh!"

"It's okay," she said hastily, hoping Peace wouldn't wake up. She'd figured on another half an hour or so for Bliss's interrupted nap, and that wasn't even guaranteed. The longer both girls slept, the more likely it was that Sunny'd be home by the time they woke.

"But I broke it." Happy frowned, brow furrowing, serious like heartbreak.

"You have so many, Happy. Crayons break. It'll be fine. I can buy you more."

He studied the broken crayon, then peeled off the paper from the broken end. He held it up to her with a small, shy smile. "I can use this side!"

The tears she'd been fighting rose again to the surface. As a child, she'd tossed broken crayons without a second thought and had never been made to feel guilty for it. Broken crayons were part of…well, just a part of life. Breaking was what they did.

This small boy, at four, knew all about how things broke, too. Throwing them away, now that was something he hadn't yet learned. Liesel passed her hand over his shorn curls.

"Yeah," she said. "You can use that side. You hungry, buddy?"

Happy shook his head. "Not dinnertime."

She didn't argue with him. Bliss still ate mostly on demand, and Peace was glad to eat at any time, especially if she was offered sweet treats. Happy, on the other hand, clung stubbornly to the schedule he'd grown up with, and though he could be persuaded to break out of it, it was never his first choice.

"Okay, well. Soon. My friend Becka's making spaghetti."

Happy had already bent back over his drawing. Liesel left him there and found Becka in the kitchen, the long table in the breakfast porch already set and the good smell of sauce and garlic bread wafting all around.

"Such service. I owe you," Liesel said.

"Hey. When I had Annabelle, you came to my house and did my freaking laundry. Do I even need to tell you how

much more helpful that was than a basket full of baby boo-
ties?" Becka shook her head. "I owed you, big-time. So shut
up."

"This is hardly the same as having a baby."

Becka gave Liesel a soft look. "No, hon, it's kind of like you
had quadruplets without even knowing you were pregnant."

That was it. Liesel lost it. She burst into racking, helpless
sobs that burned worse than the tequila had.

Becka enfolded her without hesitation. She patted Liesel's
back, and what was better, handed her a box of tissues.
"Here."

"Thanks." Liesel wiped her eyes, still leaking, and blew her
nose. "God, I'm a mess."

"Well...duh." A faint wail came from upstairs, but Becka
held out her hand before Liesel could get up. "Sit. I'll get her.
You just sit."

Liesel sat.

Becka was back in fifteen minutes with a smiling, cooing
Bliss on her hip. "Look at this big girl, she woke up soaking
wet. I stripped the crib and hung the sheets over the tub. I
didn't know where you kept fresh ones, but I wiped everything down."

"Of course." Liesel sighed. The fifteen minutes of silence
had settled her a little bit. "It's the cloth diapers. It's like she's
wearing a sieve."

Becka laughed and chucked the baby under her double
chins. "Still can't get Sunny to go for the disposables, huh?"

"She has a point about them being bad for the environment.
And about the cost. She does the laundry...when she's here,"
Liesel added and took the baby so Becka could stir the sauce
and add the pasta to the now-boiling water. There was no
way she was going to tell Becka about the fluff. Christopher's

reaction had been bad enough. "It's her kid, Becka. Who am I to tell her she has to put the baby in disposables?"

"It's your house," Becka pointed out. "You take care of those kids as much, if not more, than she does. Right? If disposable diapers would make it easier for you, I think you should just tell her you're going to use them. What will she do, throw a tantrum?"

"Who, Sunny?" Liesel scoffed at the very idea. "No. The worst she'd do is make me feel guilty for single-handedly destroying the earth with my ridiculous selfishness and disregard for the world's natural resources."

Becka's brows lifted again. "Wow. Again with the bitter. Honey, I'm worried about you!"

Liesel pressed her face to the top of Bliss's head. The sweet baby fragrance made her want to weep again. "I just thought this would be so much…easier."

"It's never easy. And you're doing a good thing. But you have to make sure you take care of yourself, that's all." Becka hesitated. "I want you to promise me you won't let this overwhelm you. You call me, if you have to. Or hell, make Chris pick up some of the slack. Hire a babysitter to take some of the pressure off."

Liesel blinked at this. "Do you think I can't do this?"

Becka sighed. "No. But I know how hard it can be, staying home with kids. And you…well, hon, it's not like you chose to quit and stay home to raise your own kids, you know? You sort of got suckered into it."

That this was very close to the truth set Liesel's teeth on edge. Becka must've seen it, because she held up her hands right away. She shook her head.

"Sorry. Overstepped. I get it. Tell me to shut up."

"I don't want to tell you to shut up."

"You're my best friend," Becka said quietly. "And it's not

that I think you can't handle kids. God knows you've been awesome with Annabelle and the boys. But, Liesel...hon... it's hard enough to do this when they're your own kids."

"And they're not my kids." Liesel's gut twisted like a ball of foil crumpled in a fist.

"I'm just saying, give yourself permission to—"

"Fail?" Liesel broke in.

Becka shook her head, but before she could say anything else, the door from the laundry room opened and the squeaking tread of sneakers sounded on the tile floor of the hallway. Sunny appeared, her blond braid swinging over one shoulder.

She was beaming. "He asked me to go to the movies on Friday. Not with a group, just us!"

She crossed to Liesel and held out her hands for the baby, who went instantly to her mother with a gurgle of delight. Sunny held Bliss high to blow a raspberry on her fat belly. She looked at Liesel with bright eyes. It was the most animated Liesel had ever seen her.

"Congratulations," Liesel said.

She tried to sound like she meant it.

Chapter
35

Patch has been sitting next to her at mealtimes as often as he can. He brought her fresh peaches after she'd mentioned that she didn't like the sort that came in cans. Sunny's known Patch forever, but they didn't become friendly until her short days selling literature, which Patch still does. He's really good at it. He has a way of connecting with people, getting them not only to pay for the pamphlets, but also to actually read them, too. She's seen people come back just to talk to Patch about the family. It's probably because he came into the family after reading one of those pamphlets himself.

Sunny knows exactly what Patch wants when he asks her to walk with him out behind the barn.

She goes with him. Happy is fine in the nursery with the other babies, and Edwina doesn't like Sunny very much, so she often sends her away. As Patch reaches for Sunny's hand while they walk, she thinks Edwina would like her less if she knew that by telling her to get out of the nursery she was giving Sunny the chance to go walking with Patch, holding his hand.

Behind the barn, Patch seems nervous. Pacing. He laughs a lot at nothing until Sunny takes him by both shoulders and stops him.

"What's wrong with you?"

Patch laughs again, a little softer, and puts his hands on her hips. "You're so pretty, Sunshine. You know that?"

It's nice to hear, but pretty doesn't really matter.

When he touches her, she closes her eyes and turns her face to keep his lips from touching hers. Patch kisses her cheek instead. He pulls her closer.

He's prepared. He brought out a blanket, some fruit, a pitcher of lemonade. Patch and John Second are good friends, that's how he can get these special things.

He isn't anything like John Second, though. That's why Sunny went with him in the first place. So when he pushes her back on the blanket and puts his hand under her dress, up over her thighs, she closes her eyes and lets him do what he wants.

It doesn't take long. It never does. It doesn't hurt, and when it's over, Patch tries to kiss her again. This time when she turns her face, he says her name like he's sad.

"I like you, Sunshine."

He's waiting for her to say she likes him, which wouldn't be a lie but it's not the truth he's looking for. Sunny'd like to make Patch happy. He's always been nice to her. But she can't say the words. She pulls her dress down over her thighs and brushes the grass from it.

She does take his hand when he offers it to help her up. Patch is frowning. He pushes her braid over her shoulder.

"You don't like me?" Patch asks. "I'd like to be special to you."

As it turns out, he is special to her, but not in the way he wants. Patch is the father of Sunny's second baby, though once her belly grows big enough to show, he stops asking her behind the barn. And once they were no longer having sex, Patch no longer seemed as interested.

Sunny hadn't forgotten that.

The dress Liesel had let her borrow had been ruined, or so Liesel said, but she had taken Sunny to the store to buy another one. She hadn't let Sunny pay for it either, though Sunny had enough money. It had just been the two of them, no kids and no Chris, but Liesel had seemed distant and distracted. Or maybe it was Sunny who'd been distracted with all the choices in clothes and trying to find something that didn't make her feel strange but still looked...

Pretty.

Pretty didn't matter, she reminded herself. Except she thought maybe it did, for Tyler. She wanted to be pretty for him.

She hadn't really expected him to come in to the coffee shop early on the day they were supposed to go out, but every time the bell over the door jingled, Sunny looked up with her heart thumping and the breath catching in her throat. It was never him, but half an hour before Tyler was supposed to pick her up, Josiah strode through the door.

"Sunny, Sunny, Sunshine." It was the way he'd greeted her so often in the past.

A wave of nostalgia washed over her. Or was it déjà vu? Something lifted inside her at the sight of him, even though she didn't let it show on her face.

"Can I get an organic soy and orange smoothie with one of those scones?" Josiah pointed at the glass case.

She served him his drink and his scone because that was her job. Josiah studied her without walking away from the counter. He held the cup in one hand, the plate in the other, like he was balancing them. Or weighing them.

"You look different," he said.

Men's clothes didn't set them apart the way women's did. Sunny had seen that when she was sent out to sell pamphlets and even more so since she'd been living with Chris and Liesel. A woman could be set aside simply from what she wore, while a man in jeans and a white shirt could pass as anything he wanted. Josiah didn't look different because he didn't have to.

She lifted her chin and kept herself from smoothing the front of the skirt she'd picked out. It hung to her toes and had been sewn of multiple colored layers of fabric that had also been twisted. She wore it with a plain, pale pink T-shirt, though she'd added a thin cardigan to cover her arms.

"Relax. You look nice." Josiah sipped from the cup. "How've you been, Sunshine?"

"Fine." Wendy and Amy both were out. They were supposed to be back before it was time for Sunny to leave, and though she enjoyed it when they were gone and she was here alone, now she wished they'd come back early.

"I'm fine, too." His grin was tempting, but faded quickly to become a look of sorrow. "You're afraid of me."

She shook her head and felt the brush of her hair all down her back. She'd pulled just the top part back into a wide barrette and left the rest to hang down. Tyler would notice, she thought suddenly, the way Josiah did. He would notice she was trying too hard.

"I don't want you to be afraid of me."

"I'm not."

Liar's tongue, she thought. Josiah knew it, she could tell. He put the plate and cup on the counter to grip it with both his hands, so he could lean closer to her. Speaking low, so nobody could overhear them, though they were all alone.

"I am not my brother," Josiah said.

Sunny knew that was the truth. She'd always known. It was the reason her mother hadn't left with him when John Second threw him out…and the reason Sunny'd wanted to go.

"I'm not my father, either. I know you're living with your biological dad. Trying to adjust. And you're doing a great job, Sunshine. You should be proud of yourself. I sure am."

The way he said it made her feel anything but proud. How hard was it supposed to be to "adjust," anyway, after being raised in a way most so-called normal people found strange and appalling? She frowned. She didn't deserve praise for just doing what people were supposed to do to be normal.

Unless Josiah could see right through her, see that she was not the same as other people, no matter how she tried.

Josiah pulled back and rapped the counter with his knuckles. "Anyway. I just stopped in to see how you were doing. I've had some people asking about you."

The question popped out before she could stop it. "Who?"

He took his cup and plate again. Two steps back from the counter. Still smiling. He rattled off a few familiar names, mostly women Sunny hadn't seen in years. Then, "Patch, too."

That was when the bell jingled and Tyler came into the shop. He made a beeline for Sunny without even giving Josiah a second glance. "Hey. Are you ready to go?"

"I have to wait for—" But there was Wendy, breezing through from the back with an apology for being late. When Sunny looked at Tyler again, Josiah had taken his drink and food to a corner table and was reading a newspaper.

He didn't look up when they walked past him.

"This isn't the way home." The tug of the seat belt against Sunny's throat was like a hand, fingers squeezing. She didn't want to sound scared or twist in her seat. *Face of stone.* She was suddenly unreasonably terrified.

Tyler beat out a pattern on the steering wheel with his fingers. Sunny didn't know the song playing on the radio, but it had very suggestive lyrics. She couldn't ask him to turn it off. She wondered if he even noticed or cared. Probably neither.

He glanced at her. "I know. It's a long cut."

She knew about shortcuts, not long. The three previous times they'd gone out together in a group, he'd brought her right home. "Tyler...thank you for dinner and the movie, but I really have to get home."

"What's the rush?" He used his turn signal, eased into the next lane, took a road she didn't know.

She didn't recognize the streets he was taking, but she could tell they were getting farther from the center of town and into a more rural area. Lots of trees on either side of the car, but no signs of anything she recognized as being close to Chris and Liesel's house.

"It's just...my dad's wife. She's been home alone with the kids all day, and she probably needs a break." Sunny thought of the twisted-down turn of Liesel's mouth lately, how infrequently she smiled and how quick she was to snap.

Tyler looked over at her with a frown. "You okay?"

Sunny shook her head. Her hair fell forward over her shoulders. She wished she'd put it in the braid she was used to. Unbound, it was heavy and hot and got in the way.

"Hey. I'm sorry." Tyler pulled slowly to the side, into one of the unmarked side roads off the main one. He didn't go very far, but the trees rose up around them and covered the car with shadows. He turned off the ignition and twisted in his seat to look at her. His arm stretched out as he put his hand on the back of her seat, fingers close enough to brush her shoulder if he twitched them.

"Tyler…"

"Sunny, I really like you."

She shook her head again. Heart thumped. She didn't look at him, afraid of what she might show him in her eyes. He'd see she wasn't like the other girls who came into the shop and laughed and joked. He'd see she was afraid, and that was stupid, because Tyler was a nice, normal guy.

"Don't…you like me? Even a little?"

Was that the twitch of his fingertips on her shoulder? Touching her hair? Sunny sat up straighter, and her seat belt tried to strangle her. She pulled it, but the stiff fabric had already cut a line into her throat.

"I like you, Tyler."

"You won't even look at me."

Stone. Look like stone. Don't show him you're afraid, that you're freaked out, that you might want to cry.

Tyler's smile was hesitant. "Are your parents really all that strict?"

"No. It's not that."

"So call home. Tell them I'm taking you out for ice cream. I can still have you home in a couple hours."

He leaned in to kiss her before she could do more than put a hand between them. Her fingers curled in the soft fabric of his T-shirt. Beneath them, his chest was hard.

She wanted to sink into it the way the girl in the movie had melted into her boyfriend's embrace. All open mouths, tongues, hands roaming. Soft sighs, low moans. The scene in the movie had fascinated her at how little like real life the lovemaking had seemed.

"What's wrong?" Tyler asked.

He kissed her again, and she did her best to kiss him back,

but his mouth was too hot and wet, his tongue went too deeply into her mouth. She wanted to kiss him because she liked Tyler a lot. She knew what happened when you didn't kiss back.

Still, when his hands slid up her body to just below her breasts, every muscle went stiff. She closed her eyes and tried to imagine the movie scene, but could not. All she could see, in fact, was Josiah's face.

"I can't." Sunny pushed at him. "I really need to get home. Liesel's been with the kids all day, and Peace gets cranky at bedtime if I'm not there to tuck her in. And I promised Happy I wouldn't be out too late."

His brow furrowed. "Huh? Peace and Happy?"

"The kids," Sunny said patiently. "Happy's four. Peace is almost three. And Bliss will be a year old in a few months."

"I don't get it…why does it have to be you?"

"Because," Sunny said, "they're my children."

Tyler recoiled, just a little. Then laughed. "Huh? Wait. You're kidding me, right?"

"No." The stone of her expression wanted to crack, but she didn't let it. "Please take me home now."

"But wait. Wait a minute. You have three kids?"

"Yes!" she said, exasperated. "That's why I have to get home."

"But…you're my age!"

There were many things about her past that Sunny was ashamed of. Many that she'd accepted she would always be sorry for. But her children were neither shameful nor something to regret.

"I know."

"But I thought… I figured…" Tyler waved a hand at her clothes. "You said your parents were so strict and stuff. I mean, I figured you were some goody-goody or something."

Sunny looked out her window. No idea where she was. No idea how to get where she needed to go. Powerless.

She hated feeling powerless.

"I thought you knew. I thought everyone knew."

"Hey." His soft touch tried to turn her toward him, but Sunny wouldn't turn. Tyler let her go. "Sure, I heard things, but...I'm sorry, Sunny. I didn't mean to hurt your feelings."

"You don't know anything about me, Tyler."

"Can't I learn?"

She looked at him. "Maybe. But right now I have to get home. Okay? Can you just take me?"

He nodded, turned the key, eased out onto the main road again. Sunny leaned forward to change the radio station from what he'd been playing to the soft-rock channel she preferred. Tyler chuckled.

"My mom listens to this station."

"That other music is lewd."

Tyler was quiet for half a minute. Now Sunny knew where they were. They'd come out from a side road onto the main rural highway heading south. In just a few minutes, the entrance to Chris and Liesel's development would be on the left. She relaxed muscles she hadn't realized she was holding quite so tensely.

"Sunny...I really would like to get to know you."

She let him drive her back to Chris's house without any more conversation. When Tyler pulled into her driveway, she was already unbuckled and grabbing her purse. If the door had been unlocked she'd have been out of the car before he could say another word, but instead her fingers slipped on the door handle when she pushed.

"Hold on a sec, it locks automatically. Let me get it." Tyler pushed a button. The door unlocked. He put his hand on her arm. "Sunny. I mean it. I'm sorry if I made you feel bad. I was just…you know. Three kids is a lot."

Liesel hadn't come running out the front door or anything, but Sunny knew she couldn't sit there much longer. She had to get inside. She looked at Tyler's hand on her arm. What would it be like to put her hand over his? To hold his hand the way those girls did in the coffee shop, so casual. Not caring what people might say or think. Just holding on to him because it would feel good to touch him and to be touched?

"I have to go inside," Sunny said. "Thanks for the ride."

He didn't try to stop her, and she was glad for that. She did stop to look back at him when she got to the front door, but the glare on the windshield kept her from seeing inside. She waved and couldn't tell if Tyler waved back.

Chapter
36

Christopher had ordered steak and shrimp and a baked potato, and he'd kept his mouth so full, one bite after another, so he didn't have to say anything. Liesel, too aware of how soft her belly and butt had become now that she wasn't running as often as she used to, had settled for a chicken Caesar salad and an unsweetened tea instead of the loaded burger and margarita she really wanted. She'd been picking at it, not satisfied.

Christopher was drinking too much. A beer when they sat down, another just before the meal came, a third with the food. Still, Liesel would've taken a sarcastic joke or caustic commentary over the silence that had fallen between them at the table in such utter contrast to the rest of the couples eating out here on the deck.

Hell, in contrast to the way she and her husband had been just a few months ago.

She'd tried, asking him about work, but he'd said he didn't want to talk about it. She'd spoken briefly of the children and had discovered she didn't want to talk about them, either. And what else was there?

"What happened to us?" she said aloud.

He looked up from the steak, a chunk speared on his fork, his jaw grinding another into a pulp he took his time swallowing. "What do you mean?"

Liesel waved a hand at the food, then him. Herself. "This. Us. Everything. It's all just… We don't talk, Christopher."

He sighed and put down his fork and knife to lean back in his chair. He drank the last of his beer and set the bottle down. "Christ, Liesel. We're talking now."

It was so far from what she meant all she could do was stab at her salad and try not to stab at him.

"What do you want to talk about?"

She looked at him, but his mouth had twisted and eyes narrowed. He was saying it to placate her, not because he really understood. She wasn't sure she did.

"Us. Life. Anything." She paused to drag a finger along her jawline. It had been almost two weeks since her visit to the salon. "I mean, you haven't even noticed my hair."

"I noticed." Christopher's eyes lingered on her face, then her hair. He looked away. "I thought you said you'd never go blond."

His former lack of comment on it had stung, but now she wished she hadn't poked him into saying anything about it at all. "It covers up the gray."

"Whatever makes you happy," was all he said.

It was a long and tensely quiet ride home, and though they came back to a dark and silent house, this time there was no furtive making out in the kitchen. No sneaking up the stairs, hand in hand. This time, there was no making love.

Chapter
37

Tyler sat in his favorite spot in the front window, typing away at his computer. He'd waved at Sunny when he came in, but she'd been in the back when he ordered his food and coffee. He hadn't yet come up to get a refill, and she busied herself behind the counter to keep herself from going to him.

He hadn't called her since the day he drove her home and kissed her. At first, Sunny'd been relieved, but as a week passed and then another, she came to realize he probably didn't mean to call her again. Now she stood and stared across the room at him. She listened with her heart, and it whispered to her in the angel's voice that she should go talk to him.

But…she didn't.

She had nothing to say to Tyler, who claimed he wanted to know her and yet hadn't called her in over two weeks. So when he gathered his things and brought his mug up to the counter, she let Amy wait on him while Sunny took care of food prep in the back. When she came out again, he was gone.

"He asked about you." Josiah said this when Sunny went to his table to clear it.

Sunny didn't pretend not to know who he meant. She gave a glance toward the back of the shop, but Amy was busy chatting with someone else. She looked at Josiah. "What are you doing here?"

"Do you want to know what he said?"

"No," Sunny said after a pause. "It doesn't matter, does it?"

"Maybe to him. But if not to you—"

Sunny shook her head and closed her eyes for a moment, thinking of how much she'd wanted to be like the girl in the movie and knowing she would never be. "I like him, Josiah, but…"

"I understand."

She looked at him. Josiah's smile, so familiar, was like a candle set in a dark window.

"He's blemished," Josiah said.

Sunny shook her head. "I don't think that way anymore."

Josiah didn't argue with her. He pushed the chair opposite him with his foot so it scraped along the floor, and gestured for her to sit. Another glance told her Amy had gone into the back. Sunny sat perched on the edge of the chair so she could get up at once if she wanted to. If she had to.

"You should come to visit us, Sunshine."

"Where are you all?" This question had bothered her since the first day he'd shown up in the coffee shop. "Sanctuary is closed off."

"We don't need Sanctuary to live a good life with the family. We have several houses close to each other. It draws less attention that way."

"Does it matter if you draw attention?" she asked, confused. "Papa said we should never hesitate to let the blemished know how they can join us."

"That was when he was living behind walls." Josiah sounded faintly derisive. "Him and my brother, living a reclusive life. How could they possibly hope to encourage anyone to join when they made it so obvious that the family is so different?"

"But...aren't we?"

"Of course. We're enlightened. But we're still people, Sunshine. And it's our goal to shine a light for all those who are blemished, sure, but how do you think we should do that? By doing everything we can to stand off from the rest of the world? Or by trying to embrace it? You should know that. You've been living outside the family now for a long time."

Did she imagine he sounded accusing? Sunny blinked and swallowed, her throat a little dry. "My mother wanted to protect me and my children. She sent us away. And I'm...glad she did."

"Are you, Sunshine?" Josiah smiled. "Are you...really?"

It was as though time had slowed, the rest of the world gone away while the two of them sat and stared at each other across the table. When he reached for her hand, she let him take it. And when he invited her again to come home with him, Sunny said yes.

Chapter
38

"C'mon, Christopher. Answer the damn phone." Liesel held the phone away from her ear at the sound of his voice mail greeting and disconnected without leaving a message.

Apparently he answered the phone when it was Sunshine calling, since Sunny had said she'd told her father he didn't need to pick her up. But now that it was his wife calling...

Bah.

That way led to crazy town, and she had to stop herself. She'd encouraged Christopher to have a relationship with his daughter, and it should have nothing to do with her. No reason to feel slighted if he spent more time talking with Sunny than he did her, when all Liesel wanted to know was what time he would be home because she needed some things from the grocery store, and Sunny was going out again after work. Liesel could've told the girl to come home. Should've, maybe. But Sunny had sounded so freaking happy, so much like a normal girl excited about spending time with a boy she liked, who was Liesel to take that away from her?

With Bliss down for a nap, Liesel moved through the kitchen, cleaning up after the whirlwind of destruction that had been Peace in search of snacks she'd been told she wasn't allowed to have. Liesel had dealt with the temper tantrum, understanding how easy it would've been to spank the little girl, but instead sending her upstairs to her room for a time-out. Happy had gone on his own to color and play with his cars.

Quiet from upstairs meant she should check and see what they were doing. Too much quiet was a warning louder than screams. Yet Liesel couldn't bring herself to leave the silent kitchen and discover just what the children had been getting into. All she wanted to do was let herself soak in the quiet.

She listened again, heard the faint mutter of the children upstairs, and again, knew it would probably be smart for her to check on them. And again, she couldn't face it. Not yet. Not one more minute of dealing with Peace's constant questions, Happy's anxieties, Bliss's baby needs.

Some frothy women's mag had come in the mail, full of articles about makeup and diets and sex tips and celebrity gossip. It was the sort of magazine Liesel had read only once in a while, not concerned with much of what was reported inside its pages, but today she took it along with a bowl of M&M's and a glass of that gorgeous tequila Becka had given her, and she went into the powder room. She locked the door.

And she pretended, just for ten, fifteen, maybe twenty minutes, tops, that she'd never wanted children.

Chapter
39

Sunny had come home.

There were familiar faces even though it had been years since she'd seen them, the men with their long hair and the women without the heavy masks of makeup Sunny was embarrassed to admit had become attractive to her. She chewed at the thin sheen of lip balm she'd applied earlier. It had only the barest hint of color, and she wore it mostly to keep her lips from getting chapped, but here in a family house she might as well have painted herself with crimson lipstick and every shade of eye shadow.

Familiar scents, too. Bundles of dried rosemary, sage and other herbs hung up in the corners of the rooms the way Papa had always instructed them. The sting of Pine-Sol from the bucket of water by the door. Even the warm and cozy smell of wax from the pillar candle on the table.

And they took her in, welcomed her as one of their own. The only judgment Sunny saw was in her own eyes in the bathroom mirror when she went in to wash her hands before dinner. There she stared at herself, this worldly girl with painted lips and her hair loose around her shoulders, her clothes not quite as modest as she knew they ought to be.

Josiah put his hand on her shoulder when she came out of the bathroom and turned her to face all of them sitting at the long trestle table. Sunny knew that not everyone lived in this house, but they'd all gathered here to share a meal with her. She should have felt honored, but felt mostly shamed that she'd waited so long to come home.

"Everyone, you remember Sunshine."

Murmured greetings, nodding heads. Sunny smiled at all of them. There was Joy and Henry and Fleur. Patch, too, looking older and giving her a smile that said he hadn't forgotten those nights behind the barn. There were babies and children she didn't recognize, along with some men and women she knew had not lived at Sanctuary.

"You sit with me. Here, at the front of the table." Josiah put his hand on the small of her back to take her to the chair next to his.

It was a place of honor, one Sunny didn't deserve or understand why she'd been given, but she sat anyway. Josiah sat next to her. He took her hand, which startled her until she saw him reach for the hand of the person on his other side and felt her own taken by the one next to her.

"Thank you for the winds that blow, thank you for the seeds that grow, thank you for the earth to plow, thank you for the love you show."

Sunny stumbled on the words that had once been so familiar she wouldn't have had to think twice about them. Nobody seemed to notice how her tongue tangled. Josiah squeezed her fingers and let them go.

Before even being served the first bite of food at every meal

in Sanctuary, everyone sat on uncomfortable benches and had
to listen to Papa, or later John Second, talk on and on about
the importance of preparing your vessel by resisting over-
indulgences. Sunny had fallen out of the habit of automatically tasting something to make sure it wasn't undercooked or
spoiled. As the platters of roasted chicken and vegetables were
brought in from the kitchen though, she didn't think she had
to worry about this meal.

"My father thought the best way to feed the soul was by
starving the body," Josiah said to her quietly as everyone
passed their plates to fill with food. "I believe in limiting indulgences, of course. It makes sense that we need to keep our
vessels in excellent condition, obviously, by avoiding toxins
and chemicals and prepared foods. But there's nothing wrong
with enjoying a meal. When it nourishes the body, it nourishes the soul, too."

The food was delicious, but she couldn't eat much. Josiah
sitting so close to her, paying such attention, was too distract-
ing. That and the conversations that rose and fell all around
the table.

This version of the family was far more politically aware
and active than Sunny could remember Papa's children being.
They spoke eagerly and with passion about working to create
awareness through their literature, not just of the ways to get
through the gates, but of political and religious tolerance. Of
health issues. Josiah spoke at length about his efforts in the
community to work with local churches and the food bank
to make sure there were organic food options for those who
relied on such aid to eat.

"Nobody should be forced to destroy their vessels with
food additives simply because they have to get their food from
charitable resources," Josiah said.

Papa had always talked while they listened, and his first true son had done the same. Josiah, on the other hand, also took the time to listen. He heard what his family had to say about any topic that was brought up.

But when he turned to Sunny to ask her what she thought about what she might be able to do at the coffee shop, if she might be able to convince her bosses to weed out all products containing harmful elements, she could only shake her head.

"They don't ask me to help with anything like that."

Josiah gave her a kind look. "You could take them some literature. The first step in getting anyone on the right path is information. You could ask them to display some of it in case any of their customers are interested."

Amy and Wendy were both adamantly antireligion. Sunny thought it had something to do with the fact that the matching rings they wore were symbolic and not legal.

Sunny shook her head. "I don't think they'd allow it. They wouldn't let a church group put their materials on the bulletin board."

"Ah, well," Josiah said after a second's hesitation. "Maybe you could just ask."

She could not say yes and felt awkward saying no, so Sunny said nothing. Josiah's eyes gleamed a little when he smiled at her. But he didn't push.

After dinner, Sunny offered to help with the dishes but was kindly turned down.

"You're our guest," Josiah told her. "Come into the living room, we have testimonies."

Sunny was not the only invited guest that night. Another young woman and an older man were both there to learn more about the family. The older man sat quietly in the corner, saying nothing, but the young woman took a seat next to Sunny.

"I'm Lisa. This is my third dinner here. It's so cool, isn't it?

But you'd know that, you're lucky. You're already part of the family, right? You're not one of us blemished."

Sunny recoiled the tiniest bit at how casually Lisa dropped the term. "I grew up in the family, yes."

Lisa leaned closer. "In Sanctuary, right?"

Sunny nodded.

Lisa grinned. "So lucky! Josiah told me about how it was there, your own place. Back to the land and everything. What a bummer his dad and brother had that falling-out with him. Josiah is a kick-butt leader. I'm totally going to join, if they let me. I just have to prove myself a little more."

"How do you do that?"

Lisa shrugged. "Well, I have to do my share of information-sharing. Got my dad over there to come. Since him and my mom got divorced, his health's gone to crap. High blood pressure, angina. I got him on this healthy diet Josiah told me about, and he's doing so much better."

Her dad was the quiet older man sitting in the corner.

"It's just that he doesn't want to sell the house, which, you know, he'd have to do to bring money into the family. Help out." Lisa said this under her breath, sharing secrets Sunny didn't want to know. "I think he's cool with most of the other stuff though, especially the part about maybe getting a new, young wife…or two. Or three."

Lisa's chuckle grated like sandpaper on Sunny's teeth. "How's he going to get a wife?"

"Oh, that's easy. See, Josiah says he doesn't agree with his father's idea about that one-true-wife thing."

"Thing?"

"You know, how nobody else should be allowed to get hooked up unless the leader of the family has his one true wife. Josiah says love should be free for everyone, and nobody should be forced to do what they don't want to, with anyone they don't want to do it with. No strings, you know what I mean? Love should be free." Lisa repeated that like it was her favorite part.

You should never do what you hate, you should love everything you do.

"It didn't really work that way, you know." Sunny shifted her chair just a little bit away from Lisa.

It didn't bother the other woman, who just leaned closer. "No?"

"No." Sunny didn't say anything else.

"I guess that's why Josiah says it should be different from how it was before."

Sunny looked at Josiah. He was making his way around the room, talking briefly with each person. He touched them all. A hand on a shoulder, a wrist, a squeeze of fingers. She thought of how his hand had felt on the small of her back, and a tiny shiver tickled her spine.

"How is it supposed to be different?" Sunny asked.

Lisa looked off with a delighted squeal. "Oh, there's Abe! I want… I have to go talk to him."

With that she got up and left Sunny sitting alone. Not for long. Josiah had made his way to her by then. He smiled down at her, and the shiver returned.

"Sunshine. I'm so glad you took me up on the invitation. I know you probably don't have a testimony for me tonight."

"What's a testimony? Is that like a report?" She hadn't pre-pared anything, though of course if he pushed, Sunny had a lot of things she could admit to having done wrong.

Josiah shook his head. "No. We don't report on each other. That was in my father's house, not mine. A testimony is the opposite. It's a listing of everything you did that was positive or good. Anything that helped your vessel toward its best state, so you can be ready when it's time to leave. Anything you did to help seekers find their way to the light."

"I haven't done anything like that." Sunny shook her head.

"That's okay." Josiah gave her another of those kind looks. His hand came down on her shoulder. "Not everyone manages to live every day pushing toward completion. That's why we have sharing, to help."

Behind him, Sunny caught a glimpse of Lisa. She was sitting on Abe's lap, her arms around him. They were…kissing?

"I'd like to share with you, Sunshine." Josiah's fingers squeezed, then moved to stroke the length of her hair.

It wasn't that Sunny had never seen people kissing, but to do it here, in the middle of everyone…and Lisa and Abe were not the only two locking lips. Others were also kissing. Not just one to another, either, but back and forth between partners.

Sunny stood.

Josiah was only a couple inches taller than she was, but there was no way to get around him without pushing him. He didn't move. Sunny put her hand on his chest, and he put his over hers.

"I know this will seem strange to you, Sunshine, seeing as how you grew up in Papa's house. Why don't you come with me into a private room, and I can tell you more to help you understand."

Come over here, Sunshine.

John Second's voice hissed inside Sunny's head.

She tried to take a step back, but the chair behind her hit her on the backs of her calves. She could go nowhere. Josiah didn't let go of her hand. He looked at her with those warm blue eyes. Seeing right inside her.

"Or you can leave," he said. "You can go whenever you

want, Sunshine. Nobody's going to make you do anything you don't want to do. I promise."

Behind him, she saw mouths meeting, hands roaming. Sunny closed her eyes for a moment, then looked at the only safe place. The floor.

"Take me someplace private, yes, please." She wanted to understand. She wanted to feel at home here. This was the family.

Josiah took her up a flight of stairs to a small bedroom at the end of the hall. A neatly made king-size bed dominated the space. It was the only place to sit, and he patted the space next to him.

Sunny hesitated, but sat stiffly, not looking at him. Josiah's shoulder and hip nudged hers, but he didn't touch her in any other way. He sat quietly for a moment or two, then twisted to look at her.

"Remember what I said downstairs? About food nourishing our vessels and our souls?"

She nodded.

"Well…it's the same with other things, too. If our bodies are our vessels, the perfect container for our spirit, and our goal is to keep our vessels in the best condition…well, Sunshine, our bodies are meant to enjoy lovemaking the same way we're meant to enjoy food."

Sunny blinked rapidly, feeling her face try to make itself into stone, but Josiah put a finger beneath her chin. Tipped her face to look at his. It wasn't a scary face, not at all. He had kind, warm eyes and a nice smile. She'd known this face for her entire life.

He kissed her, mouth parted, breath warm.

Sunny didn't move. Her mother had kissed her. Her children. But who else had ever kissed her? Nothing John Second

had ever done was this soft and warm and gentle, kind…
sweet. Tyler had kissed her, but it wasn't like this.

"Sunshine." Josiah's warm breath tickled her mouth. "Open
your mouth."

She did, just a little, and gasped when his tongue slid against
hers. She pulled away, a hand over her mouth. Mortified.

Josiah smiled. "It's okay. You don't have to be embarrassed."

Sunny shook her head. "I don't understand this, Josiah. Papa
said…"

"My father was wrong about a lot of things," Josiah said
flatly. "He and my brother perverted the message. And I know
things were done to you. I'm sorry about that. You won't find
that here. In this family, love is shared freely or not at all.
There's no place for fear or jealousy, because we are all free
to love one another."

"You don't mean love," Sunny said. "You mean sex."

If the bluntness of her words affronted him, Josiah didn't
show it. His smile turned a little sad. "Make love. There's a
difference."

He put his hand on her knee. Then inched his fingers
along the soft fabric of her skirt, this pretty skirt she knew she
took too much pride in wearing, and the hem of it crept up
over her knee. When his bare fingers touched her skin, then
higher, the inside of her thigh, Sunny put her hand on his.

Josiah stopped. They sat in silence. He looked into her eyes.

Sunny took her hand away.

Josiah's hand moved higher. Slow, slow, fingertips brushing
her skin. Her cotton panties. His fingers pressed against her.

Sunny had put her hand on his shoulder without realizing
it. Now her fingers pinched down as her head dipped. Eyes
closed. That gentle, simple pressure against her wasn't like
anything she'd ever imagined.

She knew about sex. She knew it could hurt or it could be

painless. It could take a long time or be over in minutes. She knew it could make a baby. And she knew that people enjoyed it, craved it, loved it, wanted it... She never had, but now she thought she understood what could make a woman open her legs for a man and lie down naked beneath him because she wanted to.

She shivered when Josiah kissed her. Mouths open, tongues touching. It should have been disgusting, but it wasn't.

They kissed for a long time as he touched her. Never too hard, too fast. A slow circling against her, until a pleasure built up inside her...and exploded.

Sunny cried out into Josiah's mouth. The world tipped. Her body jerked. Everything around her swirled.

Josiah laughed when she blinked and focused, but not in a mean way. He kissed her again. Then he took his hand away.

"Don't you feel good?"

She nodded, unable to talk.

Josiah tipped her face to his again, but this time didn't kiss her. "You should come back to us, Sunshine. Come back to the people who love you."

Chapter
40

Liesel had sounded strained on the phone, her voice distant. Sunny hadn't needed to see her face to imagine a frown. Sometimes Liesel said things like, "It's not a big deal," or, "Don't worry about it," mostly about things Sunny wouldn't have worried about anyway. This time, she'd said, "Come home now," and Sunny had made Josiah drive her right away.

Inside, the house was quieter than she'd expected. Cooler than outside, too, and though in a few minutes she'd think the air was too chilly, just now it felt fine. Sunny headed for the kitchen and found a tied-off garbage bag in the middle of the floor.

The faint stench of vomit was overlaid with the stronger stink of poo. Through the white plastic of the garbage bag, Sunny saw the telltale stain of disposable diapers squished up against it. She still didn't like the disposables, but since Liesel had agreed to watch her kids and was the one paying for them, Sunny hadn't felt she could continue to protest.

"Sunny? Oh. God. I'm so glad you're here." Liesel stood in the hall, Bliss on her hip. "Peace won't stop throwing up, she can't keep anything down. Happy's not much better. I don't know…"

"Where are they?" Sunny reached to take the baby, but Bliss turned her face away and clung to Liesel with a whimper. Surprised, Sunny kept her hands up for a few seconds longer, until it became obvious she'd have to actually take the baby from Liesel's arms, and probably by force.

"In the den. I have them set up on the couches. But it's been—" Liesel broke off with a shudder.

Sunny recoiled when she walked into the den. The faint odor in the kitchen had been bad, but in this room it was overpowering. Peace lay on the love seat, which had been covered in towels, a trash can with a plastic bag in it by her head. Happy was on the couch in a similar position, but he was the only one to look up when she came in. His face looked flushed, and when he saw her he sat up, eyes bright with tears that spilled out immediately.

Alarmed, Sunny went to him at once. "Happy, my sweetheart. You don't feel good?"

He shook his head and clung to her, even as Sunny tried to find a way to sit next to him without messing up the towels Liesel had put down. She didn't want to look too far into the garbage can. He clutched at her shirt, and she tried delicately to peel him off her.

"She…she maked me…"

"What, Happy?" Sunny managed to push him away enough so she could look into his face. "Who made you what?"

"He's upset because I made him put on a Pull-ups," Liesel

said from the doorway. "But he'd messed twice, couldn't make it in time to the potty—"

Happy let out a wail of shame and buried his face against Sunny's side. Liesel looked pained. Sunny stroked her son's hair.

"Shh," she told him. "It was an accident. Liesel's not mad."

"Of course I'm not. Oh, Happy, honey, I'm not mad." Liesel shook her head, bouncing Bliss a little as the baby whined. "But honey, you couldn't keep messing in your pants."

"I'm sorry," Happy whispered against Sunny's side. "I tried, Mama. I tried real hard."

Across the room, an uncharacteristically silent Peace let out a low cry and began to heave. Liesel groaned and went to her. "Over the can, Peace. Lean over!"

Sunny went to get up, but Happy wouldn't let her go. His shoulders heaved. He let out a hurking gag, and Sunny didn't spend another second in thought; she grabbed up the garbage can and twisted him around to put it in front of his face. She fought her own gag as the wet splatter of vomit hit the plastic bag, followed immediately by the rancid smell.

Five minutes later, Liesel passed Sunny a fresh roll of paper towels and some Lysol, along with a damp cloth. They worked in silence to clean up both kids while Bliss sat on the floor in between them, alternately wailing and drifting into whimpers. Sunny worked on autopilot, wiping Happy's face and trying to get him to lie back. Everything reeked, her stomach churned, and all she could think of was how grating the sound of her daughter's whining was.

"What should we do?" Liesel sounded helpless and looked bleak. She had circles under her eyes and her hair stood in sweaty spikes.

Sunny didn't feel too great herself. "I don't know."

Liesel frowned. "Should we give them some ice or

something to suck on? Or Pedialyte? Some ginger ale, maybe. That's what my mom gave me when I was sick. And saltines. I'll have to run to the store to get some. What do you think?"

"I don't know," Sunny repeated, unsure what sort of answer Liesel wanted. Or expected.

"Well..." Liesel carefully wiped her hands with a package of bleach cleaning wipes she normally used for the counters. "What do you usually do when they're sick?"

Sunny felt as helpless then as Liesel had looked. She shrugged and looked down at Happy, who'd finally closed his eyes. She looked at Peace, who could only stare, her small face wan and pathetic. "I don't know, they've never been sick."

Chapter
41

"What do you mean, they've never been sick? They're kids! Kids are always sick!" Liesel stank of sweat and puke and shit. She felt more than a little like throwing up herself. She'd been dealing with this for the past four hours and had reached her limit.

Sunny stroked Happy's hair back from his face. The boy looked as if he'd fallen asleep, which meant he'd probably have another accident. Liesel pushed a toy toward cranky Bliss, who tossed it aside.

"Not like this," Sunny said. "Never like this."

She gave Liesel one of those blank stares, and Liesel wanted to smack it off her face. It was wrong, she knew that. Sunny was doing the best she could. It wasn't her fault the kids had thrown up or shit on nearly everything in the house today.

But they were *Sunny's* kids. Not Liesel's. If anyone should be dealing with this, it was Sunshine.

"I'm going to take a shower," Liesel said because she didn't want to say any of the other million things running through her brain. Mean things. Words that weren't even necessarily true, but would taste so good to spew. "Then I'll run to the store and pick up some ginger ale and saltines. Popsicles. Some medicine. Stuff like that."

Not even a shadow of an expression twitched at Sunny's face. Liesel wanted to shake her just to get a rise out of her. How could she sit there so stone-faced? She should look worried! Or at the least, repulsed by the choking stench in the room.

"Sunny, did you hear what I just said?"

"Yes, Liesel. I'm sorry the kids are sick and made a mess."

Guilt, huge and painful, bopped Liesel on the back of the head...followed a second later by irritation. This was a pattern. Sunny or her children did something that made a mess, caused a scene, was a problem, and she apologized profusely like Liesel was some sort of...stepmonster. Then Liesel told her it was all okay, and she never seemed to believe it, no matter how hard Liesel and Christopher worked to prove to her she and the kids were a welcomed and yes, loved, part of this family.

"I'm going to take a shower," Liesel repeated. "If they puke, make sure they get it in the cans, I don't want to have to shampoo my rugs again."

Fifteen minutes in the shower worked wonders for her psyche. The irritation faded. So did the guilt. Liesel bent her head under the hot, pounding water and let it work the tight muscles in her neck and shoulders. Anybody facing the geysers of sick she'd had to deal with today would've reacted the same way she had, if not worse.

She'd hit the store, stock up on everything from hand sanitizer to tummy meds. Surely Christopher would be home in a few hours, and he could help out, too. They'd get through this, and it would be awful and disgusting, but maybe someday they'd look back on it and laugh. Or at least have a story to tell at parties when the topic turned, as it inevitably did, to the worst things that ever happened to you.

Back in the den, though, everything had gotten worse. Sunny held a gagging, choking Bliss over one can while Peace dry heaved into another. Happy wept and moaned from his place on the couch with a fresh wave of stink to show he'd had another accident.

Liesel stopped in the doorway and almost turned and ran away, but instead forced herself to move a couple steps forward. "Oh, no. Bliss, too?"

Sunny looked up, her face haggard. "Yes. She just started. Liesel, they're really sick."

"Let me call Christopher again." Liesel's stomach sunk and she looked with something like longing toward the hall. The door to the garage. If only she hadn't taken that shower, she'd have been out the door and gone by now. She'd have had an hour or so of freedom. She could still go. They still needed crackers and ginger ale…but no. She couldn't just abandon them. "Maybe he can pick up the stuff on his way home from…wherever the hell he is."

Sunny's blank look faltered for a moment, but she visibly firmed her mouth and blinked away any hint of tears. "Happy needs a shower. Bliss too, she's covered in throw up. I can take them both in with me…can you watch Peace? Please?"

The way she said it, like Liesel might refuse, set Liesel's teeth on edge, though she knew Sunny was only trying to be respectful. "Of course. You go. Let's do what we can. Peace, honey, let me get you a little water. Just a few sips."

Half an hour later, none of the kids were better. In fact, they were worse. Bliss had gone glaze-eyed, head lolling. Feverish. Peace slept, but fitfully, and Happy, who almost never cried, now couldn't stop moaning and weeping.

"I can't get in touch with Christopher." Liesel stabbed her phone to disconnect before leaving a third voice mail. "Sunny, we need to think about taking these babies to the emergency room."

"What?" Sunny looked up, eyes wide. Her hair, still wet from the shower that had been made pointless moments after they got out when both kids were sick again, clung to her cheeks. "No!"

"Hon, they're very sick." Liesel sat next to Peace and put a hand on her forehead. Burning up. "This is more than just a stomach bug. It might be food poisoning."

"What do you mean, food poisoning?" Sunny's voice caught and she swallowed hard. She scraped her hair back from her face and pulled the tangled, sopping mess on top of her head to secure it with an elastic band. "Corn syrup? Did they eat toxins?"

Sunny looked blank. Liesel thought of how when they first arrived, all three of them had been so cautious with every sip, every bite, carefully tasting everything before they ate it. More irritation pricked at Liesel. Surely the girl had heard of food poisoning that had nothing to do with her mythical and overblown fear of corn syrup.

"No. When food goes bad, like when it spoils. Like past the expiration date, or something that hasn't been properly refrigerated."

Recognition dawned in Sunny's eyes. Then a flash of something else Liesel couldn't interpret. "Spoiled food could make them sick like this."

"Of course it could!" Liesel snapped.

Then remembered.

"Christ, Sunny. The food under the beds. Did you have anything in there that could go bad? Make the kids sick?"

"I don't...I don't know—"

"Why do you even do that?" Liesel cried. "It's not like we don't feed you, for God's sake! I mean, I never asked because I figured it was just one more of those weird things you did, but good Lord, Sunny...for someone who has a bug up her ass about what she puts in her kids' mouths, you really don't make any sort of sense, sometimes!"

"It was in case!" Sunny shouted.

Happy stirred on the couch with a moan, and Bliss, who'd been dozing in her lap, startled awake with a scream.

"In case of what?"

"Just in case," Sunny said. "In case we needed it. I know it was stupid, Liesel, I'm sorry—"

"Stop being so goddamn sorry about everything!" The words bit out of her like a dog snapping. "I'm sick of it, Sunny! You act like you think me and your dad are going to toss you out on your asses for every little thing, and then you pull a stunt like that...hoarding food...that's just crazy!"

"I'm not crazy!" Sunny shouted. She looked at the baby in her lap. "Hush, Bliss. Hush!"

But the baby would not be hushed. Nor would Peace and Happy. Sunny looked at all three of her children with frantic eyes, then at Liesel. Liesel wanted to put her face in her hands and scream herself. Scream herself raw.

Instead, she took a shallow breath of stinking air and focused. "We need to take them to the emergency room and get some fluids into them or something. They're too sick. We can't deal with this. You get them ready, I'm going to call Christopher again and tell him to meet us there."

"No." Sunny shook her head without looking at Liesel,

her attention on the screaming baby. "Hush, Bliss. Mama says hush. Now!"

Liesel got on the floor beside her to squeeze her shoulder. "Sunny. Stop it. She's not going to stop crying, she's sick. We have to take them—"

"No!" Sunny shouted.

Spittle flew onto Liesel's cheek. Disgusted, she swiped at it. "What the hell is wrong with you?"

"No hospital. No emergency room! It's where the blemished go!"

"Well, I have news for you, Sunshine," Liesel said. "You're all blemished now."

Chapter
42

Sunny is seven years old. Maybe eight. She's found a kitten in the yard back by the greenhouses, close to the fence where she knows she shouldn't go, but Fleur has been in the grass with Henry for a long time, not paying any attention to the kids she's supposed to be watching. Patience is the one who told Sunny there were kittens, and now Patience stands in the dirt next to the fence and scuffs it with her bare toes.

"What's the matter with it?" Sunny squats to poke the kitten with her finger. It's so tiny it would fit just right into her hand, but she doesn't pick it up. Are they like baby bunnies? If you touch them, will the mother not come back? Why don't the other kitty mothers take care of the babies, then, the way mothers here all take turns with the kids?

"It's probably hungry." Patience is always hungry. She's got a fat face, fat belly, fat arms. Fat legs. She sneaks into the kitchen when she's not supposed to and eats snacks. Her mama's bondmate works in the kitchen, and he doesn't tell.

He'd make a report if he knew Sunny was the one sneaking something to eat. She presses her tummy now. The air's hot on her skin as she bends forward to study the kitten. Its eyes are closed. Tiny little paws press to its tiny nose. It has a little tail. The kitten is orange, and Sunny wants to cuddle it.

"So, let's feed it," she says.

Patience makes a face. "You can't, stupid. You don't have any milk for it."

If Sunny told Papa that Patience called her stupid, Patience would get into bad trouble. A switching, for sure. Sunny should make a report, but she's sure she'll forget by the time Papa asks if anyone has anything to tell. Patience won't forget anything, though. Sometimes, Sunny knows, Patience makes stuff up just to get the other kids in trouble.

Sunny stands and looks across the grass to where Fleur and Henry are still on the blanket. They've been doing the sex for a long time. It looks pretty boring. All that rolling around. But at least it means Sunny and Patience can come back here to the fence to see this kitten. The other kids are all playing crosses and naughts in the sandbox, and some of them are even taking naps.

Sunny yawns. Last night they woke everyone up to go to the chapel, but thinking of it now makes her tummy hurt, so she doesn't. She wants to look at the kitten, not think about drinking the rainbow. Papa says going through the gates won't hurt at all, but it still sounds scary.

"Kittens drink milk?" Sunny asks.

"Sure. Just like babies, do, dummy."

Patience has a mean mouth. Sunny frowns. She touches the kitten with her fingertip. It mews. "So. We should get it some milk."

"It has to come from the mother cat."

Sunny stands again to look around. This kitten is in a little nest made of grass tucked up against the fence. There are lots of cats around, but none right now. It's the only baby kitten in the grass, and it's all alone.

She doesn't think twice about it. Sunny scoops up the kitten in one palm and cradles it next to her body. Its tiny mouth opens as it wriggles against her shirt. Soft fur. The kitten's warm. Sunny strokes it. She loves it.

"You'd better put that back!"

She looks at Patience. "It's hungry, and if we don't feed it, it will die."

She knows that much. People need to eat. Kittens, too. Her own tummy growls with hunger, but they've already had their lunch and it's a long time until dinner. Oatmeal, that's what they had today. One bowl. It wasn't enough.

"You can get us some milk," she says to Patience. "Right?"

Patience's nose scrunches as she considers this. She bends over the kitten in Sunny's hands. Patience touches it, too, and coos over how soft it is.

"Yes. I guess so. But we have to be secret."

Sunny nods. She knows that. Animals aren't allowed inside the building. Just the barn and greenhouses to keep out mice. Papa used to have a dog named Jingles who liked to bark and growl, but he died.

"Patience," Sunny says as she follows the older girl around the back of the main building to the kitchen door. "Can animals go through the gates?"

Patience pulls open the door and stops to look back at Sunny. She laughs. "No way."

"Papa's dog. John Second said he gave the dog the rainbow." Sunny had heard him talking to her mama one night late when they were in bed together. About how he'd crushed up all the pills and put them in the juice. They always talked about things when they thought Sunny was asleep, and she almost never was.

In the cool dimness of the hallway leading to the kitchen, Patience stops to look at Sunny. "You're a liar."

Sunny blinks at this, taken aback. Her mouth opens. Tears burn in her eyes and before she can hush, they slip out and burn a path on her cheeks. Patience laughs, pokes her. Pinches hard to bring more tears. The kitten in Sunny's hands wiggles and cries when she squeezes it too hard.

"Liar's tongue, liar's tongue," Patience says, still pinching Sunny's arm.

It hurts so bad, but Sunny twists away from Patience's grip. The words hurt worse. "Not!"

Sunny's never told a lie in her life. Those with liar's tongues can't go through the gates, that's what Papa says, and she believes it. She pushes away Patience's hands. "I heard him!"

Patience has big brown eyes. They flash now in the shadows. "John Second wouldn't."

He'd said he did. He'd laughed, too. Mama hadn't. She'd said his name all sad, called him Jack the way she did when they were doing the sex. If she'd talked to Sunny that way, it would've made Sunny want to cry or expect the stick, but John Second had only done things to her mama that stopped her from crying and Sunny'd gotten bored and sleepy and turned her face to the wall.

But she knew he'd said it, and she knew John Second didn't speak with a liar's tongue. He couldn't. He was Papa's first true son.

"Come on." Patience pushes open the swinging doors to the kitchen and peeks around.

It's quiet inside. It smells good. Sunny's tummy rumbles again. The kitten mews, and Sunny puts her hand over its mouth to keep it from being too loud. There's nobody in here, though. That's good. They'd get in bad trouble for leaving Fleur when she's supposed to be watching them, even though she's not. And bad trouble for bringing an animal inside. And bad trouble for being in the kitchen.

All of this is bad trouble. Sunny hangs back, thinking on this, while Patience heads for the giant silver refrigerator with two doors. She opens them. Inside is all white light and shelves of food, more food than Sunny has ever seen, ever. Patience is already reaching on her tiptoes for a jug of milk. She brings it down and pours two glasses. She gives Sunny one.

"Here." Patience drinks hers.

Sunny shifts the kitten to the crook of her arm and takes the glass. She sips it cautiously, and Penny laughs again. She pushes the glass hard into Sunny's teeth.

"It's not bad, stupid. "

Sunny's had sour milk so many times she can hardly think of what good milk tastes like—sweet and cold. Like this. She gulps it. The kitten's little head turns, tiny tongue creeping out when a drop splashes on its fur. Sunny should give the kitten some milk, but it tastes so good and feels so nice in her belly, she doesn't want to.

"It's never bad right from the fridge," Patience says as if she's telling a secret. "Only in the dinner hall, sometimes."

Sunny holds out her glass. "More?"

Patience pours more, then puts the jug away. She drinks another glass herself. "Give some to the kitten."

"How?"

"Put it on your finger."

Sunny does. The kitten's pink tongue scrapes her skin. She giggles. She gives it more milk, then drinks some herself.

Patience has opened a drawer and is rustling around inside it. This makes Sunny more nervous than when she took the milk from the fridge. Patience holds up a flat rectangle in brown paper. Silver foil on the ends. Sunny can't read the white letters on the brown paper.

"Chocolate," Patience whispers. "A whole bar! I'm taking it."

"No!" Terrified, Sunny again squeezes the kitten too tight. "You can't take anything from the kitchen! Thieves don't get through the gates!"

"You stole milk," Patience points out.

Sunny's stomach clenches. Outside in the sunshine, she was too hot, but here in the shadows all of a sudden she's so cold her teeth chatter and click. She presses the kitten's soft fur under her chin.

"You gave it to me!"

Patience shrugs. She rinses both glasses in the sink and puts them with the others in the big plastic bin on the counter. "You drank it."

Sunny wants to cry. Patience is right. She doesn't cry, though. She hushes herself. Listens with her heart, but can hear nothing. The kitten squirms.

"C'mon. Let's go back before Fleur notices we're missing." Patience leads the way, saying over her shoulder, "If you're going to keep that kitten, you're gonna have to keep feeding it."

Sunny touches the soft fur. Holding this kitten reminds her of holding a baby, all sweet and soft and full of love. Her own baby! She puts a hand on her belly, which should feel too full from the milk but has a lot of room left in it. Always room left in her belly. One day, Sunny will bleed from down there like Mama does, and she'll go to Papa and see if she can be the one true wife, get him another true son. That would be a baby of her very own to love and feed.

But until then, maybe she can practice on this kitten.

"I'm going to put it in my room."

Patience's eyes get wide. "You'll get caught!"

Sunny shakes her head. "No. Not if you don't tell."

For once, Patience doesn't look like she's going to be mean. She nods. "Okay. I won't tell."

"Will you help me get the milk? If I let you play with the kitten?"

"Sure. I guess so."

Together, they sneak down the hall and up the stairs toward the bedrooms. Not all the rooms have closets, but this one does. Closets are worldly, made for keeping material things when you have too many to keep in a box under the bed or in a dresser drawer. This closet is empty but for a metal rod and a few shelves and an empty shoe box Mama put in there so long ago she'll never remember it.

Sunny takes a towel from the drawer and tucks it into the box. The kitten on top. She thinks about how the kitten has to breathe. "Should I put the lid on?"

"I don't know. I guess so."

They settle on pushing some holes into the top of the box with a pencil, then putting the lid on the box and the box in the closet. The kitten is mewing a lot. Sunny closes the closet door and presses her ear to it, listening, but she can barely hear it.

She turns to Patience, excitement tumbling all her words together. "We'll have to feed it every day! And when it gets bigger, we can train it to do tricks!"

"Cats don't do tricks, stupid."

"Papa's dog did tricks."

They're both silent while they think of Papa's dog, the one John Second sent through the gates.

"You're going to get caught," Patience says. "We'd better go outside."

In the hot summer sunshine, Fleur and Henry are still on their blanket, but now they're just talking. Patience takes Sunny behind the greenhouse and tears the wrapping off what she took from the kitchen. She breaks the stuff inside into a soft square that leaves brown smudges on her fingers. It's like poo. She offers it to Sunny.

Sunny shakes her head. "Ew!"

"You should eat it, it's good." Patience shoves the whole piece in her mouth, chewing.

Sunny risks taking the piece Patience holds out next. Patience wouldn't eat poo, would she? Oh, it's not poo at all, it's sweet! So sweet, and Sunny's mouth dances with happy when she gobbles it up. Together they eat the whole thing and lick their fingers clean.

"Chocolate," Sunny murmurs, flat on her back, her belly so tight it might just bust.

"It's good. I told you."

"Why don't we ever have any for dinner, if there's some in the kitchen?"

Patience shrugs. "It's for Papa and his true sons and his one wife."

Papa's one wife died like his dog. Papa said she tried to get through the gates all on her own before she was ready, so her vessel was here but what was inside, the secret voice, was still there, too. Stuck in the ground forever.

"Papa doesn't have a one wife now," Sunny said.

"Maybe it'll be me." Patience has chocolate all around her mouth. "Or you."

Sunny frowns. "We're too little."

Patience shrugs. "We won't be forever. If you are Papa's one wife, you get a lot of good things. I think I'm going to be his one wife, when I get older. Then I don't have to even worry about getting through the gates."

Sunny doesn't understand everything there is to know about the world beyond, but that doesn't sound right. Still, she's not going to fight with Patience. The other girl will pinch or shove her. And besides, now Sunny's stomach hurts bad.

Fleur is calling them. Patience gets up first. Sunny follows slowly. The sun beats down on her head. She drags her feet in the dirt.

Henry's gone, and Fleur has her clothes on again. She's going to take them all inside for afternoon meditations. She lines them up, all the kids who aren't babies in the nursery or old enough to have chores. Patience, Sunny, River, Willow, Praise.

Fleur's white blouse has long sleeves and lots of buttons. Her skirt is long, with more buttons down the front. Her belly pushes out the front of it, because Fleur's going to have a baby. Her hair was all down around her shoulders, but now she ties it on top of her head as she tells all the kids to get in line. She's sweating.

Sunny's tummy groans and twists. Fleur looks at her. "Sunny, what's wrong?"

A burning bad taste rushes up Sunny's throat and out her mouth. She spews the chocolate all over the grass, almost on Fleur's bare feet. Even over the sound of coughing so loud in Sunny's ears, she hears Patience laughing. Fleur shouting something. A couple of the other kids start to cry. River throws up, too.

"Oh, Sunny," Fleur says when Sunny blinks up at her. "What did you get into?"

With that bad taste still in her mouth, Sunny can only shake her head and wait for Patience to tell about the chocolate. But

Patience has a liar's tongue and a thief's hands, and she doesn't say anything.

Neither does Sunny.

Chapter
43

Liesel didn't ask her husband where he'd been or why he hadn't answered her calls. She looked at him standing in the kitchen with a kitten in each hand. Pets, he said. For the kids. Then she turned on her heel and left the room.

Three hours in the emergency room. The doctor had said it could be food poisoning or a virus, but either way she'd given all three kids shots of some powerful antinausea medicine as well as a prescription for some antibiotics for what she'd diagnosed as a previously untreated and chronic ear infection for Peace. An hour after that they were home, the kids showered and in clean pajamas, finally asleep. On the couches in the den, still set up with fresh towels and plastic-lined cans just in case, but resting comfortably. Sunny was with them in a sleeping bag on the floor between them, but Liesel doubted she was asleep.

And then there was Christopher, hours late without apology or explanation, bringing two more creatures into the house for Liesel to deal with. More mess. More poop. More of everything. It was too much.

She ignored him calling her name and went upstairs to their bedroom, where she stripped out of clothes that reeked of hospital and sickness. She left them right there on the floor and turned on the water as hot as she could stand. It was her third shower of the day, and she didn't even care. She just got in under the spray and turned her face up to the water so it would pound away the urge to cry.

It didn't work. Liesel crouched on the floor of the shower as the world spun. For an awful few minutes she thought she might be coming down with whatever the kids had, but the sickness in her stomach settled with a few slow breaths. She was just tired. Exhausted, as a matter of fact.

Heartsick.

Liesel gave in to the tears. Let them well up and out of her, less painful than a sickness but just as powerful. She pressed her forehead to the floor of the shower, thick with soap scum because she hadn't had time to scrub it in weeks. The water pounded her back, and her fingers slipped on the floor as she gripped it, trying to find something to hold on to so she wouldn't just fly away.

"Liesel?"

"Go away." She didn't want him to see her this way, didn't want to have to talk to him. She might sick up everything inside her, all the words she'd been biting back, the feelings she didn't want to admit.

Liesel didn't want to have to tell Christopher she'd been so, so wrong to ever think this could work.

The shower door rattled open, letting in a burst of cool air. Christopher stepped in, fully clothed, and shut the door behind him. Blinking, Liesel looked up at him, but before she could say a word, he crouched down next to her.

"Talk to me." Christopher didn't seem to notice his suit was getting ruined. The expensive tailored shirt, the silk tie she'd bought him several years ago for his birthday. The water sluiced over him, soaking into the fabric. His hand rested on her naked back, the pressure of his fingers light but insistent. "Please, Liesel."

It all came up and out of her, rushing, the words tumbling over one another in a jumbled, incoherent babbling she could barely keep track of but which Christopher seemed to follow just fine. She clutched at the front of his shirt, hating everything she said and yet overwhelmed with relief as it all spilled out of her. The story of the food she'd been finding, Sunny's reasons for keeping it. How angry Liesel had been that Sunny would think she needed to be prepared for starvation. How the kids had gotten into the spoiled pudding and eaten it while Liesel had been selfishly taking time for herself, even though she'd known better.

How it could have been the poison under the sink they got into, or stairs they fell down, a knife in an unsecured drawer.

"I can't do it," she said finally. "I can't do this, Christopher. I thought I could. I wanted kids so much, I thought I could just become some sort of…I don't know. Supermom. Super-wife. Whatever. But I can't do it. Everything is dirty, they need something from me every second, and I just. Can't. Do it."

Christopher sat on the floor, long legs stretched out, and cradled her to him. "You're a great mother, Liesel."

"I'm not anyone's mother!" A fresh spate of weeping shook her.

He held her for a while, saying nothing. That turned out to be the best thing he could've done, because a lot of times when they had discussions, Christopher focused so much on figuring out ways to "fix" her that he didn't really pay attention to what she wanted, which was simply to tell him how she felt.

Liesel pressed her face to his sopping shirt. "I thought I would just…love them. And that would be enough. But it didn't work that way, Christopher. I'm an awful person."

"No. You're not." He kissed the top of her head.

"They should be so easy to love!" She shook her head, eyes closed, letting him hold her while the backbeat pounding of the water somehow made everything easier to admit.

"Love isn't always enough," Christopher said.

Liesel pushed away to look at him. "Do you love me?"

He looked surprised. "Of course I do."

More tears, just a few, but somehow hurting more. "Do you love me as much as you loved her?"

Christopher didn't say anything for a long, quiet minute. "I could never love any woman the way I loved Trish."

Liesel let out a single sob, finally hearing what she'd feared all along, broken but not destroyed. But before she could say anything, he'd tipped her face to his.

"Look at me."

She did, blinking, eyes swollen.

"But I could also never, never love any woman the way I love you." He kissed her slowly with the water running over and between them. "Don't you get that?"

Liesel looked at his clothes, then at her own nakedness, and the ridiculous juxtaposition of it made her laugh. It surprised her to find any humor in this at all, but she did. It seemed to surprise Christopher, too, but he laughed along with her. Then he kissed her. He held her tight. Harder. Within minutes both of them clung to each other, heaving with laughter that sounded suspiciously like sobs. Or maybe it was the other way around. All she knew was when they tapered off, the water had started to cool.

She still felt like she might fly away, but now it was from the weight that had fallen from her rather than the world spinning desperately out from underneath her. She held her husband's face in her hands and kissed his mouth. When she looked at him, both of them blinking away water, she remembered how it felt to want to be with him instead of always hoping he'd walk away.

Together they managed to get out of the shower, and she helped him get out of his wet clothes, too. He hung them over the edge of the tub and stood in front of her. Both of them naked now, it seemed like the simplest and most natural thing to step into each other's arms. To kiss. Liesel thought there was no way she'd be interested in making love, not after the day she'd had.

She was wrong.

Chapter 44

Sunny's gone through this before, but it's no better the second time around. The pain ripples across her back, down low, then circles around her belly. She puts her hands on it, feeling the muscles tense, tense, tense…release. She lets out the breath she was holding. It's not quite time, but it will be soon.

The floor isn't clean enough yet, and there's no telling how long it will be until she's in actual labor, so she bends back to the bucket and the scrub brush. The hot, soapy water has turned her hands bright red and softened her nails so that when she presses too hard on the scrub brush, one bends back.

More pain, smaller and yet somehow worse than the rising and falling ache in her back and belly. She can't even suck at it, since she doesn't want to put her finger in her mouth after it's been on the bathroom floor and also in the bucket of filthy water. The nail is now hinged like a piece of paper that's been folded. The crease is low enough that if she pulls it off, her skin will tear, too. There's no choice for it, though, and she steels herself to hurt when she does it.

If only babies were born as fast as that, she thinks as she drops the torn nail into the toilet she's been scrubbing around.

She already knows this baby is a girl. Her mother did all the little tests, checking to see which eye had the reddest veins, which way the pendulum swung when hung over her belly, what foods Sunny was craving. There's a whole list of them, silly things, and Mama said of course not to say anything about them to John Second because he'd be angry they could even think they might be able to determine something the universe had been so careful to make a secret. But Mama was right about Happy and right about lots of other babies, so Sunny believes she's right about this one, too.

She's going to call this baby Patsy, after her mom.

But for now, Sunny scrubs. She wipes down the toilets, too. The doors of the stalls, both of them. The sinks, the mirrors. By the time she gets to that part, she has to stop every ten minutes or so to cling to the sink and pant her way through an ever-increasing round of pain.

Now it's centered almost inside her. Deep inside. The baby's head, pushing down on her, opening her. Getting ready to push its way out into the world.

When she steps into one of the three showers, the timing's perfect. Her water breaks. Hot fluid splashes down her thighs and legs, hits the tile floor. Soaks her underpants and her dress, too. It's tinged with blood.

The pain that comes next is instantaneous and somehow furious. A knife, stabbing. Sunny clutches at the shower curtain and tears it from the rings, which clatter to the floor as she stumbles forward. On her hands and knees, she feels another wave of pressure and pain building up inside her.

The baby is coming. Fast. She tries to find the strength to

scream, but all that comes out is a whistling gasp. It chokes her. She turns her head to the side, trying to cough, but all that comes up is a thin runner of spittle.

"Mama..." Her mother is out somewhere, maybe the garden or doing some sort of yard work.

Where is anyone else?

Sunny, groaning, manages to get to her feet. Careful not to slip in the puddle on the floor, she makes it to the sink. *Breathe in. Breathe out.* She pants through another wave of contractions, but the urge to bear down and push is overwhelming. She can't stop it. She squats, her body huge and unwieldy, and everything inside her stretches and surges, trying to get free.

Sunny puts a hand between her legs. She feels the softness of hair, not her own. The firm lump of a baby's head. Another pain cycles up and up and up, and from someplace inside her she finds the voice to scream.

She screams as loud as she can, and her voice echoes off the tile walls. It tears out the bathroom door, down the hall. There is the sound of running feet, loud cries. The bathroom door flies open, startled faces appear, there is someone on her knees beside Sunny, and on the other side, too. Joy and Willow. They each take an elbow, trying to help her, but Sunny can't move.

"I want my mother." This is what she thinks she says, but in reality all she manages is a series of grunts.

They are women, though, and they understand. Willow shouts out for someone to go get Trish. Joy gets a thick pad of wet paper towels and presses it to Sunny's forehead.

Sunny does not want to have her baby on the bathroom floor, but there's no stopping it. The women of her family, her sisters and finally her mother, crowd around her. They bring towels, a blanket, some cool water to bathe her face. They bustle around her, each of them with a purpose. This baby is not the first to be born here in Sanctuary, and they all know how to handle it.

"Sunny, hold on, one more time and you'll have to push," her mom says.

It's all she can do. There's no holding it back, even if she didn't bite her bottom lip and bear down, this baby would come. But Sunny waits as she breathes through the pain for her body to tell her its time, and she works with the contractions, not against them. Her body does what it's meant to do.

Something tears. More pain. There is blood, lots of it, but nobody seems alarmed even though the heat of it, the sudden bright red gush, has Sunny choking on her breath.

The baby is not coming out.

She can't stand the pain any longer, and the world grays out for a second or two. When she's clear again, Josiah stands in the doorway. Far enough away that his white shirt is at no risk of being stained, but even so…men don't usually attend the births. Even Papa wasn't there when his true sons were born.

Nobody else notices him.

They're all talking to her. Urging her though this. Wiping her brow. Joy is between Sunny's legs, fingers probing.

Sunny should be embarrassed; from his vantage point in the doorway, Josiah can see everything. He is silent, watching, but his gaze snares hers.

He smiles.

And Sunny finds the strength inside her to push again. To push hard. She bears down, pushing the baby inside her out into the world. First the head, shoulders, and finally in a great, huge gush of fluid, the entire body. The baby slips from inside her and into Joy's hands so fast she cries out, startled.

No fear, though, she's delivered babies before. She doesn't

drop Sunny's newborn. There is an instant relief, the pressure gone at least for a minute or two. A certain grateful numbness.

Then the pressure of Joy's fingers inside her again, her palm pushing on Sunny's belly. Push again, she says. The afterbirth has to come out.

Someone has taken Sunny's baby to wipe her off at least a little bit before she's handed to Sunny. It is a girl, just like she knew all along. Sunny holds her brand-new daughter to her chest, not caring that her dress is stained or that the baby is still slippery with blood and that white coating.

The women around her are crying, the way most of them do when a baby's born. The baby is silent, wide-eyed. Sunny doesn't cry either, she's too tired. She has nothing more to give but this. She wants to close her eyes and sleep forever, but she can't. They have to take her out of this bathroom and into her own room.

Later, when she's been cleaned up and stitched—it's her second baby but the first time she tore—Sunny rests in her bed with the baby tucked up firmly against her. Her milk hasn't let down yet, but that doesn't stop the infant from suckling greedily. Her nipple is already sore, just one more ache along with most of the rest of her, too. Bruises on her knees she didn't notice until now. Pulled muscles in her arms and shoulders.

Sunny dozes, but wakes when a shadow falls over her bed.

It's Josiah, and he smiles again. His hand touches the baby's head softly, softly, fingertips barely brushing the head of soft blond fuzz. He touches Sunny's head, too.

"What's her name?" he asks.

"Patsy. I want to name her after my mother."

Josiah's smile doesn't falter, but he does shake his head. "You should name her Peace. Because that's what she'll bring you."

And that was what Sunny named her child, because Josiah, Papa's second true son, had said she should.

It had not occurred to her that Josiah would remember that story, but when he asked her how Peace was doing, Sunny said, "You named her."

He was silent for a moment, only the sound of his breathing through the phone. "I remember."

"Now that my mom's gone, I sort of wish I'd named her Patsy the way I'd intended."

"Because you think it would be honoring your mother?"

"Yes." Sunny turned on her back in the cool, smooth sheets. With the window open the temperature in the room was perfect. She could hear crickets from outside. Occasionally a firefly flashed.

"Because she's gone," Josiah said.

Sunny hesitated, then thought there should be no point in lying. "Yes."

"Your mother's not gone," Josiah said. "Not really. I mean, you know that, don't you, Sunny? None of them are really gone. They're just on another plane."

Josiah had called her every night since he'd driven her home. Always when everyone else was asleep. Josiah had turned out to be the one thing she could count on to make her feel better.

"That boy. From the coffee shop," Josiah asked. "How's he?"

She was ashamed Josiah knew about Tyler. "He doesn't talk to me anymore."

"Not at all?"

She was silent for a moment, thinking of how he barely even looked at her now. "No."

"Why not?"

"He wanted me to be like those girls he talks to in the shop, the ones who go to college and wear their hair loose. They wear jeans. Lipstick. They don't have children. He wanted me to be like those girls," Sunny said. "And I'm not."

But it wasn't Tyler who wanted her to be like those girls, she thought. She was the one who wanted to wear eye shadow and glittery earrings and slim-fitting T-shirts. To paint her nails. To be someone she wasn't.

"I'd say I'm sorry, but you know I'm not."

She thought of Josiah's touch, his kiss, the warmth that had spread through her, and it made her feel hot now, though the breeze from her open window was cool enough. "I shouldn't have gone with you the first time. Liesel and Christopher wouldn't like it."

"Because they don't understand. I don't blame them. You could bring them, too, Sunny, you know we always have room at our table for more."

Sunny tried to think of her father and his wife sitting with Josiah and talking about going through the gates. Or anything, for that matter. She shook her head, her hair pulling softly against the pillow. "I'm sure they wouldn't want to."

"People are usually afraid of what they don't know. And believe me, I understand why anyone would have a bad opinion of us because of what my brother did. But you know… you're an adult," Josiah told her. "If you want to go out with me or spend time with your family, they can't stop you. And if you just told them a little bit about who we are and what we believe, I'm sure they wouldn't want to."

"My children got into trouble the last time I was with you," Sunny told him. "Because I was off with you, I wasn't there for them. They got sick, and it was my fault. They were hurt because I wasn't there to make sure they were okay, because I did something stupid…"

"Your children are as welcome as you are, Sunshine. You

know that. You wouldn't have to be away from them at all. And you're young. You could have more babies. As many as you want, and you wouldn't have to leave them to work. We'd take care of you."

Sunny was quiet. "Josiah. Do you still listen with your heart?"

A pause. "Sure. Of course."

"For the voice that tells you when it will be time to leave?"

"Oh, Sunny..." Josiah coughed. "I told you before, I think there's so much more work to do here in this world that it will be a long, long time before any of us have to leave. Maybe not even in our lifetimes."

She listened to the low murmur of the ever-present stone angel. It reminded her of everything she'd ever been taught, all she'd ever believed. "My mother had cancer, Josiah, did you know that?"

She expected him, of course, to say no.

"I did," he said instead. "I'm sorry. She came to me once when my brother was starting to lose control. She begged me to come back to the family and try to make him see that he was hurting the people he was supposed to love, but... honestly, I didn't have anything left to give my brother."

"But my mother..."

"She looked sick. I'd known your mom for a long time, you know. I was just a kid when John brought her home. And she was so funny, so full of life and faith and belief, and when she had you, you were so much like her. She looked bad. Complained of headaches, dizziness. One of our new brothers was a doctor, and he convinced her to let him check her out."

"She knew." Sunny swallowed hard. "I thought she did. It's why she sent us away but didn't come with us. Isn't it?"

Josiah sighed. "I don't know. I wish I did. But I know your

mom loved you very much. And she'd have wanted you to come to me. I'm sure she'd be so happy if you did."

Her mother couldn't be happy for anything, because her mother was gone. Nothing left in her vessel, nothing left to go through the gates, whatever that meant. The angel's voice whispered this, but Sunny already knew it.

"I hear the voice, Josiah."

She heard the shuffle of something against the phone. "What?"

"The voice Papa told us about. I hear it."

"Sunny, you know that voice isn't real. Don't you?"

"It's real."

"No," Josiah said firmly. "There is no small voice that tells us to end our lives. It was something my father made up and John Second perpetuated as a way of controlling you."

"It's my own voice, Josiah," she said, surprised he didn't know that or couldn't understand. "And it *is* real, it tells me right from wrong and what I should do, how I should live, what choices I should make. My mother must've heard it, and that's why she sent me and my kids away to my father, to protect us. She could've sent us to you, apparently, but she didn't. So what does that tell you?"

"I told you, I can't say what your mother wanted or didn't. All I can tell you is that we all love you." Josiah paused. "I always have. Please let me see you again."

Sunny listened as hard as she could, but the voice was too hard to hear with Josiah to drown it out. "I don't think so."

Chapter
45

The heat had broken, finally. Mostly because of the storm clouds that had been creeping across the sky since morning. They blocked the sun and dropped the temperatures, which had been in the mid-nineties for the past week, into the more reasonable eighties. So far, no rain, but every so often Liesel heard the far-off rumble of thunder that meant it was on its way.

"Kids recover fast." Becka sipped from a tall glass of iced tea. She hadn't offered margaritas today, but that was all right. "Thank God."

Liesel shuddered. "Yeah. Thank God. I was really worried. I'd never seen kids be so sick. Out both ends."

Becka gave her a sympathetic look. "In the realm of child-related disasters, I can honestly tell you that the very idea of what you went through has my skin crawling. That is a nightmare of epic proportions. Beans in the nose? Jumping off the second-story landing with a blanket used like a superhero cape? Cutting their own bangs? Nothing is as bad as what you went through."

"That's not true," Liesel said quietly, even though she knew her friend was joking. "I can think of lots of worse things that could happen."

"Of course you can, hon. You're a mother."

Chris had said something very much the same on the night of the emergency room visit, but Liesel had the same response for Becka. "No. I'm not."

"You're a mother to that girl out there." Becka pointed.

"Stepmother."

"So? You think that makes a difference? Her mother's dead. You're the only one she has now." Becka shook her head.

They both watched as Sunny took the hands of all three of her children. Bliss was able to stand now, so long as she held her mama's and brother's hands. The four of them circled slowly, the lilting tune of their game wafting up the hill to the deck on the damp breeze. Laughing, all of them except Bliss crouched at the end of the song, and the baby's laughter rang like bells across the lawn.

Becka sipped her tea with a sigh. "I haven't played Ring Around the Rosy in ages."

"I never liked that game. It's about the black plague, did you know that?" Liesel leaned her elbows on the table and took a grateful breath of cooler air.

"What? No." Becka pursed her lips. "That's sick."

Liesel laughed and glanced at her friend. "Yep. Check Google."

Becka pulled out her iPhone with a flourish and tapped at the screen. Down the hill, Sunny and the kids had stood up again to start all over. The kids would play that game for round after round, Liesel knew that from experience. But while she usually encouraged them to pick something else after about three times, Sunny seemed to have a lot more patience. Or maybe she just didn't know many more games.

"I'll be damned." Becka shook the phone at her. "Wow. Who knew?"

"Well, I did."

"Smart-ass." Becka thumbed her screen to read more. "It makes sense now when you look it up. Ring around the rosy means the rash. The posies were the flowers people carried to mask the stench of rotting bodies—"

"Ew, gross."

Becka gave Liesel a wicked grin. "You brought it up."

"Ashes, ashes," Liesel said. "All fall down. That's the end of it, when all the people died."

"Snopes dot com says it's not true, anyway."

Liesel shrugged.

"It was only food poisoning," Becka said. "Or a stomach virus. Kids get them all the time. And you said Sunny cleaned out all the food from under her bed, no complaints."

"She said she was sorry, over and over and *over.*" Liesel shaded her eyes against a sudden bright spike of sunshine that had pierced the ever-darkening clouds. The children were now playing some other game while Sunny sat on her favorite bench. "Oh, God. Look. She's talking to that angel again."

"It's only a problem if the angel answers her." Becka swirled the ice in her glass, rattling the cubes.

Liesel didn't say anything.

"Oh, hon," Becka said.

"I don't know anything," Liesel said hastily. "She was doing so much better. She seemed to have made peace with what happened. Her sessions with Dr. Braddock had been so helpful. Sure, she still had those idiosyncrasies about the diapers, corn syrup. Recycling, my God, you'd think we were single-handedly tearing apart the ozone layer with our bare fists if we tossed a plastic container in the trash instead of recycling."

"No, that's only if you use too much Aqua Net."

Liesel laughed a little. "She's doing really well at work. They gave her a promotion a couple months ago. She seemed really proud."

"But?"

Liesel looked again down the hill. Sunny didn't look like she was saying anything. Or even like she was listening to anything other than her children, who were performing some sort of dance in front of her.

"She's so apologetic all the damn time. And I feel like it's because she somehow senses that I'm frustrated. And so's Christopher."

"She doesn't have to be a psychic to get that." Becka snorted softly. "And you don't have to beat yourself up over it, either. The poor kid was beaten if she spoke out of turn. I'd be surprised if she didn't have a lot of hang-ups about screwing up."

"I don't want her to feel that way."

"But she does," Becka said. "Probably always will."

"Since the kids were sick, she's been quieter. A lot quieter. I asked her if something had happened at work, or maybe with the boy who likes her—"

"Yeah, whatever happened with him?"

Liesel shook her head. "I don't know. They went out a couple times. She used to kind of light up when she talked about him, and now she never mentions him at all. When I asked her about him, she clammed up and got all quiet, wouldn't tell me anything else. She gets that…look."

"What look?"

Liesel demonstrated, making her gaze go far away, her face blank. "Happy does it, too. It's like when they get upset, they go away."

"Peace doesn't?"

"Not like that. Maybe she's too young." Liesel studied the children as they now ran in a circle around Bliss sitting in the grass, playing tag. Maybe Duck, Duck, Goose. "Too much personality. Whatever it is, I know when she looks like that there's no use trying to get anything out of her. She's doing whatever it is that she talked about so much when she got here. Listening with her heart."

"Maybe she's doing something else."

That earned a laugh. "Like what?"

Becka lifted a brow. "I don't know. What did we do when we were teenagers?"

"She's not a teenager." Liesel shrugged. "I don't think she's smoking dope or getting drunk or something like that, if that's what you mean. And even if she was…well. Like I said, she's not really a child."

"The way she was brought up, I wouldn't be surprised if she didn't go a little wild. Hell, we went wild and we weren't raised in a cult."

Liesel laughed again, without much humor. "Honestly, I don't think she knows how."

"How to what?"

"Go wild," Liesel said. "Rebel. I don't think she knows how. I sort of wish she had, that would've made her… normal."

Becka made a face. "Poor kid. But how are you doing? You know you could've called me that day. I'm a hundred million times thankful you didn't, but you know you could've."

Liesel laughed. "I know. I'm doing…better. Much better. Christopher and I had a long talk. He's been a lot better about pitching in around here."

"Funny how that works, when you ask him," Becka said. "I knew I liked him for a reason."

Liesel rolled her eyes. "I thought I could do it all myself, like I was the one who said they should stay here, I should be able to take care of the kids."

"Nobody can do it all by themselves and stay sane." Becka said this with her usual firmness of conviction. "It sucks you had to nearly break down before he figured it out, but I guess he's a dude, what can you do."

"*Pffft.* It's still a lot of work," Liesel said. "For a man who's ironed his own clothes for as long as I've known him, you'd think tossing some dirty clothes in the washer, getting them to the dryer *and* folding them after wouldn't be so much like brain surgery."

"Oh, but it is," Becka said with a snort. "And then he wants a trophy after, am I right?"

"Something like that. But it's been better these past two weeks. He's even been getting up earlier so I can take a run in the morning before Sunny leaves for work. And he doesn't leave his phone off anymore, either. If I need him, he answers."

"That's good." Becka nodded. "Really good. I'm glad to hear it."

"I think things might just be…okay," Liesel said hesitantly, as though by saying it aloud it might jinx everything.

Overhead, thunder rumbled. The first fat, cold drops of rain spattered down and left dark marks on the light wood of the table. Liesel stood to check on the kids and saw a flash of lightning. Far off, but still close enough for worry.

Sunny was already up and gathering them. Not running across the grass, but herding them purposefully toward the house. Holding Bliss's hand, she helped the baby—no, she was a toddler now. Helping her walk. Bliss stumbled and fell, but Sunny caught her just as more rain started falling.

"Come on, guys!" Liesel cried. "Get inside!"

Happy and Peace, full of giggles, clambered up onto the deck. Sunny, who'd scooped up a protesting Bliss, joined them a minute later. Just in time, because another flash of lightning lit the sky, followed by a crack of thunder, and all of them ran inside the house just before the clouds opened up all the way and the rain poured down.

Chapter
46

"Sunny, Sunny, Sunshine."

Sunny looked up from the counter she'd been wiping. "You shouldn't be here."

Josiah looked around the empty coffee shop, then back at her. His frown said he was confused, though his gaze was anything but. "I don't understand. I came to see you."

"If you're not going to buy anything to eat or drink, you should go. This is my work, not a social... It's not for me to just hang out." She wiped at the counter, but it was so clean already her rag did nothing but squeak against it.

"I came to invite you to spend the weekend with us. You and the children, of course. We'd love to see them again. How old is Happy now? He'll be five soon."

"Yes. He'll go to kindergarten next year. He's going to start preschool in a few months." She lifted her chin defiantly, expecting Josiah to scold.

He simply gave her one of those kind, understanding looks.

"I'm sure the people you live with feel it's best for him to go to school."

"He needs to learn how to interact with other children." Sunny parroted what Liesel had said, though deep inside her heart and guts she wasn't as convinced mingling with blemished children would be good for her son. She wanted to believe it the way she'd tried to believe everything else everyone wanted her to accept. Liesel, Chris, Dr. Braddock.

But in her heart...she really didn't.

"We have other children in our family. Not as many as in Sanctuary, that's true. But we're growing. We need you, Sunshine. We miss you." Josiah leaned across the counter. "I miss you."

She flushed, thinking again of his touch on her and how it had made her feel. She shouldn't be ashamed, at least not according to him. But she couldn't meet his gaze, not even when he reached across the counter and took her hand, rubbed his thumb on the back of it. She thought of the way his mouth had tasted, and pulled away.

"I think you should go."

"Your place is with us, you know it is." Josiah sighed.

This time of day was always so busy, yet now there was nobody to save her from him. No customer asking for a muffin, no tables to clean off. Amy and Wendy had gone on a few deliveries, trusting Sunny to stay and mind things here. She couldn't run away.

She wanted to run away.

He sighed again and let go of her hand. "Tell me that you feel at home there, and I'll leave you alone. Tell me honestly that you feel like you belong, that you're not missing something. Tell me you don't ache for something you don't have, Sunshine, and I will walk out this door and never bother you again."

She didn't say a word, unwilling to speak with a liar's tongue though she'd done so many times before.

"You can't, can you?" Josiah spoke quietly, low enough that even if there was someone else in here, the only person who could hear him would be Sunny. "Sunshine. I know. I left my father's house, remember?"

"You were thrown out."

Josiah took a step back, for a moment looking grim before nodding. "Yes. You're right. I was thrown out. Why? Because I didn't agree with everything my father and my brother were doing. They took the message and...they ruined it. They broke it. They made it something bad."

Sunny looked him in the eye. "What makes your message any better?"

"At least I have one," Josiah said. "What do the blemished have except greed? They damage their vessels and spend their time accumulating material things, wasting their time with everything that doesn't matter. Is that what you want for your life, Sunshine? Is it what you really want for your kids?"

Josiah reached for her hand again, but this time she stepped out of the way before he could touch her. "I love you. We all love you and miss you. We have a place for you with us. Come and be my wife. Come home."

It had been a strangely quiet afternoon. Bliss had gone down for a nap after teething and being cranky all morning. Peace and Happy were playing with their favorite Lego blocks in the den and had built an entire city complete with the addition of a wooden train set Liesel and Sunny had picked up from the local thrift store.

The house was clean due to Sunny's efforts, dinner was already in the oven and Sunny had settled herself at the kitchen table with her books and notebooks to do her schoolwork.

"How's it going?"

Sunny looked up, her pencil pressed to her bottom lip. "Oh…I don't know."

Liesel took her mug of coffee and sat across from her. "Can I help you?"

Sunny hesitated, then pushed the folder of materials across the table. "I think I'll be okay with the math. I've been practicing. And the reading and writing parts, I think I'll be fine, too. But the science and social studies…"

She shook her head and frowned. "The test materials say we don't have to remember a lot of dates and things. But…I just don't know these things, Liesel. I don't have a frame of reference. The science things all sound wrong to me, I pick the wrong answers all the time."

"There are courses you can take that will help you. You don't have to do this all on your own." Liesel tapped the folder. "But you can do this, Sunny. You're a smart kid."

Sunny gave her a small smile. "Sometimes I think it would be so much easier to be…dumb. Then I'd have an excuse to just fail at this, and I probably wouldn't care, either."

"But you're not dumb. And you're not going to fail," Liesel said firmly. "You're going to ace this test and move on with your life, Sunshine, because you deserve to."

Sunny tapped her pencil against her notebook. She looked toward the hall and the den where her children played as the sounds of their lilting voices rose in laughter. She looked at Liesel. "You really think I can make it? Get my GED, go to college, get a job, move out on my own?"

"Absolutely." Liesel nodded. "I have no doubts at all."

"It was easier to live in Sanctuary," Sunny said. "We didn't ever have to think for ourselves or make decisions. I didn't have to worry about if I could pass a test so I could make a living and take care of my kids. All I had to do was obey and be taken care of."

Liesel thought about that for a moment, then nodded again. "I can see how that could be appealing. Sure."

"But it's better here," Sunny told her. "I don't want you to think I don't know that. It's better. Just…harder sometimes. That's all."

Before Liesel could say anything, Sunny laughed a little, low. "But John Second was right, then, I guess. We appreciate what we have so much more when we see just what we could have, instead."

Liesel never would've dreamed she could ever agree with anything crazy John Second had said, but she had to admit he was right in that. "It's good to appreciate what you have."

Sunny nodded. She gave Liesel a small smile that reached her eyes, her familiar blank look nowhere in sight. "I appreciate this, Liesel. I hope you know that."

"I do, hon." Liesel patted her hand.

From the den came the sound of blocks tumbling and a mingled mutter of protest. "I'll go check." Sunny closed her notebook and pushed her chair back, then ducked out of the kitchen. Liesel heard her murmuring, then more childish laughter.

Liesel looked around her silent, spotless kitchen and realized something important.

She could do this after all.

The real question was, would she ever be able to run the way she used to? Liesel knew it was just a matter of stamina, endurance. Working back up to it. But the funny thing was, the longer she'd gone without running every morning, the easier it had become to push the snooze button on her alarm and curl back up under the blankets, even though Chris and

Sunny had both been so much better about making sure Liesel had her time in the mornings.

She just didn't feel motivated the way she used to. Usually she avoided the scale, preferring to rely on how her clothes fit...the problem was, her jeans were all too tight in the belly. With Sunny home now, it would be a good time for Liesel to force herself into exercise.

In the den, she found Happy coloring. He didn't look up from his drawing at first, carefully filling in the last stroke before holding it up to her. "I drew a picture of Tiger and Noodles, see?"

Liesel looked at the picture he'd drawn of the kittens. "Wow, Happy. That's awesome. I love it. Where's Peace? And your mama?"

He flicked a disinterested hand toward the French doors. Liesel looked through the glass. Sunny was in the garden again. Not sitting on the bench this time, but kneeling alongside the path with Peace beside her. Pulling weeds, it looked like. Not that it would do much good at this point—it would be time for everything to go to sleep soon. Unless maybe Sunny thought she'd plant some bulbs for the spring.

Even just a few weeks ago, the thought that Sunny and her children would still be with them when spring came would've sent Liesel's heart racing with panic. Now as she touched Happy's hair and bent over him to watch him color, she didn't feel so freaked out. Life had changed and would keep changing. The only thing to do was keep running.

Running. She laughed to herself, shaking her head. She hadn't even put her sneakers on yet.

"Is it a joke?" Happy looked up at her.

"Oh...no, hon. I just thought of something funny." From this angle she couldn't see past the slight dip of the hill in the yard, but assumed Sunny and Peace were still in the garden.

If she was going to run, she really should get on it. Upstairs, though, she felt even less motivation than she had before. Her rumpled bed beckoned even as she tucked the sheets and blankets tight. In the bathroom, she got on the scale to prove to herself that too many cupcakes could be hazardous to her waistline.

That's when it hit her.

Hard, right in the breastbone, like a fist that punched the air right out of her. Liesel counted backward, lost track, counted again and gave up with a hitching squeak. She gripped the sink with both hands as a wave of uncertainty washed over her. Light-headed, woozy, she sank onto the cool tile floor and put her face in her hands.

Under the sink, there was a box she'd bought almost a year ago in a fit of optimism. A multipack of pregnancy tests, only two used before she'd forced herself to start waiting longer than a day or two after her period was supposed to start before checking. She had one left.

Just one.

With shaking hands, Liesel took out the box. She read the instructions, though of course she couldn't forget them. She even had a small sleeve of paper cups under the sink to make this easier. But she couldn't go, couldn't force out even a drop, which was so opposite her body's normal response to anything, that she sat on the toilet in shock for a full minute before convincing herself she just needed to relax.

She breathed. And again. Holding a paper cup between her legs felt ridiculous enough that she laughed…and then her bladder relaxed. Hot liquid hit the cup, and Liesel laughed harder at the thought that at first she'd been afraid she'd have nothing and now she had to worry about overflowing it.

It wasn't her first morning urine, which was what the box suggested, but there was plenty of it. She dipped the cottony end of the stick into the urine, dumped the rest and set the stick on the edge of the sink while she washed her hands. She deliberately didn't look at it. The test said it could take up to three minutes to show a result, and she knew from experience how long those three minutes could be.

It took only a few seconds though, for two pink lines to show in the window. Glancing from the corner of her eye, Liesel tried to assure herself she was just imagining them, but when she picked it up and looked at it, there was no question. No doubt.

Two pink lines, nothing faint or undetermined about them.

LEAVING

Chapter
47

The kitten she'd put in her closet had died after a few days. Sunny tried to tell herself now that it would've died anyway, even if she had remembered to feed it regularly, had taken better care of it, but as a grown-up the lies she told herself in childhood no longer were so convincing.

Just weeks ago her children had been sick enough to make her fear for their lives. The food under the bed, the things she'd stolen with her thief's hands, had made her children sick. She'd been trying to protect them and had hurt them instead. Just hours ago she'd watched them giggle as they played with the kittens Chris had brought home.

Now she sat with two sleeping kittens on her lap and listened to the night sounds of a dark house. When Peace woke, thirsty, Sunny gave her some sips of water and crooned a lullaby until she went back to sleep. She checked on Happy, quiet in his bed, and Bliss asleep in hers.

But Sunny didn't sleep.

She slipped outside to look at the stars, went down through the grass to sit in the garden. She wanted to listen to the angel, maybe even press her face against the stone and see if it held any heat left from the summer sun.

"You should have left with them." It's the angel who speaks, but the voice is Sunny's, inside Sunny's head.

The angel's mouth never moves.

She leans on her stone pillar with her stone wings, her stone face in her stone hands. The angel isn't real, and Sunny doesn't need Josiah to tell her that. Everything the angel has said to her over the past few months has come from someplace inside Sunny.

But why are the words in there? The thoughts? Where are they coming from?

Listen with your heart. That's what Papa always told them, and though Sunny never felt she'd reached the level Papa had expected, sitting here now on the stone bench she wonders if that really matters.

Sunny listens with her heart.

She listens hard, she listens long. She thinks of everything she was taught and believed. What she still believes, and what no longer makes any sense.

Nothing makes much sense.

Dr. Braddock had told Sunny she wasn't crazy, and Sunny believes that. But Dr. Braddock also said that the family—including Sunny's mother—were if not crazy, at least badly mistaken and led astray. Dr. Braddock did her best to make Sunny believe her mother did the best thing she could by sending Sunny and her kids away before they could all leave together...

But Sunny is no longer so sure that's true.

"It's never too late to come back to us," Josiah had told her. "We're your family, and we'll always be here for you."

But how can she go with him? Take her children from this house, from Liesel and Chris and everything they've grown so used to? Her children have become attached to material things, indiscriminate in their use of the earth's favors. Her children eat candy, watch television. Break their toys and toss them in the trash.

They have become worldly, and whose fault is that? Her own. Sunny has failed her children.

She's afraid of taking her GED test, applying to college, finding a better-paying job. She's terrified of leaving her father's house. She has to admit that she's become attached to plentiful food, the freedom of money in her pocket. She's become accustomed to the face she sees in her mirror, a girl with painted lips and hair hanging loose. Sunny has also failed herself.

She doesn't want to go with Josiah and live three or four to a room again. Back to scrubbing floors on her hands and knees. Her belly hungry all the time. Her clothes dirty and worn. And worse, owning nothing, sharing everything.

She does not want to become one of Josiah's wives. She's not sure she'd like to be his one true wife, but Sunny is certain she doesn't want to share her husband. Not with anyone.

"You should have left with all of them." The angel's voice is stronger this time. "Look at everything bad that's happened to Liesel and Chris since you got here. Look at what will happen to your children. Already they've forgotten how to listen."

With their hearts, Sunny thinks. They have forgotten how to listen with their hearts. Peace wants to wear makeup and pretty dresses. Happy will go to school. Neither of them will remember the family or Sanctuary. And Bliss will never know it at all.

"It's not too late."

No, Sunny thinks. No, it's not too late.

Chapter
48

"You have my phone number, and your dad's. The number of the bed-and-breakfast is on the fridge." Liesel paused to study Sunny's expression. She looked amused. "What?"

"You told me this already." Sunny laughed.

Liesel sighed at herself. "I know. I just want to be sure you have all the information. I'd feel better if you could drive."

Sunny hadn't yet taken the driver's test, though Chris had been teaching her every night for the past two weeks.

"You'll only be gone for two nights, Liesel. We'll be fine. You should go and have a good time. You need it," Sunny added.

They did need it. It had been months since Liesel and Christopher had had any time to themselves as a couple, and with the baby on the way romantic time alone was going to be even harder to come by. He'd surprised her with a weekend away at a bed-and-breakfast they'd stayed in while they were dating. Not too far away…just far enough.

"We'll be back some time on Sunday afternoon—"

"Liesel. Go." Sunny pushed her gently toward the door. "My dad's waiting for you."

Liesel let herself be urged toward the front door, the car in the driveway and her waiting husband. It wasn't until they were a few miles down the road, the windows open to let in the warm September breeze and the radio blasting classic rock, that she thought of something strange. It was the first time Sunny had called Christopher her dad.

Chapter
49

"One more game," Sunny says, "and then it's time for bed. What will we play?"

"Rosy Posie!" Peace dances in a circle, her blond braids flying.

Sunny shakes her head. "No. Not that one. Pick another game, my sweetheart, and then we'll have a snack and go to sleep. We'll all go to sleep."

Happy chooses Candy Land, and Peace pouts but agrees. Bliss is allowed to choose the red gingerbread man, though Sunny has to flick the spinner for her and count the spaces. They play, all of them together, until Happy is near the end and Bliss's eyes are drooping. Peace, seeing she can't win, pushes her piece off the edge of the game board and complains of hunger.

"Good thing it's time for a snack. Put the game away first," Sunny says. "We don't want to leave a mess for Liesel."

The children put away the game, then gather at the table

where Sunny gives them chocolate pudding. Their favorite.
She likes it, too.

"Tastes funny," Happy says, but eats it.

Peace has no complaints except that she'd like more. Baby
Bliss makes a face, scrubbing at sleepy, drooping eyes, and
Sunny spoons a few more bites into the baby's mouth before
offering the rest to her other daughter.

She's given them far more than she usually would have…
but they are children and pudding is sweet. They gobble it all
and lick their spoons, trusting her the way she once trusted
her own mother when she handed Sunny a paper cup of juice.

They really should have baths, but instead she simply wipes
their faces clean with a damp cloth. They throw away their
wasteful paper napkins. They put their bowls and spoons in
the dishwasher that claims economy and energy saving but is
wasteful, too.

Upstairs, Sunny puts them down in her big bed, the three
of them so small yet taking up so much space. She lays herself
down beside them, her face turned for a moment toward the
window. Outside the glass the sky is turning dark. She can
see the top of a tree but not the grass of the backyard. Not the
garden. She can't see the angel.

She can't hear her anymore, either.

For the first time in a long, long time, Sunny closes her eyes
and drifts. The bed beneath her dips and sways like a boat on
the ocean, which now she will never see. It doesn't matter.

Nothing matters anymore.

There's a weight on her chest, her throat feels tight, but
both those sensations are as far away as the stars peeking out
from the night sky. Her fingertips have gone numb. Sunny
waits to see the gates, but there's nothing but a steady, low
buzz in her ears and the taste of metal on her tongue.

She's still too heavy. She can't fly away. Her children,

they've done nothing wrong, they have nothing to keep them from going ahead of her. Through the gates. She wants her children to go through the gates, she wants to go, she wants to take them by the hand and lead them through to the great, vast world of peace and bliss and happy. Not this world, this place she can't fit inside no matter how hard she squeezes herself.

She wants to save them.

She wants to save herself.

But now the angel speaks, her words slow and dripping like honey from a spoon. From the moon. Is it Sunny's voice? Is it her mother? Is it something else? Maybe the voice of the earth, of God, a god, a goddess, someone or something out there in the night sky.

A star?

"It isn't time to leave."

That's all. There are no more words. They aren't accusation, condemnation, they aren't refusal or betrayal.

All they are is truth, and Sunny knows this because all at once there is a light so bright behind her eyes it blocks out all the stars. There is no going through the gates. All there is, is here and now, this place with nothing to get to. This life is not something to get through.

Life is all there is.

And her fingers fumble, numb-tipped. Tap-tap on the keypad of her phone. Too late, so tired, but she forces her mouth to make the words, her throat to push them out past everything she's done to silence herself forever.

"Josiah," Sunny says. "I need you."

Chapter
50

"He's beautiful." Sunny touched the baby's cheek with a soft fingertip and beamed at Liesel. "Hello, Ian. Look, Peace. See how sweet?"

Peace shifted from her spot on Sunny's lap to look in on the baby. Liesel had been afraid her nose would be put out of joint by the new arrival, but she'd taken on Ian as her "own real baby." She kissed him now.

"Him sleeping, *shh.*" Peace struggled to get off Sunny's lap and ran out across the grass to play with Happy and Bliss, who were playing tag with Chris.

Sunny watched them go. "She's getting so grown up."

"That's what they do."

Sunny looked at her. "They're beautiful, too. Thank you, Liesel. For everything."

They'd had this conversation many times over the past year, the words always the same and not really needing a response now. Liesel spoke instead with her actions. She hugged Sunny. Sunny hugged her back.

They sat without speaking to each other for a while, both of them cooing over tiny Ian's every gurgle and bit of drool. And then it was time for them to go. Chris buckled Ian into his car seat while Liesel took care of Peace, and Sunny helped Happy, who insisted he could do it himself but accepted his mother's help with a minimum of whining.

There was that awkward moment at the end of the day the way there always was after these visits, when Sunny stood and watched them drive away with her kids as she stayed behind.

"Mama," Happy said as Chris started the ignition. "When will you come home with us?"

Chris and Liesel exchanged a look, but it was Sunny who stepped in with the answer. She leaned into the car to kiss her son's head and stroke her hand over his hair. She touched his cheek.

"Maybe next time, my sweetheart."

The answer seemed to satisfy him, because he didn't ask again. Sunny closed the door and stepped back to let them pull out. The long, rolling driveway looped around the grounds, so she disappeared and came back into view three times before they finally got to the main road.

"Wave goodbye to Mama," Liesel told the children, and they did.

Sunny couldn't possibly see their faces inside the car from this distance. But they could see her, and that was what counted. They waved goodbye to her, and she waved back.

Chapter
51

In the dark and in the quiet, Sunny listened. Not with her heart, but her ears. The soft sounds of the ocean rushed over her, along with a pretty, soothing melody. The track was called "Ocean's Kiss," and was from an album Chris had loaded onto her iPod for her. She played it now on the speakers set up on her nightstand, close enough that she could reach to switch the song to any one she wanted.

But she liked this one the best.

She listened to it every night and sometimes during the day through her headphones while she went around on the walking path. She walked that path every day, never running the way Liesel liked to do. It was still good exercise.

Now she let the music send her drifting toward sleep. There would probably be dreams, but when she woke she'd know them for what they were. She didn't have trouble telling the difference between what was real and wasn't anymore.

Tomorrow she'd get up early. She might have a session with

Dr. Braddock or study for her GED. She might watch some television, though honestly nothing much ever appealed to her. She might talk to Josiah on the phone. She'd let the day take her wherever it led and appreciate whatever she had.

And maybe next week, when her father and his wife brought their son and her children to visit her, Sunny might be ready to go home with them. Maybe next time, she'd said, and she knew that one day that would become the truth.

But for now she lay in her dark and quiet bed with her eyes closed, listening to the music and the sound of the ocean… and nothing else.

★ ★ ★ ★ ★

1. Sunny's mother is the one who decides to send her daughter and grandchildren into the world of the blemished, despite everything she's always claimed to believe. Yet it's likely she knew of the abusive aspects of life within the family, specifically those perpetrated by the man she loved, John Second. Did Trish saving Sunny and the kids negate what she'd allowed to happen for years? What do you think really prompted her to save them?

2. Liesel has wanted children for a long time, yet she is surprised by the difficulties she faces in taking care of three children under the age of four, as well as a teenager. Do you think most women have unrealistic expectations of motherhood? Did Liesel, or was her situation so difficult because it was unusual?

3. Discuss how you think you would react if it was suddenly revealed that your spouse had a child you knew nothing about. Would your inclination be to welcome him or her in? Would you see them as a potential threat to your relationship?

4. Christopher never discusses his first marriage to Trish with Liesel. The arrival of Sunny in his life obviously brings back painful memories he finds hard to deal with. What do you think makes it so difficult for Christopher to relate to her?

5. Though it's mentioned that Sunny undergoes counseling with Dr. Braddock, she discontinues it after a relatively short period of time. Would it have helped or made no more difference to Sunny if she'd stayed in therapy for a longer time?

6. Do you think couples without children have fewer issues or troubles? How did not having children affect Liesel and Chris's marriage? How would you characterize their marriage before Sunny? Discuss how their relationship might have been different if they'd had a baby of their own before Sunny's arrival.

7. Some mainstream religions are criticized for what are thought to be unusual practices or beliefs—plural marriages, living apart from society, shunning technology, publicly "spreading the word." Why are we uncomfortable with some practices? Do you feel some groups have more validity than others?

8. Sunny is wary of Josiah, even though her memories of him are mostly positive. Yet in the end, he's the one

she calls for help. How did you see Josiah—as a force for good in Sunny's life, or as a potentially dangerous tie to the past?

9. The basic beliefs of the Family of Superior Bliss are taking care of the earth and the members' "vessels" through positive actions such as caring for the environment and avoiding toxins. Obviously, that message became warped. Why does Sunny cling to the past hard enough to feel as though she didn't fit in either place? Why might someone feel drawn to a join a group like the family?

10. In the end, Sunny's children are being raised by Liesel and Christopher while Sunny herself remains hospitalized and in counseling. "Maybe next time" is the message she gives her children when they ask when she'll be going home with them, and the one she thinks of when she's alone. Where do you see Sunny in six months, a year, five years? Is it realistic that she will ever get beyond the programming she experienced her whole life? Would it be terrible if she rejoined Josiah as part of the family instead of living a "normal" life?

ACKNOWLEDGMENTS

Special acknowledgments to a few people who helped me with some technical details:

Jim Thomas, retired sergeant from the Cincinnati Police Division—thank you for your answers to my questions.

Detective Leah Apple, who also provided me with some specific and important details.

The delightful limecello also came to my aid.

—If I got it right, it's because they helped me. If I got it wrong, it's all my own fault.

And finally, I could write without music, but I'm so very glad I don't have to. Turn the page for a partial playlist of what I listened to while writing *All Fall Down*. Please support the artists through legal means.

"The Banality of Evil" —Nine Horses
"After Afterall" —William Fitzsimmons
"Swans" —Unkle Bob (played it more than three
hundred times)
"Breathe Me" —Sia
"Lux Aeterna" —Clint Mansell
"Everything" —Lifehouse
"This Is Calm" —Christopher Dallman
"Josiah" —Aiden James
"Simple Gifts" —Yo-Yo Ma and Alison Krauss
"The Sound of Silence" —Simon & Garfunkel
"Beeswing" —LJ Booth
"Somebody Loved" —The Weepies
"The Chain" —Ingrid Michaelson
"Oceanic 815" —Michael Giacchino
"Lullabye" —Arcady
"All Through the Night" —Jeff Johnson and Brian Dunning
"Connamara Cradle Song" —Mairéid Sullivan

MEGAN HART

Gilly Soloman has been reduced to a mothering machine,
taking care of everyone except herself. But the machine
has broken down. Burnt out and exhausted, Gilly doesn't
immediately consider the consequences when she's carjacked—
her first thought is that she'll finally get some rest.
Someone can save *her* for a change.

But salvation isn't so forthcoming. Stranded in a remote cabin
with this stranger, time passes and forms a fragile bond between
them. Yet even as their connection begins to foster trust,
Gilly knows she must never forget he's still a man teetering
on the edge. One who just might take her with him.

precious

and

fragile

things

Available wherever books are sold.

MIRA®

www.MIRABooks.com